Mercury Dagger

A Tale From Kraydenia
Second Edition

Marius H. Visser

DRAKE
PRESS

Published 2021 by Drake Press.

ISBN 9780645092202 (Paperback)
9780645092219 (Epub)
9780645092288 (Hardback)

NATIONAL
LIBRARY
OF AUSTRALIA

A catalogue record for this
work is available from the
National Library of Australia

Acknowledgements

A special thanks to my wife for sticking with me through the late-night harassments of making her read scenes and give feedback, for pestering her with various monsters and deathly battle scenes. It's a far cry from what she usually reads and still she did it anyway. To all my friends and family that supported me throughout this project, I am blessed to have you in my life. Thank you.

To my brilliant cover designers, Cristiana Leone and Maria Ennas, I thank you for indulging all my requests and coming up with better ideas, it looks amazing.

To my fantastic editor Floyd Largent, thank you for all the late nights to push to make this book great. You guys were great and made the book look beautiful.

I hope you are all ready for the next adventure…

Cover artwork and map designed by Cristiana Leone

Cover graphics designed by Maria Ennas

Foreword to the Revised Edition

As any author would tell you, the revision leading to a second edition of a novel is done with great hesitation and trepidation, lots of sleepless nights and a strong cup of coffee every few minutes. Back in 2009, after the full effects of the great recession kicked in, I lost my job as so many others in the world did. Jobs were scarce and companies were struggling, and I needed to keep busy. So a story popped into my head one night and the next morning, I opened up my Word 2003 on a laptop that barely held itself together and started typing. I had no knowledge of the craft. I did not know what I was doing, in fact, or where this would lead to. All I knew was that I liked the story. Yes, there were a lot of mistakes made in the book. Heck, I didn't even know where to get an editor. I mean, as an Afrikaans speaking male with English as a second language, it couldn't be that bad, right? Oh boy... After the launch in 2010, money was becoming an issue, and luckily, I received a phone call from a company to do their IT Administration. So I stepped back into my corporate shoes and slaved away to get some cash flowing again. Don't get me wrong, I was grateful for the work. I took a step back then and focused on learning the art of writing and signed up for multiple courses. I wrote a few short stories and a novel, twice, but never published them. Then in 2017 we moved to Australia, and we started our lives afresh. Again, it took some time to get back on our feet. Now was the time I could finally work on my writing, and my first stop was fixing up a few things in Mercury Dagger. And this time round it is going to a fantastic editor to smooth out all the sharp edges.

And so doing the revision, I did not want to change the story itself, although I have changed some names, and added a few new scenes. I think in total I have added roughly fifteen thousand new words, give or take… and removed probably seven thousand. The rewrite took a bit longer than expected given that I wrote another novel in between, which will be published soon after I republish Mercury Dagger. Keep an eye out for it.

To those that read the first edition, I thank you greatly and can assure you that no significant changes to outcomes have occurred. If you are thinking of doing a reread with the second edition, I am sure you would enjoy this version. To any new reader thinking of picking up this novel, I thank you for considering it worthy of a read. Sit back and enjoy the journey I will endeavour to take you on.

Marius H. Visser
Sydney, Australia.
January 2021

Thank you for picking up Mercury Dagger - A Tale From Kraydenia. I really hope you enjoy this novel. If you have a moment, please leave a review on Amazon or your preferred store as this will allow me the opportunity to write more books such as this. I would really appreciate it. Reviews are especially critical in today's world. Help other fantasy readers and tell them why you enjoyed this book. Thank you!

Want to stay updated with news about my books?

* Join my mailing list at:
https://www.mariushvisser.com/contact
* Like me on Facebook:
https://www.facebook.com/mariushvisserbooks
* Follow me on Twitter:
https://twitter.com/MariusHVisser

Kraydenia

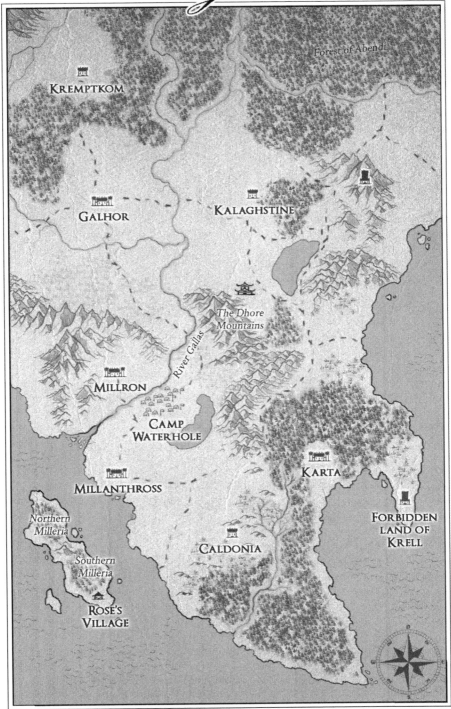

Forest of Abendi

KREMPTKOM

GALHOR

KALAGHSTINE

The Dhore
Mountains

River Gallas

MILLRON

CAMP
WATERHOLE

KARTA

MILLANTHROSS

Northern
Milleria

FORBIDDEN
LAND OF
KRELL

Southern
Milleria

CALDONIA

ROSE'S
VILLAGE

PROLOGUE

Smoke filled the dusty room as he released another puff from his cigar. He sat by the fire, old and grey, wearing his war-torn jerkin and stout leather pants. His four-legged, black-furred companion limped closer and jumped on the ancient settee beside him as he growled, 'Oh, how sorry I am that one has to get old. We are only shadows that remain, eh?'

The old warrior picked up a blanket and rose from his chair to spread it over the massive wolf as the cold winter night's wind came crawling through the cracks of the old wooden cabin.

Baldrake was once a fierce and mighty hound, being half-wolf and half-demon, or so it was believed, hailing from the depths of Hell itself. Gordon scratched the old wound on his neck as he thought back to the day the wolf had nearly ripped out his throat, and said, 'How things change so quickly.'

The once-mighty wolf lifted his head to speak to Gordon's mind with its deep growling speech, 'A thank you would be nice.'

'A thank you? For what? Almost killing me after you went back on your word?'

A growl of laughter filled his head as Baldrake replied, 'For making you look more like a man!'

Frowning, Gordon pulled the blanket off the wolf and sat down in his chair, covering himself with the blanket. The snap of teeth, accompanied by the growls of the wolf, filled the room. He stared with indignation at the wolf and said, 'Are you finished? Stop making so much noise. Besides, you barely have any teeth left. I am not afraid of you; heck, not even the rabbits are anymore.' Settling down, Gordon looked into the dancing flames. Images passed through his mind's eye as he drifted back in time...

Tired after a long day of giving speeches and advising the army battalions and their generals on tactics and strategies, Brindell returned home to find his son Gordon chopping logs for firewood and smiled as he said, 'Instead of just slamming your axe into that wood to impress the girls yonder, why don't you try perfecting your swing, follow through with the hits?'

Gordon looked up and watched as his father strolled closer, hawk-eyed and powerful, never one for backing down. Laying down the axe, he said, 'I did that for the first half of the day. I'm tired now.'

With a grin and a sheepish laugh, Brindell patted Gordon on the back as he said. 'My boy, do you even notice the girls staring at you?'

'Of course I do, father. But I suspect it pleases them even more than me at this stage.' Looking over his father's shoulder, he smiled and waved at the girls, who laughed and scurried away down the street.

Brindell laughed as he said, 'I do not know where you got your wits from, but it was not from me, boy.'

On the outskirts of town, Gordon ran the fierce gauntlet over and over as he trained his body and mind to be faster, stronger, better. The gauntlet would see you pitted against several straw-filled dummies, placed in a large oval with bales and other obstacles scattered for cover. Sprinting off the line, he shot with bow and arrow at the first three targets as he ran in, then switched to his sword and took out the remaining two before vaulting to the back of a horse. They leapt over the first bales, and he slashed his sword across the face of another straw-filled enemy. A hundred paces away, two more stood in his crosshairs. His bow was unsteady in his hands and bobbed around as the horse galloped in. He nocked the first arrow. 'Steady on, horse.' Just as he sent the arrow flying, the horse jumped over a bale, sending him to the ground in a cloud of dust as he lost his balance. Coughing as he lay on the ground, he said, 'Damn, that hurts.'

For the next twenty-five days he ran the gauntlet, day after day, for hours on end, knowing that the upcoming Rite of Passage was a daunting experience, but one that gave you the right to be called a man. A few weren't so lucky to make it through, being killed in the trying—or banished in shame. He knew what awaited him, and trained as hard as he could during the day. At night times, he duelled with his father to sharpen his swordsmanship. The last two days before the Rite, he relaxed his muscles and calmed his soul, knowing that without a content soul, he would not last long. One could lose one's temper too quickly and make rash decisions, which could cost you more than just the shame of failing in the Rite.

Brindell looked upon his boy, seeing the man he had become, and fear struck his mind as the thought of losing him ran rampant in his head. The old kitchen table rocked as he pressed on it, discussing various scenarios and different tactics that could benefit Gordon in the coming trials.

CHAPTER ONE

The crowd began gathering early, just as the sun's rays engulfed the mountain peaks to the west of Karta. The Kraydenian valley was beautiful so early on a midsummer morning. Gordon could feel the tension mounting at the thought of the day's events. His stomach churned, and it tasted like bile in his mouth.

'How are you feeling this morning, lad?' Came a sudden voice from behind. Spinning around, he saw the large bulky form of Grackis the blacksmith, who had lost his son only two years ago in the Rite. One could see how it still grieved him to attend these events.

'I am nervous, to be honest, but I feel good, thank you,' answered Gordon.

Grackis stared down at the boy and saw the sharp, hawk-eyed features of his father within him. 'Aye, but you are a tan lad, and you have grown quite a lot of muscle since I saw you last,' said the blacksmith, feeling his heart grow heavy once more. He placed his hand on Gordon's shoulder as he continued, 'Don't worry, lad, stay focused and alert. But most importantly, stay calm.'

Eager for the day's events to begin, more and more people joined the crowd and pressed closer to the arena. Brindell smiled as he saw his boy practising with a wooden sword and came over to embrace him. It was something he had never done before, and felt awkward to both, but was invited just the same. The speaker—a well-dressed skinny old man with a bald spot on his crown named Regan—took to the stage and cleared his throat. 'It's that time again, good citizens of Karta, where one of our youths ascends to adulthood after completing three daring tasks set before him this day. Today the boy known as Gordon, son of Brindell, who is well known by many, will take on the odds to be called a man.'

Regan glanced at Gordon, who stood a few feet away on the quickly erected wooden stage, the complete structure swaying with every move.

'With all the trouble you have caused in the past, young Gordon, I hope after we give you the title of "man" that you put foolishness behind you,' Regan told him with a wry smile. Everyone laughed as Gordon reddened and nodded. Clearing his throat again, the speaker said, 'The first of the tasks is a bare-knuckle fistfight, as always. We all know the rules on this one. But in case any of you forgot, the boy needs to stand his ground for three rounds with another fighter, or knock his opponent out before the final bell; otherwise, he does not go through to the next round.'

The crowd was becoming eager to find out who Gordon would face in the fight.

'In the second task, obviously more daunting, he will face another swordsman in a duel for three rounds. Whoever draws first blood will be the victor. No matter if the boy loses or wins, he still moves on to the last round, unless he declines or is too badly injured. The third and final task... and this I always dread for the youngsters... is for him to go out into the woods for as long as necessary, to hunt the Pekula!'

Gordon tensed, and his stomach churned as he heard the word. The Pekula was a fierce creature that never backed away from anything. Every year it was a different animal. This year it was a bear that had lost its mind; rage had replaced the normal mental patterns of the bear. Sadly, more and more animals were becoming like this every year. At first, the sighting of one of these creatures was almost mythical, but of late, one couldn't throw a stone too far without hitting one. A few had

5

tried to glean the reason for the change in these animals, but no credible reasons had come forth as of yet. Most had died in the undertaking.

Brindell walked over to his boy and patted him on the back. 'Do not fear, my son—I know that you have the heart of a lion. You'll be fine. The Pekula doesn't stand a chance.'

Gordon smiled, and said, 'I'm not worried, father. I will return carrying the trophy over my head.'

The usually quiet streets of the small town of Caldonia were plagued with onlookers as a man suddenly crashed through the wood-framed windows of the Blackheart Inn, to fall heavily on the main paved road, amusing many of the passers-by. Malachai stood by the broken window and shouted to the man lying in the street, 'Best be you insult no man's reading again, you filthy whoreson. Now go back to where you came from!'

Malachai had never been considered among the brightest of people, and everyone who knew him never dared to challenge him or say so to his face. He was not an even-tempered man, and you never knew that he had lost his sense of humour until it was too late.

Everyone resumed their normal activities after the sudden outburst. Malachai returned to his seat and asked the young servant girl to refill his jug with some more of Caldonia's finest ale—which was considered the worst in the countryside. She sighed and walked off.

A handsome man in a tight uniform walked over to his table. 'I see you like to hurt people, and you can handle yourself pretty well in a fight,' he said, whilst lowering himself into the chair opposite the big man.

'You better watch out, pretty boy. I'm in no mood for any more insults today. That be your first and final warning,' Malachai told the officer with a cold look in his eyes.

'Oh, I mean no disrespect, my friend, not at all,' countered the man. The servant girl returned with two new jugs of ale and set them down as she sighed and said, 'Oh Malachai, you know you'll have to replace that window, right?'

'My dear, please tell the keeper to put the window on my tab,' said the officer.

'I don't need no stinkin' handouts. I can pay for it meself,' snapped the big man.

'Oh, nothing of the sort. I merely wish to show that my intentions are to befriend you,' countered the man as he rose from his chair and bowed his head slightly. 'Let me introduce myself. I am Tudeske—Tuds for short—the regiment army major.'

Malachai studied the man: his slender figure, straight back, sharp face and long blond hair. 'You must be noble-born. What are you doing talking to me, or even doing in a place like this?' An angry shout came from behind the bar counter and Malachai replied, 'No offence, keeper.'

'Yes, I was high-born, or noble-born as you might call it, but I haven't had it so easy myself. But I'll not get into that right now. The reason I'm here is that I'm looking for a man capable of great violence.'

Taking a large gulp of his ale, Malachai eyed the major and cocked his head as he said, 'That depends on if the violence is deserved.'

Tuds smiled and sat back down before continuing, 'Look, let's not be coy. A band of thieves broke into a woman's home, pillaged it, and raped her, down in the countryside. And I care for her dearly. Her name is Lithuania, and she is an absolute angel. Never deserved that kind of treatment. I might need some... uh, "assistance"... with the issue, seeing as there would be at least eight men involved.'

Taking another big gulp of his ale, Malachai said, 'No one deserves that kinda treatment. I'm sorry to hear of her misfortune. How much would this "assistance" be worth to you?'

Tuds looked at the burly man, and said, 'Fifteen gold coins now, and fifteen when we return.'

Malachai rubbed his beard. 'How about twenty gold on return?'

The major smiled, and said, 'I think I have just found the man for the job.'

The last of the big man's ale rushed down his throat, then he said,

'Well now, when do I start?'

Both men gripped each other by the elbow in agreement, and the contract was as good as signed. 'Relax, old chum, let's have another ale and work out the finer details.'

'Never call me chum again.'

'And now, ladies and gentlemen, the moment you have all been waiting for. In his bare-knuckles fight, Gordon will face the one, the only, Tattero!' shouted Regan. The crowd roared when they heard the name. All in the city knew Tattero as The Bloodskin Mauler. He had earned the name a few bouts back when a previous opponent jumped up after the last bell to surprise-attack him as he walked away. He had lost his temper and kept on pounding on his opponent. People had rushed in to drag him from the man as he lay in a pool of his own blood. Tattero's fists had cut the man's face to pieces.

'He's big, but not fast,' came a voice next to Gordon. 'I've seen him fight, laddie, he tires quickly and depends completely on his strength. You are fast, so stay away from his fists. They tend to hurt when they connect.'

He looked up at the older man. 'Thanks, Grackis, I will keep that in mind.'

Young kids ran around the crowd collecting coins as wagers were placed on the warriors. The bookies would take full advantage of today's events. *Everyone loves a good wager, don't they?*

'Let's get this over with,' Gordon said and started walking to the boxing ring with his father and Grackis as entourage to spur him and the crowd on.

This day will get hot quickly; I will need to cool down after this bout, he thought on his way to the ring, keeping a watchful eye on the bigger Tattero as he warmed up at ringside. *Those punches don't look so slow to me.* The white floor and the blue ropes of the ring were turning brown as the wind blew the dust around. The two combatants sized each other up as Gordon climbed over the ropes and started throwing a few punches to loosen up.

'Both fighters, please join at the centre,' Regan instructed. As both fighters met, all could see that Tattero towered a full head above Gordon. The fighters shook hands before moving back to their corners.

'Round one!' came the shout as the bell rang. The fighters moved closer, fists at eye level. Tattero started with a few left jabs, but Gordon evaded them; then a sudden heavy right hook landed firmly on the side of his face, throwing him to the ground. He had never felt a blow like that before. His teeth felt suddenly loose as he pressed his tongue against them. The blow had landed true and made his ears ring. Surging up, he saw the crowd chanting his name, but couldn't hear it.

Anger flared in his mind as he charged the bigger man with a left jab that was blocked with ease, but a lightning right uppercut went straight through Tattero's defence and landed firmly on his chin. The big man's head rocked back as he stumbled and almost fell. With newfound respect for each other, the warriors circled one another once more. The bell rang, and the fighters went to their corners. Brindell and Grackis waited in Gordon's corner, cheering him on as they saw his left eye was quickly swelling shut. 'Don't lose your mind out there, my boy, you're doing great!'

'Round two,' came the voice, and the bell rang. The fighters circled each other again, starting off slowly with a jab here, a punch there. Tattero stepped in with a thundering right, but Gordon had been reading his opponent and evaded the hook to thunder his own combination of left and rights to the midsection of the big man. Tattero lost his temper and charged the boy, who could not get out of the way quick enough.

Punches thundered into Gordon's midsection and another heavy right to his face, this time cutting open the flesh below the brow. Blood streamed down Gordon's face and into his eye. His left eye was completely closed now as he stumbled back, trying to avoid more blows. Lucky for him, the bell rang. The fighters—now locked in a bear hug—did not relent, both trying to send a few quick jabs to the sides of his opponent. Regan stepped in to pull them apart.

Back in their corners, a healer rushed forward and quickly taped the gap above Gordon's left eye and cleaned the blood from his face. The world was spinning. His head ached and his face burned.

'Round three,' came the shout, and the bell rang once more. Tired now, the fighters walked straight out to each other, fists at eye level. Gordon started with a jab and was countered with a nauseating blow to his ribs. He staggered back, struggling for air as he spat up blood. Tattero gave him a moment to catch his breath. Once more they approached each other, and with a sickening thump out of nowhere, Gordon landed a right hook to Tattero's nose. The bigger man staggered back as blood gushed from his broken nose, his eyes wet with tears and swelling instantly.

I could end him. I can claim this victory, thought Gordon, but did not advance as he thought back to the moment of reprieve Tattero had offered him only moments ago. The bell rang for the last time. A sigh of relief escaped him as the crowd cheered for them both.

Tattero strolled up to Gordon as he left the healer's tent, gently squeezing his nose after they had to break it again to straighten it. The young man stiffened as cold sweat ran down his back, but there was no threat in the bigger man's movement. 'You fight well, Gordon,' he said, reaching out to shake his hand. 'Don't worry about the nose, no hard feelings. These things happen in the ring.'

'Thanks for not finishing me after that blow to the ribs. My gods, it felt like a hammer hitting me,' Gordon told him.

'Ha, no need. As I recall, you left my dignity intact when you could have won this fight. You returned the favour,' Tattero said with a smile, then turned to leave as he continued, 'Good luck with the next events.'

The second event was due soon, and Gordon needed to rest. He slumped down in the shade of a tree and fell asleep.

☿

Early morning in Caldonia, as the rays of the sun pierced through the mist over the little town, Malachai was already waiting by the old barn, as instructed by Tuds. He heard the muffled sound of horses' hooves on gravel drawing closer. He leaned in to see where exactly they were, but the thick morning mist obscured his vision. *Why is he in such a hurry?*

The horses were running at a canter through the narrow street. Tuds reined in as he neared, leading another gelding. 'Jump up, we have to move quickly,' Tuds said as he kept a watchful gaze on the surroundings. He sighed as he watched the struggle take place as the big man tried to get on the horse.

'Well, a good morning to you too,' snapped Malachai. 'What's the rush?'

Tuds pressed his boots deep into the horse's flanks and urged him on. 'I'll tell you as soon as we are clear of this place; now ride!'

Malachai urged on his horse to catch up with the man. It was not long before they were clear of Caldonia as they rode through its narrow gravel streets. As they crested the hill northeast of the town, Tuds relaxed and slowed to a walk.

'So what's the rush, Tuds?' Malachai asked a second time.

'Oh well, there's no use lying to you from the start, is there?' Tuds said expressionlessly. 'I had no choice but to steal these horses for us to travel. But don't worry, we'll give them back as soon as we return.'

'Oh, but you are a canny fellow. I thought you are a major in the army. Aren't you supposed to have your own horse? And why on earth didn't you take one of your subordinates to help you on this quest? You could have saved a lot of coin. Not that I am complaining, of course,' Malachai said as he furrowed his brow and stared at the older man.

Tuds didn't look back as he replied, 'They have suspended me from service until the outcome of my hearing.'

'Oh boy, what have you gone and done?' the big man muttered.

'I broke the jaw of my superior for not wanting to go after the band that raped the girl.'

'Ahh, those whiny bastards with their political shit, probably gave you a hundred reasons they couldn't do it,' snapped Malachai.

'Yes, they did,' Tuds murmured, then said, 'Enough on that; we should head east. I got information that they're hiding out in the mountains closer to Karta. Those bastards don't know what's coming for them. They will feel a world of pain soon enough.' He glared at Malachai as he continued, 'I want them all dead. No trials. No stays of execution.'

Malachai felt a chill running down his spine as he stared into the lifeless eyes of the other man.

'Have you ever killed a man?' came the sudden question.

Surprised, Malachai spun on his horse and looked back at Tuds as he said, 'I have once, in a fight... but it was self-defence. He came at me with a knife, and I only meant to stun him with a smack to the face, but he just fell back and never stood up again.'

'Oh, don't worry, I'm not here to investigate you. Curious, is all. By the way, what is that thing hanging on your back?'

From his back under his leather jacket, Malachai pulled clear the biggest war hammer Tuds had ever seen. 'This, my friend, is the tool that will make those bastards pay for their crimes. Belonged to my father. And his father before him. I do not know how far it goes up the line, but it has been in the family for a long time.'

Tuds stared at the hammer and marvelled at its size and exquisite craftsmanship. Covering its haft was entwined twisted brown leather strips, the pitch-black shaft a material unknown to him; the dual silver heads at the top had the most beautiful archaic symbols etched into the metal.

Night was fast approaching. The major looked around and said, 'Let's camp on the riverbank. It's getting dark, and we will need our rest for what's coming tomorrow.' They jumped off their horses and gathered some firewood, readying the camp.

Both men sat by the fire, staring into the flames after they had eaten their broth. 'Thirty,' Tuds stated.

'Thirty what?' countered Malachai.

'That's how old I guess you are.'

'Nope,' he mumbled, then said, 'And now off to bed.'

Gordon was defending their honour to make it through to the third round or best his challenger, whichever would come first. He would not give up. Swords flashed through the air at great speed. He parried a lunge to his side, then countered the move with a blow from the sword pommel to the face of Remus, his opponent.

No blood yet flowed, but Remus's eye swelled up as if a bee had stung him right on the cheek. The bell rang for the end of the second round. A brief rest in their corners and the bell rang once more for the start of the last round. Gordon waited patiently for the coming attack and evaded the horizontal slash of the sword by sliding just beneath the edge of the blade. The crowd held their breath for the instant, thinking it had cut his throat. He turned to hit Remus on his backside with the flat of his blade, and the crowd went wild as cheers rose to the air.

There was no doubt that Gordon was the better swordsman. He was toying with Remus. Patiently, he waited again for the next attack. Remus rushed forward and lunged at his throat, but Gordon spun straight past the sword to cut into the duellist's chest. It all happened so fast that the crowd thought Remus was done for. But only a trickle of blood flowed from his chest. The crowd cheered again, and Gordon won the match.

He walked down from the ring to his father. The pride shone on Brindell's face as he handed him a cloth and some water, and said, 'It's time to prepare for the hunt. Make sure you have all that you need, my boy.'

As he was gathering his gear, Brindell approached with an item wrapped in a linen cloth and handed it to him.

'Take care my boy, I know it isn't much, but it will help in your coming hunt.'

'What is this, Da?' Gordon asked as he took the item.

'Oh, just something to show you how proud I am of the man you have become. Pekula or not.'

Unfolding the linen, Gordon produced a curved sword so clean he could see his reflection in the blade. The blackened pommel had white, shining lines of bone flowing over each other etched into it, and no handguards. It was sleek and sharp, with little weight. It was a magnificent weapon. Gordon danced with the sword, slicing through the air, role-playing a duel. Walking back to Brindell, he said, 'Thank you, Father, this is an amazing gift.' Their heads came up as they heard the announcement in the distance.

'It is that time, good citizens, as darkness falls upon us, scattering us to our sanctuaries we call our homes, that this brave young man will be off to hunt a ferocious beast!' Regan announced.

Everyone came to wish him luck and ambled away, back to their homes as the sun set. Gordon started heading off towards the mountains to the west, and soon he wasn't visible anymore to the crowd.

'The gods be with you, my boy!' he heard his father shout one last time.

The night was warm, and the moon glowed high above. The wind was blowing softly against his skin as he walked for a time before stopping at the edge of the forest. Making camp, he lit a small fire and warmed some broth his father had given him. Sleep came instantly this night as he lay next to the fire on a blanket.

Startled by a twig snapping underfoot, he heard someone curse at the culprit soon after. Gordon slowly reached for his new sword, not making a sound. He barely even moved his body to not give away his awareness of them.

'What if he wakes up?' he heard the one asking the other.

'Then we kill him.'

The first man approached with caution, unsheathing his sword as he drew near. He was getting close to the bag on the ground next to

Gordon. Through slitted eyes, he watched the man hovering over him reach for the bag. He flashed up his sword and drove it through the stomach of the thief. Quick to his feet, he charged the second thief as he pulled the bloodstained sword from the man. The thief toppled over as blood gushed from his wound, muddying the ground. The second man screamed as he saw his companion fall, and charged in with a spiked club held high over his head. As the man neared, Gordon went to his knees. The sword hissed through the air as it sliced through the man's leg, severing it just above the knee. Blood sprayed as the man flailed about and slid from his lower leg. *Like covering the earth's sin with your blood, only your blood isn't worth shit*, he thought.

The attacker let the weapon fall and found himself on the ground, begging for his life as he stared up at the sword, dripping blood on his face. Blood he knew to be his own.

'What are you doing in the forest?' Gordon asked as he stood over the man. 'You will die soon if I don't stop that bleeding, so answer me, damn you.'

The pain had caused delirium, as the man spoke nonsensical words. He could not form a full sentence. Half-unconscious, his head bobbed around as he looked up at Gordon. 'We couldn't help it,' he said as darkness consumed him. Gordon cursed and tore a strip off the man's raggedy clothes, and bound the bleeding leg as best he could. He added some wood to the almost dead fire and blew on it to bring it back to life, then took up the dead man's sword and shoved the blade in. Embers jumped to the sky, bringing to life the grisly scene before him.

After some time, he pulled out the fiery sword and pushed its flat side to the severed leg to close the arteries and stop the bleeding. The sudden pain woke the man. A horrible inhuman scream echoed throughout the night air. Birds flew and animals darted from the area. It wasn't long before the man lost consciousness again. Gordon watched him for a while and knew he would not wake, and if he did, he posed no threat. He lay down and dozed off once more.

☿

The thief awoke early the next morning, only to find himself tied to a tree with torn linen. Bathed in sweat, he panicked, the adrenalin pushing aside the pain enough for him to focus. He struggled against the linen, pulling as hard as he could, but they would not break. Gordon stepped out from behind the tree and said with a grin, 'Ahh, good to see you are awake, my friend.'

'Please let me go. I mean you no harm. This is monstrous!'

'Like you meant me no harm last night when you attacked me?' Gordon countered, then said, 'Save your breath. You will need it.'

The man, in obvious pain, nervously glared at him and said, 'I will tell you nothing, you hear? Nothing!'

'Oh, I am counting on that,' said Gordon politely. 'You see, I am a man in a rather peculiar situation. I need to hunt a rather big, terrible beast, and I forgot my bait at home. Lucky for me, you came along... Live or die, that's up to you. I will have to see if the information you give me is worth saving your life. You know, the whole "effort versus reward" thing.'

The thief screamed his outrage as Gordon turned to walk away. 'What kind of monster would do such a thing?'

'When you're ready to talk, let me know. Until then, you can stare at your leg on that rock over there and think of your misdeeds.'

The man looked up and saw his leg standing upright as if he were the piece severed from it, not the other way round. 'Monstrous...'

CHAPTER TWO

Tuds jumped up from his blanket, drawing his sabre as he looked around, confused, then saw the grisly Malachai chuckle with a bucket in hand a short distance away. Drenched with water, he sheathed his sword and muttered something under his breath.

'Wow, I didn't think you were that quick, Tuds.'

He growled, 'I could have killed you.'

'Oh, don't get ahead of yourself now, it won't be that easy.'

Malachai packed the last of his belongings and said, 'Come on, little man, Daddy needs to make some rapists scream for their lives.' He lifted the hammer to his back and strolled to his horse.

'My, but we're in a good mood this morning,' said Tuds as irritation overwhelmed him.

'Come on, little man, we still have a long way ahead of us.'

Tuds looked at the big man next to his horse, busy stretching and pulling his muscles in various ways. The sheer power that radiated from the man was colossal. He had a unique look about him. White streaks encumbered his half-inch thick black beard from his ears to his mouth, with ice-blue eyes that sent shivers down one's spine. His brown hair was braided into a thick ponytail. Tuds moved to his chestnut gelding and strapped his belongings to the saddle. Both men jumped onto their horses and headed off. Silence was their companion for most of the day as they rode behind each other on the narrow horse trail. The countryside was green, but not at all lush; the desperately needed rain had not yet come. Tuds neared the crest of a hill and stopped at the top, waiting for Malachai a few paces back. As the big man's horse slowly approached, groaning under the weight, Tuds gestured to the mountain jutting out of the earth some distance away.

It was a rare sight to behold, as the snow-capped peaks shone brightly against the rays of the sun, mist covering the top. The lay of the mountain reminded Malachai of the old dragon tales his father used to tell when they went out hunting, and remembered him saying, 'Oh, quiet now, boy, you see that mountain? It is said that when dragons get too old, they would lie down on the earth to sleep. That's how these mountains formed. So beware not to make too much noise, otherwise the beast might awake, and we will be its breakfast.' He smiled then.

Tuds looked at the mountain, and said, 'Those mongrels are on that mountain somewhere; we have to find them somehow.'

Malachai stared at the man. 'Aye, I think we should make our way to the north and scout on the forest side.'

'And why do you say so?'

'Best I can tell, there's no cave on this end of the mountain, and with no forest to cover them, they will hide on the other side.'

'Well put. I'll follow your lead, then,' Tuds said as he fell in at the back.

The big man pulled out something wrapped in cloth from his saddlebag. 'Some dried beef for you, little man?' he asked, and tossed a strip over. Arms flailed in the air as if catching a wild turkey, and with some luck, Tuds snatched it from the air.

As they entered the forest cradling the mountain to the north, they reined in and jumped from their mounts. The beasts whinnied in fear, pulled their ears flat to their heads, and looked about anxiously. 'Whoa, now!' Malachai pulled on the reins and tried to calm his horse as he stroked its neck, but the horse was beyond his help. Tuds moved in to whisper in its ear and stroke its head. The gelding suddenly relaxed in his grip.

'Now, that was interesting,' said Malachai. Standing with his hands on his hips, he continued, 'Not because you have a way with horses. I am referring to the fear they both suddenly have in this area. Why do you think that is?'

'I don't know, my friend, but I do not like it one bit.'

They carried on for some time, leading their horses through the thick, lush, green and exquisite forest, green algae growing on every tree as far as the eye could see. Flowers bloomed of all colours—red, blue, yellow, purple—and the trees were humongous, almost completely blotting out the sun. It was magnificent. As the two men walked deeper into the forest, they noted that the putrid smell of rotting flesh hung in the air.

Tuds' gelding jerked himself free of his grip and galloped off some distance. He cursed as he watched the beast run. The horse held by the big man had no chance of getting free from the man's powerful grip, and was soon tethered to an old fallen tree. 'Let's go have a look to see what's happening up front,' said Malachai as his face hardened.

Both men pulled their weapons free and cautiously crept forward. The smell of rotting meat was intense now, and Tuds wanted to gag from the stench. Fifty paces in front of them, they saw movement and took cover behind a tree. Malachai peered out and saw a massive bear busily eating a man strapped between two trees by his arms. He only had one leg left dangling in the air, the other leg; a mangled piece of flesh only to the knee was being feasted on by the bear, tearing out chunks at a time. In all his life, he had never seen such a sight before. The man's head suddenly jerked, followed by a horrible scream that wouldn't stop ringing in his ears. 'By all the gods, he is still alive,' he said as he jumped up, just to see a sword flash towards his neck and stop, pressing at his jugular. Cold eyes set in the face of a tanned young man stared back at him from the end of the sword.

19

'The slightest push, and this sword will be at the back of your neck,' came the voice.

Malachai froze and gestured to Tuds not to do anything stupid. He looked at the younger man in disbelief, and said, 'You thieving rapist bastard, how can you do this to someone? What did he do to deserve this?'

Tuds was nervous enough as it was, and didn't say a word.

'I think there might be a misunderstanding here. The man being eaten by the bear over there,' Gordon jerked a thumb in the thief's direction, then continued, 'is a thieving, raping bastard. Him and his now-dead friend attacked me last night in order to kill me and steal my belongings. I'm Gordon. Please indulge me and tell me who you are and what you're doing here.'

'Name's Malachai, and this little man to your left, frozen like a tree stump, is Tuds.'

'Excuse me, but I am *not* frozen like a tree stump,' countered Tuds.

'Tuds, now is not the time for an argument,' snapped the big man, and as he spoke, he quickly withdrew his head from the sword's point, just in case. He hawked and spat as he walked to a tree stump jutting from the earth and sat down, placing the massive hammer next to him. Tuds and Gordon still stood poised, ready for a fight. 'Well then, that's good to hear. We have been hunting these bastards all the way from Caldonia. They invaded a girl's home down in the countryside and raped her. She being a very close friend to our Tuds over here made it impossible for him not to do anything about this.'

Both men slowly lowered their weapons and relaxed. A roar sounded as the bear turned from the now-dead man and charged at the three warriors. Malachai saw it first and jumped up from the log as he grabbed his hammer. Gordon turned and shouted out as he saw Tuds already charging in, 'The bear is mine!'

Tuds reached the giant bear as it raised itself to its hind legs and bared its teeth, its growl echoing through the forest. The Pekula bear lashed out with its front claws and struck him a savage blow to the chest, lifting him from the ground as deafening cracks of snapping ribs were heard. He flew and hit the ground hard. Sprawled between trees and flowers, he lay unmoving.

Gordon moved in to block the Pekula from advancing towards Tuds. With his sword raised, they charged at each other. He leapt into the air as it neared, and lashed out with his sword as he sailed above the creature, slicing into its huge shoulder blades. Malachai hung back to observe the young man in his fight. The beast reared up after the cut, black and red liquid oozing down its back. A most foul odour escaped from the wound in the creature as it lashed out again at Gordon, who moved with a certain grace between the blows. Unnaturally red eyes stared at him as the attacks continued unabated. He spun past the swipe of a claw and sliced cleanly through the right paw of the beast. Black blood sprayed from its limb all over Tuds' face, seeping into his mouth as he lay unmoving beside the beast.

The bear roared in pain and stumbled towards his attacker. With a front paw missing, it reared once more as Gordon ran in and jumped at it. The beast lashed out with his remaining claw and struck Gordon on his foot, spinning him through the air to plunge to the ground.

Malachai started to rush in, but saw Gordon up on his feet just as quickly as he went down. The bear towered above the young man, who tucked and rolled to his left and grabbed Tuds' sword from the ground. Two swords in hand, he faced the bear with a grin on his face. A whistle came from the right and the bear turned, distracting it long enough for him to run in unnoticed. Using a rock as leverage, Gordon jumped up high, directly at the bear. A perilous move. If the bear turned too quickly, he could not escape its jaws. Time slowed and sound fell away. His only focus was on the bear. *How I wish you could see me now, Da. Facing this mighty foe.* The bear turned, and he gasped as he saw the huge teeth...

Malachai held his breath as he saw the bear snapping its jaws. A glint reflected from the swords, blinding the big man as they flashed through the air. 'Gordon!' he shouted as he rushed forward.

Gordon fell to the ground and rolled into a tree as the Pekula staggered back, its lifeless body falling back to the ground as its head came off in the opposite direction. Tuds stirred and groaned as Malachai ran to his side. Disquieted and unnerved, they stared at each other inquisitively as Tuds got to his feet. 'Well now, chaps, seems that the bear had bettered me. Lucky for me it was a glancing blow,' he said as he stretched his right arm and rolled his shoulder.

'What do you mean, it was a glancing blow? I heard at least four of your ribs break when that blow landed!' snapped the big guy.

Tuds lifted his now-bloody leather jerkin away from his body and pressed on his ribs as he said, 'I don't know what to say, fellas, but I feel all right. Maybe you heard something else break, like twigs when I hit the ground. I'm sore, but nothing an ale and some rest won't cure.'

The men were walking towards their horses when Gordon spoke up. 'I don't know about you fellows, but I'm beat after today's events. I think it best if we made camp together tonight, seeing as we have the same goal.'

'Oh, and what would that goal be?' Tuds asked in obvious discomfort.

'The man I used as bait told me the entire story about how they pillaged that woman's home and raped the girl over and over. I then persuaded him to tell me where the rest of the scoundrels are hiding out.'

Tuds' eyes lit up as he looked at the young man, and he said, 'Great, so you know their location. That will help us a lot. But what does it have to do with you? Why would you want to go after this band with the risk of getting killed? Besides, what would you have done if we didn't come along? How would you have fared against at least six more men? You would have died, simply put.'

'Oh, I might have been killed, but I'm pretty sure I would have thought of something. Strength is not always in numbers, but also in how you use your surroundings, plus I would have had the element of surprise. As for the reason I am doing this—honour, respect; it's a virtue any good man should have.'

Malachai had a big grin on his face. 'You know, I think I'm starting to like you, Gordon. Just remind me never to cross you, 'cause I don't want to end up like that unfortunate idiot back there.'

Shit. Gordon suddenly stopped and ran back to the dead beast's side to pick up the claw from the ground as proof of his victory. *The head would have been better, but it is just too big. It will slow me down.* The three men walked in the direction Gordon pointed for some time, and found a clearing in the forest. Malachai dropped his pack and said, 'This will make a suitable spot for the night.'

'Agreed,' said Tuds, as he tethered his horse and sat down on a rock to nurse his ribs.

Malachai and Gordon went off to find some dry twigs and logs for a fire.

It was getting dark, and soon the fire was crackling at their feet. Malachai sat at Tuds' side, unsure how to investigate the matter further of him still breathing after the smack from the bear. The air between the men had turned thick, as none spoke for a time, avoiding the subject altogether. Gordon rose and wandered off to sit on a rock a distance away from the camp to reflect on the day's events.

Twigs cracked underfoot as the big man neared the rock and lowered himself with a sigh. Staring out into the silhouetted forest, he had a worried look on his face and said, 'I do not know about you, but I clearly heard ribs snap.'

'Aye, I heard it too. Keep an eye on him. He might have internal damage or something,' Gordon countered.

'Tell me how you got yourself into this mess. We told you why we are here. Why are you?'

Gordon sighed, then said, 'It was my Rite of Passage, and the final task was to kill the Pekula, that creature that attacked us.'

Malachai snorted, and said, 'Well, I am glad to have you with us rather than against; you fight well. The way you move differs from any man I have seen in a fight—trained, but not military. Where did you learn to fight?'

'Oh, you know… getting into trouble here and there teaches one a few new tricks. The key thing I learnt was that you should use everything to your advantage. For instance, I could use my sword to see if someone is following me by looking in the blade.'

'I guess so. But it wasn't just that. You anticipated things most would not see coming a mile away.'

'I don't really know, to be honest. I've always been fairly good at gauging a situation.'

They sat in silence for a bit before returning to camp, where Tuds had already fallen asleep, his light snores drifting around the sound of the crackling fire.

CHAPTER THREE

Anukke stood atop the balcony of his massive grey-black tower palace. One would be forgiven for thinking they had carved it out of the mountain. That is, of course, *if* you could see it. Long ago, a blinding spell had been placed on the tower to hide it from the world. Day by day, people ran the old trader's road near the mountain towards Kalaghstine, completely unaware of its existence. To everyone, it looked like a normal stone mountain a distance from the city. Old stories had hinted at rumours of a wizard who dwelled up high in its peaks, but they had become folklore and bedtime stories to scare the young.

He peered down at the city below. 'Fools, you don't even know I'm here watching your every move. For too long have I been in the shadows and treated like filth, without you even knowing who *I* truly am. Having to conceal my true identity every time I enter your filthy city... No matter, before long you will know the name Anukke and tremble at its sound.'

A knock sounded from his bedroom door.

'Soon my puppets, soon your time will come,' came the whispered words. Anukke took his time to answer. 'What news do you bring, Elgar?'

A tall man dressed in a purple robe slowly opened the door and entered the chamber. Elgar looked at the wizard and rubbed his bald pate as he said, 'How did you know it was I, my lord?'

'Oh, Elgar... still so naïve in the ways of magic. I just know these things.' Anukke stared at the skinny man before him without blinking.

Nervously, Elgar answered, 'Of course you do my lord, my apologies.'

'None needed. What news do you bring?'

'My lord—'

Anukke interrupted, 'Please Elgar, call me Anukke.'

'As you wish... Anukke. The bear—'

'Yes, Elgar, what about it? Speak up now,' he whispered.

'Well, it has been slain.' The worry showed on Elgar's face as he fumbled about the room.

'Ha-ha, wonderful!' bellowed the wizard.

Confused and unsure, the man stiffened, and said, 'What do you mean... Anukke?'

Still scanning over the horizon, which split the deep blue of the heavens with the silky green of the forest beneath like the edge of a knife, he said, 'Elgar?'

'Yes, my lord... uh, I mean... Anukke.'

'How long have you served me?'

Elgar had the feeling of bile rising from his stomach.

The wizard turned around and looked at the man standing before him, and said, 'Well?'

He stared directly at his lord without flinching, scanning his body for any threat. The long red robe covered his hands and dragged on the stone floor. Long, loose white hair waved in the winds as the yellow catlike eyes stared deep into Elgar's soul. But there came no movement to convey hostility.

'Twenty-five years, lord. Why do you ask?'

'Twenty-five years of nothing but loyal service. It's fine, I know the bear is slain; I could feel its magic malice leave it. I need you to find me the person responsible, but do not kill whoever it was. I know you are skilled with the sword. Merely *wound* him with a poison arrow; not a fatal one, Elgar, you hear? Take Parcin with you, I think he is the better shot.'

'Yes, Lord Anukke, we live only to serve you.' Elgar spun on his heel and gladly left the chamber.

The delicious aroma of barbequed meat woke the two men from their slumber. Gordon looked at the big man and said, 'Where is that smell coming from?'

'I believe it's coming from over there, laddie,' he said, pointing behind Gordon.

Tuds was busy turning three skinned rabbits roasting over the fire and called out to them, 'Good morning, chaps. I took the liberty of finding us something to eat. Hope you boys are hungry.'

Malachai stepped closer and furrowed his brow. The concern in his voice was clear as he said, 'I can swallow a cow whole, Tuds. But first, tell me, how are you not sore, old boy?'

'What can I say, old chum? I am a fast healer, I suppose.'

'Do you want to say that after a bear slapped you silly, you just got up, dusted yourself off, took a nap, went for a casual hunt, made a fire, and by the looks of it, cleared the camp?' Malachai stared at the man, then continued, 'And tell me, why are you covered in blood again?'

'Oh... must still be from the bear. Ahh, I know, now that I think about it, when I was skinning and gutting the rabbits, it got a little messy.'

Gordon joined them and said, 'We have to find the gang today. I have got a pretty good idea of where they're hiding, but it will still require some scouting.'

The three men ate in silence, the meal just too good to waste with idle chitchat. Malachai unsheathed a knife the length of his forearm and cleared some rabbit still stuck under his nails, then stuck the sharp tip in between his teeth to get the last bits, then announced, 'Aye, that was a good filling, thanks.' He hawked and spat to the side.

Tuds stared in disgust, and said, 'Well, if I have ever seen a show of appreciation...'

Gordon also thanked Tuds and walked off. They cleared the rest of the camp and got ready to move.

After walking for a while, the forest began growing denser. The horses were slowing them down and made it difficult to traverse the almost non-existent paths. Gordon turned to them and said, 'We leave the horses here.' Nods greeted his decision, and they set off after tethering their mounts.

Malachai hacked and slashed at the branches of plants and trees to make a route in the forest as the two men followed in his wake. After midday, as the sun was at its highest, the forest thinned out as they neared the foot of the mountain. Gordon noticed movement to his front left and signalled to the others to lower and be quiet.

'It's definitely them,' said Tuds as he felt his anger rising to the surface.

'How can you be sure?' asked Malachai.

'The two on either side of the cave mouth go by Dock and Murkel. They hailed from a pirate vessel that was seized a while back. Their entire existence has been about stealing and pillaging. Guess they found their new employment. The guy with the cloth around his head is called Crabs. That unholy slime of the earth will be their leader.'

Gordon studied the men, and said, 'I think we must wait until dark to surprise them.'

'I think you are right,' murmured Tuds.

Crabs left the men and went back inside the cave. Malachai felt the hairs on his arms rise, frustration taking hold of him. He jumped up and charged as he yelled, 'To hell with this!' A fierce battle cry came from him as he ran towards the two sentries sitting by the cave mouth, holding his hammer high. Gordon and Tuds jumped up to follow, drawing their swords. Before Dock and Murkel even knew what was going on, Malachai was upon them. With a mighty swing of his hammer, he almost tore Dock's head off. The body hadn't hit the ground before the hammer was reversed, sinking into Murkel's chest as he drew his dagger. Bones shattered as the hammerhead sank deeper, splitting the sternum and stopping the heart. Blood seeped from his eyes, nose and mouth following the horrid blow. Tuds came to the big man's side and shouted, 'Are you crazy? You blubbering idiot, what happened to the plan?'

'Two down, four to go, be ready,' he said as Gordon reached his side and smiled, shaking his head in disbelief.

'You know, I think I am starting to like you too.'

As they entered the cave, an arrow came flying out, sinking into Malachai's side. Not knowing what lay ahead, he charged with a sudden rush of anger. He grabbed the man holding the crossbow and lifted him high, smashing his head against the sharp rocks of the cave ceiling. Blood poured down onto Malachai from the man's crushed skull. He threw the man to the side and slumped to the ground as pain overtook him.

The others ran at the remaining three men. The first jumped in front of Gordon with a wild slash through the air, missing his jugular by a hair's breadth as Gordon ducked beneath the blade. Crabs stood at the back of the cave, shouting at the remaining thug to kill the charging Tuds. Gordon thrust his sword forward but missed as the man parried the blow. A bit off-balance, the thug gave him a shallow cut on his left bicep. He steadied himself and waited for the next attack.

There is little room for movement in this dark cave. The man lunged carelessly. Gordon stepped to the right and knocked away the sword with his left hand and brought up his sword in a flash, pushing the blade cleanly through from under the man's chin to the top of his skull and out. The sword jutting from the top of the man's head was surprisingly clean, just a thin line of blood running down the blade. He pulled it clear and waited for the major to finish. He would want this for himself.

29

Tuds was fighting for his life against a bigger man, who clobbered a right hook into his face. He staggered back with a bloodied nose and swore at the man, then charged back in. The man lacked the skill to wield an axe, swinging it around like a rag doll, hoping, more than anything, that he would hit his opponent. Tuds sidestepped a blow, flashed his sword to the left, and cleaved deep into the thug's side. Guts spilled to the ground as Tuds stepped over him. He turned to look at Gordon, and said, 'Whatever happens next, Crabs is not leaving this cave alive.'

Crabs said fearfully, 'What do you want, why are you doing this?'

'Oh, I think you know, Crabs. I want you to scream as you made Lithuania scream when *you* raped her repeatedly.'

'I raped no one, I promise.'

Moving around before Crabs, Tuds swung his sabre about. 'Oh, come now, Crabs, young Gordon killed two of your cowardly men, one confessing the entire story. *And* you left her alive. Not a very smart move on your part. I have been dreaming of the day I would look into your eyes to watch you die. Now let's end this.'

Tuds rushed in and Crabs met him, swords clanging above their heads. Tuds released his left hand from the sabre and punched him in the face. Crabs staggered back, holding his nose as Tuds lunged and stabbed him through the chest. Gordon approached as Crabs lay on the cold, wet floor of the cave. Ragged breaths escaped the man as he reached out, as if to say something.

Gordon edged closer to hear his last words. Unbelievably fast, especially for a dying man, Crabs grabbed Gordon's hand with extreme power. Gordon looked down at him and realised the man was already dead. This force was not coming from him; it was external. A bright red lightning bolt bloomed in Crabs' hand and made its way up, curling around and up Gordon's arm, snaking up his neck and into his eyes. He screamed as he heard the dead man say, 'I will open *your* eyes to the world.'

A thundering hammer suddenly came down, crushing Crabs' skull and spilling brain and bone all over the cave floor. Gordon pitched back, holding his hands over his eyes, and fell to his knees. Malachai came to his side and lowered him to the ground.

Gordon suddenly found himself rise to look down upon himself. He shouted at his companions, but they could not hear him as they stood by his body. He rose further, out over the mountain, soaring higher. *Am I dead?* he asked himself.

'Far from it, young man,' came a voice just behind him, startling him.

Unable to control what was happening, he stared at the old man floating behind him and said, 'Then what's going on here, old man? A moment ago, I was down there in the cave with two companions and unbearable pain in my eyes.'

'Oh, it always hurts the first time, Gordon, you will get used to it. Your body is still down there in the cave; your spirit, however, has left your physical side for now. So we can talk.'

Furious, he tried grabbing at the old man, but to no avail. 'So *you* did this to me! What have you done?'

'I merely sent you a message through the thug your companion killed.'

Gordon was at the mercy of this old man, and he knew it. 'Okay, then, let's speak, but don't dally. I have a friend down there who's injured. He will need help soon.'

The old man soared closer. 'More than you know. Well then, my name is Father Delios. I am the abbot at the mountainside monastery, and I have been watching you. I know of your friend who got shot with the arrow in the cave. What you don't know is that the arrow was laced with Osikama poison. If you do not get him to us in the next three days, I am afraid he will die. One more thing: whatever happens, do *not* remove the arrow from his side. The next few days will be a harrowing ordeal for him.'

Softly cursing, he looked at the old man and said, 'Thank you for the advice, Father. How do I get to the monastery?'

Floating high above the mountain, faraway mountain peaks could be seen to the north. Delios rubbed his beard as he said, 'It's going to be tough, but you have to get to those mountains to the north. The monastery is on the east side of the mountains; you can't miss it. You must hurry—his time is short, and you still have a long quest ahead of you.'

'Then why have you left me up in the sky for so long, old man?'

Delios chuckled and flew off. The ground suddenly rushed closer as Gordon was hurled back into his body.

Voices echoed in his head as he opened his eyes to see Tuds and Malachai hovering above him, and waved them away as he rose to his feet. 'How long was I like that?'

Tuds looked at him. 'Not long, a couple heartbeats.'

Gordon grabbed Malachai and helped him walk out of the cave when he saw the big man was about to faint, his face pale, sweat dripping from his forehead. Fever was about to take him.

The big man stared at Gordon as they made their way out, and said, 'What happened to your eyes? They're... different.'

Tuds also turned to him and said, 'Oh my, oh my, are you okay Gordon? Can you even see?'

'Of course I can see, what's wrong with you?' he snapped.

'Look at your eyes,' said Tuds.

Gordon heaved Malachai onto a rock and pulled out his sword to look into the blade. The reflection looking back was not the old green eyes he remembered. No, staring back at him was a pair of pale white eyes, almost ghostly. 'We'll figure it out when we get to the monastery,' he said.

'What are you talking about? I am not going to some monastery?' said Tuds as he looked around the forest.

'Fine then, but you will leave the horses here. The big guy has been poisoned by that arrow. The only way to save him is to take him to the mountainside monastery. We will need your horse.'

Malachai had no objections; he could feel the poison spreading through his body. 'Hey Tuds, just give me my gold before you leave. Twenty-five gold, was it not?'

'Oh, I'm no fool. We settled on twenty. But I'm sorry, chaps... I can't go with you on this one. I have a hearing tomorrow regarding my superior's broken jaw, so unfortunately I cannot help.'

'Ah, no worries, I will see you when I get back... or not. Now, the gold.'

He fiddled in his leather pouch, pulled out some gold, and counted it. 'Twenty gold as promised.' He shook Malachai's hand, and continued, 'Thanks for the help, it's appreciated more than you know. I hope you get better soon, my friend. I would like to drink another ale with you. Farewell.' He turned to Gordon and said, 'By all means, take my horse and take care of him. I'm sorry I can't come with, but if I don't attend, they will hunt me down and cut off my head, and I am fairly reluctant to part ways with it.'

Gordon shook Tuds' hand and said, 'If you head ten, maybe twelve miles southeast from here, you'll find Karta. You can buy another horse there. Just ask for Jonah at the stables; he'll help you out. Farewell, Tuds.'

'Thank you, Gordon, much appreciated. Hopefully, if it's the will of the gods, we will meet again one day.' He turned around and headed for Karta as Gordon and Malachai watched him disappear into the thick of the forest.

Both men swung around and followed the trail back to their horses. The air was extremely humid in the forest and Malachai was drowning in his sweat, his entire body drenched. As they reached the horses, they walked with them to the edge of the forest, where they stopped to mount. The big man had no energy left in him. Having fallen thrice as he led the horse, he was breathing like an unfit child. Gordon had to pick him up over and over. He helped the big man into the saddle and tied the horses together before they set off, heading for the mountains.

CHAPTER FOUR

For the first day of their journey to the mountains, Malachai held out strong. They pushed on for as long as they could, riding till long after dark. Tired, the horses were becoming sluggish, slow to respond to commands. Gordon pulled off the road and made camp just out of sight in a ditch, so as not to attract unwanted guests. He quickly rubbed down the horses and fed them some grain. They rode the horses hard, and he knew they wouldn't last long at this pace. But he also knew that Malachai's strength was fading, and needed to get to the healer, quick. He cooked a very basic broth for them, but Malachai only toyed with the food, barely getting any in.

'Eat,' said Gordon as he stared at his worsening companion. 'It's the only way you will keep your strength.'

'Aye, I know, laddie, but I want to vomit every time I put it in my mouth.' Malachai was visibly paler now as he turned on his side to sleep.

The night was quiet and undisturbed as Gordon kept watch. He sat for a while on the edge of the trench and heard the big guy groan out in pain while he slept. He tore a piece of his shirt and dampened it with water from his canteen. Wiping it over the brow of the man, he said, 'Come on, old boy, you still have some fight in you, push through this.'

Gordon stood up and moved away to his blanket where he lay

down, thinking about why he was doing all of this for a man he barely knew. *I don't owe him anything.* He knew he liked the man for what he represented—strength and courage. But this was something more—he was a comrade-in-arms. He closed his eyes and dreams enveloped him. *I guess you have intruded on my mind more than I thought, father. Your words follow me on this quest, 'If you are in a position to help, Gordon, then do something about it. The world is a bitter and dark place, my boy. The more we can shine some light onto it, the better we all would be.'*

Gordon ran through the bushes as arrows flew past his head, missing him by mere inches. Running for his life, he tripped and fell over the root of a tree as another arrow sailed over his head. Quick to his feet, he was running again. He turned and hid behind a tree to catch his breath, only to hear an arrow thud into the back of the big oak. Carefully watching through the woods, he saw movement from two directions.

Silently, and with great caution, he climbed the tree and waited for the men. The sound of something scraping against a branch alerted him to his left; the only sign from one of his hunters, almost completely cloaked with his green jerkin and woollen trousers. Walking with bow in hand, the man stalked through the bushes, carefully placing each footstep as he scanned his surroundings.

Just a little closer, you idiot, thought Gordon. As the man approached, he leapt from the tree with his sword pointing down. Coming down on top of the man, the blade sank to the hilt through his chest, skewering the man. Gordon heaved the sword free with some effort as it caught on a broken rib; the man died without a sound. He picked up the bow and arrow and ran low to another tree, hiding behind it. The other hunter walked now with his sword drawn towards his dead friend and cursed.

A sharp whistle came from a distance, and the assassin looked up directly at Gordon, who had already released the string. The arrow came slicing through the air as the man tried to evade it, but he was too slow. The arrow hit, piercing his left shoulder and pinning him to the tree. A second arrow came flying, pinning his right shoulder.

The man was in agony and dropped his sword as Gordon slowly approached, pointing an arrow to his head. 'Who sent you? Why are you hunting us?' he demanded.

'I will tell you nothing,' the man said.

Gordon looked at the tall man before him. His bald head was bright red from the sun's heat. He lowered the bow, then smiled as he said, 'You don't get out much in the sun, do you? I heard another man stating the same not so long ago...'

A fresh new morning arrived in Caldonia as the sun lit the trees with a bright glow, mist still hanging low, the sky an early morning blue. Tuds was already up and getting ready for his day in the courthouse. Dressed in his regimental outfit, the red-and-yellow roped bands hanging from the left shoulder around his arm distinctly shone from his grey uniform, reflecting his rank as major. He sheathed his sword and left his home.

Angry at the idea that he had to defend himself for striking his superior, he did not notice the soldiers saluting as he walked by them on the way to the courthouse. His mind was in a whirlwind of its own making. Upon entering the courtroom, he saw the five judges sitting atop the raised platform next to each other, passing a large papyrus between them. He walked to the centre of the room as one judge gestured for him to take a seat. The judge in the middle spoke with a lofty tone, 'For the charges of assaulting a superior officer, how do you plead?'

Tuds rose. 'Guilty Your Honour.'

'And for the charge of stealing a conscripted horse, how do you plead?'

'Not guilty, Your Honour. I was merely taking a ride to cool down. I have returned the animal to the stable.'

'According to witnesses, you took two horses. Where is the other?' asked the judge as he examined the papyrus before him.

'I'm sorry Your Honour, but I only took the one. If another

followed me out of the stable, that is not my fault. If that was the case, charges should be brought against the stable keeper for negligence, not me.'

The judges spoke to one another and discussed the situation at length. A busy buzzing roamed the courtroom as Tuds sat in his chair, waiting for the judges to finish. After a lengthy discussion, the judge in the middle turned to face Tuds and said, 'Fair enough then. We will drop the charges for the horses, but the assault charge is still on trial.'

The judges glanced at each other, nodding their agreement before they finally continued with the trial. 'Major, we have already found you guilty of the fact of assaulting a superior officer. You now have the chance to explain why you did what you did, in order to commute your sentence. Do you understand this?'

'Yes, I do, Your Honour.'

'Good, you may continue.'

Tuds rose from his chair and walked up and down in front of the judges' desk. 'Your Honour, as an officer of the law, I was tasked to protect the people of this town from any threat. But when I brought the information about the rape in the countryside, the information was discarded and ignored. I was told to drop the case. No pursuit was made, nor any effort for one. I thereafter lost my temper and hit my superior for not wanting to do his job—'

'Some would argue that your duties lie outside the purview of the city guard. You are military!'

Tuds shook his head. *This will not turn out well for me.*

Gordon woke up early the next morning to check on Malachai. Confusion reigned in his head about the night's dream, but there was no time to concern himself with it. Fever had taken the big man as he clutched the blanket tightly around him. His dull eyes scanned Gordon as he pulled him from the ground. The steps he took sent shooting pains through his body, but he was happy with the pain. It meant he was still alive.

Gordon helped him to the trained military horse as it kneeled and strapped his feet to the stirrups, worried that he might fall off. 'Here, take this and drink.' He pulled out a leather wineskin filled with water and handed it to the man.

'Thanks for your help, laddie.' Malachai drank deep and coughed raggedly, blood staining his hands and lips. Gently patting him a few times on the back until he was gestured to stop, Gordon sighed and moved away to his horse.

It wasn't long after they set out that Malachai fell forward to lean against the horse's neck. Gordon took up the reins and led the horse forth. Cool air was blowing through the trees this day, as clouds formed above them. Green fields spread out to their left as far as the eye could see, looking like they were maintained for a king. On their right, trees lined up densely.

Suddenly a man came crashing from the tree line, bow and arrow in hand. Arrows ripped through the sky as Gordon ducked, just in time for the arrows to sail past his shoulder. He spurred the horses on until their hunter was out of sight, then stopped and jumped down next to the trees. He slapped Malachai's horse on its rump and sent it running. Unconscious and unaware of the danger, the big man flopped about on the galloping horse down the road as Gordon ran into the forest.

A glint of metal sliced through the air. He tucked and rolled as the arrow went over his head by mere inches. Running like the hounds of hell were on his trail, Gordon tripped and fell over the root of a tree as another arrow sailed over his head. *No, it can't be. This is happening exactly like the dream...*

The galloping horse awakened Malachai as it threw him about on the saddle. He pulled on the reins with his remaining strength, and said, 'Whoa, horse. Where's Gordon?' Barely able to see, he guided the horse to a gelding grazing on the grass further down the road. There was no sign of the young warrior. Coughs racked his body again and almost sent him to the ground as he lost his balance. Walking the horse back the way he came, he scanned the tree line and heard voices echoing from beyond...

'Who sent you? And why are you hunting us?' He heard Gordon's voice in the distance.

'I will tell you nothing,' came another's pain-filled voice.

'Move, you bastard!' Gordon crashed through the brush, shoving along a tall, bald man.

Malachai tried to sit up on the horse as he said, 'What happened here, lad?'

'Do not stress yourself, Malachai. I have it under control. You must preserve your strength. I caught this son of a whore and killed his friend. They were hunting us, but I've yet to get the reason. So he's coming with us; we haven't the time to interrogate him now. You are the priority.'

Malachai grinned as he heard the word "interrogate," and thought back to the man he saw strapped between the two trees, the huge bear feasting on him. He looked down at the captive and said, 'I hope you learn to speak very quickly.'

Gordon tied the captive five feet behind his horse and bellowed, 'I hope you can run! We will not be stopping.'

By nightfall, as they neared the D'hore Mountains, Malachai was ghostly white. With no strength left in him, he tried tearing off a piece of dried beef but failed as his hand didn't respond to him anymore. Gordon quickly took the beef, tore it, and handed it back to the bigger man.

He groaned as he swallowed it. It tore at his throat, going down with unbearable pain. A few breaths later, he vomited it out. A vile green liquid came from his stomach, spilling to the ground.

'Your friend is very ill. Maybe you should let me go so you can travel faster,' the bald man said, hoping they might consider the solution.

'Just you keep walking, you old rat.' Malachai spat the last bit of bile from his mouth and wiped his beard.

Gordon felt a chill go up around him as if they were being watched. Eyes burned their way through to his very soul. Unnerved, he looked around, fear gripping him. 'Something is wrong, Malachai. We have to hurry.'

Far away, high in the tower in a dark grey room, the whispers of the wizard echoed through the chamber as he chanted. Atop the altar, jutting from the marble floor in the caress of four corroded metal stands, each in the form of a child's arm, floated the fiery ball of the Anthean. Clouds swirled within, constant chaos reigning, as fire and lightning was its nature. Anukke stared into the ball, perturbed by what he was seeing. *'This will not do, Elgar, this will not do at all...'*

Elgar could hear the words uttered to him in his mind; fear grasped at him, as he knew what the wizard was capable of. They travelled the long road for some time as Malachai lay unconscious atop his horse, dripping blood from his wound and mouth. As the darkness fell on yet another hard day, Gordon could make out faint lights coming from the mountainside. 'We will be at the monastery soon, just hold on.'

There came no answer from the big man. Gordon stared at the form on the horse. It made no movement, only swaying with the momentum of the beast as if life had already left it. 'Malachai! Wake up!' Still, no answer came. He drove his heels into the flanks of the beast, and it lurched forward. The bald man was flung to the ground and dragged behind the horse for the last push to get to the monastery.

As they approached, a silhouette of a man appeared in the darkness in the middle of the road, hands concealed in front of him in his robe's sleeves. Wind pushed hard at his back, causing the trees to sway heavily. For a short while, there was silence between him and the company as they stood in front of each other, both waiting for the other to make the first move.

'You are Gordon, I presume. He is not looking well,' shouted the man over the rushing of the wind.

'Yes, I am he, and no, he is not doing well at all.'

Clearing his throat, the man continued, 'Well then, please follow me.' Turning to his right, the man went through an archway leading up a long, misty cobblestone path up to the monastery. As they approached the monastery, the man took the reins of the horses and said, 'Why is this man tied to the horse?' Concern rang in his voice.

'He tried to kill us. Hunted us like deer... I need answers,' Gordon said as he jumped down and started loosening the rope from the horse. As if summoned by some unseen force, four more priests arrived to help Malachai from the gelding.

'Be careful, priests, he is heavier than he looks,' Gordon warned, and as he spoke, Malachai slipped down. The four priests heaved and groaned as they tried to hold on, but they couldn't bear his weight. Gordon quickly stepped in and caught the big man, helping the older priests carry him. The bald man stood with broken arrow shafts in his shoulders, blood running down his arms from the dragging on the ground. They were not lethal injuries, but they must surely hurt a lot and made him of little threat to them.

The priest from the road led the horses down to the stable and took care of them as the others lay Malachai on a stretcher and brought him into the monastery. Once inside, Gordon saw the abbot standing atop the landing of a white marbled staircase running up, left and right, to the second floor. It was unlike anything he had ever seen before, and much bigger than he'd first thought from the outside. All the walls were of white marble, and the floor was somewhat more of a shining grey. Green plants on every corner broke the sharp white of the halls. The abbot approached, his long white robe setting him apart from the other priests with their red robes. In a calm, soft voice he whispered, 'I am Father Delios. I suspect you remember me from the cave?'

Gordon nodded and looked down at the old abbot, who had only his face visible behind the hooded robe. He looked ancient. Deep-set

41

lines coursed through his face, his long, thin grey beard reaching to his chest. Delios summoned one of the priests to take the bald man to a holding facility at the back of the monastery. 'We shall deal with him later.'

With angst in his voice, Gordon asked, 'Where have they taken Malachai?'

'Oh, don't fret, young one. They have taken him to the infirmary. Come, we will walk to him. They are preparing him for healing. As soon as they are ready, I will begin the examination.'

'Thank you, Father Abbot.'

'Oh, just Father would suffice, dear boy.' The abbot smiled as he continued, 'But please, call me Delios. You make me sound old when you say it like that.'

The two men walked through a hallway at least a hundred paces long and thirty paces wide; black pillars of rock with etched white sandstone markings lined the walls all the way to the ceiling high above. They soon entered a round chamber with shining silver-white walls. In the centre of the room, between four great pillars, stood a raised golden bed with silky red sheets, where Malachai lay unmoving and deathly pale. The priests had removed his shirt. Grey-blue rings had formed around the wound, covering his whole side. His breathing was ragged as faint sounds escaped from his mouth, accompanied by a thin line of blood running to the bedsheets.

Delios began ordering about the other priests. 'Get me a silver bowl, Artoree. Magnus, get some fungree from the garden. Antelios, make ready the surgical tools.'

Turning to Gordon, the old abbot suggested, 'I think it best you leave for now, my son. I need all their concentration to be focused on Malachai, and I fear you will interrupt us. I shall call for you once we are done.'

Gordon stood frowning at the abbot, and said, 'Will he live?'

'He has weakened and is in terrible shape; the poison is spreading faster than I would have hoped. But he is strong, I can sense it. Only time will tell.'

Gordon turned to leave and looked over his shoulder back to the abbot. 'Please do what you can,' he pleaded, then left the room.

The priests returned as Delios was examining the wound. They lay their items each on its own silver table and moved to the abbot. 'Let us start then.' The abbot whispered as he took up some fungree, a green plant that made the most beautiful white flowers and had the best numbing effects when you were stung by its large green thorns. Delios squeezed and twisted the plant as if breaking its neck. The sap trickled down onto the wound, and then he dribbled a little in Malachai's mouth, 'Swallow, old boy, you will need its numbing effects.'

Delios dropped the tortured plant and took the scalpel in hand.

Slowly he cut two grooves on either side of where the arrow had penetrated. Antelios handed the claws over to the abbot and took away the scalpel. Delios saw the poison had blackened the blood as it stained the red sheets.

Using the claws to pry open the flesh from the arrow to loosen its grip, he took hold and pulled it out slowly. 'Looks like the arrow penetrated the lung,' he muttered to himself. Pulling out a small glass bottle with a green powdery substance within, he opened the lid and poured it into the wound. Instantly, as the powder mixed with blood and flesh, it boiled like an acid mixture. Everywhere inside the wound was a bubbling green-black, vile liquid. The smell of burning, rotting flesh hung in the air.

As the night progressed and the abbot laboured over Malachai, colour returned to his skin. 'Ah, the substance is finally working,' he said.

Laying his hand on the wound, he started a chant, and the other priests joined in, holding onto the abbot's shoulders. They carried on for a while before the puncture in the lung slowly closed. Time went by as the chant continued to finally seal the lung completely. Exhausted, the abbot took up a needle and some catgut to close up the wound in Malachai's side as he said, 'I need to rest, and so do you.' When he was done, he patted the unconscious man on the shoulder, then continued, 'I will see you soon. Artoree, Magnus, Antelios, thank you for the assistance; now get some rest. His fate is now his own. We have done what we can.'

The three priests stayed a while longer to clean up the bloodstains; no words were uttered. Silence reigned in the room.

As the sun rose, the rays penetrating the windows of the monastery, making the sky look like a rusted sword, Delios walked down the hall to where Gordon lay sleeping on a couch.

Sitting underneath a giant oak tree on a field of grass, he leaned back and rested his head. Looking around, the sun was high, the sky cloudless and the most beautiful blue. There was no one in sight for miles.

The winds suddenly shifted, the air growing cold. Gordon looked up and stared death in the eyes. In front of him sat the biggest, blackest wolf he had ever seen in his life. Resting on its haunches, front legs extended, it reached over six feet tall. The dark black slitted pupils; red-rimmed, stared deep into his soul.

Gordon wanted to attack but found no weapon by his side. Then the thought of running came to him. A deep and harsh voice spoke to him in his mind: 'Why do they always think of running? Do not attempt it; you will not get far.'

Gordon froze on the spot and found fear rise in him, pulling at his stomach, and said, 'Who are you? Please tell me I am not speaking to a wolf right now.'

'Ha-ha-ha,' came a harsh, forced laugh. 'So life is not as dull as you might have believed it once. Strange things happen in the real world, indescribable things. Yes, you are speaking to a wolf. Do not take it lightly, as few have lived to talk about it.'

'Well then, I'm glad that I'm not losing my mind at the prospect of losing so much more.'

'Ah, a sense of humour. I had one once. It somehow died on me a while back.'

Irritated and afraid, Gordon rubbed his eyes, hoping this would all be gone once he removed his hand. But the wolf still stared at him, calm and unwavering. 'As much as I'm enjoying our little talk,' Gordon said as he shifted

44

nervously, then continued, 'can you tell me what you're doing here, talking to me?'

'Straight to business then. I have been sent by my... someone, and that someone wants the person you are holding captive in that monastery. So if you would be so kind as to hand him over, there will be no need for bloodshed.'

'So it is who you work for, your master—'

'He is not my master!' Canines flashed from the sudden outburst, the wolf's enormous jaws snapping shut inches from his face. 'Watch your tongue, boy, before I make you regret ever using it.'

Gordon closed his eyes while the wolf was in his face. He smelled the foul breath of the animal, the hot air with every exhalation. 'I'm afraid I can't let the man go, not before I get some answers.'

The wolf shook his head in disappointment and moved back as he said, 'I like you, Gordon, and just because I do, I will not kill you here in your sleep. I will wait on the crest of the hill in front of the monastery. Bring him to me if you change your mind; otherwise, I'll have to come get him, and that, I can promise you, will not be good for any of you.'

Gordon focused on the wolf and studied its graceful movements as it walked away, and said, 'You have me at a disadvantage. You know my name, but I do not know yours.'

The wolf stopped and cocked his head slightly to the left. 'Baldrake.'

Gordon raised his arms to the sky. 'Why are you giving me the opportunity to kill you later? Why not be done with it and kill me right now?'

'Huh. You young have still so much to learn. I can sense your honour and courage. To kill someone like you this way, unarmed and nowhere to run, is beneath me.'

'Just tell me why you are doing this? What does he hold over you?'

Gordon could see the sudden sorrow fill up in the immense beast's eyes as it pulled back its ears and turned away its face. A voice filled with sorrow said, 'We all do what we must. Enough talk; make your decision. Just know that if we meet other than on the hill's crest, there will be blood.'

Baldrake turned away and vanished into the bush.

☿

45

Gordon jumped from the couch, stark realisation hitting him like a blow from a hammer, knowing that what just occurred was no dream. Staring straight at the abbot, lines creased his youthful forehead as he said, 'We have a problem, Delios. Tell me what is out there.'

With a deep sigh, the abbot took hold of his arm and said, 'Come with me, boy, it's time I showed you the real world. You've been sheltered for far too long.'

They made their way to the back of the monastery. Uncomfortable as he was, Gordon needed to take his mind off the wolf. 'How is Malachai?'

'Time will tell...'

Walking through the garden, they passed underneath an archway and approached a structure; a round stone platform, five feet high, with stairs leading up. Six pillars adorned its edges, surrounding it with their ten-foot splendour. Symbols made with rubies and gemstones cut into the stone pillars. The abbot made his way up the stairs to the centre of the structure, turned, and gestured for him to join. As the two men stood atop the structure, the abbot started speaking in a language old and unknown to Gordon. 'Panaoes, Panaoes, feltigree subdominee, artoree seblingo atietse comaniecs...'

'W-what is happening, Delios?' The wind picked up with sudden fury, and dark clouds gathered above them. As the abbot fell silent, a bright white light appeared in front of them, spinning like a whirlwind where it hovered in the air. Delios looked at Gordon. 'Look into the light and concentrate; listen to my voice.'

In the bright light, images jumped to life. Father Delios closed his eyes as he said, 'Gordon, there are things in this world you do not yet know of, creatures that may seem unbelievable to you. Look and see the Mimacranes roaming the forest; nobody really knows their true form. They can change to the shape of something and mimic its behaviour, hence their name. The only way to know that it is one of them is to throw salted water on it. The creature will burn and scream a horrific crying noise. See the fiends from below the earth, the beasts of the sky.

Those hiding in shadows. There are many more to be seen; there are sorcerers and witches, warlocks, and so much more. But for now, tell me what you saw in your dreams, and I will call up an image.'

'I was in a field under a tree, when out of nowhere I was suddenly looking at the biggest wolf I had ever seen. It stared at me with death in its eyes, and then, as if nothing could get stranger, it spoke to me...'

An image started forming in front of Gordon as he concentrated on the whirlwind. Delios waved his arms about as in a dance, then said, 'The image you see in front of you now, is that the animal you saw?'

'Yes, only the one I saw was bigger and more battle-scarred. It was black as night, and the edges of his pupils were red-rimmed.'

'Well, isn't that just grand? You had an encounter with a Gar hound.'

'He said his name was—'

'Baldrake.' The name was said with wonder.

'Yes, how did you know?'

Thoughts ran through Delios' mind as he said, 'I know of tales about him.'

Gordon, bemused at all the new creatures he didn't even know existed, said, 'Delios, how come I never heard about these creatures and sorcerers and phenomenal things?'

'People avoid such matters, fearing that to talk about them is to invite them to your home. Therefore, their tales are not well-travelled, and those that do hear them believe them nothing more than myths.'

Wanting, *needing* to know more, Gordon pushed further. 'Tell me where these Gar hounds come from.'

'Well, there was an old story that proclaims them from another world, a world they called Gar. Hence their names. They were fierce warriors on their world but were attacked by some alien force with sorcery beyond their reach and comprehension. As the story goes, Baldrake was one of the commanding wolves. They were engaged in war with the advancing enemy when sudden, mysterious magic pulled him and his whole platoon through a vortex of some kind, and they all landed up here. His platoon started a mutiny against him and cast him out. He had to kill eight of them before they let him go. Through the years, I have kept track of them. They are fascinating creatures.'

'Well, it seems your fascination will be satisfied with an up-close encounter with Baldrake himself. He wants the prisoner we have, and I do not think he is going to let this go easily.'

The abbot said a few words, and the light vanished, the clouds cleared, and the wind died down. 'Come, dear boy, we can talk more inside. My old bones are not made for the outside anymore.'

'Delios, *you* can go in. *I* need to go have a talk with our prisoner.'

Delios stared at him and wiped his face with his arm, and said, 'I think it best if we spoke before you interrogate him.'

'Very well then, let's go.'

Sitting around an old wooden table in a room on the second floor, drinking some refreshments, Delios sighed as he put down his cup, and said, 'I have been getting the strangest visions during meditation, everything has been happening according to these visions, and—'

'Please, Father, get to the point. Not to be rude, but there's an enormous and possibly hungry Gar hound waiting for me, and I don't want to keep him waiting.'

Biting on his lip, the abbot continued, 'Yes, very well. Strange occurrences have been taking place. Let me explain it to you like this. There are two sides to the spirit realm: the good and the bad. The realms have to be in balance and harmony with each other at all times, otherwise bad things happen, and utter chaos ensues. More recently, there has been an extreme pull to one side of the realm.'

'Which?'

Delios forced the words out. 'Unfortunately, the bad one.'

'This is all fascinating, but what does it have to do with me? All I want is to go back home and continue my life. My father must be getting worried about me.'

'Don't worry about that, Gordon; I have already sent a messenger to your home to explain your extended absence.'

Gordon rose abruptly, skidding back the chair, and said, 'What are you talking about, Delios?! *I* am going home.'

'Please, just listen to me. There is big trouble brewing, I can feel it. If I am right about all this, it could be the end to humanity as we know it, and *you* will not have a life to go back to! You are the only one who can stop this madness.'

Gordon collected his thoughts and walked about the room as he spoke. 'Okay, Delios, don't be so dramatic. Why me?'

'"Before the time of old and grey, the ancient ruler of none but all shall rise once more and be bound to another. Through the blood of the innocent, evil shall be reborn. Forth shall come a mountainous man and a lion with the eyes of the blind to stop the evil spread. Through evil they will battle and triumphant they must be; otherwise, the ruler of none shall plunder all who are free".'

'What was that, Delios? Are you reciting a poem to me?'

'Well, more like a prophecy. Don't you see? You and Malachai are the mountainous man and the lion who must stop the evil threat!'

Gordon laughed out loud, and said, 'How can you say it's us?'

Delios, as serious as ever, rose from his chair and shouted, 'Because of your eyes, child! When I touched you back in that cave, your eyes changed. I could feel it. That happens to no one else. You have been given the gift of foresight, haven't you? Believe it or not, but your destiny has been decided. The world's fate—that is up to you though.'

'Oh, that's just great.'

Delios pointed a shaking finger at Gordon. 'If the prophecy is true, then there will be bloodshed and lots of it.'

'Okay, Delios, let's go have a talk with our prisoner.' As they left the room, Gordon said, 'Why do they call him the ruler of none?'

'Because, my dear boy, he wanted to kill everyone. Thus, there was no one for him to rule over...'

☿

In great pain, the prisoner sat in the corner of the gaol cell amidst some wheat bales, whimpering to himself as blood ran down the poorly stitched holes in his shoulders. The priests did not care to do good work with him.

'The priests have removed the arrows, I see,' Gordon said as he moved closer.

The prisoner swore as he shifted his weight on the bale, then leaned back as he said, 'What do you want?'

With a chuckle, Gordon stared at the man and said, 'What do I want... I want to know why you were hunting us. And before you even think of lying, do be aware that whoever sent you to kill us has also sent a massive wolf to "take care" of you. So you can either come clean and tell me everything, and maybe I won't hand you over to the wolf, or you can stay your tongue or lie, and die horribly by the wolf after a tremendous amount of torture. Make your choice.'

The bound man lowered his head to his chest as he sighed. 'Okay. My name is Elgar. To be honest, I know little more than you. He did not send me to kill you, merely knock you out to bring you to him. I don't even know the name of the man who sent me; I swear it.'

Gordon opened the door to the cell and moved in. 'So, it's a man, then.'

'What's a man?'

'The one who sent you. You said, "bring you to him." What else are you not telling me?'

A low rumble and thundering paws on the stone paths made him spin around to close the cell door, but he was too slow... Baldrake lunged up with outstretched claws, tearing into Gordon's throat, blood spraying from his arteries as he fell back to the stone floor.

'Please don't, Baldrake, please...' came the pleading voice of Elgar.

'Shut up, you insignificant pup!' shouted the voice inside Elgar's head, just before Baldrake jumped on him with all fours. The jaws closed around his neck, and he felt the huge teeth sink into his flesh. *So tight. I can't breathe!*

A vicious shake from the wolf and his head tore from his shoulders.

Blood sprayed against the walls as flesh and sinew fell on the floor. Baldrake dropped the head from his mouth and turned his attention back to Gordon. Delios stood shocked, stunned to silence in the courtyard's corner, and watched as the beast approached Gordon. The warrior lay on the ground, pushing aimlessly at the wound in his neck to stop the flow of blood.

'I am sorry, Gordon; I hate turning on my promises, but I had no choice. He forced me to do what I did...' Baldrake's head came up as he heard a scraping sound drawing closer. 'No, it cannot be him...'

Gordon heard the voice trail off in his head as the wolf ran off into the forest, and he saw Malachai stumble towards them, dragging his hammer at his back. Delios rushed forward and shouted for the priests to assist, but Malachai, weak as he still was from the operation, picked Gordon up from the floor and carried him to the healing room. Delios immediately started working on him as the other priests joined in, chanting their healing chant.

CHAPTER FIVE

Deep down in the wizard's dungeon, chained in his cell once more, Baldrake lay on all fours with his head upon his paws, thinking on the day's events. Sorrow filled him as he thought back to the moment he slashed Gordon's throat.

'Oh, stop moping about,' came the voice from the staircase. 'You did well. Elgar would have told them everything. I cannot afford people knowing too much right now.'

Baldrake slowly moved closer to the wizard standing behind the iron bars. In the dark, gloomy light, his warm breath steamed from his nostrils, adding to the stories of the misbegotten demon hound. He stared into the eyes of the wizard and spoke to his mind, 'You said you would let them go if I did this for you, now let them go!'

Anukke moved around the cages, keeping clear of the reach of the wolf. 'Yes, you're right, I did say that.' He stopped and waved his finger about, then continued, 'There is just one problem with that, though. As soon as I let them go, there's nothing to keep you in check, now is there?'

'Are you really going to take the chance of not keeping your word to me? If I get out of this cage, I will rip you apart limb from limb, piece by piece, and there will be nothing that can stop me.'

Anukke sighed mockingly. 'Yes! Exactly! All that will happen if I let them go, but if I *don't* let them go, you will not dare make a move against me; you will protect me, you will obey me.' Walking back up the stairs, he slammed the door to the dungeon, leaving them in the dark.

From the corner of the cell came another voice, soft and regretful. 'I am so sorry, Baldrake; you should just leave us here and get on with your life. Forget about us, he is never going to stop.'

'Stop that nonsense, Cuorco; you've saved my hide more times than I can count. Just because you got old doesn't mean I'll forget all you have done for me. How's the young one doing?'

Lowering his head in shame, Cuorco said, 'He is still ill and not looking good, but better since they gave the antidote earlier this morning. I assumed you did what he requested of you.'

Baldrake sighed as he said, 'I did indeed. Do you remember about six years ago, when we fought together, side by side, with General Torell against those Abynesians with their war-bred dogs?'

Cuorco raised his head curiously and answered, 'Yes, I remember. Why do you ask?'

Baldrake stood staring at the dungeon door. 'Do you recall the man we named "Vasgath"?'

Instinctively. Cuorco rubbed his paw over the scar that covered where his right eye should be, and said, 'Yes, I remember him. He was insane, killed anything that came his way—man, beast, no matter what. He was a good man, though. But a greater fighter, I have yet to see.'

Deep in thought, Baldrake calmly stated, 'I saw him today at the monastery when I killed that poor boy and Elgar. I do not think he recognised me, though.'

Cuorco stepped closer to Baldrake, who stood in the dim light, still looking at the closed door, and said, 'He was never very fond of our kind. I would not cross that man. He is unpredictable and possibly crazy. But also, if it weren't for him, I would have been dead in that battle. That tiger attacked from nowhere.'

The big black wolf turned and saw the scar running across Cuorco's silver-furred face.

'I remember how I was thrown from my feet, landing heavy and losing my breath. I was still trying to regain it as I lay on the ground when I felt my right eye being pulled from its socket as the blow landed. It all happened so fast. That man charged in with no thought to his own safety and jumped at the tiger, taking it off me and its feet. He rolled on the ground, wrestling with it as I lay in a pool of my blood. I remember how they circled each other. The tiger made a critical mistake and jumped at him. Instant death followed as that hammer came down, crushing its skull.'

Baldrake grimaced and said, 'I remember seeing it from a distance.'

'Community service, working with the elderly, cleaning other people's stinking excrement? I won't have it,' Tuds cursed as he scrubbed the bedpans of the medical centre. The days were long and uneventful. Nothing interesting ever happened. And if it did, they immediately moved you to work somewhere else. Tuds did his chores to the best of his abilities every day, but it was wearing him out, slowly and surely.

Scrubbing a bedpan filled with human waste, his thoughts were dark as his hand slipped and plunged into the foul contents. His back curled as his stomach pushed up its contents. He held his gorge down and cleaned his hand with a rag. '*Kill the judges, make them pay for this,*' a sinister voice spoke in his mind.

Tuds jumped and looked around. 'Who's there? Is someone playing tricks on me? I shall not fall for it.' The hallway stood empty, devoid of any man or woman. 'What was that?'

During the walk back to his quarters, Tuds felt like smiting everyone who came in his path, thinking maybe, just maybe, the hurt of others would take away his hatred and affliction. He watched the poor souls walk past to their homes, like sheep being herded into pens. They disgusted him.

Tired and frustrated, he grabbed a bottle from his liquor cabinet and downed half of its contents. His head embraced the rush of alcohol; its numbing effects soothed his ills. It knocked his breath away and made him twist and shake as it went down his throat. Not long after, he could feel it taking effect, slowing his thinking and slurring his speech. His vision drifted as he looked up to the second floor. *Stairs, huh? What an amazing idea that was.* He made his way to his room and fell onto his bed. Nightmares came to him this night, horrible dreams of mutilated corpses, of people dying all around him. Death was in his dreams and it was never-ending. Haunting him. Tormenting him.

Drenched in sweat, he willed himself out of bed as the sun peered through the window. Exhausted, he panted; his chest heaved as if he had been running miles on end. 'Boy, that was a terrible night.'

Back at the medical centre, scrubbing down more bedpans as he had been doing for the last few days, a young man came running down the hall and entered the room where Tuds was working. He saluted, and said, 'Tuds sir, have you heard the news?'

Togy, a short, stocky man with a fringe cut hairstyle, barely eighteen years of age, stood before him. *He has no business being in the military. He is no soldier.* Tuds sighed as he stood with the cleaning equipment in his hands, and said, 'Slow down, Togy. What news are you referring to?'

'Sir, two of the judges that sentenced you have been found murdered. They were hung upside down from the ceiling with their throats cut. They say there were pieces of flesh carved out of their stomachs.'

Taken aback, Tuds tried to act calm. 'Is that even possible?'

'I don't know, sir, but whoever is capable of doing this is a monster.'

Quietly returning to his work, Tuds stated, 'There's a lot of evil in this world, Togy. The quicker you learn it, the better.'

'You don't sound very upset, sir...' came the distraught voice of the young man.

A snort escaped Tuds as he muttered, 'Well now, my dear Togy, they *did* banish me to this hellhole. Given that, they still didn't deserve to die though. Especially like that.'

'Sir, I believe they plan to ask you about last night since you were the last offender to be judged by them.'

'Thank you for letting me know; it's much appreciated. Now if you would excuse me, I have some scrubbing to do.'

Togy turned and walked out of the room, only to walk straight into one of three officers to come around the corner. 'Sorry, sir, my apologies.'

'Be warier next time, soldier. Where is Tudeske?'

'In the bathroom, busy with his community service, sir.'

'All right then, lad, off with you.'

'Thank you, sir.'

Alone behind the closed door of his room in the monastery sat Eldridge, a new intake to the order of priesthood, looking into a crimson ball of fire that illuminated the dark room and said, 'Yes, Lord Anukke, I have the blood of the two warriors here at the monastery. It was no simple task sneaking it out of the healing room.'

'Do they suspect anything?'

'I don't believe so. I will soon depart for your castle, my lord, to bring the blood.'

'You have done well, Eldridge. I will await your return.'

Antelios came running down the stairs to where Delios sat with Malachai, playing a game of woodsy as they waited for Gordon to wake up. The game involved twenty perfectly round timbers being stacked on top of each other, by which you must take out any other timber and place it back on top to grow the stack, without it tumbling down. Whoever makes it tumble is the loser. 'Whoa, slow down, Antelios. What has spooked you into a run, my son?' Delios cried out as the skidding priest came to a halt before them.

'Forgive my intrusion Abbot, but I think we have a spy in our midst!'

'Oh, and what makes you say that?'

Nervously glancing to the big man, Antelios continued, 'I was doing my rounds through the corridor for the new intakes. It was then that I heard two voices speaking, and a faint glow emitted from under a door.'

'And what was the conversation about?' asked the abbot, sitting back and taking a deep drink of water. Malachai pulled himself to the edge of the chair and listened intently to the priest's words.

'Well, I could not make out everything, but I did hear him speak about departing soon and that they suspect nothing as yet.'

'Whose room was this? I will gut him like a pig. Tell me.' Uncharacteristic of Malachai, he whispered calmly, so as not to alarm anyone.

Raising his palms, Delios intervened before it went too far, and said, 'Wait, before we take too drastic a measure. Let's wait for him to make his move. You can follow him and see where he leads you. Then, at least, we will know who is behind all of this.'

'Very well, Abbot. I wouldn't mind finding out who's been trying to kill us,' Malachai returned.

Still standing anxiously before the big man, Antelios shivered at the thought of betraying him. 'It was the new intake. I believe his name is Eldridge.'

'Thank you, Antelios. Please, do not alert anyone else of this matter, and keep me informed of his activities,' Delios stated as he waved him from the room. The young priest knew the gesture all too well. He nodded and turned on his heel to walk out of the room.

From the opposite direction came another priest, moving fast towards them.

Delios stared at the big man and muttered, 'What is with all the running tonight?' Malachai grinned through his beard as the priest approached.

'He is awake, Father,' came the voice of Artoree.

Rising from his chair, the old abbot slapped Malachai on the back. 'Come, we must go see our friend.'

Malachai had been getting stronger as the night dragged on. The last few days after the attack on Gordon had done the big man good as he rested and healed up.

As both men entered the room, the other priests left to give them some privacy. Malachai stared down at the young man, and said, 'Well, aren't you a sight for sore eyes?'

The scars on Gordon's neck were starting to fade as the healing process continued. 'I'm glad to see you up and about as well,' came his hoarse voice.

'Rest, my son. Tomorrow you will be as good as ever,' Delios told him as he smiled.

He looked back at the abbot and said, 'So, Father... was Baldrake all you had imagined?'

The big man shook his head as he shouted, 'WHAT!' Malachai pointed his finger at Gordon. 'Did he just say Baldrake? Gordon, get some rest. We will talk tomorrow once you are better. Delios, we have to talk, now!'

Half-dragging the abbot out of the infirmary and up the stairs to the meeting room, he pushed Delios into a chair as the old abbot complained, 'Stop that Malachai, you're hurting me.'

'Sorry, Delios, didn't mean to. I got a bit nervous back there.'

Malachai paced up and down next to the long table, anxiously taking a piece of bread from the table and shoving it into his mouth. Delios stared at him inquisitively. 'What is all this? Why are you suddenly so stressed?'

Malachai stopped his pacing to face him, and said, 'I told Tuds that I've only killed one man and that it was in self-defence.'

Delios nodded his head. 'Yes, I know about that. I was there.'

Flustered, his face contorted, Malachai replied, 'What do you mean "you were there"?'

'I was there in spirit. Ever since you and Tudeske set off on the quest for justice against those thugs who raped the girl, I was there.'

'Why?'

'We take an interest in such things.'

These sorts of things had never fascinated Malachai, who found it hogwash and boring, believing that people leaving their bodies and such should be left to the dead. Half-irate, he countered, 'Well, whatever. It was a lie. I'm a war veteran who has fought in countless battles. I thought I could leave my old life behind and start fresh... But that's not important right now. What's important is the fact that I know Baldrake very well. You see, I fought alongside him a while back in the war against the Abynesians, who came from the South Sea to invade our country. You might remember the times.'

Delios stared at Malachai in disbelief, his eyes wide and mouth open. 'I must say, this comes as a bit of a shock to me. I remember the war, but there wasn't much elaborated on it.'

'Yes, understandably so. They kept it quiet because we used the Gar hounds in the war.'

'Wait. Are you telling me they covered all that up?'

Malachai marched up and down in front of Delios, his hands to his sides. 'Yes indeed. See, the Abynesians had their monstrous war-bred dogs, and we had no counter. So they set the task on me and four others to convince the Gar hounds to join us in the battle to counter the dogs.'

'This is unbelievable.' Delios muttered.

'What most don't know is the fact that the Gar hounds—most of them, anyway—are honourable beasts. Though I didn't like them in the beginning, I grew to... understand them. And what I know, especially about Baldrake, is that he would never just kill someone for the fun of it. During the war, he had a nickname: "Reaper". Don't you see? He could have killed Gordon where he lay and you where you stood, but he chose not to. There must be more to this story. I hope so because if he turned against us, we're in real big trouble.'

Four days had passed since the attack on Gordon. The sweet juices from the orange ran down his throat as he swallowed another slice. He closed his eyes and was gently rubbing the scar on his neck as he sat outside in the garden when Malachai joined him. 'How are you feeling, laddie?'

'Like a Gar hound just tried to rip my head off. Guess I'll live.'

Malachai stared glumly at the trees. 'We better get our gear; that Eldridge bastard is heading off in a bit, and we should be ready to follow... I've been meaning to thank you for saving my life, by the way. I am in your debt.'

'I'm sure you would have done the same if it was me in your stead. Delios told me about your dealings with the hounds... is it all true?' He glanced at Malachai and saw him grind his teeth as he avoided eye contact.

'Yes, it is.' Gordon tossed him an orange, and the big man immediately began peeling it as he said, 'Aye, damned good oranges, these. Must have eaten forty of the things already.'

From the hall across the garden, Delios approached them slowly. 'It is time. Eldridge is ready to depart, so be careful not to be seen. We have readied your horses and packed everything you will need. Go find them in the stable. Move through the door at the back not to be seen by the worm.'

Both men stared hard at the abbot as Gordon said, 'Father Delios, thank you for your help and hospitality. If it weren't for you, we would both be dead right now. Thank you for everything. I don't know how we can ever repay you.'

Sullenly nodding and smiling at them, Delios accepted their gratitude and said, 'Fair enough. May you both be blessed in the journeys that follow. Vanquish this coming evil, then I will consider your debts paid in full, my boy. May the gods guide you. If you boys need anything, please do come by at any time.'

The spy was loading his equipment on his horse, unaware he was being watched as the two men slipped through the back and mounted their own horses. Watching, waiting from the stables atop their mounts, the two men sat looking at Eldridge, busily preparing to leave.

'That's right, you fat swine, as soon as we find your master, it's off with your ridiculously round head. I can see it now, rolling on the ground as it tumbles from your puffy little shoulders,' Malachai muttered to himself.

Eldridge said his goodbyes to his fellow priests and set out on the road. Gordon and Malachai waited just long enough not to be seen and set out after him.

Tuds had been in a holding cell for the last three days, being questioned twice daily by different officers, but they found no reason to hold him further. Once freed, he set off towards Lithuania's house, down in the countryside on the outskirts of Caldonia. A warm summer's day with a fine cool breeze was blowing from the east. Tuds found himself enjoying the fresh air more than usual after his imprisonment.

Lithuania was outside, busy sweeping the front porch when he arrived. Upon seeing him, she dropped the broom and ran to him, throwing her arms around his neck. Entangled in the embrace, she said, 'Oh Tuds, where have you been? I heard rumours you were in jail for murder. I didn't believe it, not for a moment. I have missed you so much.'

'And I you, my dove. What say you, we get better acquainted there in your bedroom? I haven't seen you in such a long time, I barely remember you. I think you will have to remind me of who you are again.'

Smiling, she said, 'Whatever, Tuds. But if you want me that bad, then you'll have to work for it.'

'Fine, then. Let's have a taste of what I need to work for.' He lifted her from the ground and carried her in his arms to the bedroom and closed the door behind them...

Later that night, Lithuania awoke to find her bed empty. 'Tuds, where are you?' *Hmph. Maybe he just got himself a drink of water or something to eat,* she told herself. Stepping softly on the wooden floor, she moved to the kitchen. But he was nowhere to be found in the house; it was empty.

Nothing stirred, except for a single window open in the kitchen, blowing cool air into the house and moving the curtains as if they were dancing about the window frame. 'Tuds! Tuds, where are you?' she shouted, but no answer came.

Finally, she went back to bed, only to find him in bed fast asleep. 'What the... am I losing my mind? No, it can't be. Tuds, wake up. Wake up, Tuds.'

Confused and tired, he sat up and yawned as he said, 'What's going on? What are you doing out of bed?'

'I... I'm sorry, Tuds, it's nothing. Go back to bed.'

Sleep did not come to Lithuania for the rest of the night as she pondered what just occurred.

He was up early the next morning and found Lithuania already making breakfast. He studied her as she cooked bacon, her slender figure and soft features swaying side-to-side as she worked away, her long dark hair flowing freely over her shoulders. Tuds hugged her from the back and sat down at the table. 'I am late, my dove, so please excuse my haste this morning.' She nodded and handed him his plate. He ate swiftly and left to continue his community service.

The walk back to town was much farther than he remembered it, and he felt much heavier, as if he was being pressed to the ground by some invisible force. Once back at the Centre, Tuds had worked his way through most of the bedpans and basins when he got a surprise visit from the famous General Blackbeard.

Disgust plagued the general's face as he watched the man trying to rid himself of the pan in his hands. Tuds reached out his hand to the general, only to receive a sneer from the man, then pulled back his hand as the general said. 'Not to stay a moment longer in this place, I will get to the point. I am willing to forego your sentence for hitting a superior if you come into my brigade under me as my major general. What do you say?'

'What about General Tobias?'

'Oh, I wouldn't worry too much about him. Everyone thinks you did the right thing by beating his pompous fat arse to the ground. So what do you say? I need people like you.'

'Well then, count me in, General.' Tuds saluted and watched as Blackbeard turned to leave.

'Splendid. Meet me tomorrow at the regimental encampment west of town.'

The songs of the cicadas echoed in the heat as the sun beat down on them. Heatwaves formed on the horizon over the road as they travelled about a mile behind Eldridge, keeping low and out of sight. Malachai rode his chestnut gelding in silence beside Gordon. In time, he took out a piece of beef and tore the dried meat in two. With a soft whistle, he drew Gordon's attention and handed him a piece. *It's like looking into the eyes of the blind,* he thought as he stared at the young man, and said, 'You know, I don't think I'll ever get used to your eyes. It doesn't seem to bother you too much, though.'

With a wry grin, Gordon stared at Malachai and said, 'My entire life I've wanted to be different, extraordinary. I believed I was, or would be— almost felt it when I was younger. Now it's simply come true. One might say that my dreams came true. It gives me an advantage.'

'How do you figure that?'

'Would you fight a blind man?'

Malachai raised his right brow and said, 'Aye, different you are, laddie. Didn't you ever have bigger dreams though than just being different?'

Biting the beef strip, Gordon said as he chewed, 'The whole having a house, a family, being in one place for the rest of my life, huh... no, that's not for me, not now in any case. Maybe later in life. What about you?'

'Enough of the pleasantries, there's someone in the road up ahead. Stay sharp.'

Up ahead, at the centre of a fork in the road, stood a cherry tree. A short old man with a walking stick, raggedy clothes, and no shoes was busy picking cherries from the tree and putting them into a straw woven basket. As the two men approached the tree, the old man slowly turned to them with an obvious limp off to his right leg, and said, 'Where ya bbbboys headin?'

'Good day, sir. My companion and I were just taking a ride through the forest, that's all,' Gordon told the old man as he lay forward on his horse.

'SSSSSorry, sonny, but I didn't know the blind could ride horses.'

Gordon and Malachai glanced at each other. 'It's a rare gift. Took me a while to get used to it.'

'Are ya boys following that young priest that cccccame through not long ago?'

'No offense, old man, but best you mind your own business.' Malachai was getting frustrated and wanted to head off.

'Meant no harm there, sssssonny.'

Gordon interposed, 'Sorry old timer, my friend just wants to get home.'

'Ya bbbbboys wouldn't be passing Kalaghstine, would ya? It's just a few miles on with this road. Ya know, old people don't walk very fast, and I would like to get home before dark.'

Malachai shook his head, but Gordon said dismissively, 'Sure, old-timer, I can take you home. Just give us a moment.'

Gordon and Malachai trotted off just out of earshot. 'What in blazes are you doing?' Malachai asked, keeping an eye on the old man by the tree.

'I don't know, but I have a strange feeling about this old guy, and I would like to see where this takes us. You follow Eldridge and see where he goes. I will take the old man home and learn what I can. Once you see where Eldridge stops, come back to this Kalaghstine and meet me at the first inn you see.'

'And what if Eldridge does not stop?'

Sighing, Gordon said, 'Then I will ride hard tomorrow to catch up. Just leave me signs on the road.'

Gordon and Malachai turned back to the old man. 'What's your name, old-timer?'

'They call me Attalus.'

Why does that name sound so familiar... I am sure I have heard it somewhere. 'Good to meet you, Attalus. I am Gordon, and this angry fellow is Malachai. Best we head off. The sun is setting soon. See you in a while, my friend.'

Malachai drove his heels into his gelding's side and launched off to the right over the hill towards the mountainside, disappearing in a cloud of dust. Gordon helped the short old man up onto the horse and followed the road to the left towards Kalaghstine at a more leisurely pace.

Dusk was approaching rapidly as Gordon crested the last hill and saw the lanterns in the streets being lit, their faint glow travelling far as the dark started taking over. Eyes strayed his way and scanned him as they trotted through the gates of Kalaghstine.

'Sssssorry, lad, people here don't take too kindly to strangers.'

Gordon pulled his hood over his head and moved through the brick facade city. It was nothing fancy, but it was clean enough, and few beggars roamed around.

Hands went flying past his head as the old man shouted directions. 'Make a rrrrright. I said rrrrright, boy! Two bbbbblocks down this ssssstreet to ya left, up three more blocks, fffffifth house on the right. That's where we stop.'

Suddenly Gordon laughed to himself.

'What's so fffffunny sonny?'

'Oh, nothing, I just saw that your first inn on this road is called "The Fairy Gall-away Inn".'

'Well, what's so funny about that, ssssonny?'

Oh, Malachai is going to have a fit about this... 'Nothing, nothing at all.'

Up in the mountainside, Malachai was moving through the trees on the side of the road, following Eldridge a mere fifty paces behind, on foot. Eldridge was no warrior; completely unaware that he was being trailed so closely, he carried on walking up the mountain, following the narrow path on his pinto horse.

Malachai was confused when he saw the road abruptly stop against the mountain. *One would think there would be a cave or tunnel heading deeper, but there is none. Hiding behind a tree like a coward. Humiliating. I should just run out and ram my hammer through his head and be done with it.*

Eldridge muttered some words in a language unknown to Malachai, and the mountain obeyed, shifting and tearing open a massive hole in its side. Two guards moved out with hands on their swords, scanning the area before leading Eldridge back into the mountain.

'What the...' Malachai moved forward to get a better look and stepped on a twig, breaking it. A loud crack sounded. One guard turned his head towards the sound and shouted, 'Hey! Who's there?' Suddenly, ten more guards came rushing out of the mountain as Eldridge vanished within.

Guards were pouring into the trees, swords and spears held high. 'Come out and play, we won't hurt you... too much... at first,' came the voices of the soldiers.

'I could never see prop'ly in this bloomin' dark.'

'Tis because ya keep lookin at bright t'ings, ya moron.'

Malachai climbed the tree before him as soon as the twig snapped. Silently, he watched them from up high. For some time, they searched the area; and luckily for him, some distance away an elk moved through the trees, snapping more branches as it darted off. 'Suppose an elk isn't a big threat,' one soldier told another directly underneath Malachai. The rest of the soldiers gave up the search.

Eventually, all the soldiers went back inside the mountain, and it sealed shut once more as if they were never there. Malachai moved silently down the tree. Once back on the ground, he stared at the mountain and shrugged his shoulders. 'Now I've seen everything. I'd better get back to Gordon and find out what we're dealing with.' Malachai rushed through the trees back to where he'd tethered his gelding and quickly jumped on his horse. It whinnied heavily with the sudden weight upon its back. 'Come on then, make haste.'

The night was quiet and unusually dark, mist floating low through the forest. Looking out from the mountainside, Malachai could make out the lights from the city. 'That must be Kalaghstine, luckily not too far away. I need ale and some rest.'

Closing in on the city, Malachai marvelled at the size of its walls, standing over thirty feet high. At a fast trot, he made his way through the gates, past the first sentry, only to be stopped by the second, with a spear pointing wildly at him. 'Whoa lad, you could put out someone's eye with that.'

'I intend to do more than that! Now, state your business.'

Calmly Malachai stared at the young man, and said, 'Laddie, if you don't drop that spear, I will drop you into the ground.'

Nervously, the sentry was looking around for backup when a voice rang out from the shadows. 'Timiell, put down your spear before you get dead. Can't you see this man is not to be trifled with?'

Timiell slowly lowered his spear and moved aside. 'Yes, Captain.'

'That's better lad, now we can continue this as a civilised conversation,' Malachai said with a grin on his face.

The captain moved forward to stand before the big man on his horse. 'Sorry about that; don't take it personal. It is their job to stop suspicious-looking people, and he is new to the campaign.'

'Now *you* have to look at *your* words carefully. Why am I considered suspicious?'

Grinning, the captain continued, 'Oh, I apologise. Did not mean to offend. It's more the manner and time you entered the gates, that's all. I am their captain, name's Chip.'

Malachai stretched out his hand. 'Good to meet you, Captain. I'm meeting someone here in town. Don't worry, I'm not here to cause any trouble.'

'Thanks. I will hold you to that.'

As Malachai started moving past them, he said, 'Say, Captain Chip, where's your first inn?'

With a chuckle and raised eyebrows, Chip stared at Malachai and saw that it was not the right way to respond to the question. Malachai's brows had furrowed, changing his expression from his calm demeanour. Captain Chip quickly stated, 'Are you sure you don't want to go to the inn further down the road?'

'No, I need to get to the first one.'

'Suit yourself then. It's just a few blocks up the road—can't miss it. Have yourself a good night, now.'

Malachai strolled through the streets towards the first building with the most lights and boards on the outside. *There's something not right with this place. Why on earth are all the boards painted pink?* Malachai spoke to the first passer-by, 'Excuse me, but what is this place called?'

An old chap with very few teeth answered him, 'As if you don't know. It's called, "The Fairy Gall-away"...' The old man stared hard at Malachai, and after a long silent pause, said, 'You people make me sick.'

'But I...' began Malachai.

The old man turned and walked off in disgust.

'Oooh, I am going to *kill* Gordon when I get my hands on him, no excuses.'

Uncomfortable with the situation, he sauntered through the doors and pushed past the crowd. Most turned from their conversation to look upon this enormous man. In the corner, he saw Gordon having a drink with his hood drawn over his head. He gestured at Malachai and to a servant girl for another jug of ale. Still, all eyes were on him as he squeezed past the tables and sat down opposite Gordon. The place looked discreet enough, except for the funny-looking thin man or woman—Malachai couldn't tell—brushing up against some other guy in the bar's corner.

'What in name of all that is unholy is this place? And why are we here? We should leave now!' he stormed.

Grinning, Gordon replied mockingly, 'I knew you would like it.'

'You hold on there... why I oughta—'

Interrupting Malachai's wrath, Gordon quickly stated, 'I hope you don't mind. They only had one room available, and it only has one bed. Better than nothing, so... I took it.'

'What! Have you lost your mind?' Malachai slammed his fists against the table, 'I will sleep in the stables... If I wasn't this thirsty...' He gulped down the ale and asked for another.

Gordon sat back in his chair as a laughing fit took him. He placed his feet upon the table and threw a silver coin to the barman, who also laughed wholeheartedly.

Steaming, Malachai roared at them, 'What's going on here? I demand to know what's happening before I start breaking limbs.'

Struggling to catch his breath, Gordon explained, 'Okay, okay. The barman and I had a bet that if I told you about the room, you would not lose your temper and still be civilised about the situation. The thing is though, I knew you were going to lose your temper. I just wanted to have some fun with you. Sorry old boy, but you were a sport.'

'Why, you little bastard!' Malachai started grinning and sat down at the table, grabbing the jug in hand and taking a huge gulp of ale. 'Let's talk about what I saw back there. But first, please tell me you're jesting about the room here.'

'Yes, yes. I got us a room with two beds at the next inn.'

Sitting at the table having a few ales, they were enjoying themselves for the first time since they set off on their adventure.

'I saw the darndest thing following that worm; I don't even know how to explain it. Eldridge was standing in front of the mountain, uttering words I have never heard, and suddenly a doorway opened out of nothing...'

'I will speak to some townsfolk and see what we can find out. You know, Malachai...' Gordon said as he lifted his jug to the air. 'This is my first time drinking ale, and I like it.'

'Seems we have a cause for celebration then, but do you mind if we celebrate at the next inn? I feel as if my clothes are being torn from my body. The way they stare at me... I feel naked.'

'Sure thing, old friend, let's move out.'

Malachai shrugged and brought his hands to the air as he said, 'I mean, it's just, *who* goes and calls their inn "The Fairy Gall-away"? Do they even understand the meaning of it, or was it by chance?'

The world spun as Gordon got up from his seat. Unable to grab Malachai's arm, he slumped back down.

With a big grin on his face, Malachai stood and asked, 'Oi, lad, how many have you had?'

'I don't know, a few.'

Getting up once more, he steadied himself and the two men walked out to the street. Once outside, Malachai untethered his horse, and they walked the two blocks to the next inn to get some fresh air.

'"The Wayward Ale." Now you see, lad, that's better already,' Malachai stated with a big smile on his face. Once inside, no real attention was given to them as they slipped by to an open table. 'Lad, this is what an inn should look like.'

People danced, music played, everyone was laughing and enjoying themselves. The wooden tables and chairs were all moved about to make room for the dancers. A fight broke out in the corner as two men began shouting something about a girl, and the big man smiled. He called over the barkeep and said, 'Two jugs of your finest ale, and two of your worst shots to begin with. Tonight, we celebrate!'

Eldridge handed Anukke the vials of blood, who took them to an enclosed chamber with a silver mirror in the centre of the room. 'Lord Anukke, if I may ask. What do you plan?'

Sighing irritably, Anukke rolled his eyes. 'So many smart people in the world, but it's the insignificant and dumb ones who ask all the questions.'

Quickly stepping back from his lord, Eldridge said, 'I am sorry, my lord. Forget I asked.'

'It is too late now, you fat swine! I am tired of not being recognised.

I am tired of hiding in the shadows. No, my time has come to rule them all. They will bend the knee to me. All of them. This blood, and this mirror, will show me the one who will be the vessel for the resurrected Bloodbane. Now, if you ask me any more questions, I will have to break your neck and offer your blood to a wraith. They will have so much fun resurrecting you, then torturing you to death, it will keep them busy for weeks. Get the picture?'

'Is that even possible?' Eldridge wondered, as his face lowered to the ground.

'Is that another question?'

'No! Sorry, my lord.'

Anukke took the blood from the first vial and threw it onto the mirror while chanting, then smeared it to cover the surface; but nothing happened. 'This one won't do. Clean the mirror, you lazy, fat excuse of a half-priest. It's time you got your hands dirty.'

Once the mirror was cleaned, Anukke repeated the process with the second vial, but still, nothing happened. 'Argh! This is useless! All this trouble for nothing.' Anukke threw the vials to the stone floor, sending the glass shards all over the room.

'Eldridge, get them to ready my horse. I have a trip to take.'

Upon reaching the castle courtyard as he came down from the musty aired staircase, Anukke stopped and looked upon his horse standing amidst his guards: a black beast with silver armour covering its chest and flanking the sides of its head. *Come, Shadow, tonight we ride into the camp of murderers and thieves.*

'I need two guards to come with me,' Anukke whispered; but all in the compound heard him clearly, as if he were talking into each of their ears. None stepped forth. All the guards nervously glanced at each other. 'You two next to my horse, saddle up and be ready; we ride out soon.'

'But sir,' the one guard protested, 'It's dark out. Strange and terrible creatures roam these lands at night!'

Anukke stared at the man with his head cocked to the right, while silently uttering words under his breath. Everyone was now staring at Anukke, waiting for his response. Suddenly everyone jumped back as they saw the guard drop to the ground, unable to breathe as his face turned red and his eyes bulged from their sockets. In front of their eyes, the armour of the guard was giving in on itself, crushing the bones and organs of the guard. After a final thunderous crunch, the guard's heart burst open, killing him instantly. Anukke stared at the other men and said, 'Is there anybody else who would defy my orders?'

Everybody looked down and continued with their work, trying hard not to be noticed.

'If I come back down, there had better be another one of you ready to take his place, or else, I kill the lot of you... you bunch of spineless cowards.' *If I didn't need you to guard this castle, I would have killed you all at this very moment.*

A while later, Anukke appeared at the bottom of the stairs once more, carrying an old, black, charred wooden staff. Three horses stood ready for the trip. Two guards atop their mounts flanked his black steed. 'We are ready, sir; your horse awaits you.'

'What are your names?'

The two riders glanced at each other as he patiently waited for their reply. The first rider spoke up, 'I am Vintrian, loyal servant of Anukke.' He was a hard-looking man with a broad flat face and short square red hair. *Big built, and looks strong,* thought Anukke.

The other rider spoke up, 'I am Vargus, loyal servant of Anukke.'

The wizard stared at the man, seeing a vague familiarity. 'Who is your father?'

'My father was called Elgar, sir; he died recently on one of his quests for you.'

'I know who he is. Do you know the manner of his death?' Anukke asked as he walked closer.

'No sir, I only know he did not make it back to the castle.'

Anukke glared at the soldier, and said, 'You will know soon enough if you disobey me.'

The wizard mounted his steed and stroked its head. *Run, Shadow, and run fast. We head for the Forest of Abendi.* Upon hearing the words, Shadow pitched back his ears and bolted out of the courtyard, followed by the two guards.

CHAPTER SIX

At the crack of dawn, the light shone through the curtain's cracks straight into Gordon's eyes. He woke slowly, muttering a curse at the sun, and with great effort, turned over in his bed to find a young, good-looking maiden next to him. 'Who the...'

He rose with great effort, pushing down with his hands to sit up in the bed. His vision blurred as he looked upon the big man getting dressed near the window.

'Aye, lad, you sure know how to celebrate, I will give you that,' came the voice of Malachai, still busy dressing.

Gordon looked around inquisitively. 'Why does it feel like a donkey kicked me in the face?'

With a slight chuckle he glanced at Gordon and said, 'With the amount of liquor you poured down your windpipe last night, I'm amazed you're still breathing.'

'Who is the girl?' came his raspy voice. He cleared his throat and rubbed his scar.

As Malachai pulled on his leather jacket, he announced with raised brows. 'One of the servant girls of the inn. I saw you leave with her last night and thought it well not to interrupt. You would've gutted any man to be with her. Said something about her being the most beautiful woman in the world, and you can't live without her... and such. The usual drunken nonsense.'

'I can't remember anything,' he said, looking down at the sheets, then rubbed his eyes.

Malachai looked at him and pulled his hammer close. 'Aye, you better get dressed and send her on her way. We have a long day ahead of us. Once you're dressed, come down to the bar, drink some water and eat something. You will feel and hopefully look much better. And I would recommend a bath.'

As Malachai left the room and closed the door, Gordon fell back to the bed, sighed, and with a great moan, got up again.

Gordon pressed against his stomach, and said, 'Oh, for all the gods in this world, I *never* want to drink again.'

Malachai burst out laughing. 'If only I had a silver for every time I heard that.'

As they walked through the streets of Kalaghstine, leading their horses by the reins, people glared at them.

Gordon glumly looked ahead. 'Let's get to the liberatum and search the archives; we need some information on this mysterious mountain of yours.'

'What happened with the old man last night? You never mentioned him.'

The two men barely looked at each other during their conversation as they walked on. 'Not much. I dropped him off and he invited me for tea. I drank some and left. No more. I still can't recall where I heard his name before.'

As they reached the liberatum at the corner of the road, they saw a skinny old man wearing ragged clothes with torn shoes, his long, filthy hair covering his face as he screamed at the people passing by, 'He is watching us! Watching us, I tell you. Why is nobody taking heed of my warnings?'

For the first time since they took to the streets this morning, both men glanced at each other questioningly and walked to the old beggar. Gordon called out, 'Hey, old man. What are you talking about?'

The old man, excited for the interest shown, quickly leaned closer. 'Beyond the unseen castle walls in the mountain, the wizard awaits. No one can see, but yet there he be. Alchemist knows more but unwilling to tell.'

'Come, he's obviously mad, let's go,' Gordon said, annoyed with the old man.

Malachai grabbed Gordon's shirt and pulled him back as he said, 'I don't know why, but I believe this old fool; there's something in his words that makes sense of what I saw.'

Gordon pulled away from the dirty old man, looked down at his shoes, and with a sigh said, 'All right then, what do you suggest?'

Malachai, never being the one to lead others, shrugged and looked down at Gordon. 'Ya know, I don't like making choices for other people, it's usually easier if it's just me. But I think, laddie, that we should go speak to this alchemist and see what he knows.'

'Fair enough; I'm too drunk still to worry about the end of the world today.' Gordon glanced back at the seemingly senile old man, then continued, 'Hey old man, where does this alchemist live?'

The old man pulled back his hair to reveal a dark grin, and said, 'Come, I show.'

'Lead the way, then,' he said with a disinterested look on his face and gestured to the old man.

They rode in a triangular formation, Anukke at the head, his long black cape fluttering over the back of his steed, Vargus on his left and Vintrian on his right. They were riding hard, the dust from the road kicked up behind their horses as they pushed their mounts.

'My lord, we have been riding for half a night and day, and you have not yet told us where we are heading,' Vintrian said, gloomily looking at

Anukke.

The sun was shining high in the sky, and the air felt thick. Anukke didn't look back to the man as he answered, 'Well, it's because you haven't yet asked me. Now that you have, I'll answer. We're heading to the forest up north, the Forest of Abendi.'

Vintrian stared at Vargus with a wide grin and cursed under his breath. 'Why did I have to pick the short stick? It seems I always lose.'

Vintrian looked back towards Anukke and asked, 'My lord, not to defy you in any way, but what is our plan once we enter the forest? Abendi will have defences all over, and—'

'I'm counting on that, Vintrian; leave the entrance to me, just stay close and kill anyone who lunges at me. But whatever you do, don't go after them. This forest has a nasty habit of never releasing you if you stray from the path.'

Soon they were at the entrance to the forest, a thin winding road leading deeper. Cautiously, the three men entered atop their horses, keeping a vigilant watch around them. The light grew dim, the sun's rays blocked out by the big trees of the forest. Sudden flames erupted in front and behind the riders as four men on either side of them jumped up from the ground under the bush. Covered in the brush, it made it near impossible to see them in the forest. Shadow, still rearing up to the flames, settled back down at the command of the wizard. Vintrian and Vargus both drew their swords instinctively but saw they were heavily outnumbered and looked around nervously at their enemies, waiting for the first to attack. Anukke, serene as always, spoke to the men with a grin on his face. 'Well, this is a very good trap that you have made here. I congratulate you.'

A lean man with a sharp face spoke up. 'I am afraid, stranger, that this is where you part ways with your goods. Hand them over to us.'

Anukke chuckled and said, 'I do not believe that we will do that just yet.'

The man before them also laughed. 'I admire a man that is not willing to part with his possessions, but unfortunately, that will mean your death!' Just before the men could charge in, Anukke uttered a few

words while moving his hands around as if tying a knot in the air:
Pantoree anflamino. Suddenly the flames in front of them shifted and
moved, burning their way quickly to surround the men at the front and
rear, forming a circle around them. The flamed walls surged high above
the men, trapping them in their fiery prison. 'Now, if you don't listen to
me, you pig-piss-covered dog, I will make this circle grow smaller until it
burns you to a pile of ash.'

From behind the flames came a whimpering voice: 'Yes, yes, I'll
listen.'

Vintrian and Vargus stared at each other in disbelief while Anukke
questioned the man. 'I need to speak with Abendi in person, so I need
you to take me to him, and I don't want any more unwanted intrusions
on the way. Any funny business from your side and I'll turn you into a
very undesirable creature, like a three-legged dog or a ten-toed one arm
sloth,' hissed Anukke's voice. A little while later the man behind the
flames spoke once more, 'Okay, I'll take you to him.'

Anukke lowered the flames, and the relief showed on the men
trapped inside.

Tuds' squadron was being outfitted to move down to camp Waterhole
at the river following the border of Caldonia and Millron, off to the
west. 'The current company stationed there needs to be relieved,' came
the voice of General Blackbeard as he looked at the soldiers, then said,
'Now that I've promoted you to major general, I will watch you closely.
So...'

Tuds turned to his right and observed the general. 'Don't worry, sir,
I will not disappoint,' Tuds said, taking in the older man with his long,
curly black hair hanging loosely to his broad shoulders, a pitch-black
beard cut in a triangle from his chin to halfway down his chest. He was
rarely seen without his black-furred pullover and brown leather leggings.
He must have been a very powerful man in his youth, thought Tuds. 'Are
there any problems that we might encounter, sir?'

Blackbeard turned to Tuds. 'Ya should always expect trouble, son.'

With that, Tuds turned back and observed his squadron milling about, getting ready for departure. He cupped his hands together in front of his mouth and yelled out, 'Borka, attend!'

From a distance, a lean-muscled man with a round face and widespread eyes jogged towards Tuds. As he approached, he stopped and saluted. 'Borka has attended, sir.'

Without looking towards the general, Tuds said, 'Make sure that all the men double-check their equipment and take extra provisions. Get an extra wagon if you have to, but get it done. Relay my message to the cooks and healers that they must also take extra provisions. Now off with you.'

Blackbeard stood at his side with a wide grin. 'Yer definitely learning. Now I'm going back to my quarters; I am sure you can handle everything here.'

'Thank you for your confidence, sir.' Turning away from the general, Tuds cupped his hands again as his voice rang out, 'Major! Headcount!'

A slight figure appeared at his side. 'Fifty engineers, two hundred infantry, a hundred cavalry and fifty bowmen, sir!'

Tuds stared in disbelief, and said, 'What in the blazes is this?' A young, attractive woman, with long flowing brown hair, deep green eyes, wearing tight-fit brown leathers and a rapier at her side, looked back at him.

'I beg your pardon, sir. I am Gweniviere. General Blackbeard wanted me moved to your squadron. I was with the Seekers for some time before being placed by the general.'

With a chuckle, he lowered his face and asked, 'Do you really think that I should believe that a young girl like yourself was with the Seekers?'

'Yes sir, I believe you should because it's the truth. I'm more than willing to show you that I'm capable of handling myself in a problematic situation.'

Tuds, with a wide grin on his face, stared at her and said, 'Well then, I believe a demonstration is in order.'

'So be it.'

Tuds looked over the encampment and bellowed out, 'Borka! Bring your sword.'

Gweniviere slid out her rapier, and with no sign of emotion on her face, walked to meet the oncoming combatant. The two warriors started circling each other, swords held up, points touching each other. Soldiers ran up to form a circle around the two, with Tuds standing at the front line. Borka rushed in, faking a jab to his right, trying to throw Gweniviere off balance. It didn't work. She read his moves swiftly and toyed with him. Swords met each other, the clashing of steel ringing throughout the camp. Wagers were being placed as the duel continued. Shouts filled the air as soldiers showed their support. With a fierce left cut, Borka swung his sword at Gweniviere's head. She ducked and rolled smoothly past the blow. Coming back up, she swung a blow with the flat side of her blade straight onto the buttocks of Borka, making everyone laugh.

'You fight well, soldier,' said Gweniviere as she stepped back, then continued, 'but what you lack is patience and focus. Do not...' Borka rushed in once more, sword held high above his head with both hands on the hilt. He swung the blade down, but Gweniviere expected the clumsy move. She saw his anger had flared and blinded him. She parried the blow and before Borka knew what was going on, he was kneeling on the ground before the major, her dagger pressing against his neck. 'Relax soldier, *that* is an order!' Gweniviere said with a stern voice that suddenly calmed the raging anger in him.

Being bested by a girl is one thing, but being best by your superior is another. Tuds stepped forth and spoke to the entire unit. 'This is Major Gweniviere. As you have seen, gentlemen, do not take her lightly. Now continue packing.'

Gweniviere helped Borka up and sheathed her rapier. The soldier stood dumbly before her and lowered his face to the ground as he said, 'I am sorry I lost my temper during our duel, Major Gweniviere.'

'Think nothing of it, but learn from it. And please call me Major Gwen.'

☿

The men edged out into a well-hidden campsite and were halted by two men with large spears. 'Halt! Who goes there?'

The lean man escorting them stepped forward. 'It is I, Belvadere. You may lower your spears. These three have come to see Abendi.'

About forty men that they could see huddled around campfires, drinking and laughing as a pig was roasted over a fire. Belvadere turned and said, 'I will call for him,' and walked off.

After some time, the guard returned and beckoned them to the centre campfire, where Abendi sat on his elaborate stone throne. The leader of the band of rogues said, 'Well now, strangers, what brings you to this neck of the woods? Surely you know we don't take kindly to strangers in these parts.'

Anukke stared at the man on the throne: an average man, it seemed, with a carved-out tree stump for one of his legs. Interesting. A square face, short black hair, and a short beard all around. Looking at the man, he realised Abendi is not in control of this camp because of the fear he bestowed, or by strength and power. No, it was his mind that made him their leader. He was a genius when it came to stealing and committing murders without getting caught, and his men loved him for it.

'I am Anukke, and these are my guards, Vintrian and Vargus. I am planning something rather big, and I need some men. How many do you have at your disposal?'

Abendi rubbed his beard for a while in consideration and then said, 'And why would we help you, mage? Or better yet, why don't I just kill you?'

Flustered and surprised, Anukke calmed himself quickly and said, 'If you know I am a mage, then I don't have to demonstrate that I could kill you this very instant, long before your men will get to me.'

Abendi burst out laughing as his guards joined in. The wizard's anger flared. He uttered words unknown to man, flashed out his arms in an arch... But nothing happened. Abendi looked at him in silence, as did all his men, then burst out laughing again, even louder than before, throwing their arms in the air mockingly. Abendi, struggling to contain himself, said, 'Did you really think that we would let a mage waltz into this camp without taking precautions to ensure our safety? You disappoint me, Anukke.'

The wizard cursed softly under his breath, his teeth tightly clenched. Abendi stood from his throne and hobbled over to stare into Anukke's eyes. 'I have my own mages, and they cast a spell all around this camp to neutralise any other magic in this area. You're worthless in here!'

Vintrian and Vargus looked around nervously, knowing their leverage has disappeared. Anukke grinned at the man. 'I apologise for my outburst. Sometimes my anger gets the best of me. But as I said, I am planning something big, and I require your services. The pay would be very generous.'

At the mention of payment, Abendi pulled back and started smiling. 'Now why on earth didn't you say that in the beginning? You would have saved yourself a whole lot of embarrassment, you know. I think it best if we were to speak further in my quarters regarding this matter. Guards show these men some hospitality; give them food and wine. Also, bring some to my quarters for the mage and me.'

Vintrian and Vargus joined the men and women while Anukke followed Abendi to his quarters, a rickety old cabin with little in the way of furnishings. Abendi gestured at the wizard to sit, and said, 'Relax. Do you smoke, mage?'

Anukke disliked being given a title that did not portray his magnificence, and said, 'Please, call me Anukke. And no, I do not smoke.'

'Oh well, suit yourself. You shall stay here and be our honoured guests until we finish our negotiations.'

☿

Gordon and Malachai walked behind the crazed old man as he muttered the whole way he led them down the street. He came to an abrupt halt and started screaming at the top of his voice, 'We here, we here! This the place, we here! Now you give me food and gold!'

Gordon looked around, puzzled, then said, 'Wait a moment—'

Malachai interrupted. 'Yes, just wait a moment, you old coot. You said nothing about payment.'

Gordon looked at Malachai and mumbled, 'Give him something, and let him be on his way.'

Malachai sighed and turned back to the old man. 'Here, take this.' He reached into his pouch and produced a few bronze coins. 'Now get out of here, you old buzzard.'

Gordon turned with a puzzled look on his face. 'Remember that old man I gave a ride back to town?'

Still irritated about giving coin away, Malachai replied, 'Yes, what about him?'

Gordon chuckled as he replied, 'This is his house.'

Malachai furrowed his brow and said, 'Now that *is* quite a coincidence, wouldn't you say?'

The house was ordinary looking, with a well-maintained little garden out front. As the two men approached the door, it swung open to reveal the short old man standing at the entrance. 'I have been wwwwwaiting for you, sssssonny.'

They looked at each other, with not the faintest idea of what was going on. 'Good day to you, Attalus. How did you know we would come to you? I mean, *we* didn't even know.'

The old man turned around and walked back into the house, gesturing them to follow and sit at the table. The smell of tea lingered in the home; and after a while, with the ringing of spoons in cups, he brought them tea from the kitchen. Malachai was awkwardly unfamiliar with tea and drank it hesitantly. Seeing Attalus lifting his little finger up to the air as he held the cup in his hands, he clumsily tried imitating the old man. But with his enormous hands, he could barely get his finger in the cup's handle.

Gordon was working so furiously in his mind regarding the old man's name that he didn't even hear him speak. 'I got it!' Gordon put down the tea and stared at the old man. 'You're the son of Anomus, the ancient god of healing!'

The old man almost dropped his cup at the outburst. A fountain of tea spurted from Malachai, drenching Attalus as he shouted, 'What!'

Attalus set down the cup and stumbled off to his room to get dry clothes, mumbling all the way down the hall. Malachai, more confused than ever, sat on a couch nearby. When the old man returned, Gordon resumed the topic. 'I remember now. My father used to tell me stories of the gods that once walked the world a long time ago; *that's* where I heard your name.'

Attalus looked at them and said, 'You are partly right. I am more the son of the son of Anomus. I am the son of Attalus, also called Attalus Junior, of course.'

Malachai stared in disbelief at the old man. 'Junior! You look at least a hundred years old!'

The old man frowned at that. 'More like seven hundred. But who's counting?'

Malachai almost fainted. 'Sure, why not have a god thrown in the mix? What else needs to happen on this quest?'

Once again, the old man frowned. 'Don't be so dramatic, sssssonny, I'm more of a demigod. In the final years during which the gods roamed the world, my father fell in love with a mmmmortal woman as his father had before him. I was the result. When he ascended, I stayed behind.' With a sigh, he continued, 'Now you know my story. What's yours?'

Gordon shrugged his shoulders. 'I doubt we will have a better tale than that.'

Malachai, still stunned, said, 'Aye laddie, that be true.'

They sat in deep conversation around the table regarding all that had happened.

'Yes,' said Attalus, 'The story of the invisible ccccastle at the side of the mountain is true, as is the story of the wizard who lives there. I have always kept a cccccclose eye on him, making sure he doesn't get too far with his endeavours. I fear I missed this one. Therefore, I am ssssssorry. I'll help where I can, but I fear I will not be of much use. I am getting too old.' Attalus scrambled to the back of his house, to return a little while later carrying a bag. 'Here, take this. Just rrrrread what I have wwwwwritten on the bottles and use it accordingly.' He handed it over to Malachai.

The group ate a hearty meal and shared more stories as they sat around the table, then Attalus told them of a secret way into the castle. Presently, the companions thanked him and rose from the table to walk to their horses. Saying their goodbyes, they mounted and rode down the street in the dark of night as the old man shouted, 'You be welcome here anytime!'

It was a wondrous night out; the stars were shining bright, and the moon was high and full—a bad thing for two would-be burglars, making them far too visible. The two men backtracked along the trail to where Malachai saw the mountain open up. They went on foot for the last few hundred yards, making their way stealthily through the woods. Now crouched behind a tree, Gordon looked up to the mountain. Malachai stood behind the tree, pointing to where the road abruptly ended, and said, 'There, that is where the mountain—'

'I know,' he said as he scanned the area and continued, 'I can see it.'

Malachai frowned. 'What do you mean, you can see it?'

Gordon looked back. 'Just that. I don't know why, but I can see the castle. It must be a side effect from my eyes changing. The castle looks vague, as if it's behind a thin veil or something, but I *do* see it.'

Malachai just shrugged and said, 'Well, I suppose it's a good thing for us. Just one more strange thing today. If I go mad, would you feed my dogs?'

Gordon raised his brows. 'What are you talking about?'

'Oh, nothing, don't worry. I don't have any dogs. I'll be fine.'

'If we follow the old man's explanation, the secret way into the castle is on the other side, at the back. We'll have to wade through a swamp, and pry open an old tunnel that should give us entry. That will take us to the lower levels of the castle. Once inside, there will be guards, so let's try not to get caught until we get to the wizard and Eldridge. I believe they will be at the top, in the tower somewhere. As soon as we find them, we need to act fast. Before the wizard can cast any spell, I need you to knock him unconscious somehow. Use your imagination for that. I'll get Eldridge. As soon as we have them, we'll need to leave quickly. Once we're clear, we can ride for the monastery and question them. Then, my friend, we can go home.'

Gordon glanced one last time at the castle, looking up at its massive stone walls, too high to scale unnoticed. The doors in front were of thick oak, reaching over twenty feet high. He glanced back. 'You ready, old man?'

Malachai rumbled, 'Old man. My foot! Old man. Will get shoved up... We'll just have to see about that.'

They rose and moved out. A long, winding path took them around to the back, where they spotted the swamp, just like Attalus said. A nasty stench flowed from the swamp, a foul smell of death and decay. Malachai stepped into the water and waded deeper, sinking waist deep. 'Argh! Won't get the stench out of my nose for days!'

Gordon stood on the side and smiled as he said, 'If your eyesight were any better, you would see that there's a perfectly good path over this swamp, but I see your plan. The dead raccoons and rats will probably make you blend in with the surroundings.'

'Dead raccoons? Rats?' Malachai looked more closely to see the dead things floating in the water. With his teeth clenched against a scream, he swore under his breath and hurried to get out of the water. Gordon was already at the other side of the swamp, waiting for him as he clasped his hand over his mouth to stifle the sound of his laughter. Once the big man shrugged off some of the filth, he saw rocks protruding above the water's surface, which one could use to skip across. Once on the other side, he stopped in front of Gordon. 'Ya know, lad, if you hadn't saved my life, I would bust you in the jaw right now.'

Gordon pointed out with his finger. 'There. The tunnel is barred with a metal grate.'

Malachai still only saw a mountain, but moved closer and readied his hammer. Striking where Gordon pointed, the metal shifted from the mountain, then he shimmied the grate. Moving the hammer back and forth with great effort, he caused the grate to fall clear, not making much noise as it sunk into the soft mud. Now, as it lay on the ground, Malachai could see it, for the first time being able to distinguish between mountain and castle. They peered in and entered the low tunnel.

Keeping low and to the shadows, they made their way up the stairs. As they approached a landing, Malachai peered around the corner and saw one guard turn in their direction during his patrol. They waited until he was next to the stairs, then Malachai snapped out his arms and broke the guard's neck before he even had a chance to react. He then dragged the corpse into a dark corner, hoping he wouldn't get noticed too soon.

Soon they were at the topmost floor, going from room to room, peering in. 'There...' Gordon's whispered as he pointed towards an enormous door around the corner from them. 'That must be it.'

Both men drew their weapons and opened the door with great care. Once inside, they saw a figure standing at the balcony, peering down to the courtyard below. They looked around but saw no one else. Malachai swiftly and soundlessly moved towards the figure. Gordon thought, *he moves quite stealthily for such a big man.* With a heavy thud, the figure dropped to the ground. It was the fat fake priest—Eldridge. Throwing him over his shoulder, Malachai glanced at Gordon. 'The wizard ain't here. Let's get out of here. We can question this one.'

He nodded, and they made their way down the stairs once more. As they reached the exit level, something caught Gordon's attention that caused him to stop. It was as if he could hear a voice speaking inside his head—not to him, but to someone else. 'Wait a moment, Malachai, I know that voice. Follow me.'

The big man sighed but followed as they went down into the dungeon, slowly and cautiously. They reached the door descending into the lowest dungeon. As Gordon opened it, the talking in his mind ceased. Looking around the dark dungeon, he could see no guards, only big metal pots scattered around, a fire burning in each, lighting the dark room a little. *These are like giant candles.* Once they came to the bottom of the stairs, they saw the big metal cages. At first, they appeared empty; but then something stirred in the dark corner.

The two men crept closer, trying to see what was in the cages. Both jumped back when they saw the eyes of a massive Gar hound staring back, slowly making its way to them. For the first time in a very long time, it formed words in a hoarse tone: 'Vasgath...' and with that Baldrake appeared in the ominous rippling light.

Malachai dropped his hammer and Eldridge to the ground. 'Reaper.'

Cuorco also stepped into the light. 'It has been too long a time, Vasgath.'

Malachai watched the old wolf drawing closer and said, 'Cuorco.'

Gordon stared at the big man.

'Lower your sword, lad,' Malachai said as Gordon moved in to take revenge on Baldrake for nearly killing him, but found his sword ripped from his hand as he stepped in close. 'Gordon, please listen to me. I need to find out what's going on here. Let me speak to them first. You go see what you can get out of Eldridge.' Malachai handed back the weapon and moved to the cage.

Gordon stomped off to the side of the unconscious fake priest as Baldrake stepped closer to the bars and spoke aloud to him, 'Young one, I am glad to see you alive and well. Please believe me when I tell you I did not want to harm you. The wizard—'

Gordon drew his sword again and ran at the wolf, slicing through the air, missing Baldrake by inches before Malachai stopped him once more. 'You nearly killed me, you bastard!' Gordon shouted. 'Just look at my neck, because of you. And what *about* the wizard, huh? Did he put you under some spell or something? Is that your excuse?'

Baldrake sighed a deep, sad sigh. Tears rolled down the wolf's face.

Malachai knew them well enough to know that he was telling the truth, and said, 'What means did the wizard use to get *you* into his service, old one?'

Gordon glared at Malachai for using such a respectful tone. Baldrake moved towards Cuorco, and said, 'The little one over there is very dear to me, Vasgath. The wizard's men ambushed and captured him and Cuorco while I was out hunting. I came back and followed the tracks here, where they got hold of me and put some sleeping spell on me. When I awoke, we were in the cages, and before us stood that wizard, telling us he needed my services. At first, we refused to help him, but then he poisoned the pup. He said that every time I didn't do what he needed of me, he would not give the pup the medicine to stop him from dying. I had no choice.'

Malachai looked at Gordon. 'I'm going to free them; they will come with us. We can take the little one to the monastery.'

Gordon couldn't believe what he was hearing, and said, 'If you let them out of those cages, they will kill us, or I will kill them.'

Malachai suddenly flared with anger, shouting, 'No one is killing anyone! You got that? If any of you steps out of line, you will answer to me! Now get Eldridge awake.'

Just then, they heard shouts of alarm coming from all over the castle.

Gordon stared at them and said, 'We will deal with this later. First, let's get out of here.'

Malachai cracked open the cage with a mighty blow from his hammer, tearing the doors from their hinges. The chains on the wolves' feet also gave way after a few blows. He then rushed to pick up a big wooden beam lying on the floor and jammed it up against the door leading into the dungeon. 'How is Eldridge?' he asked.

'Awake but unwilling to cooperate.'

From behind Gordon came a voice, 'Let me try. Do you still want him alive and able to travel after he has spoken?'

Gordon stared at the beast as he passed him, and said, 'No.'

Baldrake turned to the fat priest. 'Good. I suggest you tell them everything they want to know.'

Eldridge, stricken with fear, started laughing hysterically. Baldrake lunged forward, putting his massive jaw over the fat priest's knee, and with a sudden crunch of bone, he tore off the leg from the knee down. Blood spurted out onto the floor as the leg dropped next to Eldridge. Screams of pain echoed through the dungeon.

As Malachai ran over, Cuorco nudged with his nose at the little pup, who was still lying unmoving on the floor in the cage. Cuorco said, 'He will not make it to your monastery, Vasgath. We need medicine now to help him.'

Malachai called Gordon over and handed him the bag they'd gotten from Attalus. 'See what's in here that would help the pup. I will go to Eldridge.'

The guards were pounding on the door to the dungeon now, trying to break it down. Cuorco stared at Gordon as he went through the bottles until he finally found one with a label that read, "*Healing Elixir—pour down throat*".

He turned the pup over and pried open its mouth. Ragged, almost non-existent breaths escaped it, and he felt a sudden wave of sympathy for the wolves, thinking he would have done the same if the situation was reversed. He poured the elixir down the little wolf's throat and made sure he swallowed it. Only a pup, he was already about waist height to a man. Staring at Cuorco, Gordon said, 'Is there another way out of this castle?'

Cuorco nodded. 'There are two ways—the one you know, the other a pathway that leads from here to the courtyard. From there, we will have to fight and open the gate to get out. The courtyard will be better if we have to fight, as we will have room to do so. In the staircase, we would have to fight one at a time.'

Gordon looked around. 'I agree. The guards will still think we're in here until they break through that door. We will have less resistance.'

Gordon spoke to Malachai. 'Could you get anything out of Eldridge?'

With a nod and a grin, Malachai said, 'Got all we could out of him, but cost him an arm and a leg.'

Gordon didn't laugh, though Malachai thought it was an excellent play on words. The big man ran over to the pup and lifted him over the back of his neck. 'Okay, I'll be unable to help in the fight. I can't move well with the mass on top of me. You three will have to clear the way.'

Cuorco led them to the passageway. First Gordon moved in, then Cuorco; then came Malachai and the pup on his shoulders, and lastly Baldrake, covering the rear. They swiftly moved through the passageway and came up to the entrance of the courtyard.

Six guards saw them and moved in. Baldrake quickly killed his first by lunging straight at the neck, severing the arteries. Memories of Baldrake ripping at his throat sent chills down Gordon's spine. The wolf glanced up and went for his second kill. A guard running towards Malachai was suddenly on the ground just in front of him, as Cuorco pounced on the man and ripped at his face. Gordon was engaged in combat with another and quickly pierced his sword through the guard's armour and his heart. The man slumped backwards to the ground.

The wolves still tore at their victims when Gordon saw Malachai fighting for his life as a guard attacked him. Unable to use his hands and arms, he was parrying as best he could, using his legs as shields, kicking at the lunging spear. It sliced into his calf muscle as Gordon ran and leapt forward, taking the man off his feet. The guard struck the ground so hard his helmet flew off. Battle lust had taken Gordon; he grabbed the fallen helmet and started beating the guard until there was no face left. Blood soaked the ground. After some time, he realised the others were staring at him. He dropped the helmet and ran for the gate, which was operated by a wheel about thirty feet to the left. He spun the wheel as fast as he could turn it.

More guards came back up the stairs from the dungeon now, heading for the courtyard. The gate was open but would close as soon as Gordon left the wheel. Malachai propped himself in front of the great door and shouted, 'Run! I will hold it!'

The big man leaned his great mass against the door, as well did the two hounds, pushing with everything they could with their flanks against the door. Their claws dug into the ground as the door slowly pushed them back. The guards came into sight, running at them with swords held high. Arrows came flying towards them, thudding into the door.

Gordon left the wheel and ran as fast as he could. He saw them pushing with all their might against the massive door, but it was too heavy to hold. Malachai turned red in the face and his thick leg muscles bulged as he drove his feet into the ground. He jumped through the gate, and the others followed suit. Once outside the castle, they ran as fast as they could through the forest to their horses. Fear gripped their mounts as the wolves neared. They bucked and whinnied, trying to break their leads.

Gordon calmed his horse as best he could before he strapped the injured wolf-pup on the back of his gelding. The two warriors rode down the mountainside at full gallop, with the wolves bounding next to them. Cuorco stared anxiously at Gordon, with the pup bouncing up and down on the back of the horse. Baldrake saw the worried look on the older wolf's face, and the thought of losing the little one saddened him to a point where he could feel his heart giving in. Shaking his head, he pulled his mind away from the thoughts and realised he was already mourning the pup's death. *He is not dead yet, damn you! He will survive! Curse these thoughts.*

Pulling ahead of the horses, Baldrake spoke to Gordon in his mind. 'Gordon, there are no words I can utter to portray the grief I felt when I lunged at you. I have lived a very long time, and I have seen the value of life. I tried all I could to defy the order given me by the wizard. But in the end, it was futile. I hope that one day you can forgive me. I, therefore, give my life over to you, to do with as you please—until the day I die, or you set me free.'

Gordon heard the sigh of the saddened wolf echo in his mind as the voice faded away, but did not answer.

CHAPTER SEVEN

The journey back to the monastery was relentless; a two-day ride without stopping, both warriors pushed their mounts to the brink of death. The wolf pup wasn't looking good at all, his tongue hanging out of his mouth as if he were already dead. Clouds had gathered, blocking out the moon's bright light. An icy wind picked up from the east, cutting through the two men as they pushed their mounts for the last stretch through the archway of the monastery. *Strange weather for this time of year, with it still being summer. These gnawing winds were usually only felt in late winters,* thought the big man.

They dismounted in a rush as they reached the doors of the monastery. Working fast to get the wolf pup from the horse, Gordon took the young one in his arms and hurried towards the front door. Glancing back, he yelled over the howling winds at Malachai, 'Get the horses out of the cold and rub them down, it will be the death of them.'

Malachai irritably took up the reins of the two animals and shouted back, 'What do you take me for? An idiot?' He led them to the stable and immediately brushed them down. An abundance of food and water awaited them. He stood back to watch them as they ate and drank greedily to get their fill. Unknown to him, Cuorco stood in the shadows of the night, studying him from a distance.

Unable to knock with the heavy pup in his arms, Gordon kicked the door open and walked in, followed by the massive Baldrake. Priests jumped up in sudden alarm, completely unaware that someone had approached their haven through these howling winds. Screams erupted as they saw the wolf move into the room close behind Gordon. The sight of the wolf ripping Elgar's head off his shoulders was still fresh in their minds.

'Delios!' Gordon shouted as he lay the pup down on a couch at the entrance, then shouted again, 'Calm yourselves! Delios!' A few of the priests moved closer, thinking it would be futile to run if the wolf wanted to do them harm, and rather calmed themselves as they joined the pup's side.

Father Delios appeared at the top of the stairs. 'Good Lord! What's going on here? What is all that racket?' He rubbed his eyes and gasped as he opened them. 'I can't believe it.' His legs worked autonomously as they guided him down the stairs towards Baldrake. 'Gordon, what is this?' The old man asked dubiously, stunned.

The young warrior moved away from the couch to reveal the wolf pup lying there, motionless. Gesturing to Delios, he said, 'Don't worry, Baldrake won't cause any problems; he's with us now. There's no time to explain, Father.'

Delios stood in front of the pup with his mouth agape. Shocked, he didn't hear a word Gordon said.

'Delios!' came the voice next to him. 'I need you to focus.' Gordon shook the old abbot out of his trance and said, 'He is very ill, Father—we need to get this pup to your healing room, now!'

Delios shook himself and called to Magnus and Antelios to meet him in the healing room, then said, 'Gordon, bring the pup and tell me what happened.'

As they ran down the hall to the healing room, it surprised Delios to hear it was Baldrake, not Gordon, who started speaking with him. 'The wizard's men ambushed us. Anukke, the sorcerer, poisoned the pup and forced me to do his bidding. If I complied, he gave the pup the antidote; if I didn't... he would die. That's why I did what I did to

Gordon, and nothing grieves me more. I do not know what it is he gave him, but I can tell you this: it has a foul odour to it, and through the dark, it looked like a dark bluish substance. The pup has been gradually becoming worse ever since, dreaming of other creatures ripping him apart, killing him every time he closes his eyes. Since two days past, they have not yet opened again. Please, help him.'

Gordon lay the pup down on the golden bed and gestured for Baldrake to follow and leave the priests to do their work. Instead, the wolf walked over to the pup and placed his head against the pup's and said, 'Fight little one. Your time has not yet come.' Both left the room and headed to the antechamber, where Malachai and Cuorco joined them.

Cuorco lay at the foot of a chair, and spoke to Baldrake's mind so no one else could hear: 'Do you think he will make it, brother?'

'I do not know. These priests will do everything they can to help. Just keep hoping,' he replied as he closed his eyes and turned away.

'Vasgath has changed. He is not the man he was in the war,' Cuorco stated.

'And this surprises you?'

'It's just... I thought nothing could break him so.'

Baldrake looked at Malachai and bowed his head in respect as he said, 'This man, Cuorco, went through a hell no man should endure on that battlefield. Any other man who endured what he did would have gone mad or killed himself. I'm amazed he's doing this well.'

Cuorco also looked at Malachai and lowered his head. 'I watched him outside tending to the horses. Never did I see a caring side of this man before now. I also saw something else...'

At the tone of Cuorco's voice, Baldrake met his eyes.

'He huddled in a corner, swaying back and forth, his arms cradling his legs as tears streamed down his face. I touched his mind to see what ailed him so, but all I saw was darkness. He was begging for forgiveness.'

This news saddened Baldrake. 'We all bear scars from war.' He looked towards Cuorco. 'I have pledged my life to Gordon for what I have done to him—'

Cuorco sat up suddenly. 'You can't!'

Baldrake hushed the raging wolf. 'Calm yourself, my brother; all will be fine. I know you feel you owe Vasgath for saving your life. So consider your debt paid, as I will watch over him on this journey.'

'Who is this pup to you?' Gordon asked suddenly.

Baldrake hesitated, then looked up and said, 'We are a dying breed. He is the first "Gar hound," as you call us, to be born from this world. It was a difficult birth; his mother very nearly died from bleeding. Until he happened, we were unable to procreate with your wolves. Our numbers are plummeting. So from him will come the new generation of Gar hounds. He carries in him the genes to start anew. He is my son... I have named him Beldrin, meaning "Hope" in your tongue.'

Gordon sighed as he heard the full story and spoke to him earnestly, 'I'm truly sorry for what you've all been through, Baldrake. I hope he comes out of this just fine.'

'Thank you, Gordon. That means a lot.'

Malachai stared at them both. 'Aye, me too.'

With that, he nodded and lay down on the marble floor.

'You are not getting away from me so easily,' said the harsh voice while darting in and out through the bushes. The night was bitter, and the ground hard against the bootless hunter, the moon high and shining bright. He saw movement a hundred paces in front of him, moving swiftly through the bush. With no shirt and a makeshift spear, he charged. The wolf he was chasing was scared and running for its life... There are very few things more deadly than a scared and cornered animal. The chase was on. The wolf stopped under a large oak, thinking it had eluded its hunter. Sniffing, its head cocked to the air, trying to smell for him. Suddenly, the wolf picked up the scent; and before it could dash off, the hunter jumped from the tree to stand before the wolf. Teeth gleamed with ferocity while the wolf's claws dug into the ground, throwing dirt to its rear as it clawed at the earth. The two stared at each other and circled slowly.

With a sudden launch from its strong hind legs, the wolf caught the hunter off guard, throwing him to the ground and causing him to drop his spear. The wolf was on top of him, his jaws slamming shut only inches from the hunter's face.

Pushing hard against the beast's head with his hands, the hunter tugged and rolled and got up from under the wolf. It jumped once more with lightning speed, but this time the hunter was ready. He caught the wolf's head in the air and viciously jerked it to the left. A bone-splintering sound came from within, and the hunter knew the wolf's neck was broken. Momentum took the beast further, landing on top of the hunter and taking him to the ground. The wolf was alive no more.

The caws of a crow awoke Tuds just before dawn to the stark realisation that he was not in his cosy bed in his warmed quarters, but rather, naked and covered in blood in the middle of nowhere. He rose from the ground and watched as the foul bird swooped down from the tree to feast on the carcass of a nearby animal. The sun would rise soon. His men will be getting up to start their duties.

'What the blazes is going on? How did I get here?' He looked at the carcass again, and saw the fangs of the wolf, then said, 'What did I do last night? I'll have to get back to camp before everybody wakes. Maybe I can sneak in from the rear,' he argued with himself, trying to figure out what was going on. He knew the terrain, and judged his location not too far from the encampment.

'Damn, it's cold. Why am I naked? Damn this! I'm going to catch my death in this cold.' He sprinted off in the encampment's direction. It was about a mile's run back to the camp. *I will have to be careful to not be seen by the sentries*, he thought as he ran.

Once back, he slipped unnoticed into his tent and washed the blood from his body. Barely finished, standing half-naked with drops of blood still on his face, Gweniviere threw open the flap to his tent and entered as she said, 'Major General.'

Tuds quickly grabbed a towel and wrapped it around his waist, then chided her, 'Don't you know how to knock? Hmmmm? Were you born in a cave?'

She didn't turn away and stood with a grin on her face as she stared at him. 'Sorry, sir, but we have company. We need you at the wall. Oh, and please sir, be more careful when you shave. You have some blood on your face. We don't want you to cut your own throat, now,' she said as she turned and left the tent.

'What?' Tuds quickly used the towel to wipe his face and looked down on the few bloodstains on the white towel. 'If only it was a shaving accident,' he mumbled to himself.

Four men in fine cream garments were awaiting Tuds at the entrance of the encampment on the other side of the River Gallas. Tired from the last night's excursion, he strolled up the stairs to the top of the wall, where he looked at the men on their horses. They didn't look like soldiers—more like diplomats. *I dislike diplomats; they talk for days on end and are ultimately incapable of making decisions.* He shouted from the wall over the river, 'Who are you, and what do you want?'

The four men stirred on their horses as one replied in a smooth old voice, 'We ride from Millron. We have need of your services. Counsel selected us to meet with you. Can we talk in private?'

Tuds descended from the top of the wall and looked at Gweniviere as he said, 'Lower the bridge. Send them to the war room.' She nodded in response and left to give the orders. He turned and headed for the war room to await their arrival.

Gwen entered and announced them as they followed behind her. The four gentlemen entered and saw a big rectangular table in the middle of the room with a map of the whole countryside stretched out and pinned to the table, with toy soldiers on the map in various places and formations. Tuds spoke up from beyond the table, 'This is our strategy room, gentlemen. Please forgive that we do not have something more to your liking; this is the best we have for now. Please sit.'

The four men took their seats around the table; the man who spoke at the river sat down at the head. Tuds gestured to Gweniviere to join them for the meeting.

'So, gentlemen, what brings you here today?' he asked as he looked upon the four.

The man at the head of the table spoke up, 'I am Markus. This man on my right is Ritz, and the two on my left are Powell and Nemets. As I said, the counsel of Millron chose us to ride out to your encampment so we can ask for reinforcements from you.'

Tuds half-laughed at the words. 'Why on earth would we send in reinforcements for Millron? And exactly to whom do you need reinforcements against? You know that the Kraydenians and Levians have not seen eye-to-eye for a long time.'

'I know,' said Markus, his gaze steady. 'You are closest to us. Our sister cities are too far away to get reinforcements to us in time. There's an army marching towards us the likes we have never seen. Murderers, thieves, a full barbarian horde. They have plundered and killed as they have made their way towards us.'

Visions of men dying and blood flowing down the walls of Millron filled Tuds' mind. His blood boiled within, his heart racing at the possibility of war. *Why is this?* he thought, then breathed deep to calm himself. Tuds listened carefully to the man called Markus, then asked, 'Where did you see this army? Do you know who they follow? What's the purpose of this war?'

Ritz replied, 'We do not know who they follow. Our scouts came back two days ago. The horde was last seen in the valley northwest of the D'hore Mountains, crossing the River Gallas. We are afraid they will reach Galhor within the day.'

Tuds fidgeted with his hands and stood up from the table as he said, 'And what makes you believe this army intends to attack you or Galhor?'

'We do not know,' Markus admitted. 'But we would rather waste the time to get reinforcements and be prepared than not have them if we need them.'

He bowed his head in acknowledgement. 'Well put, Markus. How many men are we talking about here, and how many soldiers do you have?'

'As estimated by our scouts, they are around four thousand men...

and women.'

Tuds suddenly glanced back to Markus with his brow raised. 'And women?' It was uncommon that women would join in on the battlefield.

Markus hesitated, then continued, 'Yes, it appears so.'

Gwen raised her voice over the men. 'Do not underestimate women, sir. They might be just as trained as the men. I can take out any man in our uniform... and this you know, sir.'

All the men stared at her now, while Tuds stood rubbing a beardless chin, then said, 'You are right, Major. One should never underestimate his enemy. Markus, how many men did you say you have?'

Markus stared at the others and gestured to Ritz to answer, 'We have around a thousand five hundred men.'

Tuds walked about the room as he worked it through in his mind, and said, 'We only have four hundred men here, and I can only take three hundred of them away. We need the other hundred to stay behind and keep the camp. So I don't see how we can help. We could send word to Caldonia.'

Gwen jumped from her seat and stormed as she said, 'Sir, you can't seriously be thinking about this. We have no agreements with them or any treaties—'

Tuds gestured for her to be silent, and said, 'I have noted your objections, Major. Now please wait outside for us to finish.'

In a flush of anger, she stormed from the tent.

'Now, gentlemen, where were we? Ah yes, we could send word to Caldonia to send men from there, but they might arrive too late, depending how long the battle continues.'

The four men smiled until Tuds spoke again. 'Of course, there would be some terms on our side...' The smiles vanished.

The four men rose from around the table and made their way back to their horses. He watched them spur on their mounts, then heard the animals' hooves sound out as they rode over the lowered bridge. *Half the day has been wasted talking to those baby-kissers. At least we got some good out of it.*

The sun was high in the sky as Tuds walked to his quarters. The previous night's events had taken its toll on the man. He was tired and annoyed that the memories still evaded him, hoping some sleep might bring them back. As he ducked to enter the tent, he sighed as he saw Major Gwen waiting for him and sauntered past her as she raged. She was furious with him, especially for sending her out of the room. Biting her lip in anger and frustration, she stood with her arms crossed about her chest. 'What was that all about, sir?'

Tuds looked at her and calmly said, 'Do not forget your place, Major.'

She grabbed the girandole, ready to throw it at his head, and shouted, 'I was with the Seekers! Do you even know who they are?'

He slowly moved to a nearby table, sat down, and poured himself a drink. 'Do you want one, Major?'

Gwen shook her head in disbelief and rather indelicately placed the girandole back on its stand before saying, 'No, I do *not* want one. The Seekers were the most feared group we had in service. They got done what no others could. I am a master assassin, not some dim-witted, no-good major worth less than the sweat stain on my shirt! I was transferred here to help you with your position. To see that you do your job!'

Tuds calmly took another drink. 'I know all about you, Major. But you must understand something. I was given this post by General Blackbeard because I have initiative, not because I am some dim-witted assassin who can kill with extreme prejudice. So if you will calm down and listen to me, I can tell you why I agreed to this.'

Major Gwen sagged down into a chair, knowing he had the full right to punish her for her insubordination. She calmed herself and said, 'Fine, I'll listen.'

'The reason I'm considering this whole shebang is that I made them sign a treaty to respond if we were ever in crisis. They'll pay, house, and feed all soldiers we send in for reinforcement. The best of all, we've secured the trade routes through their country. Kraydenia has wanted the trade routes opened to them through Levia for a very long time, and now we can finally get them.'

'Yes, but at what cost? We can't stand up to four thousand soldiers with less than two thousand combatants of our own!'

Tuds took another sip of his drink. 'That's true, Major. Send a rider to General Blackbeard explaining the situation, outlining exactly what's at stake here. Tell him that in the meantime, we're moving out to Millron. If he wants us to return, he should send out a rider to recall us; otherwise, he should send reinforcements to aid us. Now please, Gwen, give the orders. I'm tired—I had a rough night.'

It was midday when Father Delios exited the infirmary. Pale and depleted of energy, he trembled as he slumped down on the couch next to the big man, waking him from his slumber. He had been up all night working on the little pup. Sprawled on couches and the floor, they all woke up and stared at the abbot as he caught his breath. Malachai scanned him from head to toe, and said, 'By the gods, you look awful, Abbot.'

Father Delios managed a grin, then looked towards the wolves before him. Baldrake was the first to speak. 'Delios, master of the monastery, how is the little one? Is Beldrin...'

Delios cut him off as he placed his finger across his mouth and waved for them to enter the infirmary. Malachai helped the old man lie down on the couch, where he lapsed into instant sleep. The companions entered the chamber and looked upon the golden bed. Beldrin lay with his back turned to the party as they approached. Baldrake stopped halfway, closed his eyes, and turned his head away. 'I can go no further; I dare not look.' Tears welled in his eyes.

Cuorco stopped beside him and said, 'Come, brother, you must face your fears. What's done is done and cannot be undone. If you don't face him now, you will never again have the chance.'

Malachai and Gordon watched him silently as they stood at the doorway, wanting to help him through this, but they knew they were helpless. A soft groan sounded as the pup stirred in the bed. Baldrake looked up as he heard a faint voice inside his mind, 'Father? Father, is that you?'

Baldrake rushed forward and came around the bed to look upon his son. Beldrin's eyes were barely open, his breathing ragged, but better. The old wolf rested his head against the young pup's and said in a firm, clear voice, 'Do not speak, son. I am with you. You need your rest.' The others joined him and smiled at the pup.

'Son, here are Gordon and Malachai. They are the reason we are free and you are healed.'

Beldrin looked at them through slitted eyes and whispered, 'Thank you.' His eyes closed as sleep took him. The lone eye of Cuorco darted between them as he stated the obvious, 'We should let him rest and retire for the night as well. We could do with some food and rest to regain our strength.'

Malachai nodded. 'Aye, agreed. I could eat a horse.'

With their spirits lifted, Baldrake was the last to leave as they departed the room. Gordon glanced at the one-eyed wolf and asked, 'What do you eat? I mean, can we get you some kibble or what?'

Malachai looked at Gordon in sudden surprise and burst out laughing. Baldrake walked past them towards Delios and with good humour turned to Gordon as he said, 'Tonight, I would not mind. Although I don't know if Cuorco would agree. His appetite for fresh meat is relentless.'

Gordon suddenly jerked his head back to Cuorco, who licked his lips while staring at him with his lone eye. Malachai saw this and laughed even harder. 'Aye, suppose you better keep your wits about you,' he told Gordon.

'I'm only jesting,' said Gordon as he waved his arms about and looked at the silver wolf.

Baldrake turned away and walked to the abbot on the couch, hearing Cuorco explain the etiquette of making jokes. Their voices trailed off as he neared the sleeping abbot and said, 'Master of the monastery, I do not know if you can hear me, but I truly thank you for your kindness.'

The company walked to the dining hall where they sat and laughed as stories were told. Four long wooden tables with chairs all around filled the room. Gordon and Malachai had taken their seats at the table whilst the wolves sat on the floor. Priests moved from the back room, bringing out plates covered with silver lids and bottles of wine. Everyone was silent as they awaited the reveal of the food. They raised the lids to reveal large steaks and potatoes with garnish and some tomatoes on their plates, with platters being brought in filled with breads and cheeses. The wolves' mouths watered as they saw the massive pieces of half-cooked steaks and a bowl of milk placed before them. They all dived into the feast, eating profusely. Now and then Cuorco would lift his head up, food falling from his mouth as he said, 'I must have died and gone to Valanaar. Only the valiant dead kings of old could surely eat like this.'

'What's Valanaar?' asked Gordon as he stuffed a potato in his mouth.

Baldrake looked up, his mouth covered in juices from the feast. 'It is where we will join our fallen brothers and sisters after death.'

Anukke stood beside Abendi, their army of murderers and thieves at their backs. Soldiers were running wild on the walls of Galhor. Men were sharpening their blades and getting their fill of food. Tonight might be their last night alive. Campfires were burning everywhere, becoming brighter as night settled in. Anukke picked up a rock and threw it as he said, 'We kill everyone! We leave no one alive; do you understand? I need as much blood as possible to flow.' The wizard laughed as Abendi gave the orders to his men.

Galhor was situated on the open lowlands of Levia; the fields of the farmers stretched out for miles, and with no mountains, it seemed one could see to the world's end. Three men on horseback rode out from

Galhor's gates and stopped a few hundred feet before them.

'Seems they have beckoned us for negotiations. I fear my terms will not satisfy them,' the wizard said as he leaned in and kicked his horse forward.

'I am Count Benjamin, and we are here to negotiate this ridiculous challenge.'

Anukke stared at the man with cold intent and uttered a few words unknown to the man. The clouds above gathered, and the winds howled their anger. The riders turned their mounts around in circles to calm them; the beasts clearly wanted to bolt. Confused, they still milled aimlessly before Anukke when a blinding flash came from the clouds, followed instantly by a thunderous crack so loud it deafened the men on their horses as it struck. It smashed the count and his horse to the ground, and the smell of burnt flesh immediately filled the air. The other two horsemen from Galhor stared at Benjamin in horror, frightened and wide-eyed as they saw the charred and melted flesh before them on the ground. The immediate grass around them was burnt black, but no fires sprang up.

Stars shone once more as the clouds dissipated. Anukke shouted at the other two men, 'Tell your king that come tomorrow, Galhor will burn!'

The two men turned their mounts and pushed their heels hard into the beast's flanks. Abendi looked at Anukke with raised brows as he said, 'So much for negotiations.'

Dawn was yet to approach when the attack started. War cries sounded out as the horde moved in closer. Their three mages positioned themselves at the complete left, right, and rear of the horde, waving their arms as they chanted their spells to life. One of Galhor's captains stood on the wall and let fly his arrow as the barbarian horde came into range.

Everyone on the walls waited in silence as the arrow sliced through the air, eager to see the first of the horde fall to the ground, never to rise again; but instead, it shattered in mid-air, as if it had hit an invisible wall. 'What sorcery is this?' the captain asked as he lowered his bow, then said, 'How can we fight against an army like this? Fire at will!'

Every bowman on the wall let their arrows fly, hoping that a few would penetrate the invisible wall. Hundreds of arrows filled the sky, but none made it through.

The advancing army halted, and Abendi gave the order for his bowmen to fire. With military perfection, the foot soldiers formed into rows, and all the bowmen ran to the front through the opened paths and let their arrows fly. Men toppled from the city wall as arrows found their marks. Screams of pain erupted as some sliced into legs and arms to cripple them.

Massive boulders rose from the walls to the sky, flung by the catapults to crash through the invisible wall and crush the horde beneath them. For a moment, they felt victorious as they saw the boulders penetrate. Shouts went up all around the wall.

The horde reached the wall, placing ladders along its length to get to the top. At the northeast gate, guards were pushing at the door, bracing it as the horde rammed it with a battering ram; the door was starting to give already. Splinters went flying as the battering ram hit again and again, but it was taking too long for the likes of the horde.

'Burn it!' yelled one barbarian. A torchbearer ran forth to light the battering ram. The burning contraption rammed the gate over and over. The door caught alight, but the flames died quickly. Having foreseen this, the guards of Galhor had soaked the door in water during the night. But this did not help for long. The gate burst open and the horde streamed through. They were unstoppable, killing everyone who stood in their path.

The Galhorians poured oil down from the sides of the wall, covering a multitude of the barbarians. A torch followed, and chaos ensued as they were set alight. Multiple barbarians caught in the fire, now rolled around on the ground, trying to extinguish the flames as arrows rained down on them. By then their brethren were everywhere on the walls fighting, swords swinging, heads rolling.

Galhor had one more trick up its sleeve, one intended only for survival. Most of the women and children had been evacuated through tunnels beneath the city. Built years before, they extended for a mile underground and opened up in the nearest forest. From there, they could make a run to Millron.

The rivers ran red with the blood of innocents this night; the soil absorbing the dark liquid as best it could. Mist covered the earth in the gloomy forest, obscuring sight. Small twigs breaking underneath a foot made him turn, but not hastily. He had never felt this calm. He looked upon his visitor and spoke in a sad voice: 'Father Delios, where are we? Why does this sight sadden me so?'

Delios sighed as he said, 'You are in a spirit walk, Gordon, and I have joined you as... a guide. This is the prophecy, becoming reality. The evil is spreading and killing the land. Slowly it will darken the forest until no living creature can enter it. Much innocent blood has been spilled tonight. His strength will grow because of it. Soon, he will make himself known.'

'What can we do against an evil such as this? Just look at the forest! It's dying before our very eyes. The river is the colour of blood; the fish are dead, already floating at the surface. The forest reeks of despair. How can we fight an enemy who works against the elements?'

'You are wrong about one thing. The river is not the colour of blood; it is blood. But there is still hope, Gordon. I have ventured to the island Milleria through one of my spirit flights. I encountered a sorceress who might help you in your fight. Now that you have learnt that this Lord Anukke is the sorcerer responsible for all that has been going wrong, you need some way to fight his magic. I believe this sorceress is the only one who can help you. She is called Rose.'

'Why, Delios? Why would she help us?'

'I do not have all the answers. Some you must figure out on your own. Now come, we must get back.'

'I don't even know how I got here, Delios.'

The old abbot grinned and said, 'This spirit walk is part of you now; it is a gift from your new eyes. They are attached to your soul, and the soul sees more than you can imagine. You will get used to them. Just will your soul back to your flesh and it will be so.'

The sweetness of the orange quenched his yearning as he pushed another slice into his mouth. *I can't recall ever having such a delicious orange in my life before coming to this monastery.* Mist hung in the valley, covering the trees and landscape down below. He looked over the grey vista as the sun was about to make its appearance when Baldrake joined him.

The wolf saw him looking towards the cage and lowered his head as he said, 'I will leave. I can see this haunts you still.'

Gordon looked back at the wolf as he walked away and said, 'I have never had oranges as good as these. Here, taste one.' He threw a slice through the air, and Baldrake snatched it in his mouth.

He chewed and rolled the slice in his mouth, then said, 'Juicy. But I dislike its sweetness. It is overwhelming.'

Gordon rolled his eyes and continued, 'That's the best part. Oh, never mind. Hey, Baldrake, please tell me what you see when you look into my eyes?'

The wolf walked back to the young man to stand mere inches from his face and gazed deep into his milky eyes, unblinking. After a while, he pulled his deathly black eyes away and sat on his haunches as he said, 'I see a young man who has a duty to fulfil. What that duty is, I do not know. I can't see the future, but what I can see is the heart of a person, and in you, I see courage and determination. I also see that you miss your father dearly; you have a longing to make him proud, and would do anything to accomplish that.'

Gordon rose and threw the orange peels into the garden. 'Come, let's go wake the big guy.'

Together, the two entered the monastery and walked up the stairs to

Malachai's room. The priests who passed them were in awe of how the warriors complemented each other, both walking with a certain grace and calmness to match. A tanned young warrior with milky ghostlike eyes and his black hair pulled back into a ponytail, swinging side to side. A muscular wolf walking beside him, black as night. Black slit eyes, the rims gleaming red as blood, his tail swinging side to side. They looked like a formidable pair.

Loud snoring could be heard as they neared the door and crept into the room. Malachai slept soundly, snoring so loud you could play the violin next to him and not hear it. Gordon grinned to the wolf and said, 'Keep a close eye and don't make a sound.'

He approached the bedside, taking care not to make a sound as he pulled out a paper bag, filled it with air and raised it to just above the sleeping man's head. Baldrake spoke to his mind, 'I do not believe this to be a good idea.'

Gordon smiled and whacked the bag, bursting it with an extremely loud pop. Before the echoes of the pop had faded, Gordon dangled in the air, his head pressed against the ceiling as he hung from the grip of the big man's hands. Malachai stared at him with eyes as cold as winter frost. The swiftness of the big man ruffled Gordon. He smiled and muttered, 'Well, I'll be a monkey's uncle. You move quickly when needed! Now please put me down and get some clothes on you.' Malachai looked towards Baldrake and said, 'You think I should let him off so easily?'

'I do not.' The wolf's teeth gleamed as he pulled his face into what Gordon could only assume was a smile.

Malachai had a nasty grin on his face. He walked to the nearest window and peered down while holding Gordon in the air and said, 'I don't think so either.'

'Oh no you don't, big guy, I was just joking.'

He lifted Gordon over his head with little effort and tossed him out of the window. A scream followed, and then a mighty splash of water. They heard Gordon's curses coming from the animals' water crib down below and laughed. Peering out of the window, they saw him spluttering about.

'You knew there was a crib down there, didn't you, Malachai?' Baldrake asked as he laughed his roaring laughter.

'Well, I assumed... more hoped, really.'

The companions were all up and eating a hearty breakfast when Delios entered the dining hall and said, 'Good to see you all had a good rest; you will need it.' With a big grin he added, 'Also, I heard Gordon went for a quick swim this morning in one of our drinking cribs for the animals.'

Malachai laughed harshly. 'He sure did.'

'Oh, grow up,' Gordon countered and thought even the Gar hounds were laughing now.

Delios silenced them by waving his arms up and down. 'I have someone who would like to join you for breakfast this morning.' From behind the abbot's long silvery robe came Beldrin, slowly making his way closer to the companions. Everyone leapt from their seats and welcomed the young pup.

'By the teeth of Valin, I am glad to see you are better, my son. We all are!' Baldrake shouted.

Beldrin joined his father and Cuorco on the floor and ate silently as Gordon explained what he had seen in his vision and the urgency of the matter. Malachai rubbed his beard and then stuffed another piece of bacon in his mouth, closing his eyes as he chewed the meat. Gordon snapped his fingers before the big man's eyes and said, 'Are you even listening? Can you stop eating until we finish this conversation?'

'Aye, I can't help it. It's so crispy. I've heard enough anyway. It seems like an adventure to me. Seeing that we have to save the world and all.'

'No, there won't be any, Malachai,' Gordon said.

'There won't be any what?' Malachai asked, annoyed at the interruption.

'There won't be any payment, I knew you were going to ask.'

Malachai turned away, his face flushed red with anger as he muttered to himself, 'Blasted... idiotic...' *Saving the world, and we don't get paid for it. Don't seem right to me, is all.*

Gordon continued, 'I'm not asking for any of you to join me, but the company would be appreciated. This could be a very dangerous journey, and I, for one, wouldn't judge you for not wanting to come along. Either way, I'm going ahead.'

There was silence in the room for a long time before Baldrake stood and said, 'I will join you on this quest. However, I have been thinking about Cuorco and my son. They will not come with us.'

Cuorco and Beldrin both reeled at this statement and started arguing. 'No father, you cannot do this. I will come with you.'

'As will I,' Cuorco stated.

Baldrake surged to his feet and barked out, 'Quiet! I am still your rightful commander, and if you do not want to listen to me, your father or friend, then you *will* listen to your commander!'

All in the room went silent, staring at the black wolf as he sat back down. He cleared his throat and said, 'I am sorry, son, I cannot allow you to come. You are too important, and I do not want to put you in harm's way. No, Cuorco will stay with you and teach you our ways, how to fight and survive. When we are done with the quest, I will find you.'

Baldrake felt a sting as he said the last words, for he knew his fate would be decided not by himself, but by the one he swore fealty to. *I have to obey when the time comes. A Gar hound keeps his vows, after all.* He could only hope that Gordon would let him go after this quest.

Cuorco nodded and said, 'So it shall be, brother. May your travel be swift, your enemies slow, and your kills merciful.'

'Thank you, brother.' Baldrake lowered his head in respect.

Gordon rose from the table, walked to the doorway, and turned. 'So, we are all in agreement, then—we head for the island of Milleria to find this sorceress, Rose. We'd better get our gear checked and packed. We should leave as soon as we are able. Delios, would your priests be so kind as to pack some food and water for the journey?'

'Yes, of course, we cannot send you out with nothing to fill your bellies.'

'Thank you, Delios.' Everyone rose and went their separate ways.

Beldrin sat underneath a great old willow outside the monastery in solitude, thinking about the discussion in the dining hall, when he realised Baldrake was sitting next to him. 'I have spoken to the master of the monastery, my son. He has agreed for you and Cuorco to stay here for as long as it pleases you. However, he wants you to stay at least until you are completely healed. He assured me you and Cuorco are welcome here always. I must go; I will come back for you when the quest is done.'

A shout came from the front of the monastery. 'Baldrake. We are ready to ride.'

Beldrin did not say a word or show any feelings as Baldrake turned to leave. Rather, he looked away into the distance.

Everyone was gathered in the courtyard at the front of the monastery, watching as Gordon and Malachai mounted their steeds. Still at unease with the wolves, the horses pulled their ears flat against their heads as Baldrake sauntered over to stand next to them.

The priests stood at the top of the stairway, with Delios and Cuorco in the middle. Sitting on his haunches, he was the same height as the abbot. But Beldrin was nowhere in sight. As the party moved off, everyone was shouting their best wishes; and just as they rounded the outer garden wall of the monastery, Beldrin came skidding around the corner, running towards them as he shouted, 'Father...' Pebbles flew up as he skidded on the gravel and came to a halt before them. 'Father, forgive me. I behaved like a spoiled human child. You do what you must; I understand that.'

The two wolves moved closer and pushed the top of their heads together. The two warriors on horseback felt the sudden emotion between father and son. They moved apart as Beldrin said, 'May your journey be swift, your enemies slow, and your kills merciful.'

Baldrake lowered his head. 'Farewell, my son. Until we meet again, in this lifetime or the next.'

With that, the company departed on their way to the island.

The day looked promising, the sky bright blue and cloudless. Gravel crunched underfoot as the small company walked their horses down the road, with Baldrake hanging on the left next to Gordon. Dense and dark, the forest lay to their left, and the mountains rose to their right. Malachai tore a dried piece of beef in three while riding and whistled to get the attention of his fellow warriors. Both Gordon and Baldrake cocked their heads his way as he tossed them the pieces. Still chewing on his piece of beef, Malachai said, 'So tell me again how we're getting to this island.'

Gordon sighed. 'This will be my third time explaining it. Did you not listen the last two times?'

'I tried, I really did, but you explain like my great, but *very* dead, grandmother. There was just no way I could pay attention. Ya know, it took her three days to tell a story.'

Gordon grimaced. 'Okay, okay. It shouldn't be far down this road, as shown on our map. In fact, you see that rock sticking out of the ground at the base of the mountain, the one that looks like a finger about three hundred paces away? There's a pathway leading through the mountain to the valley beyond. Once through this mountain, we can make camp in the valley. From there, we cross over the D'hore Mountains and run into flatter plains until we reach the port. Then we find a ship to take us to the island.'

Malachai was looking in all directions and swatting at a fly that was annoying him, oblivious to what Gordon had just said.

'Malachai!' Gordon called out.

Startled, the big man shook the reins of his mount and almost leapt into the air. With raised brows, he turned and demanded, 'What was that for?'

'Were you even listening to me?'

'Of course I was,' Malachai lied and spat on the ground.

Same old Vasgath, testing everyone's patience. Baldrake thought. Problem was, no one ever dared lose their temper with him. The consequences could be dire.

As the company reached the finger-rock, they halted, staring down the narrow corridor leading through the mountain. Barely wide enough for the three warriors, the fissure stretched for miles. Malachai glanced back at the group. 'It looks like some god was unhappy and tore the mountain in two. Say, Gordon, why is it we didn't notice this tear in the mountain when we came this way from Kraydenia?'

Gordon shot him a quick smile and said, 'Because the last time we came down this path, you were dying with that poisonous arrow in your side, it was at night, and I was too busy trying to save your fat arse. Baldrake, you take point and keep your nose high. I need you to smell for trouble. I assume you have a very keen sense for it?'

Baldrake bowed his head and replied, 'Indeed. I would like to hear this tale about Malachai's fat arse and how you came to save it. I would have you tell me this story in more detail.'

'Oh, so much tact coming from the wolf. Who would have guessed?' Malachai spat again to the side, then said, 'I think there's something in my throat.'

Gordon smiled and nodded to the canine as they moved deeper into the eerie tear in the mountain. Both Malachai and Baldrake had taken to Gordon as their leader on this quest. Even though he was still young, he had a talent for leading... and besides; he was the one who'd gotten them into this. It was his duty to get them out.

Gordon had fashioned himself a harness for his sword's scabbard, which slung over his right shoulder down to his left hip, giving him more freedom to move around without the sword flopping to his side. Over his white cotton shirt, he wore a brown leather jerkin to match his brown leather pants. Slowly, as they made their way through the fissure, Gordon took up his bow and nocked an arrow from the quiver at the side of his horse. Malachai was scanning the clifftops restlessly for any movement.

They walked for about a mile in this manner before Baldrake stopped and scanned the cliffs. 'Someone or something is up there, following us,' he said. Malachai, trailing five feet behind Baldrake, pulled on his reins and lifted his right hand, palm open, and Gordon halted. All three scanned the clifftops in silence for a moment. Baldrake jerked his head to the left, indicating some small stones tumbling down the cliff, dust trailing up. 'Move to the side of the mountain!' he growled.

Gordon and Malachai dropped from their horses with lightning speed and hastened to the mountain's side, taking refuge under an overhang. Gordon, arrow nocked, was looking frantically for a target.

Baldrake is gone, Malachai suddenly realised. 'Did you see where Baldrake went?' he hissed.

Gordon cursed under his breath while he looked around and said, 'No!'

'He must have gone after whatever he saw,' Malachai whispered.

From above, they heard a sudden vicious growl, followed by screams and shrieks of terror. A body, blood-smeared and mauled, fell from just above them to the left, hitting the ground with a dull thump. It lay unmoving. Cautiously approaching the body, they held their weapons ready. Gordon looked down at it and quickly turned his face away, wanting to vomit. The body was that of a man deformed, his skin very pale, translucent even; one could see through to his intestines. His eyes were completely black, as were his veins where they coursed under his skin. The head was completely hairless, mouth lipless, and his teeth looked as if they had been sharpened by a file.

From above, Baldrake spoke: 'They are a human race banished from civilization, driven to dwelling in caves and feeding upon any meat they find, including other humans. They are called Crawlers. We should hurry and get through to the valley; there will be others coming for the dead one.'

Malachai and Gordon looked up to see Baldrake standing at the entrance to a cave ten feet above. He leapt from the cave to land silently

115

on the ground before them. Gordon only then realised how stealthily Baldrake could move. *An animal landing from that height without a sound should be impossible...*

The two men mounted their horses and set off at a full gallop to get away from the Crawlers. Listening carefully, Gordon could hear more of the screams and shrieks behind them, getting closer. When he turned in his saddle, he saw hundreds of the once-humans descending from the mountain's sides to the Crawler lying dead in the middle of the path behind them. They tore off its limbs, and gobs of meat flew as they ravaged the carcass. From in front, Baldrake bellowed, 'They will not follow us into the forest; it forbids them. Hurry!'

Hundreds of Crawlers were already chasing them, jumping from the side of the mountain, trying to grab them, to pull them down from their horses and feast upon them. Somehow, they had adapted to this way of life, mutated to become faster, more agile, almost able to keep up with the horses at full gallop. Gordon let fly one of his arrows and saw it sink deep into one of the Crawlers. The creature pitched forward, and all those around it stopped to tear it apart.

One was about to jump onto Malachai's horse when Gordon screamed caution. Malachai had his huge hunting knife drawn, and as the Crawler grasped at him, his blade plunged from the bottom of its jaw through to the top of its hairless skull. He pitched it off the horse; more Crawlers stopped to feast on the dead. The forest was in sight now, and the Crawlers slowed in their pursuit, returning to their caves when the riders entered the tree line.

About six hundred paces into the forest, they stopped to calm and rest the horses. Riding them like that too much would be the death of them. Quickly, the men rubbed down their horses to ease their hot, tense muscles. Gordon took carrots from a bag on his horse and fed them to both mounts.

Taking the reins, they then ventured deeper into the valley. Gordon pulled out a map and studied it as he walked. 'There should be a pond to the north, not too far,' he said after a bit. 'We will make camp there, near the waters.'

'Aye, the horses could do with some rest and water,' Malachai said as he marvelled at the variety of trees and flowers around them. Birdsong filled the sky; the air was cool, and the wood's wind calm. A herd of elk darted away to their left. Animals were in abundance, as they saw wolves, squirrels and all kinds of other animals, even a bear that ran away as soon as it saw the group, too afraid to venture close to the massive wolf that strode beside them.

Gordon looked around and said, 'They fear you, Baldrake.'

Baldrake turned his head and said, 'They should,' then moved away from him.

'Don't worry, lad, animals understand each other. He must look and act superior to all, otherwise, they will challenge him. He must radiate power and authority,' said Malachai.

'I guess so. Must be strange to have to compete with other animals all the time.'

Malachai kicked at a rock and sent it flying as he said, 'I would argue men are worse than animals, lad. I think it's easier for him than us.'

Baldrake lifted his nose to the air. 'With that, I agree. The world of man knows nothing but chaos. Come, we are close; I can smell the water in the air.'

There was more than water to be sensed. Cocking his ear to the sky, Gordon heard faint, pleading cries for help and the splashing of water coming from the pond's direction. Letting go of his horse's reins, he darted forward, slamming through the brush, and soon vanished from their sight. The two warriors turned to stare at each other, and Malachai grinned as he raised his brows and said, 'That's what happens when you eat too much. Ya can't hold it all in forever.'

For a moment, it looked like Baldrake pulled his face into a snarling smile, but that vanished just as quickly as he said, 'I hear a cry for help! Gordon must have heard it as well, and ran to their aid. Let us go! He might be in trouble.'

Leaving the horses, they hurried through the forest, angry at themselves for letting him go off like that. *He might be dead already...*

thought Baldrake and quickened his pace as he leapt over a fallen tree. Once they broke through the last line of brush, they halted to see Gordon swimming out to a hapless victim splashing and sinking in the middle of the pond. Malachai stopped next to the wolf, hissing breath through his teeth. 'What is that?'

Baldrake shook his head and replied, 'I don't know that creature, Vasgath, but one thing is for certain... it can't swim.'

Malachai stared glumly at Baldrake. 'Is that humour I hear?'

Gordon pulled the dishevelled creature out of the pond and laid him down on the pebbles next to the water. He was definitely of human origin, but much smaller. The little man was breathing deep and ragged as he coughed rapidly to expel some water from his lungs. Gordon yelled out whilst he lay next to the little man on the ground, also trying to catch his breath, 'Don't just stand there, help him!'

The two walked closer to the rapidly coughing little man, inspecting him as they neared. He was a funny-looking thing, tiny and frail. Smaller than a dwarf, like a small child, but old. The eyes were too big for his head as were the ears; a thin white beard ran all the way from ear to ear surrounding his mouth, and short wet grey hair lay flat against his head. Malachai knelt beside him and helped him into a sitting position as he said, 'There, there, fellow. You're fine now, our Gordon here saved you.'

The little old man spoke as rapidly as his breath allowed, 'Saved Melche. Yes... yes... yes, he did. Melche would have drowned if he hadn't.'

As the little one turned, he saw the massive wolf standing there before him, and with a scream of terror he darted back into the water—where he started drowning again. Gordon sighed, 'This time old boy, you go get him.'

Malachai walked into the pond and raised the little fellow out of the water by the straps on his clothes. Dangling in the air, he still screamed for help as if drowning. Malachai put the obstreperous old fellow on the pebbles once again and said, 'It's all right little one. The wolf won't bite you.'

Slowly, he opened his eyes and stared at the wolf. 'You will not eat

Melche the mekkel?'

Baldrake spoke in his most gentle tone to the little one, 'No, I will not,' and still the sound of his voice would have chased away most children, sending them running to their parents. Then continued, 'Is that your name? Melche the mekkel?'

With a sudden outburst of laughter, the little one jumped to his feet and said, 'No, you poop. What name is "Melche the mekkel"?'

The wolf turned to Malachai and asked enquiringly, 'Poop?'

'Must be in shock.' Malachai shrugged.

Gordon sat up and said, 'His name must be Melche, and he must *be* a mekkel, whatever that is.'

Melche smiled, his mouth wide open as he nodded and said, 'Yes, yes. That it is.'

Gordon glanced up to the big man. 'You two go get the horses and bring them back. Get them fed and watered. I'll get some firewood and start setting up camp. Melche, you're welcome to stay and rest until you're better.'

The old fellow jumped up and down as he shouted, 'Melche *must* stay. Melche owes a debt to you.'

Baldrake and Malachai looked at each other, then walked off to the horses rather than trying to sort this out.

Gordon just sighed and dropped back to the pebbles on the ground, closing his eyes.

CHAPTER EIGHT

The night did not progress as expected. Rest did not come easily, and as for relaxation, there was none. Camp was made, but it took nearly double the amount of time than it should have, thanks to Melche. At first, as Gordon erected the tents, Melche stole the rope and booby-trapped the campsite by spanning it low off the ground around the perimeter.

Horse leads in hand, Malachai walked back with the horses and tripped over the rope, falling face-first in the mud with a loud thump.

Gordon turned at the noise only to see the mekkel run and hide behind a tree while the big man was getting up from the ground. He walked over and saw the rope on the ground, then said, 'That sneaky bloody mekkel, I wondered where this went! No wonder I couldn't find it.' He chuckled and quickly covered his mouth as Malachai looked at him from behind a mask of mud.

Furious, the big man shouted, 'Come out here, mekkel! I should wring your neck!'

From behind the trees, they heard a high-pitched voice sound out, 'Melche sorry. Only wanted to make camp safe. Please do not hurt Melche.'

'Well, the trap worked as intended. Cut him some slack.'

Malachai walked over to the pond and washed the dirt from his face and dried it with a cloth. 'Come out, Melche, I'm not angry anymore.'

The mekkel darted out from behind the tree and threw himself around the big man's leg.

'Get off me, you little animal!' Malachai shouted, stomping about as the little mekkel still clutched on.

'Melche sorry!'

Gordon and Baldrake sat a distance away from the charade, laughing at the big man's expense. The milky-eyed warrior turned to the wolf and stated, 'That little mekkel is quite fast for his age.'

Baldrake looked on with what could only be perceived as a grin, and said, 'That he is.'

After they had settled down, the two men dragged a large piece of timber from the woods and sat down next to the fire. Baldrake lay on the far side of the fire and closed his eyes.

Suddenly, the clangour of metal rang out, and instinctively they jumped up and reached for their weapons, only to see Melche with Gordon's sword, role-playing a fight with a goblin.

The sword swung wildly through the air. The three had to duck and weave as the blows were dealt with very inexperienced hands. Twice the length of the mekkel, the sword threw him off balance as he battered it against the tree. 'Take that, you hobgoblin, and that, and that, and that!'

Gordon jumped in, caught the hilt of the blade, and said, 'Melche, what are you doing!'

'Melche is teaching this goblin a lesson,' came his high-pitched voice, dignified as ever.

He sighed and lowered his face as he muttered, 'It's a tree, Melche, a tree... not a goblin! You are hitting my sword against a *tree*. Now please, get some rest. We all need it.'

The white hall of Galhor was befitting a glorious king no longer. Blood-smeared and black-charred walls surrounded its new occupants.

They had wrought significant damage to the city and its castle from the battle they had waged. The streets were foul with corpses and detritus; the city lay in ruins, smoke drifting up to the clear night sky. Chaos reigned supreme, and atop the throne of the king sat the wizard, rolling two small silver balls the size of plums in his right hand. Head down, he studied the exquisite floor design. The black stone, glittering with the mix of a fluorescent rock, was something to behold.

'Is everything ready?' he asked Abendi.

'Yes, it is. But—'

'But nothing!' Anukke interrupted. 'You shall do what I pay you to do.'

Rising from the throne, he strolled to the balcony overlooking the massive courtyard. As far as the eye could see lay bodies, the mutilated corpses of the brave men who gave their lives to protect a few, scattered throughout the city. Hundreds of wooden pillars had been erected, with the surviving soldiers tied with barbed wire a few feet from the ground, suspending them in the air as it cut into their flesh, blood running freely from their wounds. *I bestow unto you, Ortega, all these innocents. Take their lives to live once more.* Anukke turned his gaze to Abendi and commanded, 'Bring me the king.'

A while later one of the barbarians walked in, dragging a man who had his hands bound with rope, his left leg leaving a trail of blood behind him, broken in multiple places. Blood ran from the top of his head down the front of his face, staining his frosty beard and dripping to the floor.

'Now, now, king. It's not good manners to stain *my* new floor,' said the wizard mockingly.

Next to him stood the crippled king, staring down at the ghastly sight below. Tears streamed down his face. 'This is madness,' he said in a trembling voice.

Anukke stood, arms folded, and with a wry grin he said, 'I thought you would like to see the last of your city before death takes you.' Leaning forward over the balcony, he called to a barbarian in the courtyard, 'Douse the captives with oil, then burn them.'

What followed were the horrific screams and death cries of the last defenders of the city as they were torched alive. Anukke slowly turned to face the king, a glinting dagger in hand. He moved forward with one quick motion and slit the throat of the old ruler. As the king slowly sagged to the floor, clutching at his throat, blood sprayed out through his fingers and hands onto the floor. He gurgled out, 'Why?'

'You bore me... king.' He turned and walked off towards the throne, and said, 'Abendi, we must discuss our next strategy.'

'Of course, Anukke. I believe we must travel south to Millron and strike them hard.'

'That's the problem with the youth of today; they don't think ahead. Millron would have been notified of our march to war and would have gone for support. So they will have a much bigger army than what we just faced. No, we will have to be more... creative this time round.'

Abendi stood rubbing his beard and said, 'What do you have in mind?'

The wizard rose and moved closer. 'Gather a thousand of your best warriors and tell their leader to meet with me before we head out. I have a special task for them. Rest for the night. In two days, we ride out. We will set up camp just out of sight of Millron and kill any scouts that may patrol. Millron must be blind to us.'

Tuds had arrived at Millron early that morning with his company, and ever since had been negotiating the terms of their trade agreement, signing all necessary documentation. After all the politics, he barked out orders for preparation of the defences in the oncoming battle. With his heavy overcoat waving in the wind, Tuds and Gweniviere walked through the dust-filled air—kicked up by the soldiers running around fulfilling their orders: gathering equipment, taking weapon supplies to certain locations, digging trenches, sharpening blades.

Trenches were being dug on the outside along the wall, barricaded with long wooden spikes, and filled with an oily, liquid tar-like substance. Tuds studied the city as he walked. Starting at the northwest were the massive grey walls stretching to the southeast around the city, connecting to the mountains that encompassed it all the way further. A six-hundred-foot sheer cliff face stared down at them.

'Gwen, arrange for the Millronian general to meet me in my chambers. We have to discuss their strategy of war and I suppose... follow their lead.'

Gweniviere regarded him with worry on her face, then nodded and said, 'I hope you know what you're doing, sir. We still await word from General Blackbeard for an answer to our situation.'

Tuds stopped at this and said, 'Well let's pray to the great Baliël that he sends troops.'

The three wooden gates, northeast, southeast, and southwest, were being doused with water. Southeast being the main gate, and the biggest would likely not be their focus. Smithies were called in to fasten metal backing plates to all the gates to reinforce the structures. Eight watchtowers stood guard: two on either side of every gate and one each to the far corners of the city, manned day and night by the best bowmen. Weapons were being sharpened and oiled, bowstrings smeared with fat. Conversation was kept to a minimum, as all knew too well what had happened at Galhor.

Women and children who escaped through the tunnels from Galhor had arrived the previous day, sharing their horrid accounts of the battle that took place. 'Galhor stood no chance,' they said. 'There was no honour in them. They attacked without remorse or compassion. Women, children... It did not matter to them,' they said.

As the day wore on, Tuds and Gwen walked the ramparts until the general and his two majors arrived. Leading the group to a gazebo with a table and some chairs, he gestured for them to sit. *This young man cannot be the general. Surely not. He's just too young. Probably not even fifty. Age comes with wisdom, and generals are wise,* Tuds thought as he eyed the men, then said, 'General Floghorn, I presume.'

As everyone sat, the young general nodded and rolled out a map of the city and its surroundings, then calmly stated, 'This is Major Bell and

Major Lice. They will attend our meeting; I hope you don't mind. I'd hate having to repeat everything said here to them later.'

Tuds gestured to his left as he saw the two majors staring at Gwen. 'This is Major Gweniviere; she will also join us.'

The general nodded with a grin. 'Let's begin then, shall we?'

Major Lice rose from his chair and started. 'We have dug the trenches, here and here, and filled them with the oil mixture, watered the gates, and reinforced them with metal sheets. We filled the towers with archers and spotters. Light infantry will man the wall.'

Major Bell cut in from there. 'Reserves will be at the bottom and go wherever they're needed. Stretcher-bearers will have a fight on their hands, as most fighting will be on the wall. We have two medical facilities near the gates. In total, we number eighteen hundred men, sir. That includes your men, Major General Tudeske.'

Major Bell, you make me think of my friend Malachai. You're almost the same stature. He just likes a hammer and not an axe. I wonder how the big man is doing. I hope he's okay. Bell's cleanly shaven head and face made him look much younger than he was. Lice was the opposite, being much shorter and leaner with red ruffled hair and sideburns to match.

Tuds stood, absorbing the information, then said, 'Spare a hundred men to run with the stretcher-bearers. They'll need aid getting through the fighting. Place four of your trebuchets at the bottom of the walls and four on top of the walls. As long as they can lob rocks just over the walls, that would be great. They'll make for invisible targets and do a lot of damage. You heard the stories of the invisible wall made by their sorcerers. The soldiers could only get through with their arrows once the barbarians were at the wall, so there was no advantage from firing arrows at a distance. Keep the men low on the walls until they are close enough to breach the invisible defence. We can only speculate that they'll use the same tactics here. Once the barbarians reach the wall, Major Lice, have your archers in the towers send the fire arrows to the trench you dug. And have the heavy infantry bracing the gates.'

Gwen sat passively listening to the tactics being played out, and as they finished, she whispered, 'Baliël be with us all.'

The four men acknowledged her statement and walked away.

Gordon awoke early the next morning and found the mekkel lying close to Baldrake, almost as an infant would. Rubbing his eyes, he walked closer. 'What the... What is that? Baldrake?'

The wolf blinked open its eyes, yawned, and spoke to his mind, 'Well rested?'

Gordon laughed and moved away as Malachai joined them. The big man chuckled and also moved away to the dead fire.

'What is it you find so funny?' the Gar hound asked as he followed them to the fire.

'It seems you have been made a pet. The mighty Baldrake... a mekkel's pet,' Malachai said as he chuckled again.

The wolf turned his head and saw the object of their amusement. A blue ribbon had been tied around his neck to form an enormous bow at the top. 'If you will excuse me, I will kill the mekkel now.'

Melche still lay motionless on the ground, sound asleep, as Baldrake approached. 'How can one hurt such an innocent-looking thing?' he asked the others. Malachai walked closer and untied the ribbon as he whispered, 'Let's break camp silently. Move out before he wakes.'

'You mean to leave him here?'

'Well, yes. Unless you want to wear makeup tomorrow.'

Baldrake glared at the man. 'No, it is an excellent idea. Let's move.'

They packed their gear in silence and set out into the forest, all while Melche slept soundly.

After travelling for about a mile through the forest, Malachai said, 'At least we will have lost the mekkel for sure by now.'

Baldrake spotted a small deer to their left and gave chase. They were all hungry, and the thought of meat made their mouths water. The men moved on foot through the forest, their mounts trailing behind them.

'I am glad to see you two getting along,' Malachai said as he climbed over a dead tree stump.

'I still don't trust him, old boy. I tolerate him for the quest. We need him... I mean, he *did* try to kill me. And was I not at that monastery, he would have succeeded.'

Malachai sighed at the response and said, 'I was once like you; I didn't trust the Gar hounds either. But in time, I learnt they are trustworthy, more so than man, I dare say. I fought alongside them; hell, I even saved Cuorco's life.'

Gordon studied him as he spoke and saw the emotion that statement brought to the big man. 'What happened?' he asked.

'We were at war, and out of nowhere a massive tiger jumped Cuorco from the forest, tore his one eye right out of its socket. I stepped in and got rid of the tiger.'

'No, I meant...'

Suddenly, a man dropped from the tree in front of them with sword in hand, saying, 'There is no need for bloodshed. Hand over all your gold and weapons, and we will be on our way.'

Gordon curiously looked at the man as he said, 'You must not be a good thief, seeing as there are two of us and only one of you.'

All around them men rose, covered with brush to hide themselves. Six men surrounded them now. 'I'm sorry, you were saying?' came the arrogant voice from the man at the front.

Malachai pulled free his hammer and Gordon unsheathed his sword, getting ready for a fight. To their left, they heard a dull thud as something fell to the ground. As all the men turned, they saw the massive wolf standing fifty paces away from them with a dead deer at his feet. 'What is this?' Baldrake roared. With bared teeth, he grinned as he saw the shock register on the thieves' faces as they realised it was him speaking.

Malachai chuckled as he said, 'It seems the tides have turned once more, lad. Give up now, you swine, and we will spare you.'

Before the thief could even answer, one of his men at the back was attacked, screaming as he went down to the ground. Gordon used this distraction to his advantage and leapt in to meet the leader, clashing with steel. The thief was skilled with the sword and held his own against the young warrior. Malachai followed suit and moved to the first on his right. Baldrake lunged towards the thieves on the left.

Baldrake dispensed with two of the thieves quickly and looked about to see Malachai send a crushing blow with his hammer to a man's chest. The thief toppled over without a sound. Attacked from the side by the last thief, Malachai parried the blow and sent a right hook to the man's face. Knife in hand, trembling and wide-eyed, the thief staggered back. Malachai dropped his hammer and rolled his shoulders. The thief jumped wildly at the bigger man, knife flashing through the air, cutting into Malachai's leather arm guard. On the second attack, the big man caught the thief's knife hand and pulled him closer. He grabbed the thief's jugular with his free hand and squeezed; the spasms stopped.

Gordon was still busy fighting with the leader while the rest of the thieves lay on the ground, motionless. The man was well-trained, dealing blows in between slashes from his sword. The fight raged on. 'Your men are dead! Stop this now and we will spare you,' Gordon said as he parried another blow.

The thief glanced at the men on the ground and shouted as he lunged forward with his sword.

Baldrake and Malachai walked over to the thief who had been attacked first, who was still wrestling to get his attacker off his face, bleeding from scratches and bite marks.

Melche had been tracking the company since he woke and as soon as he saw them surrounded, charged in and pinned himself to the face of the thief, biting and scratching as hard as he could. Malachai stepped forward and said, 'Let him go, Melche. We have our eyes on him now.'

Freed of the mekkel, a harsh right hook landed square in his face, knocking him out cold.

The duel between Gordon and the thief continued, and Gordon parried a thrust meant for his face, following a slice to his midsection. He jumped back just in time to avoid the cut. With sword and dagger in hand, the thief circled the young warrior and rushed in. *Always let your enemy come to you,* Gordon thought. Sidestepping a vicious blow from the thief's sword, he quickly returned a sweep with his own and caught the man unguarded.

Hot fire tore through his arm. Slowly, the thief turned to face Gordon and saw his sword, still in the grip of his hand, lying on the ground a few feet away. He looked at the sky and saw the vultures approach, some already settling and waiting to feast on his dead friends. 'So it has come to pass,' the thief said as he dropped to his knees. 'Please finish it.'

A merciful death, then. Gordon walked to stand behind the man, his sword resting with the tip to the back of the thief's neck. With a sudden downward thrust, the sword sliced through the spine and heart. The body toppled over and slumped to the ground, blood oozing from the stab wound. He glanced up and walked to Malachai, saying, 'What attacked that thief?'

A chuckle came from the man as he moved away and said, 'See for yourself.'

Smiling a big smile, the mekkel leapt out from behind the big man.

With a great sigh, Gordon thanked the mekkel for coming to their rescue, hoping that if the favour was returned, he would go on his way. Unfortunately, that did not work out as planned either. Melche turned and said, 'Melche sees now, you will not survive without Melche. Therefore, Melche the mekkel shall stay with you, and protect you.'

As the meat from the deer was roasting over the fire, Gordon and Baldrake sat next to the mekkel and said, 'Melche, we are on a perilous journey. We ride into the heart of danger. You will not be safe. Go back home, be safe.'

'All the more reason for Melche to join, then,' was his answer.

No matter what they tried, it would not sway him. Finally giving up, Gordon said, 'Fine, if you are coming with us, you will do as you are told. Agree?'

'Yay! An adventure. Melche has new friends!'

Gordon produced the map he'd received from the abbot and spread it open on the ground in front of the group, and said, 'Currently, we are just before the D'hore Mountain range; once we pass over, it's lowland. We can follow the River Gallas all the way to the Ventrian Sea. Once we reach the ocean, we can go down the shoreline to the ancient golden city of Millanthross. At the port, we will have to find a ship that can carry us to the island.'

'So we camp tonight in the D'hore Mountains?' Malachai asked as he raised his brow.

Gordon looked up and saw the momentary discomfort in the man's eyes. 'Yes. Why?'

'It's just... nothing.'

He rolled up the map and placed it back in his bag, and said, 'Good, then it is settled.'

The day wore on as the company moved through the forest, reaching the mountain path as the sun started fading away for the night to follow. The D'hore Mountains were enormous, spreading far and wide as if all the mountains were fighting for location. They could have walked around the mountains, but it would have added another week to their journey, and time was a luxury they didn't have. The path they followed was narrow, probably an old animal trail. Walking single file, Baldrake took the lead, with Melche skipping along happily behind him. Then came Malachai, with his massive hammer resting on his right shoulder and the reins of his horse in his left hand, with Gordon at the rear, guiding his horse over the rocky terrain. The steep mountainside, tinged with an orange hue by the sun's dying rays, quickly tired the companions as they pushed ever upward. Out of breath, Malachai huffed and puffed the last few steps before Baldrake said, 'There. A clearing. We can rest up there for the night. Vasgath, I don't believe I have ever seen you this unfit.'

'Oh, shut it. I'll regain my strength again.'

As they reached the small clearing, more level than the rest of the area, they stopped to make camp. Grass covered, it looked to be carved out of the rock as it spread out under an overhang of the mountain. Tired and hungry, they slumped down to catch their breath.

'I'll take first watch. There are critters in this mountain I don't care for,' the big man said and moved to the cliff edge to look over the beautiful valley far below them. 'Get some sleep. I'll wake one of you to take the next turn.'

Sleeping soundly, the company lay under the open sky, stars shining bright, the night air hot, the fire still burning bright in the centre of the group. A rapid drop in temperature occurred as Baldrake stood watch. He looked to the sky and said, 'Something is not right. Gordon, Vasgath! Wake up,' he roared.

Confused, they felt the sudden chill in the air as they woke from their sleep, and the mekkel pulled a blanket around himself.

Gordon stared at Baldrake questioningly as he said, 'What's wrong?'

'I do not know, but I feel something dark, magical... approaching.'

With an exploding scream above them, the threat dived at incredible speed towards the companions. As it neared, fire erupted from its mouth. The flames raced towards the group and the warriors jumped for dear life off the clearing, rolling further as they landed on the steep slope of the mountain. As the creature passed overhead, Gordon saw the rotten flesh hanging from its face, the face of a long-dead creature, the bone of the maw visible from beneath the torn, pulled-back flesh. There was no blood; the wound had to be an old one. The eyes were dull, lifeless, but furious.

Malachai was up and running for higher ground as fast as his legs could carry him, the dull glint of his hammer reflecting in the night's moonlight. A ball of fire erupted once more and hit very close to Gordon, setting his clothes on fire. With a quick drop, he rolled down the mountainside, hitting rocks and falling long distances, thinking a few broken bones were better than being burnt to ashes.

On a large rock protruding out of the mountainside stood Malachai, waving his arms at them. Baldrake, seeing his plan, howled, trying to get the creature's attention. As soon as the creature noticed him, it dived and flew just above the ground at breakneck speeds. Baldrake turned and ran as fast as his legs could carry him about forty feet below Malachai, luring the creature towards the big man. The creature followed, breathing deep to launch another fireball towards the wolf. It did not notice the threat from above.

Jumping the distance from the rock, hammer in hand, he fell in silence. The timing was perfect. Malachai landed on the creature's thick, rotting neck just behind its head. It shrieked with fury, tossing its head left and right, but Malachai sat steadfastly. With all his power, he lifted the hammer and brought it down on the dead dragon's head. Bones split beneath the blow. He brought the hammer down again and again and again. The creature dipped in its flight and crashed heavily against the mountainside. A cloud of grey dust exploded into the night sky.

Gordon couldn't make out what had happened. Limping to where the creature had crashed, he passed a small figure lying sprawled in the dust between the rocks and stopped. Melche lay unmoving. There was no heartbeat. Gordon picked up the little mekkel and moved to where Malachai lay, sprawled on the ground with a massive gash on his head. Baldrake was already there, his head low, eyes closed. Gordon lay the mekkel down beside the wolf, and said, 'No, no, no, no. Not him too. Baldrake, see what you can do for the little one.' Stumbling to Malachai, he saw the blood running from a mortal wound on the big man's head. He lifted Malachai's head from the ground, holding him close. The bond that had been forming between the two warriors was great, and to see his close friend die like this tore him apart. Malachai opened his eyes slowly and whispered, struggling to get the words formed, 'Aye... it's time, laddie. You can't save me this time. Tell Baldrake I am so...'

With that, his head fell back and his face relaxed. Serene and calm, he stared upon the stars. Gordon gripped the warrior as tears started flowing down his face. 'I will avenge you... brother,' he said. Standing up, he saw the creature clearly, its massive wings broken in many places. The mouth containing rows of teeth.

'A dragon?'

Baldrake moved closer, and said, 'No. A dead dragon.'

Gordon looked at him with irritation and said, 'I know it's dead! Malachai just killed it.'

The wolf sighed. 'I am sorry, you misunderstand. It was long dead, it was resurrected... magically.'

Gordon turned back to look at the creature. 'The sorcerer?'

'Yes.'

Gordon slumped as he said, 'So this is what we're going to face.'

Startled, Gordon awoke from his sleep and called out softly as he moved between his companions to shake them. 'Wake up, wake up everyone.' Baldrake woke quite fast and shrugged off the little mekkel as he clung to him, waking Melche. Malachai struggled to open his eyes and groaned, 'What's happening?'

Gordon quickly put out the fire and looked at them. 'We're going to be attacked by a dragon. A dead one, but... alive. Resurrected. Look, there's no time to explain. Just trust me. We have to get ready, now!'

The wolf looked to Malachai inquisitively but did as he was told. All prepared for the alleged attack.

Pacing through the camp, Anukke looked around, with Vintrian and Vargus flanking him. The "barbarians", as they were called, were drinking and laughing at jokes being told around blazing fires. Sudden commotion stirred the camp awake as an unannounced rider made his way through towards the sorcerer. Men jumped in front of the rider and dragged him down from his horse, then ushered him to Abendi's tent. As Anukke entered, he watched as the leader of the barbarians interrogated the rider and said, 'I know this man. He is one of my guards. Let him up.'

'Next time, let us know beforehand if you're expecting someone. He might have been killed.'

Anukke glanced at the man, then nodded. Turning to the rider, he said, 'What news do you bring, Sustan?'

Impressed that his lord knew his name, the man rose quickly and approached, kneeling before him as he said, 'There was an attack on the castle, my lord. Two men got in and freed the wolves. They mutilated poor Master Eldridge.'

Anukke stared at Sustan grimly. 'How do you mean?'

Sustan rose from the ground and said, 'My lord, you should have seen what they did to him. It was horrible. We found his leg in one corner of the room and his arm in another; we fixed him as best we could. He lives... barely. Lucky for him, the intruders dropped a bag containing some healing elixirs, otherwise, Master Eldridge was done for. We did not know where my lord was heading. That is why it took so long to get the news here. He knew of some mirror that my lord used and figured out how it worked and called up this location.'

'The mirror, did you bring it with you?'

'Yes, my lord. It's tied to the horse. We thought you could use it here.'

'Very good Sustan, you did well. Take it to my tent. I will join you shortly.'

'Yes, my liege.'

Soon after, Anukke entered his tent and looked about as he said, 'Oh, how I miss Galhor. This pigsty is unbecoming.'

Having left Galhor to get in position for the attack on Millron, he had been sleeping in a tent, and it has been most frustrating for him. The constant wind, the foul smell of the barbarian horde, all of it just infuriated the wizard. He looked at Sustan next to the silver mirror and said, 'Leave me. Wait outside with Vintrian and Vargus.' Then he moved to the mirror, pulling a dagger from his belt. Slowly, he cut his left hand, and as blood started trickling down to the ground, he slammed his palm down on the mirror's surface. He uttered magical words and rubbed his hand in a circular motion, '*Elforvee resoratee comos draconis kaloha serb.*'

The mirror shimmered and vibrated, the solid silver surface turning liquid. From a pouch at his side, he drew forth a small piece of a scale and carefully extended his arm to the liquid silver. As soon as the scale touched the surface of the mirror, it was swallowed. The mirror shook violently, as did the tent and the ground beneath their feet. With a loud magical explosion from the mirror, a bright blue-green wave erupted outwards for miles. The occupants of the camp threw their food to the ground and jumped for their weapons, thinking they were being attacked.

The mirror, still liquid in form, awaited its instruction.

'Find the wolf called Baldrake and his allies. Kill them all!' Anukke said angrily, with clenched fists.

Hiding in the dead of night, crouched behind a grove of old oak trees, Gordon watched the night sky with intense focus. It was cloudless, with a full moon; stars were shining brightly, so movement was easy to spot from miles away. Suddenly he noticed the mekkel standing before him with his hands to his hips, looking deep into his milky eyes.

'Melche wants to know, how you can see?' he asked as he furrowed his brow.

Gordon grinned and said, 'Well, old one, I was blessed by Baliël himself. I remember the day like it was yesterday. We were hunting these bad people for doing wrong to a woman, and when we found them, we had to fight for our lives. For days we fought, and eventually, we got to their leader. As soon as I struck the deathblow, he spoke to me his last words—words from Baliël himself. He said, "You are the chosen one". As I touched the man, lightning red as fire coursed up my arms and into my eyes, blinding me. Later, when I could open my eyes, they looked like this. I can still see, I just look blind.'

Melche stood with eyes wide and mouth gaping while he listened to the story. 'Can Melche touch them?' he asked while moving his little hands closer to Gordon's face.

Marius H. Visser

He pulled back quickly and raised his brows as he said, 'No, you may not! If anyone touches my eyes, they will go mad and die a horrible death.'

As quick as lightning, Melche withdrew his hands, saying, 'Melche will never touch.' Gordon grinned, happy with the outcome.

Suddenly the temperature dropped drastically, and he let out a bird's call to warn Malachai, who was sitting high in a tree a few hundred feet further down the tree line, holding one end of a rope. The dragon flew above them, searching vigorously with its blind, dull eyes.

Turning to Baldrake, Gordon said, 'You know the plan. Let's get to it.' He looked down at the mekkel and continued, 'You did well, old one. But now it is our turn. Hide behind those trees over there,' he pointed to some trees standing a distance away from them and said, 'and don't come out until we call you, no matter what.'

Melche nodded and darted off.

Running into the open, Gordon waved his hands and shouted as Baldrake howled out loud. The dragon turned on its back in mid-air, swooping down towards them. Black-scaled and smelling of death, it flew low to the ground as it came at them. They turned and ran back to the tree line as fast as possible; to stop or slow down now would be suicide. The two entered the trees, closing on Malachai's position a few hundred feet away. The dragon drew air into its fiery lungs and set ablaze everything all around them. The heat was intense, flash-burning bushes and trees as they ran.

With the beast at their backs, they ran straight past Malachai who pulled on the rope as soon as Gordon shouted, 'Now!'

The dragon followed suit, weaving through the trees to get its prey. Too late did it realise it had been set up. A massive bunch of spikes held together by rope swung towards it at great speed. The beast reared in mid-air, pulling up its head and pitching its tail forward. Heavy spikes collided with the beast, driving into the rotting flesh, bone, and dead organs, crushing its body. The rope snapped, and both beast and spiked pile dropped from the air, hitting the ground hard.

The already-dead beast lay on the ground, stirring but ultimately too broken to go any further. Malachai quickly jumped from the tree and pulled free his hammer as he approached, saying, 'Aye—today, you devil, is not your day.' He hoisted the hammer above the dragon and brought down the killing blow, hitting the beast between the eyes.

Gordon came from one side and saw Malachai standing before the dragon, almost the size of its head. He called to the little mekkel, who came skipping from the trees where he'd hidden. Clapping his hands with joy, he said, 'See, Melche told you it would work!'

Gordon smiled. 'Yes, you did. You also said that you invent things. What sort of things, exactly?'

Melche stood and rubbed his palms together as he said, 'Where does Melche begin? Melche needs to make a list, yes Melche does.'

Frowning at Gordon, the big man said, 'You know, he will not stop speaking about his inventions for days.'

'Yes, I know, but he also saved our lives with this idea of his. This can be his reward.'

The mekkel was so busy trying to align his thoughts that he didn't even notice the discussion between the other two.

CHAPTER NINE

Boulders and arrows filled the sky, only to shatter against the invisible wall high above the barbarian horde. The wall of Millron was easily defensible, being built more as a fortress than a city.

As the barbarians pushed their ladders to the walls, the archers in the towers shot their flaming arrows into the trenches, lighting the oily tar mixture and burning everything that came in contact with it. They poured more oil down the wall to add to the blaze. The day wore on as the battle continued, the ineffective battle rams smashing against the gates, causing minor damage. Scores of barbarians died in vain at the bottom of the walls.

The first day had gone the way Tuds had hoped. Scores more barbarians died than what their losses were. He had stationed Gweniviere at the front wall with the troops to be a driving force for motivation and hope for the men, and she was successful, hacking and slicing at anyone who made it up the brutal climb. The horde sounded their horn to fall back, to regroup and rest for the night. To tend to their wounded.

Stretcher-bearers rejoiced as the enemy pulled back, giving them the break to run without having to fight to get to the wounded up on the wall. Most wounded were carried down with arrows in their chests.

Gweniviere looked out over the battlefield below as the horde retreated, seeing them carry their dead and wounded back to camp. Crows and vultures started feasting on the abundance of meat.

'Major, get yourself cleaned up and rest for the night. Have that cut looked at as well.'

She glanced at the blood streaming from her left arm and said, 'Sir, we—'

'That's an order, Major.'

Gweniviere nodded to Tuds and said, 'Yes, sir. Will get it looked at right away.'

'You fought well today, Gwen. The men look up to you. I need you at your best come the morrow.'

'Thank you, sir, I will not let you down.' She turned and left the wall to look for a healer and a bathhouse. The blood was making her itch all over.

War cries and war drums sounded out early at dawn as the barbarians walked onto the battlefield, marching to the wall once more. Gweniviere stared at the rushing horde and shouted to her men beside her, 'Keep low, men! Do not let the urge get the better of you. Wait for them to get close! Then we fight.' She knew they were listening; their silence only meant they were focused. *Why don't they change their tactics? Surely they saw that this will yield them nothing.*

No arrows were fired from the wall until the horde was too close to use the wall of magic from the mages. And the slaughter started anew. Soon, the battle was going the same as the previous day. The thoughts of all the souls in Millron were with victory until screams of horror and pain echoed through the city from the rear.

With all their attention to the front wall, they'd left their rear wide open, thinking nobody would come down from the cliffs. But they were very wrong. In silence, a thousand barbarians had rappelled down the side of the mountain and entered the city unopposed. Men, women, children, were all cut down where they stood as the barbarians moved through the city to reach the gate and open it. Tuds and a handful of men had left the wall and ran to meet the threat from the back. Sabre in hand, he dropped the first with a cut through the jugular, a second with a lunge that stabbed the man through the chest. Cutting left; an arm fell to the ground. Cutting right; blood sprayed over his face. His sabre sang as it sliced through the air, hacking and killing everything in his path; he seemed unstoppable.

Gweniviere ran down the wall to support her major general in the fight for their lives.

Battle-raged, blood pumping; Tuds wasn't himself anymore. He could feel himself being drawn from his body, pulled from this world, his thoughts being replaced by dark, deathly visions as he fought on. He couldn't even remember what he was fighting for anymore. His body working mechanically as a death dealer, his mind drifted away...

Deep inside his mind, he stood on a long narrow stone bridge, the sky an orange hue, the air hot and stale. His nose burned from rising gasses.

'Where am I?' Tuds asked himself.

As he looked down over the bridge, he felt the heat hit him like a blow to the chest. Far below, a river of molten lava coursed through the rocky mountain fissure. Screams of terror and the dying surrounded him, but he saw nothing. He looked up and saw a figure approach him on the narrow bridge, clad in silver armour with no helm. The man bowed to one knee before him. As he rose to full length, Tuds studied him. Looking into his keen, sharp green eyes, he saw no sympathy. Big, bigger than he remembered Malachai to be, and cleanly shaven, with long black hair flowing down the side of his face. A monstrous broadsword hung to his side. A weapon for a king, the golden haft shining brightly with the red ruby at the back, set in what looked like the claws of an eagle. The man spoke: 'I am honoured you came all this way,' he said in a low, calm voice.

Tuds was rattled and utterly afraid. He stepped back as he said, 'Who are you? And where am I?'

'I am known by many names in many places. Here, you can call me Ortega Bloodbane. Where you are is of no importance. I do not wish to bore you with the details of who I am. It is a long and tragic story.'

Tuds' head was spinning as he backed away. His foot caught on a rock, and he fell over backwards, landing on his buttocks as he said, 'What's happening, why am I here?' He got back to his feet.

'Ahh, now that is the question. I have been dead for a very long time, trapped in this ghastly place, to live out my days seeking refuge from the next sundering. It follows me constantly, ground breaking open at my feet if I tarry too long. I grow tired of it. One in your realm has reached out to me. I am growing stronger, but I still require one thing.'

'What's that?' Tuds did not know why he even asked. It just slipped out.

'You. As my vessel.'

Here before this god of a man, Tuds felt himself uncontrollably expelling the piss from his body, staining his pants. 'Why me?!'

'You were not my first choice, but here we are, nonetheless. I will oblige you with this answer; you deserve to know.' Ortega paced back and forth as he spoke. 'A long time ago, when they were getting ready to trap me here, they needed my blood for the spell to work. I can only assume that this wizard found my blood and has been infecting the creatures with it, driving them mad and forcing people to kill them. He knew blood would flow, and at some point, when someone came to slay it, I would find a connection to a new host. One that accepted me with his lust for violence. Since my blood merged with yours after the fight with the bear, I have been biding my time, growing stronger day by day, filling your head with murderous thoughts. Don't you remember? Kill the judges, kill them all! Oh, how they squealed like pigs as we strung them up. How about that wolf hunt we went on? Exhilarating, wasn't it? I have been patiently waiting for you to become what you became on that battlefield.'

Tuds stood trembling before Ortega and said, 'So you have been with me all this time? I thought I was losing my mind. What do you mean, "what I became"?'

Ortega burst out with horrible laughter and said, 'Power-hungry, a ruthless killer. Now you have become what I need for you to sustain me. It is time for me *to end this, Tudeske. I promise I will make the next part as painless as possible. Just stand still.'*

Tuds grabbed numbly at his sabre and pulled it free, his fingers fumbling about the hilt as he cried, 'No! I will not allow you. You will have to kill me.'

Ortega cocked his head to the side, and with a smirk on his face, said, 'Okay, maybe this will hurt you after all. Besides, your sword will not help you now.' The unsheathing of Ortega's blade and the attack came all in one move. Tuds barely parried the heavy blow, which knocked him off balance as he staggered back, barely on his feet. Standing inches from the edge of the bridge, Tuds launched his own attack but was easily parried. Ortega blocked a slice from Tuds with his armour and thrust his blade out. It happened so quickly. Slowly, Tuds sank to the ground, blood frothing at his mouth. The broadsword had penetrated a lung. With a savage yank, the blade slipped free from Tuds' limp body.

'Once more I will rule this world!'

With a vicious kick, he sent Tuds over the edge of the bridge, his body tumbling down, swirling in the air, and finally vanishing into the molten lava river.

Still fighting the barbarians, Tuds' eyes glazed over as his body hacked and slashed at the threat, his mind nowhere to be found. He suddenly stopped and thrust his sword deep into the red-stained ground, and knelt on one knee. Looking about confused, the barbarians lowered their weapons, not knowing what was happening when a shock wave of enormous power rippled out from Tuds' body in all directions. The limbs of those directly surrounding him were shattered with the blow. Others were thrown against the walls of buildings with such force that some died of the impact, crushing their skulls or breaking their necks. Gweniviere was among those thrown, luckily hitting a pile of stacked hay bales, the wind knocked out of her. Her vision swam as she fell unconscious.

Tuds slowly rose to his feet and looked at the world through different eyes—the eyes of Ortega Bloodbane.

Anukke suddenly ceased the heated argument he was having with Abendi and looked up towards the city, saying, 'He is here. I can feel his power. Never have I sensed a power like this.'

Walking out of the tent, he flung the flap closed as Abendi ranted on in his argument to retreat. Running after the wizard, he called out, 'Who is here? What is going on?'

Anukke, not turning to regard the man, shouted out, 'Pull your men back! You have accomplished your task.' He walked into his tent and drew a circle on the ground with his staff, as he had been doing every time they went into battle to spill blood. In the circle on the edges, he drew five smaller rings and moved to the centre of them all. Raising his hands, he started chanting and said, 'As the blood of innocents runs through the grounds of mortals, I offer all those as sacrifices to you, Lord Ortega.' Fire erupted from his palms and the circles he drew in the ground, but the wizard stood unscathed in the centre. Power coursed through him in convulsive fits as his eyes turned black as night. His back arched, and his body hovered above the ground, scraping his toes over the soil. 'Show yourself. Come, Lord Ortega. Join me, and together we can rule this world,' he said, reaching out his communication towards the resurrected lord.

Ortega stood looking at his surroundings to find any threats, but saw only the devastation, then smiled. The sun was high, and the smell of death filled the air. Blood stained the walls of the city, and an annoying voice in his mind kept wanting him to *join* him, to rule the world. His smile vanished at the irritation and he spoke back, 'Anukke, I presume.'

The wizard's eyes flared wide at the reply. 'I have waited for this moment for far too long. I bid you welcome once more to the world of mortals. If you know my name, then you already know that it was I who was responsible for your return,' he said in excitement.

'And for that, I shall spare your life... for now,' Ortega replied in a calm and collected tone. He reached down and plucked his sabre—Tuds' sabre—from the ground and stared at it with disgust as he said, 'Now, this will just not do.'

Chanting a language of magic, he stood with his eyes closed in full battle gear, his arms extended above his head, hands reaching to the skies. In an exploding, blinding light that burnt the eyes of onlookers, he was gone. The light faded, and dust began to settle.

Gweniviere saw her major general disappear in the light and thought she had struck her head much harder than she first believed. But when she rubbed her eyes—the pain subsided slightly—Tuds was gone, nowhere to be seen. She came to her feet slowly and climbed to the top of the wall to look down at the retreating army of barbarians.

'Tuds, I do not know how you did it, or what it was you did, but it worked. Wherever you are, I will find you.' Cheers and shouts of joy went up from the soldiers on the wall.

Sheathing her sword, she turned and made her way to the main hall where the counsellors sat discussing tactics. Bursting through the door, Gwen walked closer and stared at the men around the table. Markus stood up, anger flaring in his face as he said, 'What is the meaning of this! How dare you—'

She cut him short and shouted out, 'It's over! The battle is over! We're victorious!'

'What do you mean?' All the men sprang from their chairs, staring at her, ready to burst out in tears of joy.

'They're retreating. I don't know exactly what happened, but they are retreating. They have lost too many men to continue,' she stated.

Shouts echoed through the hall as the men cried out their relief. Markus fell back in his chair with clear relief on his face, and said, 'Where is your commander? Where is Major General Tuds? Send for him immediately. I wish to congratulate him.'

Gwen dropped her head to the left, trying not to look at them. 'I'm afraid... he's gone. I do not know what happened. It must have been the magic users among the barbarians. I saw him jump in the midst of those barbarians that came to ambush us from the rear, killing left and right. He was incredible. Then a spell was cast, aimless, killing most of their own men. Everyone was flung through the air, me included. Most died from the impact of the shock wave. The last thing I saw was Tuds standing with sword in hand, and then suddenly an explosion of light so bright, I thought I would never see again. Then... he was gone.'

Markus stared at Gwen in silence; covered in blood, her sadness was clearly evident behind her warrior mask. 'That is... a terrible loss. I'm sorry Major. He was a fine man,' he said to Gwen.

'The weather these days speaks of the end of time. First, it rains, then suddenly the sun shines, then out of nowhere hail comes down on us half a day later. The blasted clouds don't know what they want anymore,' Malachai said while trimming his beard with his hunting knife. He spat on the hard-pressed ground; the mucus almost bounced away like a rubber ball.

'Argh, Malachai, that is *disgusting*, damn!' came the voice of Gordon as he neared the bigger man.

'Aye, that it was. Lucky there are no women among us to have seen.'

'What will we do without you, big guy?' Gordon asked mockingly.

Malachai shrugged and said, 'I believe you would lead long, boring lives.'

From their right, another voice, harsh and deep, pitched in, 'And I believe we would be able to sleep at night without your vexatious snoring and hold down our food while not having to look at you push a whole rabbit down your trap,' Baldrake said with that snarly grin on his face.

Out of nowhere, something landed on his back with a thud. Startled, the wolf started running, only to see no one following; then he heard the shrill voice ring out, 'Heya, giddy up pony! Gordon! Why is there no saddle on this horse!' Not believing what was happening, he reared like a horse and threw the little mekkel to the ground hard, then turned to confront Melche. 'Why you little—'

Gordon quickly intervened, 'Whoa. Baldrake. I'm sure he's... sorry. Just let it go.'

'What! Just let it go? Why, this is punishable by death! The humiliation... I mean... a horse!'

The little mekkel stepped out from behind Gordon's legs and said, 'Actually, Melche thought you were a pony.'

Baldrake's eyes narrowed on Melche, and Gordon thought for a moment he would have to draw his sword. But the wolf turned back around as he said, 'Mekkel, if you ever do that again, I promise you will be my next meal.'

Melche jumped around excitedly. 'A mekkel! Where?'

Baldrake just lowered his head, shaking it from side to side, and surrendered.

Malachai appeared next to Gordon, still trimming his beard, and said, 'That was very brave of you.'

'Why? What was?'

'Getting between a Gar hound and a potential victim... it's just not smart. The only reason I can think of why Baldrake didn't attack was out of respect.'

Gordon cocked his head and furrowed his brow. 'For the elder?'

'No, you ninny, for you.'

Malachai and the horses carried on walking after Baldrake and called back to the mekkel, who was still hiding behind Gordon. 'Melche, it would do you good to heed the words of that wolf. We didn't call him Reaper for nothing.'

After they'd walked a while, Malachai approached Gordon again, and spoke in a hushed tone, 'When we get to the River Gallas, what is your plan exactly? Why don't we just cut across the lowlands with the horses?'

Gordon glanced at Malachai, who knew immediately that he had hoped not to have been asked that question.

'All right. See, there's a boat shack on this side of the river. We're going to get a small boat there and follow the river down to the coast. I just have a gnawing feeling the wolf doesn't like water. That's why I said nothing, but that would be the best thing for us. It will save us time and energy. I just don't think Baldrake will be happy.'

Malachai rubbed his beard as their conversation carried on, then said, 'Oh dear, when are you planning on telling him?'

'I'm not. You are. Seeing that you know him so well.'

Quickly retreating, Malachai waved his arms about as he said, 'Oh no I'm not.'

'Yes, you are, but only when we reach the river.'

Melche started singing a very annoying song, making up the words as he went along:

As we trot through the wild unknown,
the adventure grows and grows.
The blackened wolf with wild unrest,
will take off Melche's head so.

Killing dragons is much fun,
I'll do it in my run.
Melche the Mekkel is not tall,
but still he'll never fall.

With milky eyes and sword untouched,
Melche wonders what it's worth?
Now Melche don't know what to sing,
so let's just finish with a hymn.

Gods below and gods above,
spare us through this time of rough.
Keep us clean and keep us kind,
never let our minds unwind.

'Would you please shut that mekkel up!' came the voice of Malachai. 'I'm going to lose my head with that irritating little thing!'

Apparently hurt, Melche shot Malachai a glance from the side and stopped singing. Gordon paused and raised his hands to his face, blocking out the sun's rays as he said, 'Over there, that shack. Let's see what they have. Maybe we can get some more food from them.'

The wooden shack stood about fifteen feet from the river with little wooden boats lying everywhere. Some had been damaged, and tools lay in them as repairs were being done. Malachai was anxiously watching the wolf to see if he would put it all together, but he looked as calm as ever. Melche immediately ran to the first boat on dry land, jumped in, and started steering the "ship," making pirate sounds.

The men walked into the shack, where they found an old, grey-haired man sitting behind a desk, fast asleep.

'You think he's alive?' Malachai asked as he shoved Gordon in the ribs.

Just then the old man made a loud snort and woke from his sleep. Startled by the sudden appearance of these strangers standing before him, he fell off his chair. Quickly, Malachai moved around the desk to help the old man up, and said, 'We're sorry to have startled you like that, sir. Did not mean to.'

The old man stood up and dusted off his clothes. He was a big man and must have been a feared warrior once in his life. 'It's okay, lad. No harm done. My name is Gunthar. Where ya boys from, or rather, headin?'

Gordon moved forward to meet the man's gaze. 'I'm Gordon, and this here is Malachai. We are on our way to the coast. We need one of your boats that can carry at least three and if you have some food to spare, it would be appreciated.'

Gunthar smiled. 'There's not a lot of business these days, so I hope you have the means to pay for this here transport.'

Gordon sighed heavily and said, 'I was rather hoping we could trade our two fine horses, as we could not take them with us even if we wanted to.'

Gunthar rubbed his unshaven face while looking at the two. 'Well, I suppose I can always sell them later on. There's a boat in the water, at the dock; you can take that one. She's old, but she will hold.'

Gordon smiled and extended his arm, which Gunthar gladly gripped in the old traditional warrior's handshake; their hands grabbing each other's arms just below the elbow. 'Thank you, Gunthar. You have a warrior's soul. I hope we meet again.'

Gunthar leaned down and pulled some dried meat and fruit out from under his desk and tossed it over to Malachai as he said, 'I don't know what ya boys are up to, but by the looks of it, you'll need that. Here's some water as well. It's not a lot, but I hope it helps.'

'It sure will.'

Walking to the dock, Gordon spoke to the group, 'Okay, we've arranged to take that boat and leave our horses behind,' he pointed to the boat and continued, 'This river leads to the coast, where we will continue further to Millanthros on foot. Let's get to it, then. We can camp farther downriver tonight.'

Baldrake strolled to the boat and jumped in without complaint. But the mekkel stood frozen on the pier, just shaking his head from side to side as he looked at the vast amount of fast-flowing water pushing the boat. Everyone was already on board, shouting at Melche to get in, but to no avail. Baldrake launched himself out of the small wooden craft so ferociously it almost tipped, making Malachai curse as he shifted his enormous weight.

Running down the pier at the frozen little figure, Baldrake scooped up the mekkel too quickly for him to even think about getting away. Screams exploded from Melche as he dangled from the wolf's mouth, his hands and feet already kicking at the air as in a swimming motion, 'Why do you hate Melche so? No! You are tearing my clothes! No water for Melche!'

As the wolf jumped on board, Gordon quickly untied the ropes and set off down the river. The mekkel thrashed on the floor for a good while before exhaustion took him. He ceased in his death throes and sat nonplussed in the small craft, studying its quality; it was a small wooden boat about twelve feet long and six feet wide. A mast about ten feet high stood in the middle, steered with a rope at the end of the sail, which the big man was holding on to. Gordon sat in front, scouting the area with Baldrake next to him. Melche had forgotten his fears and was now climbing all over the boat, stepping on toes, using Gordon and Baldrake for leverage to get higher and closer to the water.

The tranquil river had the most serene views; the banks were lined with beautiful big trees of all sorts, but the willows reigned supreme. The sun was bright and the sky clear. Baldrake sat with his paws hanging over the side of the boat, staring at his reflection in the water. As his paw dipped into the cool liquid, he was thinking about his son and worried he might never see him again.

Woefully unaware of his inner turmoil, Malachai intruded on his thoughts and said, 'Aye, Baldrake, I thought wolves are afraid of water.'

Baldrake did not turn, but said, 'No... well, I suppose some are, same as with your species. There is very little in this world that we fear.'

'What do you fear?' Gordon asked from the front.

With a long pause and an inner sigh, Baldrake whispered, 'Seeing my son die before me.'

Gordon looked away and said, 'No, I meant—'

'I know what you meant.'

Malachai belched loudly and wiped his mouth. 'I'm sure the lad is fine. He is with Cuorco and Delios in the monastery. I think he's being spoiled there, maybe too much. The only danger he should be mindful of is getting too fat.' His stomach growled, and he continued, 'How I miss those steaks right now.'

At that point Melche fell into the water, barely making a splash as he hung too far over the side, looking at the fish swimming underneath. Malachai dipped his hand in and hauled him back into the boat. Coughing rapidly, the mekkel sat still for the first time, his cheeks flushed red as he stared at his companions.

The day wore on; the sun getting low, and the companions, all tired of the long day's journey, began seeking refuge for the night. Iron grey clouds were gathering, and it seemed to Gordon that even the sky was collapsing. 'We'll probably have to fix that too at some point. Probably some damned prophesy about that as well,' he muttered to himself. The light was dimming, and all things started losing form as the dark settled in.

Malachai steered the boat to the closest bank, and as they neared, Gordon jumped overboard to drag it further up the muddy embankment. Satisfied that the boat would not drift off, he went to lie down on the grass further from the river. 'Malachai, you take first watch, then wake me. Baldrake, you can take the last watch,' Gordon said with closed eyes. Melche was silently busy with something, and nobody complained about that, rather enjoying the peace while it lasted.

The road was muddied, and the horses were struggling in the slippery mess caused by the rain as it beat down on the soldiers making their way back to camp Waterhole. They had left Millron behind them, with a lot of pyres burning at their backs. Out of two hundred and fifty men, only half had survived.

Being the highest-ranking officer left alive in the squad, Gwen had taken over leadership in Tuds' absence. She looked up. It was impossible to tell how far the day had progressed with the thick clouds above. She blinked as the raindrops fell in her eyes and caused her to lower her head.

Making their way across the open plain towards the River Gallas, they were tired and wet to the bone. As they reached the river, a shout came from the border control point high on the wall of Camp Waterhole. 'State your name and business... And don't try anything funny. We have archers fixed on you as we speak.'

Gwen lowered her hood and called out, 'It's me, Yurgen... Gweniviere. Lower the bridge.'

A creak sounded as they released the chains to lower the bridge, and she made a clicking sound with her mouth. The horse walked across the bridge and stopped halfway as she tugged on the reins, letting the supply train move past her to enter the camp. Gwen brought her hand to her face, trying to keep the water from her eyes as she looked down the river and shouted, 'Yurgen! Get me a spyglass, quick!'

Running down the wall, a short, stubby man with broad shoulders came to her side and handed her the spyglass. Pulling it open, she peered through. 'Baliël's tits, what is that?'

Yurgen's eyes went wide as he pulled on his earlobes, saying, 'Blasphemy! Baliël is a man!'

'Shut it, Yurgen!'

Through the long looking glass, her view was obscured and very blurry through the rain. She handed it back to Yurgen and said, 'What does that look like to you?'

'Looks like a small boat with some kind of enormous dog in front, struggling towards the camp.'

'Just behind the dog, look at the size of that man and his hammer. Does that look friendly to you?'

'Great balls!' Yurgen said as he looked back at his major, and continued, 'What's your orders, sir?'

'Archers, ready your aim!' she yelled out loud, pointing towards the small boat. All the archers on the wall nocked their arrows at the sign of trouble and trailed the craft as it neared the camp. Now more visible to the naked eye and within earshot, Gwen called out to the travellers, 'You boys lost? It's a rare thing to see people coming this far down the river. Where ya headin?'

'We are travelling west, to the coast. Got some business there. But we sure could use some accommodation for the day until the morrow, maybe. This rain and wind are relentless,' came a voice from the small boat.

Gwen leaned closer to Yurgen and whispered in his ears, 'Tell the archers not to let them out of their sights.' Yurgen quickly ran back up the walls to relay the message.

'Come on up. We have some extra rooms available.'

Gwen motioned to two guards near her to help them out of the water. They threw ropes to the straggling boat in the middle of the river, for them to pull themselves to the side. Malachai heaved as he pulled on the rope. The current pushed them hard, being much more violent than anticipated. The big man had to use much more of his strength than he expected he would have needed. His biceps bulged with the veins pressing at the skin.

The two guards hadn't noticed the full size of the "dog" that was in the boat due to the heavy rain and wind as they performed their duties, and as the boat reached the embankment, Baldrake jumped out next to the guards, standing at eye-level with them, and calmly sat on his haunches. Suddenly alarmed, the two guards screamed and ran towards the bridge, with no desire to look back. Gwen quickly called out to the archers not to fire, as she felt the sudden tension and fear in the air, and rightly so. Staring at the beast, she whispered, but her voice carried nonetheless, 'What in the name of Ulexis is that?'

Baldrake ambled towards the bridge, followed by Gordon, then Malachai and finally the mekkel, after he fell out of the boat, face-first. The wolf approached her, bowing his head down to the right, and said, 'We thank you for your hospitality.'

Speechless, she stood with her arm still staying the archers, then shouted, 'They are guests tonight. Do not fire!'

Grinning his wolfish grin, Baldrake knew how he had startled them, and moved on into the camp, awaiting the others. Few people had encountered Gar hounds, and he knew they were rattled by his presence. The looks of awe he received from the passing soldiers only made him push out his chest more, boasting with his muscular, furry body. Gordon and Gwen walked up from the bridge through the gate as he explained, 'He's a Gar hound. I know, right, takes a bit to get used to. Scared the hell out of me the first time I heard him speak.' Unconsciously rubbing at the wound on his neck, he continued, 'He will not cause any issues. I promise.'

Still not convinced, Gwen said, 'I'd like you to join me in the war room in a short while. Please give me few moments to restore some order here, as we just came back from the battle at Millron, and these idiots have probably not followed any of the orders left behind for them.'

Showing them to their quarters, she turned and shouted to the soldiers, 'Everyone gather up. We have lost the major general. For the time being, as ranking officer, you will obey my command. Anyone who has an issue with this can come to me about it.'

One man at the back shouted, 'We'z won't take no orders from a girl!' A thud was heard, and suddenly the man lay on the ground clutching his broken nose. One of the men who'd stood with her on the wall stood over the fallen man and said, 'Don't worry, sir. I think he'll learn to take orders right quick.'

The companions sat in the tent, drying out their clothes, all too glad to be out of the unceasing rain. Melche lay on a bed already snoring, his little body convulsing into shakes because of the cold. Baldrake knew in the back of his mind, although he would never admit to it, that the only thing that would make the little mekkel stop snoring is if *he* were near. He sighed and silently jumped up on the bed. Melche threw his arms around Baldrake's tail, and immediately the snoring ceased. Baldrake found himself amused at the situation: a killer wolf general, lulling a defenceless little creature to sleep...

Far away, in the dead of night, on a cliff high above the roaring sea at the top of the peninsula, while no rain fell, the clouds were looming dark and heavy. A sudden lightning bolt flashed from above and split open the earth with a thunderous crack. The winds were rushing, the night air frigid. From the crack in the earth came a strained and bloody hand, grasping the ground to pull itself forth. As the battered body rose, fresh scars were visible all over; blood trickled to the ground. Trembling from exhaustion and pain, Ortega slumped back down on all fours. 'Curse this weak body.'

Breathing heavily, he lifted his head up and made to stand once more. His legs wobbled beneath him as he walked through the forbidden lands of Krell. *Finally home, then.*

Cursed upon his imprisonment, the land was devoid of any living creature. Hopefully, now, animals would start returning to this once beautiful forest.

The night was dark and cumbersome as he made his way deeper inland, away from the edge of the cliff. His deep wounds started healing as he ambled on. Looming through the trees was his enormous castle, and as he set his eyes upon it, he mockingly said, 'I wonder if anyone is home.'

As he sauntered in, he saw the devastation a few hundred years can do to the material world. Dust lay inches-thick on the floor; chandeliers lay in the mix. Rats had chewed through almost everything. Windows and walls were marred and shattered, crumbling to the ground. The staircases were broken halfway up, and the stone floor had turned black and was beyond human repair. Ortega stood in the main hall, looking about his ruined castle with disgust. With a sigh and a shrug, he lifted his arms to the sky and said a few magical words. As he chanted, a furious wind came swooping in, blowing away all signs of dust, and slowly all things started falling back into place as the castle neatened itself. The chandeliers rose to the ceiling and were fastened once more. Candles flared on the side of the walls, and the broken stairs were joined back together. The stone floor turned back to its original colour of dark, shining green.

Finally satisfied with the room, he turned his attention to his throne and walked closer. Bone and iron tusks adorned the elaborate chair. He glided his fingers over the armrest and smiled before he sat down. Blood dripped from his nose to the ground, staining the floor. 'I need to get this damned body stronger, physically and mentally, or else I will kill it,' he said aloud.

'As soon as I am strong enough, I will awaken my army.'

Anukke was furious. Pacing in circles about his chamber, he cried, 'How is it possible?! He was supposed to be weaker than that! He should not have escaped. And in whose body is he? How did he get into that body?' Walking past a chair, he grabbed it and tossed it against the wall, breaking its legs. So angry was he that he used his hands, not his magic. The frustration was eating him alive.

Anukke walked down the spiral staircase and entered the chamber where the silver mirror stood once more in the centre of the room. Muttering to himself, he said, 'Where could he have gone?' As he reached out to the mirror, he paused, his finger inches from its surface. 'But of course. How could I have been so stupid?' he said with that strained voice and lowered his hand. 'I should have foreseen this, laid a trap at that old castle of his.'

Walking to the window overlooking the courtyard, he called out, 'Vargus, tell the men to make ready. We leave in the morning for the forbidden lands of Krell.'

'Uhm... You know, my liege, there is a reason it is called forbidden.'

'Yes, Vargus, I know the story. Are you refusing my command?'

'No! No, my lord, just adding information, that's all.'

'Very well, make ready the weapons and prepare the soldiers. We might have a battle on our hands soon.'

When the mage disappeared from the window, Vargus quickly drew a deep breath and started rallying the men.

She could hear hushed voices in conversation as she neared the war room where the companions waited for her to arrive. As she entered, the conversation ceased as eyes followed her to her seat. Gwen looked at the map still laid out with the tactics of the battle at Millron and sighed as she said, 'Well then, why don't you boys tell me what's going on?'

Gordon and Malachai gave each other concerned looks, then the young warrior said, 'It's not that we don't want to tell you. It's more that we think you won't believe us.'

'I'm sitting across from a wolf the size of two men, and it spoke to me, and I haven't run away or drowned myself in the river. So why don't you try me.'

Gordon pursed his lips and began speaking, 'I was on my last task for my rite of passage. To hunt and slay the Pekula.'

'The what?' Gwen frowned.

'It's a general term we use for an animal that has lost its mind, basically. In my case, it was a bear. I happened to run into a thief that was trying to steal my belongings one night in the forest, and I restrained him, so to speak.'

'Aye, you did a bit more than restrain him,' Malachai said as he chuckled. Then, as everyone stared at him, he said, 'Sorry. Continue,' and cleared his throat.

'The thief was rambling on about some girl he and his fellow thieves had raped. After a bit of intense questioning, he was nice enough to tell me where the rest were hiding. At the same time, the Pekula wandered by, and that's when I ran into Malachai over here. As it went, he and another fellow named Tuds were hunting—'

'Whoa! Wait a second. Tuds, as in Tudeske? Long blond hair, quite a charming fellow. Thinks a little too much of himself? *That* Tuds?' Gwen asked, astonished at the notion that these strange characters knew her major general.

Both men nodded in return to Gwen, but it was Malachai that spoke. 'Aye, that would be the one. How do you know Tuds?'

She planted her palms down on the map and stared at it as she said, 'We were at the battle for Millron, against those blasted barbarians. That's where we came from before you arrived. Something happened to him on that battlefield, something I can't explain.'

The coarse voice of Malachai sounded out, 'Try.'

She stared at the big man as he sat with his arms folded. 'Yes, of course. The battle was going well. We thought we had them on their heels. But they were cunning; they had planned this long before arriving. They rappelled down the sheer cliff of Millron and ambushed us from the rear. Tuds fought with everything he had, then suddenly, for no reason at all, he stopped, thrust his sword in the ground, and knelt down as a massive shock wave exploded from him, throwing me through the air and killing a lot of men closer to him. Then... he was gone. Just disappeared into thin air. I bet it was those sorcerers.'

Malachai's mouth hung slightly open, shocked by the story, and he said, 'Well, where do you think he went or was taken, lass?'

With a sigh, Gwen said, 'I wish I knew.'

Gordon turned to Malachai and said, 'It seems our adventure with Tuds is not yet over. I have a feeling we will run into him at some point.'

A loud thump made them all turn their gazes to the one side of the table where the mekkel sat. The boredom had been too much for Melche. His head had slipped from his hands and hit the table as he fell asleep. Jumping up on the chair, he held his head as a lump formed and stared at the others as they tried to conceal their laughter. He shouted, 'Who put this piece of wood here? Melche demands justice!'

Gwen, surprisingly serious, said, 'At once, my mekkel friend. We will investigate the matter.'

Turning back to face Gordon, she chuckled and gestured for him to continue his story.

As the night wore on, Gordon told the entire story to her as she listened to every detail. At some points, Baldrake and Malachai would fill in the missing pieces, but when it came to the meeting of the little mekkel, Melche utterly took over the conversation.

'There Melche was, a helpless old mekkel stuck in the blackest of swamps as a scaly, slimy swamp monster circled Melche, biding its time to strike and drag Melche down into the pit of its lair, where it would feast upon Melche's tiny bones. But!' he jumped up on the chair with his fist to the air, and continued, 'Out of nowhere came this hero!' he pointed at Gordon. 'With nothing but his wits and naked bum, he dived into the swamp and grappled with the beast for over a day... underwater... All Melche saw were bubbles, and Melche thought, *oh no, the beast is coming back*. But then, just as Melche lost all hope, he thrust himself out of the water, victorious from battle. This hero dragged Melche to the side and saved Melche's life. Melche pledged his life to this hero, hoping that one day, Melche could return the favour.'

So the night passed with stories of glory and a few pints of ale, flowing freely as the major brought in a new cask. The big man almost had a tear in his eye as he gulped down the liquid. He looked at the major and said, 'You are too kind, Major.'

Gwen nodded and sipped at her ale and enjoyed the festivities, knowing the rest of the squad was on duty, watching for any trouble.

Grabbing a bowl, Malachai poured a jug of ale into it and put it in front of Baldrake. 'Oh no, Vasgath, I have seen how inebriated people act. It is unbecoming.'

'Oh, shut up and drink, you big kitten!' Malachai slapped the wolf on the back and walked off.

'Maybe just one sip. I am no kitten.' Cautiously, he licked at the liquid and snarled at the bitter taste. Then said, 'Maybe another sip to conclude my findings.'

The sloshing of liquid was heard, and then the bowl being pushed on the ground. Malachai looked up and saw the froth on the black wolf's face, then heard in his head, 'More!'

Baldrake launched himself out of the room and scared the soldiers as he sneaked from the darkness to stand before them with a soft growl in his throat. He found it very amusing for some time until Malachai pointed out that arrows were still trained on them.

A foul odour drifted from the remedy Gordon was brewing over the fire, something his father used to make after a night with too much ale. Mist hung low as the morning sun peeked its head over the plains when the once more composed, focused, and still, Gar hound approached and sat on his haunches next to him, looking ever so far in the distance as though he could see into the future with that deathly gaze. 'Please, my friend, do not let me *ever* drink that horrible liquid again. My head feels unwell this morning.'

Gordon drew closer a bowl and poured some of the remedy into it and said, 'Here, have some of this. It should make you feel much better.'

Baldrake hesitantly sniffed the yellow liquid and pulled his face into a snarl as he said, 'Dear Chronus! What is that?'

'Just drink it. Don't be such a baby.'

Disgusted, Baldrake drank the contents and choked halfway, coughing repeatedly, his breathing ragged in between the fits. The mekkel ran up and smacked his small palm on the flank of the wolf. More out of shock than anything else, Baldrake stopped coughing. He shook his head with brows raised, and stared at the mekkel as he jumped on the bench next to Gordon and said, 'You're welcome.'

Malachai came out of the tent, half-dressed as usual in the mornings. With only his pants and his hammer, he moved past his companions as he said, 'Morning, lads. Care to join me for some exercise?'

The mekkel's hand was first to go up and wave about, as if needed to be picked for the position. Immediately Malachai regretted his enthusiastic invitation, and said, 'Well then, come along, old fellow.'

The two walking off to an open area had a comic look, the giant and the little mekkel doing exercises together. First, they loosened their muscles and did some stretches as not to sprain anything. Melche imitated all of his moves as he twisted his pelvis and pulled his arms and shoulders, then swung them round and round. But when Malachai started swinging his massive hammer, the old fellow stared at him with arms crossed and scowled at him. 'Melche needs a weapon too.'

Malachai stopped when he saw the little mekkel's face, then pulled out his hunting knife from the sheath at his side and handed it over. With eyes wide and arms outstretched, Melche received the knife with glee. 'Melche never had a knife as big!'

'Oh no! That's just for practice, old one.'

Gwen came from her tent and moved over to Gordon and Baldrake, and said, 'He is a rather large fellow, isn't he?' She gazed at Malachai as he exercised.

The wolf turned his attention to the big man and said, 'People have always marvelled at Vasgath's size.'

'Who is Vasgath?' Gwen asked.

'I beg your forgiveness, it was a... what do you humans call it? A nickname we gave him during the war. I was referring to Malachai. He has always stood out among other men.'

Gwen watched the big warrior and saw how much grace he had with that massive weapon, swinging it from left to right, up and down faster than most men could swing swords.

'A man I would not like to meet on the battlefield,' she said as she turned away, then continued, 'Will you be staying another night?'

Gordon rose. 'No, we must go forth to the coast. We should be able to reach it in another three days. Thank you for your hospitality.'

'If what you say is true, I will send word back to the general. We need to get out in front of this threat before it's too late. Thank you for your candour. Not everyone would have been so open about this. But you, I see, still have faith in man. You still trust, never lose that.' She turned and left them as Gordon nodded his thanks.

Back in the boat, the companions headed for the coast. After the initial concerns they had with the means of travel, they had come to agree that travelling on the river was by far the better idea. The companions all conserved their energy as the craft was guided by the current, making good time.

'The days are getting colder every morning,' Malachai stated flatly. 'Winter is approaching much faster than I thought... or hoped.'

Baldrake watched him from the corners of his eyes, and he could see the torment in the big man's face. He knew instantly why the cold worried him so. *Oh, Vasgath, what did they do to you in that war? It was winter back then, as I recall, and since then you have hated the cold. How I wish I could help you, old friend.*

'What is that you are drawing, old one?' Baldrake asked as he peered down over the mekkel's shoulder.

Melche stopped drawing, looked up over his shoulder, and replied excitedly, 'It's a flying machine. All we would need to make it would be some long pieces of wood and some dead cows.'

'And how would this... flying machine work?'

'Well, we'll use the cowhides, stitched together, as the wing.'

'But do birds not have two wings to make them fly?'

'Ahhh, therein comes Melche's brilliant invention. Melche will make one great wing, spanned across the body of the structure. It won't be able to move like a bird's wing. No, it would soar like the eagles in the sky. So when you jump off a very high cliff, you could soar quite some distance before hitting the ground.'

His usual scepticism gnawed at him, but Baldrake went along with it and said, 'That's all good, old one, but where does one sit?'

'They will hold on to this piece of crossbar underneath the wing; nothing else will support them... yet. Maybe Melche can add some ropes to hold their feet.'

Baldrake rolled his eyes and looked to the sky as his stomach pulled into a knot. *Oh, how glad am I not to be human right now.*

Gordon was also listening to this elaborate scheme of the flying machine. Compelled to keep out of the conversation by the notion of him falling through the air in that death trap, he avoided their eyes. But as if the mekkel could sense that he was listening, he turned to him and asked excited once more, 'Could we please build this? You can be the first flying man, just imagine!'

Caught off guard, he stumbled into catastrophe as he said, 'Ah, sure...'

With a smile as broad as the ocean, the mekkel jumped up, screaming, 'Yippee, Melche is going to be famous!'

A chuckle came from his right as the big man looked at the distant trees, guiding the boat along, and Gordon knew at that point what he'd got himself into. Looking back at Baldrake he said, 'Thanks...'

The days went by slowly, and occasionally they stopped to make food or camp. Melche had fashioned a fishing rod from materials he had gathered and trailed some dried beef off the side of the boat. A hard tug on the line and Melche jumped up as he shouted with joy, battling with the beast he caught. The companions cheered him on as he got the fish to the boat and hauled it over. Flapping its tail as it thrashed in the boat, Melche quickly jumped on it and held it down. Adrenalin rushed through the little mekkel as he shouted, 'What now! What now?' He felt a tap on the shoulder, and as he looked up, he saw the big knife in Malachai's hands.

The big man said, 'You have to gut it, but be careful not to cut the stomach. Here, use my knife.'

As Melche stuck the fish with the knife, Malachai said aloud, 'Congratulations, my mekkel brother, your first kill.'

Melche lifted the heavy fish and said, 'Dinner?'

They took turns to steer the boat and keep watch throughout the night; even the mekkel had a turn at the helm. On the break of the fourth morning, Malachai woke the rest of the group with his usual loud banter, banging on something while shouting, 'Wake up, you lazy pigs! Rise and shine, girls!'

All were up instantly after that rude awakening. Still dusting the sleep from their eyes, Malachai pointed to the horizon, and as they all turned, they saw the beauty that lay before them. A little stretch ahead, the river broke off into hundreds of small branches flowing into the sea, and above the vast open ocean was the sun, rising as every morning; but somehow no other morning was like this. The beauty of this sunrise was unlike any other on the mainland. The companions marvelled at it; it was as if the sun was burning away the clouds above the ocean, clearing the smog away. The bright orange-pink hue that mixed with the clouds made it seem as if astronomic birth was taking place right that very instant. Malachai angled the boat to the far left most branch and brought the boat skidding to a halt on the beach.

'We go south from here to Millanthross—the Sea Breeze City,' Gordon said to his companions as they got out of the craft and made their way down the beach.

Malachai furrowed his brow and said, 'I thought you called it "The

Golden City" before?'

'It apparently has a few of these names. Apparently, it is called the Golden City because, as the sun rises, the reflection of the sun on the sea, turns the walls to a golden colour. The Sea Breeze City, well, that you can work out on your own.'

Dead leaves drifted in the wind, floating down to cover the roads as they settled to the ground. Anukke sat atop Shadow, riding at the forefront of his hundred men. At the back, a few wagons were pulled, which housed weapons, water, and food.

Travelling south-southeast for the last fourteen days had been an unfriendly affair to all in the country. Some smaller farm villages along the way were burnt to the ground by Anukke's soldiers; others were destroyed by Anukke himself. Word of his destruction was spreading all over Kraydenia—stories of thunderstorms forming in the middle of the day where there were no clouds, striking down on the villages with the anger of the gods, burning fields, houses and stores. Anukke's soldiers had run through the villages, hacking left and right, slaying everything that moved. People had become afraid to even leave their homes.

Misfortune struck them at night after one of their raids. Camped three days' travel from the forbidden lands of Krell, the wizard was in his tent, practising some new form of binding magic, when he heard the screams from outside. He rushed out and witnessed what caused the peril in their voices. Draghnai had invaded his camp this night...

Being a descendent of the infamous dragons, they were very rare, much smaller, but just as ferocious. Four of the beasts had attacked without warning, setting fire to tents and wagons as they scorched the earth from above. His heart beat furiously as he thought of what he could do to stop this attack.

Magical words formed from his mouth as he stared at one beast circling above him in the sky. '*All timai et forna kei topia dem vorla ait slem!*' As he finished the words, he slapped his palms together. The draghnai shrieked in pain and fell to the ground uncontrolled to crash into another wagon, tipping it to its side. Another draghnai had been killed by archers who were now taking aim on the next. The last two turned their attention to the sorcerer and came at him head-on. Flying low over the burning camp, they closed the distance fast.

Anukke could have sworn he saw a smirk on the one's face just as it blew fire from its mouth. Again he spoke magical words, and just before the draghnai reached him, he raised his hands into the air and a massive wall of fire erupted from the ground with incredible heat. The wizard could smell the burnt flesh of the one draghnai as it flew through the wall of fire. In a ball of flame, it plunged to the ground. The other had turned fast enough not to be singed. It turned and left the area.

Soot covered his face as he walked through his camp to inspect the damage, and yelled, 'Vargus! Report! Damn you!'

Out from the rubble of a burnt-down wagon, Vargus crawled out, half scorched to death. His whole left arm and half of his chest had been burnt to a crisp. Anukke regarded him and said, 'Don't move.' More magic flowed from the wizard, and the torn, burnt flesh closed up and healed, but left scars.

'Thank you, my liege,' Vargus gasped.

'I want a report immediately. How many men have we lost? How much water do we have left? Are the horses still alive? What about our weapons? These are the questions I need answered.'

'Right away, my liege,' Vargus said as he got to his feet, still in obvious pain. He swiftly walked back through the camp to disappear in the smoke haze.

Anukke moved back to the confines of his tent and awaited Vargus' report whilst pondering about what just happened. Draghnai were very rare creatures, and even more rarely did they hunt in a pack. They were solitary creatures of swiftness; get in, get out. That was the way they hunted. Not a full-frontal assault like this. After some time, Vargus returned and entered the tent. 'My liege, your report.'

'Well, speak, damn you, I don't have all night.'

With no more pauses, Vargus continued, 'Forty men are dead,

165

twelve are seriously injured. Luckily, we removed some food from the wagons earlier, before they hit it. I tried saving the rest by hitching up some horses to get it out of camp, but I was too late. The wagon and those horses are all gone. We will have to split the food up onto the remaining two wagons. Also, nine horses in total died.'

'Very well, we will have to make do.'

CHAPTER TEN

Four days had passed since the attack by the draghnai, and now Anukke was staring up at Krell's castle. Battered and bruised, he and his men walked into the courtyard, weapons drawn and not knowing what to expect. The light was fading fast, the tensions high.

'Well, well, what have we here? Is this a band of soldiers to stop me once more?' came a voice from a figure at the top of the stairway. 'I would advise you to be very careful of your next words and actions.'

The soldiers nervously looked around as ten draghnai settled down at the top of the wall surrounding them. A billowing dust cloud kicked up from their furiously beating wings.

Anukke quieted them and said, 'So it was you who sent those draghnai to our camp a few nights back.'

Shrewd laughter followed as Ortega replied, 'But of course. Who else would have the power to control all these draghnai? You know, they are magnificent creatures. I have been trying to gain control of a few dragons, but alas, this body is still weak.'

So, you haven't got all your power restored yet. That still gives me a chance. With a smirk on his face, Anukke said, 'I was unaware that there are still dragons left in this world.'

'Oh, don't be naïve, of course, there are. They're just hiding. Before we continue, I have to show you something. I have been waiting for this moment for some time... Arise, knights!' he bellowed.

Anukke's men shifted around nervously, holding onto their weapons. 'Do not do anything stupid,' he told his soldiers bluntly.

The earth beneath their feet trembled and gave way to the graves of the knights below. Slowly they crept up and out of their tombs to stand once more before their king. He had resurrected thousands of them. *One would have thought they would be just bones, barely clinging together, and one good hit should make them fall apart—but one would be remiss.*

The spell had kept them intact, as if they only died the day before. The only sign that they were not alive anymore was the fact that some still had axes and spears embedded in their bodies; others still bled from the deathblows of the swords that caused them.

The last hole fell open, adorned with a stone, crested with the king's sigil. Out of this grave came a man stories were still told of. He was Anthelos, the king's private guardian and most trusted servant. No one had known how Anthelos had died those many years ago, and now he walked to stand right in front of Anukke, looking more alive than most of the wizard's soldiers at this moment.

'Ah, Anthelos. It's been too long,' Ortega said as he walked down into the courtyard. 'He willingly gave his life for me, so I may call upon his services once more upon my return. He was never killed in battle.'

Anthelos bowed down before Ortega and said, 'I bid you well, oh great King. I am your servant once more if you wish it so.'

'This is what I call undying loyalty. Of course, Anthelos, as always. Now arise, my first knight, and take your seat at my table.'

They were outnumbered thirty to one. Anukke was thinking as fast as his head would allow him. His blue robe flapped in the wind as Ortega approached to stand a few feet away, next to Anthelos.

'So, what will it be?'

A long moment of silence and no movement came to pass, before the wizard bowed his head and dropped to one knee, and said, 'I am here to serve Krell. I am the one who resurrected you. I am the one who gave you the strength once more to be in this world. Spare me, so I may serve and bathe in your glory and power.'

Rubbing his hand over the stubble on his chin, Ortega said, 'I haven't heard that name uttered in a very long time. But call me Ortega. And what of these men who came with you?'

Raising his head, he stared at the cold eyes of the man, held them fast, and said, 'Do with them as you wish, my lord. But they fought valiantly for you in the past to set you free. They will fight even harder to keep you free.'

All the men behind Anukke shifted nervously, for they all knew the history of this man.

Standing with no armour, just a cotton shirt and leather leggings, Ortega looked down at the subjugated wizard, his long blond hair swaying in the wind as he said, 'I am glad to accept your service and that of these men. I have... how shall I say... learnt from previous endeavours that killing everyone doesn't help me, though it is very satisfying. No, *we* will build a kingdom, *we* will destroy those who oppose us, and *we* will force the others to join me! I will build an empire unlike the world has ever seen. Nothing will stand in my way! I will be feared and loved and respected, for there is no king like me!'

The undead soldiers lowered themselves before Ortega, paying homage to their king. Slowly, after seeing the dead bow down, one by one, Anukke's men lowered themselves to their knees. Soon the whole massive courtyard was bowing at his feet. Fire erupted into the sky from the draghnai in celebration of the return of the king.

'For once, the rumours are true,' said Malachai as he stood upon the golden shores of Millanthross, the Golden City. 'It is beautiful.'

It wasn't that big a city, but they had built it with pride. Every road was of cobblestone and swept daily. The shops were all of a very rare white stone they used for the walls. Houses in the northern district all had pitched roofs and were higher than the rest to have a better view of the sea. Rivers ran throughout the city, and small domed bridges connected roads wherever you looked. White gulls were perched everywhere, some walking through shops looking for something to eat; the more cunning jumped on tables where people sat enjoying a meal, trying to steal scraps. It was a pleasant place with minimal quarrels among the residents.

As the group wandered through the city, stares were hard to avoid, bearing in mind that the group was composed of an abnormally large man with a massive war hammer on his back, a mekkel that just wouldn't shut up, a young "blind" warrior with a sword strapped to his back, and of course to top it off, a huge pitch-black Gar hound the likes of which only stories have been told. Stopping in front of a small fresh fish market, Gordon spoke to the group. 'Malachai, you and Melche go to the port. Baldrake and I will find us suitable accommodation.'

Malachai immediately interjected, 'No way, you swine, after the stunt you pulled at Kalaghstine! I believe I should look for accommodation whilst you sort out the boat issue.'

Onlookers found the big brute's shouting very un-Millanthrosian, and a straight-backed, finely dressed man walked up to Malachai whilst he was going on about what happened in Kalaghstine and tapped him on the shoulder. 'I say, do excuse me,' came the fine, high-pitched voice.

With the whole group's sudden attention, Barnicus Bree felt a sudden chill go through his body, his spine wanting to give in under the stares, but he stammered on to say what he came to say, 'W-Would,' he cleared his throat, then continued, 'Would you be so kind as to have your little "discussion" somewhere else? We are trying to have a civilised conversation over here, and you are ruining the experience.'

Malachai grabbed Barnicus Bree by the collar, heaved him into the air with one hand, and just before he threw him over the side and into the river, he said, 'No one calls me uncivilised!'

Barnicus Bree flew over the small retaining walls and fell into the river like an old washcloth being thrown away, splashing and screaming for dear life, 'Help! Help! I can't swim.'

Gordon cursed under his breath and glowered at the man. 'Really? Why, Malachai? Why?' Quickly pulling off his shirt and trousers, he jumped into the river and dragged Barnicus Bree to the nearest side.

Malachai looked at Baldrake and shrugged as he said, 'One would think people who live next to the sea would know how to swim.'

Melche was off to one side, laughing and imitating Malachai's response to Barnicus Bree. Amusingly he picked up a stick and said, 'You will not call me uncivilised,' and threw it into the river. Only the stick didn't fall in the river. It hit Gordon on the head whilst he was getting out of the freezing water.

'What are you trying to do, Melche? Kill me?' Gordon yelled.

Instinctively Melche ran to hide behind Malachai's legs, crying, 'Melche sorry!'

Gordon and Barnicus came back to the top, where his companions waited. 'I am Barnicus Bree, heir to office of mayor of Millanthross! I will have you executed for this, you hear me, you brute?' Barnicus was screaming at the top of his voice.

Gordon intervened, 'Sorry sir, but don't you think that's a little rash? Especially considering if he throws you in again, I might not be there to save you? Malachai, please apologise to the man and let's be on our way.'

Considering Gordon's words, Barnicus immediately extended his arm as soon as he saw the big man's face turn into a scowl and spoke loud enough so that all could hear. 'I accept your apology. But see that it doesn't happen again.'

Gordon quickly clothed himself as he said to Malachai, 'Stop making trouble, big guy. We have enough as it is. Now, go find us accommodations. We will meet up here tonight just after sundown.'

Baldrake spoke to Gordon through his mind, 'Do you think it wise to let those two out on their own?'

'Malachai can take care of himself, and I believe the mekkel has sort of taken to him. They'll be okay.'

Walking through the streets towards the docks, Baldrake and Gordon barely talked, as he still didn't trust the wolf. The docks weren't as "civilised" as the district whence they came. Boats, small and big, drifted everywhere in the harbour. Guards patrolled the area, especially past "The Hallow", an old half-stone, half-wooden tavern that seemed as if they'd started to rebuild it but stopped halfway. In front of the tavern lay two men and a youngish girl on the wooden decks, as drunk as pigs at a wedding. The autumn sun was glowing, but it generated little heat as the icy winds blew over the ocean inland. Gordon and Baldrake made their way towards the tavern, hoping to find a captain willing to take them to the island.

The one problem they had was gold. They didn't have enough for accommodations *and* a trip to the island; they didn't even have enough for adequate accommodations.

'Can I be of assistance to you?' came a voice from just behind them. Turning, Gordon and Baldrake saw three of the guards that were patrolling the docks standing in front of them with their hands on swords, half-drawn. Baldrake snorted and grinned his wolfish grin, and spoke to Gordon's mind. 'Why is it you always attract trouble by doing nothing?'

Gordon raised his brows to Baldrake and silently communicated to the wolf, 'You have been around Malachai too much, and your sense of humour is becoming more like his. It's kind of strange. I think I liked you better when you were all business and no fun.'

'I asked you a question. What is your business on the docks?'

Gordon and Baldrake gazed at the guards, and it was Baldrake who spoke, with the most authoritative voice he could muster, 'What is the meaning of this? I should rip your limbs off for the arrogance you show. Do you even know who you are speaking to?'

Gordon rolled his eyes and muttered to himself, 'Oh great, here we go again. I travel with children, the bunch of them.'

The guards were so dumbstruck by the awe-inspiring authority that radiated from Baldrake that they sheathed their weapons.

'Who, may I ask, are you?' asked the guard, trembling in his boots.

'Why, you insolent fool.' Baldrake moved forward, stepping with such power that two of the wooden crossbeams cracked under his foot. 'I am the great general of the Gar hounds, and this is my blind counsellor, Gordon. But even with no eyes, he sees better than you three idiots!'

Confused and afraid, the three soldiers saluted Baldrake and said, 'Sorry sir, it's just that we didn't recognise you. You wear no markings of a general.'

Walking forward slowly, fury shining in his eyes, Baldrake closed in on them and said in a low slow tone, 'Boy, do I really need markings?'

'I-I guess not, sir, forgive me.'

Baldrake moved back and said, 'Now, I have business to attend to. We will need shelter for the night. For your insolence, be so kind as to arrange something, soldier. I do not have time for this.'

'Right away, sir. Should I alert General Fawn that you've arrived in town?'

'No, it will not be necessary. We need a ship to take us to the island, Milleria.'

'Well, sir, I believe you might be able to convince Captain Bellark Bree.'

Gordon and Baldrake exchanged glances and turned back to the guards as Gordon asked, 'He wouldn't have any relation to Barnicus Bree, would he?'

'Actually, he is his brother, sir. How do you know Barnicus?'

'We ran into him earlier today,' Gordon announced.

'Well, you should be able to find Bellark at the tavern. He just unloaded some cargo and will probably set out soon. Also, I will arrange accommodations for you at the soldier's quarters.'

Gordon stuck out his arm like a blind man and waited for the guard to close in, grab, and shake it. 'Thank you, soldier, we must be on our way.'

The guards all gave a courtesy nod, spun on their heels, and went off in the other direction.

Gordon looked to Baldrake and acknowledged, 'Very well played, my friend. Not only did we get information on a ship to take us to the island, but also a place to sleep for the night for free. Very nice indeed.'

The stench in front of the tavern was almost unbearable as the piles of vomit lay everywhere, urine stains marked the surrounding areas, staining the wood platform to a putrefied white-yellow colour, and fish guts lay everywhere. Just before they entered the tavern, a gruff voice called out to them, 'Well now, there's something ya don't see every day.'

Fifty feet away from the tavern, a fat but burly fellow with a large, thick black beard and long black hair tied in a ponytail was sitting on a bucket drinking ale, leaning over a wine barrel he was using as a table. Gordon and Baldrake stopped and turned to the man. 'And what would that be?' Gordon asked, half irritated.

The man gestured for them to join him, and as they closed in, the man said, 'Ya boys drink? It's on me—can't miss the opportunity to sit with a Gar hound.'

Baldrake curled his lip as soon as he heard the word *drink*, and countered, 'Sorry, but I do not drink, as I am afraid it has bad... effects on me. We are in search of someone by the name of Bellark Bree.'

The man's face turned stern, and he rubbed his beard as he said, 'Is that so, lad, and what do you want from this Bellark Bree? I might just know where ta find him, ya know.'

Gordon said, 'We need transportation to the island of Milleria.'

'Wait a second! Yer the 'blind' man who saved my brother. Though only after one of your companions threw him in the river.'

'Ahh, yes, sorry about that. So you must be Bellark.'

Laughing wholeheartedly out of the blue, Bellark stood and extended his arm as he said, 'Captain Bellark Bree at yer service, and don't worry about my brother, we tend not to see eye-to-eye on a lot of things anyway. Besides, he was probably an ass about something. If ya men come back here in two days' time, early in the morning, I'll take ya over ta the island... for a nominal fee, of course.'

'I thank you, Captain, we'll be here.'

Walking side by side through the streets of Millanthross, Gordon and Baldrake looked around for opportunities to make some coin. They tried everything. One of the more successful schemes involved them standing on the corner of a street, while Gordon held out his hands, bellowing aloud, 'Step right up, folks, see the amazing Gar hound speak. See his magnificent power and gaze into the eyes of death. This is a once-in-a-lifetime opportunity.'

A few people came to see the wolf; some even brought their young to pet the beast. Others were completely frightened out of their boots. This brought in some coin for them, but not enough.

Then Gordon tried swindling some gold from guys playing dice, as he had done when he was younger in Karta. He even signed Baldrake up for a hunting contest, to which the other hunters protested out loud. Forced to withdraw, they moved on to a different scheme. Gordon had won a small duelling contest, and as people believed him to be blind, his story spread rapidly throughout town. People raved about this blind warrior, and Gordon played along with it, either holding on to Baldrake's mane as he walked through the streets or clutching a wooden stick he used as a guide. Coin were thrown at the pair to get a fight.

As the sun set and night settled in, people quietly moved to their homes as it got colder. They had made enough money to buy winter clothing for the group. Gordon clasped his robe about him as the wind blew through the streets. As they approached an intersection, Baldrake stopped and turned his attention to a shop that had a Gar hound puppet on show in the window and said, 'I believe we Gar have become some kind of icon for these people... fools.'

Awaiting any kind of sarcastic remark from Gordon, he stood staring at the doll. But to his dismay, he saw in the window's reflection that three armed men had surrounded Gordon about fifty feet back.

Gordon had his back turned to Baldrake and one attacker, who charged with a knife. Two men came at him from the front. Gordon parried the first blows of the men in front of him, and then he saw it; the glint of a blade flashing at his back. He knew it was too late; he knew he could not deter the blow. As he turned to face his attacker, a black mass took the assailant off his feet with blinding speed. All Gordon heard was a faint yelp.

Quickly spinning on his heels and swinging out his blade, he sliced through the leg of one man. Falling and rolling on the ground with only one leg, the man screamed out for help as the unmistakable red liquid stained the cobblestone road. Gordon stood ready for the last attacker. 'Who sent you? What do you want?' he yelled to the man.

The man only laughed, then charged. Gordon launched himself through the air, somersaulting over the man, and flashed his blade out, cutting the man's back wide open. He swiftly got behind the attacker and turned the blade in his hand to hold the edge against the attacker's throat, then asked once more, 'Who sent you?'

The man made to laugh, but he only gurgled blood as Gordon drew the sword across his throat. He fell to the ground, clutching at his throat.

Gordon looked around to see what had happened to the third attacker but saw only Baldrake's body lying on the ground.

Some people were looking out of their windows by now, to see what the ruckus was all about; they quickly closed the shutters and locked them tightly after seeing what was going on. Quickly, he ran over and knelt at the side of the wolf and looked him over for injuries. The thick fur made it difficult to see anything, although his hands came off stained with blood.

'Baldrake! Where are you hurt?'

Slowly, Baldrake opened his eyes and looked at Gordon as he spoke, 'I think he got me in the side with his knife. But I think I did him one better.'

As Baldrake tried to rise, Gordon saw the man lying underneath, his jugular ripped out. He grabbed the swaying frame of the wolf and saw the blade dangling from his side. With a quick jerk, he pulled out the blade and tried to stop the bleeding with a piece of cloth he tore off the shirt of the dead man. Looking around, he screamed aloud, 'Help! I need some help. Please, is there no one who will help?'

Running to the window where he'd seen a figure peering out earlier, he jumped up and pulled open the wooden shutters. A frightened old lady stood inside, cradling a young boy. Gordon stared at them as they stared back, terrified. Trying to lower his voice, he said, 'Please, they hurt my friend. I need to get him stitched up. If you would just give a needle and some catgut. Those men attacked us. Please don't just turn away.'

The old woman released the little boy and told him to go to his bed. After the boy had left, the old woman said to him, 'You wait with your friend, young man, I will be down shortly.'

'Thank you.'

Dropping back to the ground, he first stopped at the other man, who was trying to get away by crawling on the cobblestones with one leg. Taking his sword, he spun it around in the air next to the crawling attacker. As the man pulled himself forward, Gordon swiftly brought down the blade and relieved the man of his hands, and said, 'If you don't have hands, I don't have to tie them up.'

Returning to Baldrake, he saw the agony in the eyes of the wolf. The blade had struck deep but had missed the vital organs. One could see in the blood's flow that no major arteries were cut. 'You old fool, why on earth did you do that?' Gordon asked as he sat by the wolf.

Pelting breaths came from the animal as it tried to sit on its haunches but soon lost consciousness. The old woman came out and moved over to the wolf with a needle in hand. 'My, but he is a big beast. Is he your dog? I love dogs, had one myself once, but not as big as this one.'

Gordon looked at the old lady inquisitively. 'Uhm, yes. He is... my dog. His name is Baldrake, and if he weren't here, I would have been dead. He took the knife in his side, instead of me. Is he going to be okay?'

After some time, the old lady had Baldrake stitched up and said, 'You must take better care of your dog.'

'Thank you, I will.'

City guards came running up the street as more onlookers peered through their windows. Immediately, the guards pushed Gordon to the ground and arrested him. Tying his wrists with rope as they started hauling him away, one guard recognised him and shouted, 'Stop right there. This man is the counsellor for the general of the Gar hounds.'

Hearing this, Gordon immediately recalled the three guards they had met earlier at the docks. 'Yes, please. The general is injured; he needs help. Please let me go. Those men over there on the cobblestone attacked us. One of them is still alive. Take him in for questioning.'

They untied him and hurried to the wolf's side. Lifting Baldrake onto a stretcher, they ran down the street to the army infirmary. Healers ran in, and at first paused as they saw the massive wolf, perplexed why they were called in at this hour to work on the animal. The guard said, 'He is the general of the Gar. We do not want hundreds of them coming through Millanthross to seek revenge for his death. So I suggest you help!' The healer nodded and started examining the wolf. Gordon thanked the officers and left to meet Malachai, who was probably furious by now. He ran as fast as he could through the streets to the little fresh fish market where they had separated earlier in the day.

Malachai sat outside, drinking ale and cursed under his breath as he saw Gordon approach and said, 'Well, well, well. Look who we finally have here.'

'We can fight about me being late, later. Now we must get to Baldrake's side. We were attacked on our way back here. Bastard stabbed him in his flank.'

Malachai jumped up and slammed his glass on the table, nearly breaking it as he said, 'What?! Where is he now?'

Gordon sighed while he looked around. 'He is at the army healers; they are looking after him. Where's the mekkel?'

'Think he said something about going to a blacksmith or something like that.'

'And you let him go? Great!'

Running to the nearest open smithy, they could but only think of all the trouble Melche had got himself into. Upon entering the shop, they could hear Melche shouting his pitched scream, 'Unhand Melche, you insolent fool!'

Drawing their weapons, they rushed in, breaking down the door leading to the fire pits... Only to see Melche on a table re-enacting one of his elaborate stories—which of course had never happened—to the blacksmith, who sat listening intently to the little mekkel.

The bald old blacksmith jumped up with his one remaining eye wide at the sudden intrusion and bellowed, 'What is the meaning of this?'

Gordon immediately sheathed his sword and said, 'Sorry sir, we heard the noise and thought—'

'And thought what?' interrupted the blacksmith. 'Thought that I may have thrown this little mekkel into the fire pits? You should be ashamed! He has been nothing but fun. Very clever too, you know, and he knows his way around weapons. Maybe I should hire him to work for me.'

They looked at each other, both having the same idea. Gordon walked forth to stand in front of the little mekkel and said, 'Well, Melche, we will miss you very much. But if it is your desire to work for the blacksmith, then you should do it.'

Melche slumped down onto an old steel chair and dropped his head. 'But Melche promised Gordon he would take care of him. Gordon saved Melche's life.'

He lowered himself to his knees and said, 'It's okay, Melche, you saved Gordon... I mean, me, when that band of thieves came out of the bush. And you saved all of us from that dragon.'

The blacksmith said, 'Oh, now that sounds like another story, my mekkel friend.'

Melche's eyes shined back at the blacksmith as his smile formed. Gordon then continued, 'Besides, we are just going to the island; we will come back this way. If you then want to come with us, so be it.'

Melche lifted his head and smiled as he said, 'Thanks Gordon, Melche has always wanted to work with weapons and shiny things. Malachai, please bring Melche something back from the island. A piece of raw iron would work nicely.'

The big man knelt by the little mekkel and extended his arm. 'Will do, old one. You take care of yourself now, you hear?'

Both men rose and made their way to the door, where Gordon turned around and said, 'Farewell, my friend. We will meet again.'

They ran down the street towards the infirmary to see how Baldrake was doing.

Lying on all fours with his head on his paws, Baldrake saw his friends approach and pushed himself up to sit on his haunches. Immediately, his wound tore and blood stained the bandage around his flanks.

'Lie down, Reaper, you're not as young as you once were. Relax, we're here, old friend,' Malachai said with a forced smile on his face. Gordon went to call for a healer to have a look at his reopened wound.

'They *shaved* me, Vasgath! Am I some house cat to be shaved at the whim of some healer?!'

Malachai chuckled as he stared at the wolf as his head lolled about.

They had given him herbs to numb the pain. Baldrake was quite happy in the grand scheme of things, responding to Malachai as he lowered himself. 'You know, Vasgath, right now, I do not believe that we will grow old. Not like these other people.' With his head, he gestured to a grey-haired old fellow on the next bed.

Malachai frowned and said, 'What do you mean? I think those herbs are doing their job pretty well.'

Baldrake shook his head left to right a few times, and said, 'It makes my head swim, but at least I feel no pain. What I meant is, in our minds, we will not grow old. We cannot allow it.'

'What happened back there when they attacked you? You are usually much more careful.'

Sighing and looking away out of shame, Baldrake spoke, his voice barely audible, 'I was careless. Distracted. I stopped at a shop where they were displaying Gar hound puppets. Can you believe that? Anyway, I turned around and saw Gordon in the middle of the road, with his sword drawn. Three men came at him, two from the front, one from the back. That's when I charged in as fast as I could. I went for the throat of the thug at Gordon's back, but before I had him, I felt the knife sink deep into my side. I was stupid; they could have killed him.'

Gordon came back, dragging one healer along by his shirt. 'No one wants to hurt anyone here, so I'm asking you politely to fix my friend.'

Trembling feverishly, the healer tried to examine the wound but found his hands shaking terribly. Baldrake stared at the man and said, 'You have no cause to fear me.'

Gordon heard voices from outside the tent growing louder in confrontation with each other as they neared.

'Aye, I have urgent news for the Gar hound and his companion, now let me through!'

'I know that voice.' He ran to the entrance of the tent. 'It's okay, let him through.'

Puzzled, the guards exchanged glances with each other after Bellark Bree lifted the flap and entered the tent. 'How do you think he knew who was out here? And how is it he looked straight at us with no eyes? He followed our movements,' the one guard said to the other.

'I guess he has excellent hearing or something,' the other guard replied.

Gordon was listening on the inside of the tent to their conversation and poked his head back out as he said, 'That I do.'

Abruptly turning around, the guards apologised.

Bellark stood before them and said, 'Well lad, seems someone's out to gut you and your friends. And by the looks of things, they're not playing very nice.'

Gordon looked at his companions as he said, 'Captain Bellark Bree, meet Malachai. A companion of ours.'

Bellark and the bigger man nodded in acknowledgement to each other. Malachai pulled free his hunting knife and stuck it into the wooden frame of the bed as he spoke to the captain, stretching out the words, 'Well met, Captain. Now tell me, what do you know of this attack? How did you find out about it exactly?'

'Well... Ya see, I was busy out on the docks, pulling in one of the ropes for the fishing nets. And as ya might have seen, there's a graveyard out just past the docks. I faced that direction as I was working and saw some strange movement up there and foolishly thought to investigate.

As I made me way up to the yard I saw the darnedest thing. Thought me eyes were playing tricks on me. Ya would probably think me mad, but I swear it. The graves split open, and I saw dead men climbing out of their tombs! It's those things I followed and saw them attack ya, but I was afraid... Ain't every day ya see the dead rise, ya know. I thought it was the end as we know it... Anyway, I wanted to warn ya but it was too late, they had already attacked ya, so I ran off like a coward to get the guards.'

Malachai was scratching his beard with his one brow raised, thinking about what Bellark said. 'Sounds like the work of a sorcerer to me.'

Bellark interrupted Malachai, 'Sorry, laddie, I have to go. I just came here to tell you the schedule has changed. I'm leaving tomorrow morning at first light. Be at my ship, the *Holland Bell*—you can't miss it. It's the big black one at the end of the docks with the large red sails.' Bellark turned and left the tent.

'Baldrake, do you think you will still join us on this journey?' Gordon asked as he sat down on the bed next to the wolf.

'I heal quickly; just be sure to come and get me on the morrow. You might need to carry me to the ship, but luckily, it's not far. Once aboard, I can rest until we reach Milleria. After that, I should be fit to walk and soon hunt, fight even.'

Gordon and Malachai nodded and turned to leave for their sleeping quarters.

Back in the stuffy room, tossing and turning in his bed, Gordon was sweating, gripping the sheets as he spoke out loud in his sleep. Malachai rose from the other side of the room and came to his side, trying to wake him, but to no avail. Gordon was fast asleep, his dreams haunting him...

☿

The Holland Bell was being thrown every which way. Like a mere speck of dust on the ocean sands, the ship stood no chance against the onslaught of the massively powerful sea. The crew ran around frantically, trying to secure the sail's ropes to regain control of the ship; others were trying to secure the cargo that was being flung everywhere.

The vision faded, and another took its place.

Tuds was screaming for help as he fell into an endless pit. The sides were unreachable, the depth inconceivable. Gordon tried reaching out to catch him, but he could not reach him.

Once more, the vision faded.

The island of Milleria was mountainous, every mountain in sight trying to reach higher into the heavens than the next. It was beautiful and peaceful... until the trumpets of war blew all around the companions. Then chaos ensued.

'Wake up, you fool!' Malachai shook Gordon viciously, and with a final slap to the face, he finally awoke; the visions of his dreams and the sight of the big man standing over him blended together and confused Gordon completely—rightly so. 'Where am I?' he asked.

Malachai sighed with relief and said, 'You gave me quite the scare there. Didn't know what was going on with you. It was just a nightmare or something. You're still in the soldier's quarters.'

Gordon sat up and rubbed his eyes. 'No, they weren't just dreams or nightmares. They were visions.'

'What do you mean, "visions"? Like what, like you can see the future "visions"? Are you sure you weren't injured in the attack, maybe you knocked your head or something?'

Gordon rose from the bed and walked over to the window to stare out into the night sky. 'You know when that dead dragon attacked us, and I told you about it before it happened? I had the same sort of vision. Only in that vision, *you* died killing the dragon. The same thing happened when you were hit by the poison arrow and Elgar attacked us on the way to the monastery. I knew that something would happen. I think some events I'll be able to stop, some I won't.'

Malachai slumped down in an old, raggedy chair that creaked as he set his weight upon it and said, 'Oh, Floghorn's pits. Since when has this been happening?'

'Since my eyes turned.'

Jumping up from the chair, the big man paced around the room. 'Well, are you going to tell me what the visions were? We need to be prepared.'

Gordon sighed and said, 'That's just it. This time the visions made no sense! Some of it did, or so I thought, but I don't know...'

Malachai slumped back down into the chair, cradling his head in his hands. Gordon turned around to face him and said, 'I can tell you this, Tuds is in trouble. He was calling out to me. We should be very cautious on this trip; many dangers lie ahead.'

CHAPTER ELEVEN

It was still night out when they boarded the *Holland Bell*. 'Ahoy my friends,' came the voice of Bellark Bree. Walking from the stern of the ship he said, 'Oh dear lads, ya think the wolf is seaworthy? Looks a bit green if ya ask me.'

Baldrake was lying on the stretcher they'd used to carry him to the ship. Lifting his head, he looked at Bellark and said, 'It's good that we didn't ask you then. I will be fine by the time we reach the island.'

'Oh hell, suit yourself. You lads can move down to the lower deck; I made a room ready for ya three.' Bellark barked some orders to the crew and moved away.

Lifting the stretcher, they moved Baldrake to the room, where they unloaded their equipment, then closed the door and walked back to the main deck to give the wolf a chance to rest. The two men milled about the crew, trying to help wherever they can. It was about a two days' trip to the island, and Gordon didn't realise just how sick the sea could make one. For most of the day, he hung over the sides, hugging the rails as he spilled his guts into the sea. Malachai was rather enjoying himself, as he had become the one to defeat in arm wrestling. Sailors lined up to have their chance at victory over the big man.

As everyone was busy, Bellark thought to take it upon himself to see how Baldrake was doing. Dipping two mugs into a water barrel, he brought one to Gordon and said, 'Ya should drink some water, lad, need to keep yerself hydrated. Ya'll feel better in a while.'

Barely able to hold on to the mug, he could not speak, and just nodded his thanks as he drank the water. It didn't take long before he turned to hang over the side again.

Bellark knocked on the door to the companions' room and walked in to find the wolf sitting up on his haunches, trying to pull out the stitches with his teeth, but his head wouldn't reach. With furrowed brows, he said, 'I don't believe those are supposed to come out yet.'

Ignoring the comment, Baldrake continued his pursuit of the stitches. The captain set the mug down in front of him and continued, 'Drink. You need to keep your strength up. I will see what's bothering you with the wound.'

Baldrake viciously dipped his mouth into the mug and lapped the water. In between breaths, as water gushed down his throat, he said, 'It itches; I am healing. They need to be removed.'

Bellark thought the wolf mad and chuckled as he unwrapped the bandage. Brushing back the overhanging fur around the shaved wound, Bellark was baffled by what he saw. 'How is this possible? The wound is already closing.'

'I told you. You don't have to worry about me. I am a fast healer.'

Bellark took his knife to cut the stitches, then slowly and meticulously pulled them out with his nails. 'Aye, ya can be glad the blade didn't go deeper. It would have pierced the lung.'

'Of that I am aware.'

Moving back to the door, Bellark said, 'Ya get some rest, that wound is not fully healed.'

For the better part of the day, everything went well; Gordon even stopped throwing up after some time. Birds were flying high and dolphins were swimming next to the ship, leading the *Holland Bell* through the treacherous seas. The sky was blue, and the sea was calm; for that moment, everything seemed okay in the world.

☿

'Are they dead?' Ortega asked as he moved to the edge of the throne.

Anukke stood facing him and bowed, his red robes flowing over the hay-strewn floor. 'No, my king. They eluded death once more.'

Ortega stood and unsheathed Nightslinger, a sword forged of magic and steel at the fire pits of Tarsis by Bloodbane himself; an enormous blade, but yet lighter than it appeared. The bright red crystal embedded in the pommel made the silver grip and dragon-winged cross guard gleam red as fire.

Moving closer, he raised the sword, pointing it to the wizard's face, and said, 'Fail me again, and I will send you to the depths whence I came.'

'I will not, my king. They will suffer for their insolence.'

Anukke left the king's tent and walked through the encampment to his own tent, where Vargus and Vintrian were awaiting their master's return. Anukke entered and waved for them to follow. Vargus stepped forth and lit a candle on the table in the centre of the room and said, 'My lord, what are your orders?'

Anukke stared at the two men with hatred burning in his heart—not just for mere man, but for his new king too. 'With an army that's already dead, one would have thought that we could resurrect them after they die again... or not die at all. But I was wrong. It seems everyone who joined his army all those years past was forced to take a vow to fight for him once more should he ever return. Even in death, they would be resurrected as the king saw fit. There are thousands of his soldiers buried all over the world. But once they are resurrected and killed, it's over. They cannot be called upon again. Their vow is then fulfilled.'

The two soldiers looked at each other uncomprehending. Vargus said, 'Sorry, my lord, we don't understand.'

Anukke leaned forward on the table, the bright candle glowing in his eyes, and as he spoke, the candle flared. 'It means, my stupid little pet, that Ortega does not have an infinite army. Once they are gone, it's just him. For now, just carry on with your orders as normal. When the

187

time comes to act, you will know. Now leave me!'

Both soldiers turned and left the tent.

The wizard flipped the table over and drew on the back with a piece of coal. He drew a rough sketch of two small, curved blades, one facing up and the other down, with a waving ocean line connecting the two blades from grip to grip. 'The bottom of the sea will be your fates,' he said as he climbed onto the overturned table. Magical words escaped his mouth, and as he chanted, he waved his arms about as if leading an orchestra. He twirled his hands in the air and brought them crashing down. Sweeping them back up and from side to side he continued, '*Eko servme ier, vatre am cor-ospon...*'

The sea was rampant; the ship pitched up and down, rolling left to right. Captain Bellark and some of his crew were running around on the deck, tying the snapped ropes from the mainmast, while others fastened the escaped cargo. Crates and barrels of liquor had broken their bondages and rolled about briskly in the cargo hold. Shouts came from the hold as a man was crushed by one of the barrels.

The storm was pounding the life out of them. A few of the crew were taken down to the lower deck, having sustained some serious injuries as it threw them about. Some broke only their legs or ribs, some worse. One man was hanging over the side of the ship, a broken beam having pierced him through the chest. Malachai and Gordon were trying to help where they could, grabbing ropes and securing cargo. Baldrake was still in the room below deck, trying to recover; he was still too weak to be of any help. Lightning flashed from the dark clouds to strike the water with a mighty crash.

'Land ho!' Came a voice from the top of the mainmast.

Captain Bellark, Gordon, and Malachai ran to the bow of the ship for a better view. Squinting his eyes to see through the rain, the big man shouted out over the crashing monstrous waves, 'We ain't gonna make it, Captain!'

'Of course, we will, sonny,' Bellark stated overeager and was interrupted by a massive blow to the hull of the ship. Suddenly pitched to the left, the ship yawed and sent them rolling on the deck. A loud crack was heard over the thunder, and Captain Bellark knew they were taking on water. He looked over the side and confirmed his suspicions when he saw water gushing through a wide gash in the hull. Another crack followed; he turned and saw the mainmast snap. The barrelman fell from up high to disappear in the ocean below.

He sighed, then snorted as he said, 'Well, we *were* going to make it. Next time, ya keep yer big mouth shut!'

The *Holland Bell* was taking on water fast, bending under the sheer weight of the sea. Loud creaking sounds reverberated throughout its structure. Bellark went down to see how bad the damage in the side was, leaving one of his crew to steer. Shortly after leaving, the horizontal mast of the spanker came loose and knocked the new helmsman unconscious, leaving the wheel to head in its own direction. Malachai rushed forward and fought through the falling crewmen to the wildly spinning wheel to grab hold of it. He strained his muscles to gain control. Any lesser man's arms would have been pulled out of their sockets by the wheel. After fighting it for a few intense moments, he turned the ship back on course for the island and sighed with relief as the gusts suddenly died down. The storm dissipated as the sun poked its head over the disappearing clouds. They had never seen a more beautiful sight after a storm like that.

'This was no normal storm, my friend,' came the voice of Gordon as he stood, arms folded and leaning with his back against the top rail of the ship, looking over the chaos on the deck.

'We're not out of this yet. The ship is sinking, and we're too far from the island. We will *not* make it,' Malachai responded as he looked over the side. The ship was halfway underwater by now and was barely moving. He left the wheel and said, 'Aye, that's it, we'll have to swim from here. We're about a mile out. I'll carry Baldrake—he'll be lighter in the water.' As he walked to the stairs, the ship rocked and shook everyone off their feet. 'Abandon ship! She's sinking!' Malachai screamed aloud.

To their astonishment, the ship didn't sink, but rose. Creaking and moaning, the *Holland Bell* lifted from its watery grave. Water gushed from the wound at her side, spilling back down into the sea. All onboard were frightened and confused at what was happening. Slowly and surely, the *Holland Bell* made her way to the island's shores, floating just above the ocean's surface.

'The gods have heard our prayers! We are saved!' Malachai roared and lifted the mighty hammer above his head.

All on the ship forgot their shock and terror as screams of joy sounded throughout. All except Gordon. He didn't join in with the celebrations; instead, he stood at the bow looking over the shores for signs of movement; and he soon saw it. Lady Rose walked out of the thick of the tree line, gracefully moving her hands in the air, the intense focus showing on her face as she lowered the ship to the shores of the island.

As the ship pushed its bow firmly into the strand of Milleria, the crew cast ropes down the sides and vacated the ship as fast as possible, dramatically throwing themselves on the ground and yelling their praises. Back in his cabin, Baldrake limped to the door and looked at Malachai as he approached and said, 'And how do you propose I get off this death trap?'

The big man frowned, and in the most serious tone he could muster, said, 'Cats do land on their feet when they fall, don't they?'

Baldrake just snorted and calmly replied, 'You know, I should eat your heart for that comment, Vasgath. You know I am not feline.'

Just then Gordon came through the doorway bearing the stretcher, and said, 'Come, let's go, we will carry you down.'

I would rather starve to death. 'Fine, let's go.'

They strapped Baldrake to the stretcher on the deck while they got ready to take him down, but then, the wolf and the stretcher drifted to the sky. Both men just stared at the wide-eyed wolf as he descended to the ground and heard his last words trail off in their heads, 'This is not funny!'

Once on the sandy beach, Baldrake turned his wide gaze to the left and saw the sorceress; a mature woman with a light brown complexion and braided black hair. She was a lean woman, dressed in a green-and-red linen dress, wearing wooden trinkets around her ankles and wrists with the deepest green eyes.

As she approached the wolf, she spoke through the mind, 'Korviete (Greetings), maksouel (warrior).'

Astonished but composed, Baldrake replied, 'Korviete, tinde (lady) Rose. It has been a long time since I heard my home tongue. I thank you for greeting me in such a manner.'

'It is my honour to have you and your friends as my guests.' Gordon and Malachai approached and bowed before her. 'Oh, stand up!' she laughed. 'There is no need for that. Help him out of the ropes and stop making a scene.'

Malachai walked over to Baldrake and untied him as he whispered, 'I don't understand; I have never bowed before anyone. But I just had no control. I don't like this.'

Lady Rose walked over to Captain Bellark, who had started the assessment of the damage to his ship as soon as he set foot on the shores.

'Captain Bellark Bree, you and your men can go up three miles northwest from here. There you will find lodging, food, and artisans who should be able to get all the material needed for your repairs. You're welcome to stay for as long as is necessary. You and your men will have no trouble here; just don't cause any. Otherwise, you will answer to me.'

'Aye, thanks, milady. Will keep the boys outta trouble. Repairs will take about a week er two.'

'Go into town, and if anyone gives you problems, tell them you come with the blessings of Lady Rose.'

Bellark nodded, turned away, and continued shouting at his crew.

She re-joined the three companions and said, 'You will come with me; I have need to speak with you.'

☿

After their long walk through the woods, they emerged from the trees and set their eyes upon a small village consisting out of round mud huts with straw-thatched roofs. There was no proper structure to the village, no plan in the layout. Everyone just built their little hut wherever they saw fit. The locals were a very dark-coloured race, running around the village with smiles on their faces as they greeted Lady Rose and her guests. This was a Neolithic culture that thrived, a happy people who took more to the natural life, but not primitive at all; they were very clever, seeing fit to preserve life rather than destroying it.

The journey to the southern end of the island was silent. Gordon and Malachai walked at the rear, exchanging only glances, while Baldrake walked next to Lady Rose, speaking his almost-forgotten language with her.

Finally stopping before a hut that was fairly larger than the rest, Lady Rose turned to Gordon as he said, 'Excuse my insolence, but I thought that a sorceress like yourself would live in great towers and have long nails and evil thoughts of gaining power, ruling the world and such. From what I have seen, you have the power to do it.'

'Just because I have the power does not mean I yearn to use it. Now let's go inside and have something to eat.' She entered the mud-covered hut first, followed by the companions. Upon entering, it was as if a shift in time and space had occurred. The inside of the hut resembled no primitive mud dwelling. The interior was vast, with milky white-and-green agate stone floors everywhere. Stairs spiralled up to the next floors, rooms branching off in all directions. Massive stone eagle statues stood on the sides of every doorway. Everything was beautifully crafted.

Stunned to silence, no one spoke as they marvelled at the interior. Malachai eventually broke the silence and said, 'Where are we? Did we get smaller or something? Because there is no way this is the inside of that mud hut.'

Lady Rose, unwavering from the path she was leading them on, said, 'I adore beauty in my old age, and a mud hut just doesn't work for me anymore, so I changed the interior just a bit with a little magical help. From the outside, the hut is more an illusion than anything else.' She led them to a large room, where they were seated near a hearth on a large, red-stained leather couch.

Baldrake went forth to lie at the foot of the hearth as he spoke. 'Lady Rose, please tell my companions what you have told me on our way here.'

Gordon unbuckled his weapon and set it down next to the couch, then said, 'Yes, please do. Also, tell me how you know our names and how you knew we were bound for the island?'

Rose stood and added some more wood to the fire as she said, 'I know of all that is happening from where you come. I knew Anukke a very long time ago. He was different then... we both were.'

Malachai leaned forward. 'You were in love.'

Baldrake came to his haunches, bared his teeth, and growled as he said, 'You neglected to mention this to me. How are we to trust you? Is this a trap?' Slowly he moved closer to Rose, the saliva dripping from his massive fangs to the floor. 'If this is a trap, I will tear your heart out, sorceress!'

Frightened, she backed up against the wall as she stared into the wolf's eyes, knowing, at this distance, that she could not cast a spell quick enough to stop an attack.

Gordon said calmly, 'I think you'd better speak quickly and accurately. I don't think he is in the mood to play games.'

Rose took control of her fear and said, 'Yes, we were in love—a very long time ago, but the power consumed him. I watched as his will to control his power failed him. He became a vile thing. Unredeemable. I could not bear to watch him murder innocent people anymore. I finally got the courage to stand up to him. We fought for days, weeks even. It came to a point where it was not just words anymore; we started using our magic against each other. Nearly killed one another, but in the end, I could not, and neither could he; and so he cast me away to this island, where I have lived for over twenty years. He imprisoned me here,' tears rolled down her face now as she continued, 'but he could never stop my soul.'

'Ease off her a bit, Baldrake. I need her to think clearly,' Gordon said as he leaned forward on the couch.

Rose composed herself and sat down on the couch before them, and said, 'My soul took flight a few weeks back and found an old man in a monastery willing to listen to my story.'

Malachai was busy sharpening his hunting knife on a stone he had taken out of his pocket. 'And just what is your story?'

'There has always been a sort of connection between me and Anukke, since our first joining. Sometimes when I sleep, I get glimpses of him, of what he is up to.'

Gordon sat back on the couch and said, 'And you saw what he had planned, and took flight to warn Delios. He then waited for us to arrive to give us this quest.'

Malachai looked at Gordon with a raised brow and asked, 'What do you mean, flight? She can fly?'

'No, big guy. Spiritual flight. She left her body here. I did it once; wasn't all that fun.'

Rose said, 'Yes, that's exactly what I did. I told him to send the one who was destined to fight Anukke to me for help, the one preordained in the prophecy. Face it, you don't stand a chance against a sorcerer like him as you are. He would strike you down long before you could reach him.'

'Get to the point already. Why did we come here? What is it you can offer us?' Gordon said as he slammed his palms on the couch.

Quickly rising, she merely spoke one word, 'Anflamino!' Flames erupted from the fireplace, burning a bright blue as she said, 'I care not that you do not trust me. But I will not be treated with disrespect in my house again! Do you understand me?'

They shifted around nervously on the couch under her stare, and Gordon said, 'I apologise, Lady Rose. It has been a long journey.'

The fires retreated, and the heat died as she walked over to the cupboard in the room's corner. From the top drawer, she pulled a map of the isle, unfurled it, and walked back, leaving it suspended in the air.

Malachai muttered, 'Why doesn't she just get a table? They work just as well. Even better. You can put your ale down too.' Gordon shoved him in the ribs to keep quiet.

The map lay outstretched in the air as she pointed to the top section of the map with her slender index finger. 'There is a man who lives in a cave in the northern region of the Tannak territory. He has something that belongs to me. Unfortunately, I cannot go in and take it by force; it would mean war between the two tribes. He also has something in his possession that would aid you in your quest. It needs a spell cast on it to bind you to it. If you bring me back what is rightfully mine, I will cast the spell upon the item and you can be on your way. This will give you a much better chance against him.'

Gordon smiled and said, 'So the old saying is correct: "Beware of witches and favours." It doesn't seem that we have any choice in the matter. Or am I mistaken, Lady Rose?'

'I am no witch, but no, you don't. Not if you want to succeed.'

'Then I guess we head for this Tannak territory.'

Milleria had very little in the way of flatlands or open plains. Most of the island was mountainous rock or forest, and where our heroes went, they could not go on horseback. Together they set out for North Milleria to find the items and bring them back to Lady Rose.

Baldrake had almost completely healed by now and was running from time to time to exercise his stiff muscles. It has been almost a week since he was stabbed, and ever since, he had gotten no proper exercise. The slightest bit of movement stretched his taut muscles to the point of tearing. Time would prove the best healer of all.

For the first day, they had little to no problems as they passed through many small villages, most looking like the village they'd left. The Miknak people, also known as "The Tribe of Rose," were very calm and good-natured. They lived a more primitive lifestyle than the Tannak, who had built roads and cities and developed a currency system, where the Miknak still relied on each other's generosity to help where needed.

The two tribes had been locked in conflict for the last decade. The Tannak believed that Lady Rose was holding back the Miknak people in further development of their lives, whereas the Miknak believed the Tannak would destroy nature in their greed for development. The two tribes fiercely hated each other.

The moon shone high in the sky before the companions stopped to make camp for the night. They pushed themselves to get as far as possible and stopped just a few miles shy of the border of the Tannak. Baldrake sat, watching the two silent warriors go about their business; Gordon was scanning the surrounding area of the campsite for any threat, analysing every defensive stance they could take, should the need arise. His loose and heavy mohair cloak shifted slightly in the passing wind. Malachai looked completely out of character in his new clothes; the intended loose-hanging full-length robe pulled taut against his skin and reached only to his knees, the material stretching with every muscle that bulged. He was busy making a fire to cook the small deer they had killed earlier in the day. Baldrake had already eaten two of the deer's legs. *Why do they insist on destroying food so?* he thought as he made his way to the distant Gordon.

'I never thought I would say this, but that little mekkel has grown on me. At least if he were here, there would have been some laughter,' came the voice of the wolf next to him.

Damn it! I didn't even hear him approach. Not wanting to make a scene, Gordon calmly replied, 'Aye. Me too. I hope he's safe.' Turning with arms folded, he asked, 'Do you believe in what we're trying to do?'

'I would not be here if I didn't.'

'Yes, but why us? Why not some other sorry sods?'

Baldrake could hear the hurt in his voice and knew deep down that he missed his father, his friends—the life he once knew. Immediately he thought of his own son and lowered his head. *Where was he? Is he safe? Is he maybe on his own adventure trying to save the world, just like Gordon?* He pushed out his chest and stood proud as he said, 'On Gar, my homeworld, we have a saying: "If one misses his destiny, the world could cease to exist the very next day." This is our destiny, and if we fail, who knows what might happen? We have been put on this path and all we can do is try to finish strong.'

Gordon turned back to the dark. 'You are a wise old wolf.'

Both turned and headed back to the fire, where Malachai had just finished cooking the deer. Sitting in peace, the men ate while the wolf took first watch.

CHAPTER TWELVE

Walking through the forest, Gordon heard hymns drifting through the bushes. As he pushed through the brush, an old man sat by the side of a lake with his feet dangling in the water.

'Oh, Gordon, I am glad you could make it,' said the old man.

'Delios, is that you?' He asked as he moved closer to the lake.

'Of course it is me! Who else would it be?'

'What are you doing here? How're Beldrin and Cuorco? Are they in any trouble?'

Delios climbed to his feet on the bank of the lake. 'They are fine, my boy.'

Boy—a title he tried to shed. But coming from such an old man, everyone was a boy to him. He did not mind the title. Gordon leaned against a tree, folded his arms, and said, 'Why did you call on me, then?'

'I was a little worried... and little Beldrin wouldn't stop nagging me to speak to his father. How is he doing?'

He smiled and said, 'You old softy, Baldrake is just fine. He took a knife wound to the chest a few days back to save my life, but he is healing fast.'

Sudden, inexplicable pain ripped through Gordon's head. He screamed as he stammered and fell to the ground, rolling and shaking with the pain, cradling his head between his arms. Delios and the lush green forest disappeared, and the pain subsided.

An extraordinary weight was pulling on his arm. As he opened his eyes, he looked down a massive cliff, clutching the arm of his companion. Malachai was dangling from the side of the cliff, holding only to Gordon's arm. The snow-covered mountain was slippery. His body slipped further down the edge, but wouldn't let go, though the big guy was too heavy for him to pull back up. Malachai knew he would be the death of them both, and with tears in his eyes, said, 'Don't let my death be in vain, my brother. Finish what we started!' He opened his hand and shook off Gordon's grip on him.

'No!' came Gordon's cry. Tears ran down his face; snot ran down and out of his nose as he watched his friend, brother, and companion fall down the cliff and vanish through the mists.

He rubbed at his burning eyes and rose from his blanket to add more wood to the fire, wondering about the visions he had been experiencing, troubled by their meaning. A voice came from his left. 'Can't sleep,' Baldrake stated more than asked.

'Quiet. I don't want to wake Malachai.'

With a snort, Baldrake replied, 'You do not have to worry about that. He could sleep through a storm and not notice.'

'I spoke to Delios in my sleep. Beldrin and Cuorco are doing well; they just miss you.'

'Thank you for telling me. It eases my mind, knowing he is safe. What troubles you this night?'

Gordon sat staring into the flames as he thought about the vision. It gnawed at him from within. Should he speak to Malachai about his vision, of what he saw?

'Gordon.'

'Huh? What was that?'

'I asked what troubles you so tonight?'

'Oh, sorry. Got distracted. Nothing. Don't worry about it.' He rose as the sun peeked its head over the valley and kicked Malachai softly on his feet, saying, 'Wake up, we need to get going.'

☿

After they had crossed the border into North Milleria, they immediately noticed the difference between the two tribes. Vast pits with tunnels carved into their sides plagued the region as the Tannak mined for iron, destroying the forests to gain the metals. They had walked past three of these pits already, watching the camp as the workers laboured on with picks and shovels at its base. Connected with a much more extensive road system, they had culled the forest to make way for the modern society; it left the companions with few places to hide from prying eyes. The people of the Tannak were a very hardworking and suspicious bunch. Anything out of the ordinary would be reported to the high cleric, and that was usually when the hangings took place.

Avoiding the roads, they ploughed through the thick snow as they made their way to higher ground. A hard climb up the slope of the mountain awaited them. The less-travelled path was treacherous underfoot, the snow slippery. Gordon stopped to inspect the surroundings. The mountains were enormous, jutting out from the low-hanging clouds as far as the eye could see. Rich in iron, they had a rusty red-brown look in the areas not covered with snow. The valley down below wasn't visible anymore as he looked down at a blanket of clouds surrounding the mountain with mostly pine trees, running along its sides.

The day's running was hard, but they had made good time and mostly went unnoticed, sticking to the forests and the mountains and caves. Before dusk settled in, they stopped at a cave entrance to spend the night. Tired and cold to the bone, they went inside and started a little fire to heat the broth Lady Rose had given them. There was silence as they worked and ate, too tired for conversation. They collapsed on their makeshift beds to sleep.

In the middle of the night, Gordon awoke to find Malachai's bed empty. Cautiously and precariously, he moved about the cave with sword in hand, walking light-footed so as not to make a sound. At the cave's entrance, the big man stood, hammer in hand. 'Aye laddie, all peaceful out here. You can put away that sword of yours,' he said without turning.

A rasping sound as the sword slid back in its sheath sounded then, and he moved to stand next to Malachai, and said, 'How did you know I was there?'

With a faint chuckle, he said, 'I met this young fellow a while back who told me he uses his surroundings in certain situations. I guess you can say I followed his teachings. I saw your reflection in my hammer.'

Gordon smiled as he said, 'I shall remember to be more cautious next time.'

Malachai settled the big hammer on his broad shoulders, and as he stared out of the cave, said, 'I have always liked the mountains, you know,' he gestured in the distance, then continued, 'Even in the dark, you see their power. Their beauty.'

In the distance, in the dead of night, the snow-capped mountaintops shone brilliantly under the big moon above. 'Yes, they are quite magnificent, aren't they?'

Malachai suddenly reached into the buckskin jacket pocket underneath his robe and pulled out two big cigars. 'Now, this here is for after we kill the wizard. Got them in Millanthross. No smoking this before then, ya got that?'

Gordon raised an eyebrow and looked at the mountains as he said, 'This stuff will kill you.'

'Oh, don't be a cry-baby. There's plenty more where we're headed that will do you more harm than this here cigar.'

Gordon sighed and said, 'Give me that. Thanks.'

'In the name of the high cleric, Veal Temur, come out of the cave immediately! Slowly and peacefully! Mercy shall be shown to those who do not oppose us!'

Pain lanced through his head as he opened his eyes. Gordon pressed his fingers to his temples as he rose unsteadily to his feet, and said, 'What is that? What happened?'

'I don't know. It's coming from outside. What happened? Last thing I remember was talking to you.' Malachai rose a few feet away and staggered closer.

'Not so loud, my head is pulsing,' came the eerie voice of the wolf. 'I can't remember anything either. Someone or something did this to us.'

Slowly, the three crept up to the entrance of the cave, staying as low as possible.

'Come out! We know you are in there. Come out, and try nothing stupid,' came that same voice.

Peering out of the dark cave, they looked upon the faces of the men who accosted them. Their only way out of the cave was straight down the mountainside, blocked by ten soldiers.

'We can take them,' said Malachai as he brought his hammer up.

'I love your enthusiasm, my friend... but no, we can't. Look closely, beyond the men in front. They have archers hidden amongst the trees, all over. We would never make it. No, you're going to have to trust me.'

Hectar, the high cleric's personal guard, sat atop his horse, looking to the cave, waiting for movement. Sure enough, three figures emerged slowly from the dark.

'Throw down your weapons! And do not make any sudden movements!' Hectar said as his horse nervously backed up and circled.

Malachai stared at the man. *Now there is a man I would like to fight.* The Tannak stood at least as tall as him and was just as muscled. Hectar's face showed his age, though, with deep lines on his forehead and the crow's feet around his eyes. He wore the colours of the clerics: a bright red tunic, bound in brown leather guards covering his chest, arms, and legs. His axe hung from the side of his horse. The rest of his troops wore their standard battle uniforms: black breastplates over chain-mail suits, red capes dangling at the back.

'You seem a bit out of place from the rest of your squad,' Gordon said as he neared them and tossed his sheathed sword to the ground.

'Arrest them!' Hectar growled at his men. Five of the armed guards dismounted and moved towards the companions.

'On what charges? What did we do to warrant this?' Gordon called out.

'Conspiracy against the high cleric,' Hectar said, as he leaned forward on his horse, then continued, 'Take them away, and tell your pup to behave.'

After a considerable amount of time and trouble, the guards eventually got Baldrake muzzled and Malachai to stand still to have his hands tied. They marched the three off to Vilencia, the capital city of North Milleria.

The city itself wasn't as big as the cities on the mainland, but it was big enough. Unlike cities on the mainland, Vilencia was not walled in; it spread far and wide. At first, a few small homes appeared as they walked, each with a big plot of land between them. Then a little closer, until they were virtually on top of each other. A bakery was on their left, and Malachai closed his eyes as the scent of the goods filled his senses. A few paces down the road to their right stood a sign for a barbershop.

Screams erupted from the little shop on their right as Hectar chuckled and said, 'Must be getting a tooth pulled.' Gravel roads led to houses and shops that branched off from the perfectly cobbled road leading to the castle at the centre of the city, where they were being marched to. Once inside, they stood in the main hall before the high cleric with their hands bound. With a vicious swing of a spear to the back of the knees, both Malachai and Gordon went to the ground. Baldrake turned and gave the guards a threatening look and spoke through his mind to the guard, 'You dare touch me or my friends again, and I will break this bondage and rip out your heart.'

The guard looked around frantically for this voice speaking to him. At some level, he knew it was the wolf, but he would not believe it and instead turned around and marched away.

The high cleric rose from his seat and came to stand in front of the prisoners, and said, 'Place *them*,' he pointed to Gordon and Malachai, then continued, 'in the mines. Kill the demon-wolf!'

Immediately Gordon stood and said, 'Begging Your Highness, do not kill him. We did nothing to deserve this fate.'

The cleric glared at the young warrior and said, 'Any and all who come into North Milleria and sneak around like you three are up to no good. You will not have the chance to prove me right. Give me one reason I should not kill this wolf.'

'Well... just think of it. If you put him on display, everyone on Milleria, North *or* South, would come and pay to see that you have captured this demon-wolf. You would be revered.'

Rubbing at his beardless chin, the old cleric thought about this proposed solution, then said, 'I think I might have a better idea than that.' Pointing to one of his guards, he said, 'You. Throw them in the dungeon for now.'

Sitting in the dungeon's corner on a hay bale, Gordon said, 'I've never heard of a cleric being treated as a king, with the power to do what he wants. I still want to know what happened last night.'

Malachai, nonplussed, just shook his head. Baldrake lay in the centre of the cell, licking his now-healed wound, then said, 'We need to find a way out of this place. We can't stay here long.'

'Oh, we'll get out, don't worry, even if I have to tear every man, woman, or child's body in half to do so,' Malachai muttered as he rubbed his hands together.

The rattling of keys made the companions stir, then look up as a guard approached to open the door. 'Seems it's off to the mines with you lot. Except for the wolf. He stays here. Gonna be entertainment instead.'

Nervously glancing at each other, Baldrake spoke through the mind to Gordon and Malachai, 'Don't worry about me, I can take care of myself. As soon as you two get a chance, take it and get out. We will meet up later.' He could but only look on as they were shackled and ushered out of the dungeon. Additional men had been sent to escort them to the mines, to make sure they do not escape.

Silent, Baldrake sat alone, imprisoned in the dungeon, awaiting his escort to this entertainment room. Thoughts ran through his head. *Would Malachai be able to get through this? I haven't seen that look in his eyes for a very long time. What did they do to you, Vasgath? You were gone for months before we found you, bloodied and barely alive. Worse so was the camp they held you in. The carnage was surreal.* "Even if I have to tear every man, woman, and child's body in half, we will get out." *Please, Vasgath, hold yourself together.*

Four guards with ropes and spears walked in and surrounded Baldrake, staring at each other with fear in their eyes, waiting for the first to make a move. One man to his left said, 'Okay, demon-dog, it's time for you to come with us.' He swung the rope in the air and cast it at the wolf, trying to snare his head, but Baldrake snatched it in his jaws and jerked violently on it. The guard went flying into the iron bars, then slid to the floor, where he lay groaning.

Shouts went up as the remaining guards rushed in with spears in hand. Baldrake shifted and caught a clumsy thrust from the guard. The spear went flying as he threw his head around to impale the one guard in his chest. More spears were thrust at him, but he leapt out of the way. Before the guard could pull back to thrust again, the wolf was on top of him with fangs bearing down. A sickening crunch sounded as bones split under the mighty bite. Screams erupted from the man as his arm was crushed just above his wrist. Alone now, the remaining guard stopped to rethink his situation as he stared into the wolf's eyes...

'You have two choices,' came the overly calm voice of the wolf, 'You can either come at me with that spear, and I can crush your head, as I did his arm. Or you can let me walk by my own free will. Choose wisely.'

The crowd went crazy, shouting their dissatisfaction and cursing as Baldrake walked through the massive curtains, escorted by two armed guards. He walked with a proud gait and stopped to inspect his surroundings. Standing in an arena with high walls on the sides, four gates entered from the north, east, south, and west. There were five raised platforms in the arena, one at the centre and the others at the four corners of the rectangular hall. At the far northern wall stood the high cleric, shouting with arms raised high to get the attention of the crowd, 'Fellow Vilencians! I have called you here today to bear witness to the demon hound we have captured!'

Once again, the crowd erupted in delight, cheering and shouting their praise to the church. The high cleric shushed the crowd once more and said, 'Tonight we will pin this demon lord against his barbaric brothers, his underlings. Tonight, we will watch them tear each other apart! No more will the church sit and do nothing! Let the games begin!' And again, the crowd cheered.

Out of the gates came three normal wolves, growling at everything that moved. Baldrake jumped atop the centre platform and calmly awaited them. As the wolves approached him, he said, 'Brothers! I do not wish to fight you. I have no quarrel with you.'

'But I do!' came a voice from the shadows of the gate. A big Gar hound sauntered out with his head held low.

'Chaulle? Is that you?' Baldrake jumped down from the platform and pushed through the smaller wolves, ignoring their snapping at his flanks. 'What are you doing here?'

'I should ask you the same thing... traitor.'

Baldrake bit his lip and turned his face away. That word stung more than a thousand blows. He turned back and said, 'You know very well that I never betrayed you.'

Chaulle cut him off with a bark to attack. Their reaction was instantaneous. Baldrake barely evaded one wolf's teeth as it slammed shut just below his throat, and as he righted himself, he broke the back of another charging wolf with a vicious smack to the spine. Searing pain suddenly ripped through his back leg. A wolf had latched on with his jaws, jerking to break the thick bone of the Gar, but all he did was tear some skin. With a flick of his leg, he grabbed the wolf at the back of the neck and quickly bit down hard. The snap and yelp that followed made the crowd nauseous.

The dead wolf dropped from his mouth and fell limp to the ground. 'Is this what you wanted? To see the death of innocent wolves?' His words echoed in the hall as the crowd grew quiet. The last wolf circled him now, limping due to an injury to his back leg. Baldrake charged, the wolf charged, fangs ripped through the air. But it was inevitable. Staring down with sadness in his eyes, he turned around to face Chaulle, his mouth gleaming with the blood of the wolves.

'Why! Why did you do this? You just sent those wolves to their death for no reason,' Baldrake blazed with anger. 'Answer me!'

With a chuckle and a grin, Chaulle said, 'To see if you are even worthy of killing anymore. That's the problem with you. These wolves are not our kin; they never will be. But you are incapable of seeing that we are going to die on this planet, because of you!'

The two Gar hounds circled each other. Baldrake growled, 'No! Soon these wolves will be a part of our society—I have fathered a son! One like us! From one of them! Don't you see? We can rebuild our kind. Our life, right here.'

'Lies! All lies! You are despicable! You would say anything to save your hide! Enough!'

Chaulle attacked; Baldrake lunged forward, claws extended and mouth open. The two wolves collided heavily, jaws snapping at each other's throats. Falling to the ground, both wolves stood on their hind legs, slashing their claws at each other. Chaulle bit deep into the front flank of Baldrake and sent the general skidding with a shake of his head. Blood flowed from the wound as they circled each other. They charged again and collided in the air, but Baldrake stayed low and grabbed Chaulle by the front paw, biting down hard and breaking the thick bone.

Chaulle fell to the ground, rolling from the momentum to come to a stop in a cloud of dust. Blood ran from both wolves. Before Chaulle could push himself up on his three legs, Baldrake was on top of him, pushing him back to the ground. 'Stay down, or I will end this.'

Slumping back down with a yelp of pain, Chaulle muttered, 'Just kill me. There's no hope for us. We are dead anyway.'

Baldrake stood up from Chaulle and moved to the side as he said, 'No. There is hope. I was not lying about my son. He is named Beldrin, and he is a fine young wolf. I have other... friends in the mine. They're going to break out soon, and so shall I. Come with us. We could use your help.'

High on the walls, the crowd was booing the show of mercy.

'Thank you all for coming. I am afraid our evening's entertainment has concluded. Please be sure to come the morrow, though; we have something great in store,' Veal Temur said before he turned and left the hall.

Guards ran out from the gates to surround the two wolves. Baldrake ambled away with his escort and looked back as Chaulle slowly got to his feet, his broken paw dangling in the air as he limped away.

Cold and wet, the floor of the gaol cell was a breeding ground for sickness. Blood flowed from their backs as they sat huddled with another fifteen prisoners of the mine. After only one day, they were whipped, stoned, spat on, and humiliated by the guards patrolling the area. Gordon lay coughing blood, his body trembling terribly. One prisoner approached him as he lay on the ground and was grabbed by Malachai as he jumped to his feet and lifted the man high off the ground by his shirt's collar, then whispered to him, 'You touch that man, and you will die! Do we understand each other?'

A frenzy of commotion followed as the other prisoners all fled to the distant corners at the sign of danger and sat huddled together as the two men conversed.

Still in the air, the prisoner pleaded, 'Please, I didn't mean to... I was just going to give him this...' Producing from his jacket pocket blue-coloured leaves, he showed them to Malachai and said, 'His wounds are infected; he is fevered. This will help. I swear it.'

Gently, he lowered the man, and said, 'This better not be any trick.'

He was a rag-tag old man, with marks of old lacerations covering his body. *More scars than a man who has survived a hundred wars*, Malachai thought as he watched the man walk over to Gordon. He placed a big red leaf on the ground, then bunched up the smaller blue leaves and ground them as much as possible, occasionally spitting onto the blue leaves as he worked at them. He then rolled up the big leaf into a small ball with the blueish paste inside and fed it to Gordon. 'Swallow it whole; believe me, you do not want to taste it, and I don't want you vomiting everything out.'

Unable to speak, Gordon nodded as he trembled with fever and did as he was told. The big man kept an awfully cautious eye on what was happening.

After some time, the coughing lessened, then stopped altogether. Weak, but now able to think for himself, he extended his arm and said, 'Well met, my friend. And thank you. I might just survive this yet because of you. I am Gordon; that big fellow over there is Malachai. Sorry, he is a bit overprotective.' Out of breath and exhausted, he let fall his arm to the ground, and immediately Malachai was at his side. 'Gordon! Are you okay?'

Trying to wave him off, Gordon looked at him with a smile. 'Yes... I'm... fine.' The words came in between gasps of air.

The old man lowered himself and gripped Gordon's hand as he said, 'I am Phineas; welcome to the pits.'

Later, during the night, while all the prisoners were asleep, Gordon softly called out to Malachai; and after that didn't wake the sleeping giant, he threw a small stone at him.

Startled, Malachai looked around and eventually saw Gordon waving him over. All the prisoners were still asleep; some coughed, some snored, and some twisted and turned, moaning from the aches and pains they had endured. Looking around the cell, he asked, 'How long have these people been here?'

'I don't know, but I wish I could help them,' Gordon said, his voice sounding much more alive than before. He sat up as Malachai slumped down next to him and said, 'Okay, today didn't go very well. But I believe that this happened for a reason.'

Malachai scratched at his beard and said, 'Coming tomorrow, you mustn't slack in your duties. This is no joke. You won't last long here. That said, I saw something suspicious while we were being beaten half to death, down in the quarry,' he shook his head. 'But it was probably nothing.'

'Please, Malachai. Anything might help us. What did you see?'

Deeply concerned for his friend, he sighed as he said, 'While they were beating us, I saw a cave, or tunnel rather, heavily guarded at the bottom of the pit. They don't guard any of the other tunnels at all; they just patrol them every so often. *This* one is different.'

Gordon was thinking rapidly, trying to sum up all he could, then said, 'We have to get into that cave. Lady Rose said the man lives in a cave, right?'

'Aye, she did.'

The day was bitter, with a thin layer of frost covering the ground and snow drifting slowly down from the heavens, but the sweat still ran down the faces of the prisoners as they pushed the heavy mine carts filled with rubble and ore. Some were digging in the caves; some filled the carts, while others hauled them away to the dumping site. At the lower level of the pit, Gordon made himself look busy, moving rocks around near the guarded tunnel, waiting for the opportunity to slip in. A loud stream of curses followed as Malachai's cart tipped over and sent the contents strewn all over the ground, attracting the attention of the guards. Nearby prisoners shouted their curses, knowing what would happen next, and started arguing with the big man—soon a fight broke out between the prisoners.

With no other guards in the area, the guards stationed at the entrance to the tunnel had to intervene. Leaving their posts, they made their way to the brawling men and started pulling them apart from each other. Gordon slipped into the cave unnoticed.

The cave coursed deep but wasn't dark. Lanterns hung along the walls, illuminating the corridors. And the deeper he went, the more he realised that someone must, in fact, live down here. From room to room, he would see a chair in a corner, a couch in the opposite corner, a table in the middle of nowhere, then drawers in a room with a bed. All the furniture looked to be of fine quality.

Then, at the end of one corridor branching off to the left, he saw an enormous iron door standing ajar and made his way closer and thought, *whoever lives here must have great trust and loyalty from his men.* He opened the door slowly, hoping it wouldn't make a sound, but the screeching hinges were deafening to his ears. *Someone must have heard that.* Finally, with the door open, he peered inside and saw a bright golden, almost red, blazing light coming from within an iron-barred vault only four feet across, with a big, old steel lock on the door.

Jewels and precious artefacts lay scattered on the floor, but they were not the objects of his attention. The light was blinding, and as he looked closer; he saw it came from a crystal at the top of an old staff... a wizard's staff—Rose's staff—placed on a stone pillar standing four feet high. Next to it lay the shield of Nethas.

Hearing voices, Gordon ducked and dived to get out of the tunnel, quickly making his way back to the entrance unnoticed. Lucky for him, the guards were still busy with the mess made by Malachai. Eerie silence met his ears as he exited, followed by a loud crack from a whip. Then he saw the big man and his stomach pulled into a knot.

Stretched over a barrel with his hands tied, the skin on his back peeled open as the whip came down again and again. Malachai didn't make a sound; he wouldn't give them the satisfaction. He merely kept his eyes forward and bit down on his teeth.

After the severe beating they gave him, they untied him from the barrel and let him slip unconscious to the ground. 'Stay back!' yelled a guard as Gordon approached his friend. 'Stay back, or you will be next!'

Gordon halted a few feet away and saw the splashes of blood and bits of flesh lying on the ground next to the barrel. He clenched his teeth as he bunched his fists. The guards walked away and spat on the big guy, then one stared Gordon in the eye and said, 'Take him away before I get too excited.'

Phineas grabbed Gordon's arm and pulled him away from the guard before he did something he would regret, then walked over to Malachai and said, 'Let's get him in the wheelbarrow and take him away.'

They lay down thin sheets on the icy floor for the big man, and before Phineas could move away, Gordon gripped his arm and said, 'Please, help him.'

'Are you mad? Help the man who almost got me a whipping? I think not!' Indignant, Phineas turned to walk away, but Gordon gripped his arm again and said, 'I will get you out of here, Phineas. But you have to help him.'

A wishful face stared back at him before Phineas said, 'No one escapes this place. We will all die here. That includes you, my friend.'

'Trust me, Phineas. We cannot stay here for long; this was always temporary.'

Studying Gordon's eyes, Phineas jerked his arm free and muttered a curse as he fetched more of the leaves, then moved over to Malachai, who lay unmoving on the sheets.

'You better not be lying to me. Well, come on, don't just stand there, help me turn him over.' With some care, they flipped the big man onto his belly and administered the herbal paste on the wounds at his back. Then they turned him back, and Phineas shoved a ball of the leaf paste down his mouth, holding closed the big jaws to ensure he did not vomit it out. 'It should stop him from getting infected. Won't do anything for the pain, though.'

'We're not lying. Just don't spread the word. Thank you.'

The day had been hard, and Gordon was very unhappy about the fact that he was happy to be back in these cages.

Time passed slowly as Gordon lay waiting for the big man to wake, thinking on ways to get out of the pits. He heard the groaning of the big man as he slept and thought of Baldrake, wondering if the old wolf were even still alive.

☿

With weapon raised, blood running down his legs, the fighter moved about the arena, catching glimpses of the black mass of death moving stealthily behind the high stacked bales of hay added to the edges of the field. Even the crowd did not want to betray the whereabouts of the wolf, as they had begun to enjoy watching the wolf in his deadly games of cat and mouse. It was like being hunted by a ghost; first, you would catch a glimpse of him on your right, then a glimpse on your left, then out of nowhere, he would stand above you or next to you, and it would be too late.

The fighter moved on, trembling with fear. Baldrake was not at all pleased that he had to kill all these men and animals, but he knew that something bigger was at stake here. He knew he needed to get Gordon and Malachai their weapons; he knew they would need him in the coming battle. The fighter suddenly stopped and stood with his axe rattling in his hands as he felt and heard the warm breath on the back of his neck. Slowly he turned, wetting himself as he did so; and just as he looked into the eyes of the demon wolf, Baldrake opened his jaws and clenched down on the man's neck. But instead of ripping out the man's throat, he felt a wave of compassion and closed the airway of his victim until he stopped moving.

At first, it was only once a day they brought him out, then twice a day. Now he barely had time to rest in the cell before being escorted back to the arena to perform another execution. The high cleric found that instead of just a public hanging, he could make a fortune by letting them die in the arena, or rather, showing his 'mercy' by giving them a 'fighting chance' for their life against the demon wolf.

Little did Veal Temur know that every time they ushered the wolf to the arena, he was busy laying out his escape route. He had seen Gordon and Malachai's weapons lying in a bag on the floor of one of the rooms as he walked past, and noticed guards shaking ice from their jackets on one passage, indicating that it must be the way out. The guards were getting more comfortable around him as he made jokes with them about the oncoming execution he would administer. Some guards even asked him to kill the prisoner in certain ways.

☿

Malachai was sitting on a wooden bench, leaning against the iron bars of the cell, eating the cold slop the guards threw at them when Gordon joined him and whispered, 'I'm sorry for what happened. But know this—the pain you suffered wasn't in vain. I found the items, both of them.'

Every move Malachai made brought more pain. Putting down his empty bowl, he said, 'So where are they?'

'I didn't have enough time to get them out. I'll have to go back for them at the same time we make good our escape.'

Shouts from the guards roused everyone as they unlocked the cages and hit the iron bars with their wooden batons. Everyone filed out of the cages and were ushered to their respective duties.

'Aye, the sooner the better.' The big man nodded and rose as the guard approached.

Digging in the tunnels, Malachai lay the shovel over his broad shoulder and wiped his forehead as he said, 'Who lives in that there tunnel at the bottom of the pit?'

Looking around to see if the big brute was hopefully speaking to someone else, Phineas was disappointed as he saw Malachai staring straight at him. 'Hectar lives there. He's the high cleric's personal guard. Why do you want to know?'

Malachai shrugged. 'Just curious, I guess.'

'Well, don't be.' Phineas turned and started shovelling again. He could feel the big man staring at him and was obliged to speak. 'How are your wounds?'

The shovel dropped to the floor with a loud clangour. 'They're healing quickly, thanks to you,' Malachai said as he walked to stand at the entrance of the tunnel, gazing over the mining pit. A broken-down wooden lift stood on the side of the pit that used to run all the way to the top, high above. Now, to the right of the lift, a wooden walkway filed up all the way to the top; this was their only way up and out. Once they get out of the pit, the rest was fairly simple: make a run for the hills and get lost in the forest. Malachai stared at the walkway and rubbed at his beard, and said, 'Do we have any rope lying around?'

'There should be rope in those crates over there,' Phineas gestured to his left.

CHAPTER THIRTEEN

The morning began the same, the routine never changing. They were shoved out of the cages and pushed along to file out before the guards to be assigned a duty for the day. Gordon knew the assignment roster by now and waited near the end of the line to be placed near the walkway. They would start the hard, labour-intensive day soon. The guard yelled out, 'Sector thirteen for you lot,' and gestured to a section of the inmates.

Strange and unbecoming stares followed Gordon as he walked to his sector to labour on for the day. Unease gripped him. *Do they all know what we plan? This can't be my imagination.* Trying their best not to get noticed this day, he and Malachai stuck to their work with their faces to the ground, avoiding any conflict or guard.

As nightfall approached with the end of their shift, Gordon left his sector to collect the ropes they had stashed the day before and ran to the walkway leading up and out of the pit. Hugging the sides, he waited for a chance to run under the walkway to quickly start climbing. Time was a factor tonight. Dozens of guards patrolled up and down the walkway, keeping a keen watch on the workings of the prisoners down below. Burning from the constant chafe of the sharp rocks he had to move all day long, his hands were bleeding as he gripped the underside of the walkway and started his ascent. It was a tedious climb to the top, having to grab at the nearly vertical struts holding up the structure, stepping on the supporting beams, gripping ropes and climbing further until he neared the top of the pit when he heard a voice shout from below, 'Hectar! Come out and fight me, you coward!'

Gordon looked down and saw that the guards had huddled all the prisoners together with Malachai standing a few feet in front of the line, swinging his arms and stretching his muscles.

He cursed and thought, *This is happening way too fast. I needed more time to get down.* He looped the rope around a tree a bit further from the edge and started his descent as fast as he could.

'Get back in line, prisoner! Or do you wish for another whipping?' one of the guards called out as he unclipped the whip from his side.

Malachai crossed his arms as he glared at the guard and said, 'You touch me tonight and I will break every limb in your wretched little body... boy!' Turning back to the cave, he yelled, 'Hectar! Come out here and face me like a man, you ball-less fop!'

Infuriated by the prisoner's lack of respect, the guard charged at him with his spear and swung down with such force that the shaft snapped in half as it was caught in mid-air. Puzzled, the guard looked at his half, then at the other half still grasped by the big man.

'Now, boy, didn't I tell you not to touch me tonight?' He threw the spear as the guard turned to run, catching him across the back and sending him tumbling down the slope.

Circled by a dozen guards now, Malachai stood ready, waiting for his next attacker, when a shout rang out, 'Leave him! I want to teach this one some manners.'

Hectar ambled out of his tunnel and headed in his direction.

217

Graceful and strong, a dangerous combination. Let's hope he ain't quick as well. As he approached, the guards shifted out of the way as Hectar said, 'You have a big mouth.'

'Aye, and big muscles to back it,' countered Malachai.

Hectar chuckled as the two men sized each other up and circled one another. 'It's a shame I have to break you, but I can't have a prisoner starting riots and giving hope to the others. It would sow too much chaos.'

Malachai grinned and said, 'Too bad indeed.'

'Get back to your cages! Now!' shouted one of the guards to the prisoners, and Hectar turned and said, 'Belay that order. I want them to watch as I crush their dreams once and for all.'

Shouts, curses and cheers echoed in the pits as guards and prisoners alike stood watching the confrontation, waiting for the first blow to land.

'Why are you doing this?' Hectar asked.

Malachai shrugged and said, 'I don't like not knowing who's better.'

Hectar shook his head and pulled at his lip. 'Admirable, but stupid. You're probably one of those that can't even read. All brawn and no brain.'

Malachai broke out laughing, clutching his stomach as he forced it out. Confused, the guards looked at each other, then all joined in, laughing at the big man. A loud crack was followed by a dreadful thump. The laughs ceased instantly as everyone gasped and saw Hectar lying on the ground, blood running from his nose and mouth.

Oh, please get up, please get up. Malachai stared down at the unmoving body for a while and, with a sigh of relief, he saw the big mass stir. A guard was at Hectar's side, trying to help him up, but was immediately pushed away as the big man struggled to get to his feet and said, 'Get away from me, you fool.' He held his jaw and moved it about. 'You move fast for a big man. I will not make the mistake of calling you stupid again.'

Malachai threw a few punches and countered a few jabs when a monstrous left landed on the right side of his face. His teeth immediately felt loose, and the iron taste of blood filled his mouth. He spat on the ground and said, 'You hit like a little old woman. Is that the best you got?'

The two men charged at each other and engaged in a bear hug. Malachai was able to turn to throw his opponent over his shoulder, but Hectar was too heavy even for him. Realising he was in a compromising position, he quickly sent an elbow to the ribs of his opponent and heard it hit true as the air exploded from Hectar's mouth.

Hectar staggered back, searching for air as another blow landed on his face, tearing open his brow ridge. Any lesser man would have been finished after a blow like that. Hectar, however, recovered quickly. As Malachai charged in to finish his opponent, he unexpectedly caught a fist square in the face, breaking his nose. Blood gushed out as his left eye swelled shut.

Staggering back and struggling to breathe, they fought on. No one realised that Malachai was slowly herding the fight ever closer to the dilapidated old lift. The fight was intense but was slowing as the two men tired. Dazed, Hectar rose from the ground after a monstrous uppercut, his vision swimming. Air was driven from his lungs as he realised too late that his opponent had charged in, driving his shoulder deep into his ribcage. His feet left the ground as he was carried backwards until he came down hard on the rusted and broken gear system of the lift.

Groans and creaks echoed from the lift as it tilted to one side, and ropes snapped in loud succession. Pulleys were freed as the lift plummeted down, crashing into the walkway and bringing the entire structure down with it. Prisoners and guards alike ran for their lives to get away from the falling debris. Guards on the walkway jumped to their deaths as the structure collapsed. Billowing clouds of dust obscured the area as the structure hit the ground. Wooden beams and guards fell from the sky onto those unfortunate enough to be below them. It was another full hand of chaos. During the ensuing madness, Malachai grabbed Phineas and slipped out of sight to join up with Gordon at the rope tied at the top of the pit.

'Ooh, he really did a number on you, big guy. You look terrible,' Gordon said as he saw the two men approaching.

'Oh, shut up. You should see *him*.' Malachai chuckled and said, 'Do you have the items?'

Bending down, Gordon picked up a small round shield about twenty inches across and another item, wrapped in a dark blanket, and said, 'Come on, we have to go.'

Phineas stared at the two with eyes wide. He stuttered and mumbled as he grabbed the rope to begin his climb to freedom.

This night I have broken a proud man, and how did it make me feel? Nothing... I feel nothing. Maybe if he was a good man, I would have felt something... but I don't know. Guess I won't know if he has a son. A daughter, perhaps, waiting for him to come home. To surprise and lavish them with gifts. No. It does not matter. He protects and does the deeds for a wicked man. Halfway to the top. These bastards got what they deserved. Malachai pulled himself higher with his bloodied hand, then glanced back over his shoulder to look at the chaos below. *Things are only going to get worse now, and for that, I apologise.*

After the agonising climb to the top, they ducked out of sight as guards franticly ran past to help the others trapped at the bottom of the pit, even as the prisoners battered them with rocks and tools, taking the opportunity in the chaos to ignite the old lift. The blaze spread rapidly. Phineas turned to them and said, 'Thank you. I will not forget this.'

Both men nodded and the big guy said, 'Keep low and out of sight. Run as fast as you can to the forest, and don't look back.' They turned as Phineas set off to their right to disappear in the darkness. Running for their lives with no weapons and barely clothed, they would not last long in the bitter cold of the mountains. They would need to wait out the night in a cave somewhere, or they would die.

A horse whinnied in the distance, and shouts rose to the air. Gordon knew they had found the rope. *Shit. Should have cut it. They aren't far behind.*

Thick snow blanketed the area, playing tricks on the mind as the moonlight reflected from the white surface. As quick as they could, they trudged through the thick blanket, contending with the bushes and trees as they came into view. Unsure of their direction, they just ran to get ahead; there was no time to figure anything out right now. Malachai slammed through the bushes and tree branches as he led the way through the forest's darkness. Gordon turned to see how far the guards behind them were, and as he turned back, he saw the big guy was gone... He skidded to a halt mere inches from the edge of the cliff as thoughts raced in his mind.

'No! Not this!' Gordon remembered his vision and fell to the ground, sticking out his arm as he heard a snap and a scream. An excessive amount of weight suddenly pulled on him as Malachai grabbed his hand. The thick root he was holding onto had snapped and fallen down the mountain as he dangled off the side.

Gordon held on with everything he had, but the slippery, icy slope would soon see him slowly dragged over the edge. He could feel the muscles in his back wanting to tear from the weight they held onto. Turning red in his face, the veins on his forehead and neck bulged out, ready to burst, but he would not let go. The horses were drawing closer, and he heard a guard shout, 'This side!'

'Let me go, Gordon. I'm proud to call you a brother. Don't let my death be in vain. Finish what we started!' Malachai opened his hand and shook off Gordon's grip on him, and fell in silence down the cliff—just like in Gordon's vision.

'No!' Gordon cried out as he watched the big man fall, their eyes locking until he disappeared through the mist. Tears ran down his face; snot ran down and out of his nose.

'Don't make a move!' said a guard as he nocked an arrow and pointed it at Gordon, where he lay whimpering in the snow. A dull thump came from his right, followed by an angry growl. The guard twisted in his saddle and saw the flash of Baldrake's fangs just before they sank into the back of his neck. Momentum carried them crashing into the thick snow as the wolf ripped at the guard's armour, tearing it to pieces as blood stained the white of the snow until there was no movement beneath him. Baldrake looked up and said, 'I am truly sorry.

He was a fine warrior.' Moving closer, he crouched next to the desolate Gordon, and continued, 'Get on, we need to run. I can't get you up on my own.'

'He's gone, Baldrake,' Gordon whispered. 'He just let go.'

'What he did, he did for a reason. Don't let that reason go to waste. Get up! Fight for him as he would have for you.'

Dragging himself off the ground and out of the snow, Gordon clambered onto the wolf, who rose and said, 'Hang on tight; this might be a little bumpy.' Baldrake walked up to the bag he dropped earlier and picked it up in his mouth. 'Here, take these.'

Cold and wet, he raised his hand from Baldrake's sticky mane to his eyes, the darkness making it hard to see. 'Is this blood? You're soaked in it!'

'It's not all mine. Don't worry,' the wolf said as he darted off into the forest, his vision as clear as day in the ominous night. To Gordon everything was shapes and blurs, haunting him for his failure to protect his friend. Every tree looked as if it was trying to snatch him from the wolf's back with long taloned claws; every big rock was a troll waiting to tear him in half. But no other animal could touch him this night as Baldrake glided through the forest at extreme speed, the beating of his paws on the ground a distant drum to Gordon's ears.

For two days and two nights, Baldrake ran with Gordon on his back, stopping only at night to rest for the coming run the following morning. On the third day, he stopped just out of sight of Rose's village and, huffing and puffing, said, 'Better not to let them see you weeping on my back like a deprived infant.'

'How can you be so cold?' Gordon asked as he slid off the back of the wolf. 'Our friend just died, and you don't even blink.'

For a heartbeat, the Gar hound lost control and lashed out, snapping his jaws shut and snarling to reveal his fangs right before Gordon's face. Growling, he said, 'I have known Vasgath far longer than you. I fought side by side with him, and I would have died for him if I had the choice. He was a great man, and I respected him. Don't you ever forget that!' Turning away, Baldrake stomped off through the village, ignoring the men and women who ran to their huts, pointing at him and cursing in their language. Not looking back, he left Gordon behind with the items.

'I couldn't have been more of an idiot, could I? I'm sorry, my friend,' he said as he sighed, but the wolf was too far to hear. He saw for the first time how deeply he had wounded Baldrake with his words.

Waiting for them by the front door, excitement got the better of Rose as she rushed forward and said, 'Where is it?'

Begrudgingly, Gordon handed over the wrapped item and brushed past her into the house. He found Baldrake already lying in front of the fiery hearth, which was magically burning its due course. Upon entering the room, Rose made some hot elm's root for herself and Gordon to relax their nerves. Warming some milk over the fire, she poured it into a bowl and gave it to Baldrake. They sat and sipped the drinks in silence for a while before Lady Rose said, 'I'm glad to see that my little interference worked out well enough. Otherwise you would have probably never found the items.'

Gordon, half asleep, wasn't sure he had heard correctly. Placing his cup down on the ground, he said, 'What did you just say?'

Baldrake was lying in front of the hearth, not paying attention, but at the tone of Gordon's voice, he pitched his ears and listened. Rose, thinking nothing of it, shrugged and said, 'Yes, I notified Veal Temur of your whereabouts.'

Gordon rose from the couch, his voice soft and trembling as he said, 'So it was *you* who made us fall into that deep sleep. *You* who called those guard scum on us.'

'Well, you didn't think I would leave it to chance, did you? Where is that big friend of yours anyhow?'

'Dead! Because of *you!*' Gordon shouted, his rage returned. He picked up the cup and hurled it across the room straight at Rose's head; she expertly stopped the distraction in mid-air with her magic, only to be blindsided and taken off her feet by a monstrous tackle. Struggling for air, she tried to breathe and felt the bite of the blade against her throat. She looked up into Gordon's eyes and shivered as he pushed a little harder, then held her breath.

'Give me one good reason I shouldn't slip with this blade,' he growled.

Bewildered and frightened, Rose mumbled, 'Because I still have to cast the spell on the shield.'

Baldrake stepped closer and said, 'Let her up, Gordon.'

Unwillingly obeying the wolf, he backed off and let Rose push herself up to the couch to lean back against it, a trickle of blood running down the side of her throat.

Shaking her head, she rubbed her throat and looked at the blood on her hands as it came away from her neck, then said, 'Thank you, Baldrake.'

'Thank me? Oh, my dear, you misunderstand; I am probably more intent on sinking my teeth into your neck and ripping out your spine than he is on cutting off your head. I just need to know why. Why did you betray us like that?'

'I did it to help you. If I hadn't gotten you locked up, it would have taken you weeks to find those items. I'm so sorry about your friend. I truly hoped for all of you to return safely.'

Baldrake sat on his haunches, eyeing the sorceress with much hatred as she explained herself.

'It was the only way I could get Veal Temur to believe that I had nothing to do with this,' Rose continued.

'By setting us up,' Gordon said as he fell back on the couch.

'Yes. For that I am sorry.' Tears flowed from her eyes and down her face as she spoke.

Baldrake turned to face the fire, and said, 'How long will it take for you to cast the spell? We need to get back to the mainland.'

Gordon jumped to his feet. 'We can't just let her go, not after what she's done!'

'Unfortunately, we must,' Baldrake said as he kept staring into the flames, then continued, 'She did what she had to, to protect her people. We must honour that. Remember this, Gordon: if we live without rules or a code, we will be no better than those we are trying to stop.'

Wiping more blood from her neck, Rose said, 'It will take half a day. It is a complicated spell.'

'In the coming morning we will hold a funeral for Vasgath,' the wolf calmly stated, then looked back to Lady Rose and said, 'The day following that, we leave. Is Captain Bellark's ship ready?'

Knowing this could cause more problems, Rose quickly answered, 'Actually, they have already left. But don't worry, there is another means to get you back, and it is much quicker and more comfortable. I promise.'

Gordon's head sank into his hands as he mumbled, 'Just great.'

On the hill next to the village, the three stood before a cross planted in the ground. Malachai's massive hammer stuck out from the soil; the haft plunged into the earth. A studded wooden crossbar tied just below the head of the hammer carried a sign that read, "In remembrance of Malachai, our brother."

Gordon cleared his throat and said, 'For the short time I came to know you, I have seen you care more for others than you do yourself. An honourable man you were. A warrior at heart. I will miss you.'

Baldrake joined in, 'Vasgath, I never thought the day would come that I would stand before a human's grave, mourning the loss of friend, warrior, and brother. But you made that happen; you showed me that there is honour in your race. Never did I see you humiliate the dying during the battles as so many countless of our comrades did. You always let them die with dignity. Rest in peace, my friend. I will see you beyond the gates someday.'

Rose bent down and placed a white rose atop the hammer's head, kissed her middle and index finger, and pressed them to the metal head of the hammer as she said, 'I am sorry for the role I played in your death. For that, there is no forgiveness. I only wish to make up for my failures now. I await your judgement in the afterlife. Fare thee well.'

Throughout the day, they could hear the chanting echo through the village as Rose bound the magic with the shield. Strange flickering lights and eerie noises were heard as winds howled their anger, threatening to destroy the village with their magical malice. Gordon lay on the couch, resting while Baldrake paced up and down in front of the hearth, impatiently waiting for the sorceress to finish.

Dusk had approached, accompanied by the bitter, icy winds. The cold air drifted through the house as they heard the door unlatch, swing open, and latch back into place. Gordon came to his feet and peered at the door to see Rose enter, holding a magnificent shield in her hands.

'This cannot be the same shield, can it?'

'Yes,' she said with a smile.

'I can't believe it. Well, I can. But... how?'

'The magic reforged the shield. As I said before, this is no ordinary shield. Otherwise, I would not have sent you on your mission.'

He smiled as he strapped the leather bindings to his arm from the back of the shield, and said, 'This is magnificent.'

The plain, round, silver shield they'd brought back from the mines had been reforged into a bigger shield with a golden hue, and the most spectacular design etched into the metal. 'Is that a dragon on the front?' Gordon asked.

'No, it is a phoenix. Some believe them even greater magical creatures than the dragons.'

Sliding his hand over the rim, he jerked his hand away and saw the blood on his fingers. A very sharp concealed blade lined the inside of the rim all around. *That could be useful.*

Settling down on the couch, she said, 'Trust in the shield. It will protect you.'

CHAPTER FOURTEEN

R ose had stayed up all night crying about the death of Malachai. She felt, deep inside her, a voice telling her that she did what she had to, for her people and for herself. *But at what cost? The death of an innocent man; a good man, I judge.*

Trying to keep her mind off the haunting images, she had packed some things for Gordon and Baldrake all while they slept soundly in their rooms upstairs.

Rose literally thought of everything by trying not to think at all. She packed various foods, several blankets and pillows, canteens filled with water, some flint rock and iron pyrite. She conjured up clothes, hoping they would fit, even for the wolf. Like a mother whose firstborn was going on his very first camping trip alone, she carried on obsessively.

Early in the morning, Gordon came through to the kitchen and found her still packing, running around bewildered by the thoughts in her head.

'What are you doing?' he asked as he looked at the piles of items lying around on the floor and table. With barely any room to walk, he squeezed past one pile, trying not to collapse it, then slowly and reluctantly pulled out a pink formal lady's hat from one of the clothing piles. 'Are you okay?' he asked as he looked at her.

'You don't really care about that, but yes, I'm fine. Go wake Baldrake. You two need to be on your way.'

Dropping the hat back on the pile, he turned and stalked from the kitchen to the lounge and sat down on the couch in front of the ever-burning fire. Baldrake joined him soon after, yawning as he jumped on the couch opposite him. 'Where's Rose?'

Mockingly, Gordon gestured with his thumb towards the kitchen and said, 'I think Malachai has been haunting her. She's caving. Go see for yourself.'

Jumping off the couch, he moved to the kitchen and, upon entering, noticed the point of Gordon's conclusion. Concerned but unwilling to show it, he announced his presence, *'Korviete, Tinde.'*

Startled, she looked up and said, *'Korviete, Maksouel.'*

Gordon waited for a loud outburst from the wolf, but it never came. *If the big guy was here, it would have been more fun.* Annoyed, he decided to find out what had spoiled his laugh and walked back to the kitchen. Rose was sitting on a chair, her face in her hands, covering her eyes, her elbows resting on the table. Baldrake sat next to her, whispering in a language unknown to him, and yet he thought he could understand what was being said.

Silently, he turned and left to ready his gear, and awaited the wolf. After walking around the house for some time, keeping himself occupied by looking at paintings and studying the craftsmanship of the art, he went back down to the kitchen to move things along. Only a few neatly packed items remained; all the chaos that was there before had just disappeared.

'I am ready for you to depart. Please take those as a token of my appreciation. They are just a few items I packed for your journey ahead.'

The reluctance in him to be nice to her gnawed at him. He wanted to throw it in her face, but he sighed and slung the pack over his shoulder. 'Let's get moving.'

Rose ushered them through a long corridor lined with scribbles of paper. She noticed them staring at the pieces and said, 'For every time we fought, I wrote it down. I don't actually know why, but it felt like it helped, so I created this hallway to remember everything I hate about him.' Turning left down a passage, they carried on; and on the third passage to the right, went through a big, empty hall. They stopped before a door at the very back that looked as though it just led outside to the village. She said, 'This is as far as I can go. Once you step through this door, you will be back on the mainland, close to Millanthross. Remember the spell; I cannot go through this door. But because of you two and a great man who gave his life for this cause, I may one day again set foot upon the mainland. Good luck with your journey.'

A long, awkward moment of silence followed as Gordon stared at Rose with his murky eyes, then said, 'Thank you for your kindness and help.' Then he turned and vanished through the door.

'*Aghtjer* (Farewell), *Tinde* (Lady). May we meet again at more suitable times,' Baldrake bowed his head and also walked through the door.

Flames rose high as black smoke drifted up to the sky, blanketing the city with ash. Buildings, houses, and shops were destroyed, their charred remains standing vacant, debris lying everywhere. Blood stained the still standing parts of the walls, and bodies lay at their feet. Crows were feasting on the carcasses, squawking at them as they walked through the deserted streets of Millanthross. Streams of blood ran down the cobbled roads and into the rivers.

'What madness is this? Why would they do this?' Gordon asked as he looked upon the horrible sight.

'Madmen don't need reasons.'

Baldrake stopped and pitched his ears, and said, 'Wait, I hear something.'

Listening intently, they stood in the middle of the street, carefully surveying the area. A clatter came from a distant garbage bin at the corner where the barbershop used to be.

'It could be a trap,' Gordon said as he unsheathed his sword and stayed to the side to set their own ambush. Nodding in agreement,

Baldrake cautiously walked closer; and suddenly noticing the stench in the city as the wind wafted it into his face, he almost vomited. Shaking his head to clear his mind, he walked on, keeping Gordon in the corner of his eye. Upon reaching the bin, he smacked it with his paw and sent it tumbling down the street. A scream, followed by some more clatter, rang through the dead city as the bin rolled on the cobbles. The trash stirred and groaned.

Baldrake lowered his voice to a deathly growl and said, 'Move very slowly out from the bin, and throw any weapon on the ground.'

The contents of the bin shook as a little figure emerged, trash covering its entire body and face. Unable to see with all the old rotten food and rubbish stuck to its face, the figure pleaded, 'Please, do not kill Melche, Melche has nothing you want!' Hearing the sudden low laugh, the little figure cleaned the mess from his face and said, 'Baldrake, is that you? It *is* you!'

Running to the wolf, trash falling from him as far as he went, he jumped up and flung his arms around the front of Baldrake's broad chest, hugging the wolf.

Baldrake laughed and was filled with joy to know that the little creature had survived this terrible onslaught.

'Well, well. Now *this* is a surprise,' Gordon said as he sheathed his weapon and approached. Melche turned, saw the murky-eyed warrior and ran up to him. Instinctively Gordon held out his arms to await the little mekkel, but to his amazement, all he got was a kick to the shin. 'Ouch! What was that for?' he asked as he hopped around on one leg.

'That's for leaving Melche to die here in this place!' the mekkel said as he stood with arms folded.

'Sorry, my friend, but I thought you would be safer here than where we went,' Gordon said, still rubbing his shin. 'Besides, I bet you have great new stories you can tell us now.'

With his hands to his sides, Melche looked like a furious little teapot. 'Do not move and say nothing!'

Confused, they stood in the middle of the cobbled road as Melche put his two index fingers to his mouth and whistled, then shouted,

'Come out, men! Melche knows these two.'

All around them, from the broken-down shops, sewers, and rubbish bins, came men and women holding anything they could use as a weapon. About fifty people surrounded them now, carrying knives, gaffs, shovels and pitchforks for protection.

Unclipping a scabbard from his belt, Gordon handed Malachai's huge hunting knife to Melche and said, 'A leader needs a trusty weapon.'

Awestruck at the thought of wielding the knife, he held out his hands with eyes wide and clipped the scabbard in place with great care, unsheathed the blade, and swung it around with both hands. 'He gave this to Melche? Where is he? Where is the big guy? Melche has missed him, Melche needs to train with him.'

Gordon knelt by the old mekkel and put his hand on his shoulder as he said, 'I am sorry, Melche, he did not make it back with us.'

'But he was supposed to come back.' Lowering his head, it was clear Melche's heart ached for the loss of his friend. A quick sob escaped him as he tried to hold back the tears. 'So much death and destruction. What did we do to deserve this?'

'Where are the people responsible for this chaos? Are they still near?'

'Yes, the main force has left, but a few stayed behind. They are just on the outskirts of the city.'

Gordon rose and looked at the people surrounding him, and said, 'Brothers and sisters! Will you join us to fight these bastards?!' At first, only a few muttered and shoved around. Growing impatient and angry, he shouted, 'Don't you want to see the people who have slaughtered your families, your brothers and sisters, mothers or fathers at the end of your blade? Do you not want retribution for the crimes committed here? Stand with me and show these barbarians what we are made of.'

Weapons clanged against each other and were lifted to the air as shouts went up.

Barnicus Bree walked up to them and reached out his hands to lay them on their shoulders, but quickly retracted his arms as the thought of having to touch them echoed in his mind. 'I am sorry about your friend.'

Melche gazed upon the people surrounding them, and said, 'Go to the gates; we will meet you there. Melche needs to take them to Melche's shop first.' Tugging on Gordon's clothes, he continued, 'Come, Melche has something to give you.'

Running through the streets, Baldrake trembled as he looked upon the sights and thought back to the war on Gar. But even that brutal war did not compare with this. He had been in plenty of battles, and he had known and seen his fair share of cruelty. But this he could not consider war. No, this was just murderous intent. Small children hung from spears thrust into the ground, crows feasting on the small, limp hanging bodies. Women lay at the bottom of those spears, hacked to pieces as they reached for those children. *They must be the mothers of those poor children, made to watch them die before getting hacked up themselves.* 'Sick bastards! You will pay!'

Gordon stopped as they entered town square and saw the bodies piled up in the centre, the now-dried stream of blood snaking its way down the street as big as a river. Melche didn't stop, ignoring the deathly scene altogether, and ran straight into the blacksmith's shop, gesturing for them to follow. 'Come, quick.' Melche slammed the door shut and jammed a table against it.

'Follow Melche,' repeated the mekkel as he ran to the back of the shop, past the fire pits and down a flight of stairs. Rounding a corner, he came to a locked metal door and removed a key that hung around his neck and forced it into the keyhole.

The latch of the lock released its hold, and the door slid open with loud creaks. A musty odour coming from the room made them pull their faces away for a few heartbeats, and when they looked back, they marvelled at the creations before them.

Melche jumped up and down excitedly, clapping his hands as he said, 'You like? You like? Melche made them for you.'

'I knew you had some talent, Melche, but this is incredible.' They moved into the vault, staring in amazement at three wooden stands displaying the most amazing armour they had seen. Gordon approached the set resembling his build and looked back at Melche.

'Try it on, Melche did not make it to be looked at,' glowered the mekkel.

Gordon donned the armour and was astounded at how light it felt. Covering only the essentials, it would not slow him down in a fight. Melche stared at him and said, 'Made with two things in mind; manoeuvrability and speed.' Two fierce eyes were on the chest, enveloped by fire. The detail, incredible. 'Melche wasn't sure if you had any, so Melche gave you stomach muscles.' He chuckled as Gordon smiled at his joke. Each forearm had a separate piece of armour stretching from the hand to the elbow. Four metal wolves' fangs rose from these guards and around his neck as well, the curve of the fang moving away to stop a blade swung at his neck. There were pants with metal plates bound into the sides of the upper and lower leg, front and back. Gordon traced his finger over the matt-black armour and smiled.

Melche was helping Baldrake into his armour as Gordon stood admiring the work when the deep and husky voice of the wolf made him turn around. 'What do you think? Would I still scare my enemies if they saw me like this?'

'I would definitely say so, my friend.'

Completely scaled to improve movement, the armour rattled and clicked as the dark silver scales glided over one another as he moved. It ran all the way up his neck and to his head, where a solid metal piece resembling his features covered his eyes and down his snout with two massive metal fangs. There was no lower jaw. But the most impressive were the solid metal pieces going down his front legs to his paws, only half-open at the joints. Metal nails scratched and tapped on the floor as he moved. 'I don't want to sound ungrateful, but one of my greatest talents is stealth.'

Melche paused and said, 'Melche will file the nails down a bit. Not a problem.'

There was a third set of armour, one with a hammer as an emblem on the centre of the chest. It was much bigger and full-length—sized more for a warrior who faces their enemies head-on, without fear or doubt.

'Thank you, Melche. This is a magnificent gift and will surely be used a lot in the coming days,' Gordon said as Baldrake nodded in agreement. 'We have to go.'

They turned and left the shop and the other armour behind.

Melche ran back to the armour and stuck a note on it before he wheeled around and ran for the door. 'Wait for Melche!'

Running through the remnants of Millanthross, Melche had fallen three times already as the long hunting knife kept swinging between his legs, sending him head over heels as his foot got caught and landing chin first on the ground like a shot-down dragon, a small cloud of dust erupting from him every time. The main gate facing inland to the northeast stood wide open and untouched by the assault, as though the enemy were welcomed into the city.

On their return to the pitchfork-wielding mob of townsfolk hiding behind the walls, they crouched and moved closer to the gate, stealthily sneaking forward to peer out at the diminished enemy force. One of the mob members came closer, holding a shovel in hand and nervously glanced at the three, and said, 'Sorry to interrupt, mister Melche, sir, but we were wondering what the plan of attack is.'

Gordon and Baldrake looked at each other with narrowed eyes before the young warrior said, 'Yes, Sir Melche. Please tell us what the plan is here.'

With a nervous chuckle, Melche gestured for the man to leave them and await his orders. 'Okay, so Melche might have exaggerated just a very teeny bit about the fight to the death with the dragon, and those ten murderers Melche disarmed on our way here, saving your lives and putting you all in my in debt.'

Baldrake cocked his head and said out loud, 'But Melche, I clearly remember that it was Vasgath who dealt the death blow to the dragon, and I am sure there were only six robbers on the road, and I believe you clung only to one of them.'

Irritated and angry, the mekkel stalked off and said, 'That's why Melche said Melche exaggerated a little!'

Gordon climbed up the stairs on his hands and feet to get a better view, keeping below the parapet of the wall. *Two big tents. Probably for the soldiers. And one smaller tent; must be for their commander. Near to the gate, these soldiers are not worried at all about any retaliation. They believe themselves invincible after their 'victory.' I can use that to our advantage. They will probably get drunk tonight. About twenty men that I can see, a lone guard standing at one corner, half-asleep by the looks of it. If only you were here, Malachai, then you could have led these folks to war. Although we outnumber them two to one, we don't stand a chance.*

Gordon sighed as Baldrake joined him and slumped down with his back to the wall. The "Ell-Shadack," or "Once-Dead," as they had come to be called, were hardened warriors and skilled fighters, not mere townsfolk parading around with pitchforks and shovels. Taking the piece of charcoal he'd picked up from a burnt-down shop, he drew various strategies on the floor to figure out which one would suit them best.

Baldrake studied the strategies as he walked along the wall. The first was a full-frontal attack in the daytime. The second was at night when the townsfolk would surround the camp and attack, shouting loudly to frighten the warriors. The third was only a sneak attack, with one man moving into the smaller tent at night. Fourth was to use some of the townsfolk as a distraction to pull some fighters away from the camp so the rest could attack the remaining fighters and their leader. And so the strategies carried on...

'Something is wrong with this setup,' Baldrake growled at Gordon.

Glancing up from his work, he saw the wolf looking through a peephole in the parapet and said, 'Has there been anything that wasn't wrong in the last few months? I think I have a way of evening the odds quickly,' he threw the piece of charcoal away. 'We wait for night.'

During the better part of the day, they took the courageous

townsfolk to a more secluded part of the city and taught them how to wield their weapons, attack their foe using a bow and arrow, and what a good defensive stance should be—bare essentials that might just save their lives.

The camp was silent and ghostly, as all soldiers were asleep, drunk in their beds. Gordon crept through unnoticed as he poured oil over the two big tents. Standing back, he took a branch from a campfire and cast it on the nearest tent. It erupted in flames, engulfing those within and spreading fast to the tent beside it. Howling men came crashing through the burning walls from all sides. Baldrake gave the silent command to Melche, and watched as a volley of arrows silently graced the night's sky to plummet into the ground and soldiers, killing most. Some were not so lucky to die instantly by the arrows as they fell to the ground, burning to their deaths in excruciating pain. With the unskilled archers a good distance away, Gordon and Baldrake had taken cover to ensure their safety. *This is nothing less than slaughter,* the wolf thought, displeased at the way things concluded. Relaying another message to Melche, the arrows stopped their flight.

'I must say, I am impressed. Didn't think you had it in you to be so cruel,' came a voice in the winds.

Suddenly, the high-burning flames died down and the soldiers rolling on the ground saw that the flames on them were no more. Amazed, confused, and glad to be alive, they rose from the ground and looked at each other; then, suddenly, all dropped dead to the ground in harmonious splendour.

'Ahh, such a nuisance they were,' came the voice again.

Baldrake circled the remaining tent, roaring aloud, 'It's him! It's the wizard!'

Gordon cut through the tent flap and entered the dark little room of the smaller tent.

'Why are you looking for me in there? Do you really think I would be that unprepared?'

Gordon moved silently about and out of the tent, looking around to find the wizard, shield raised and sword drawn. Out of the cover of darkness, Anukke walked up to stand before him, then laughed mockingly and covered his mouth with the tips of his fingers as he said, 'My dear little pet, you cannot possibly believe that you can defeat me with that.'

Without blinking or averting his gaze, focused and centred, Gordon replied, 'I am not here to defeat you, wizard. I am here to eradicate you from this world.'

Anukke turned away and dropped his arms to his sides. 'But I am an unarmed man. Would you really kill an unarmed man?'

Walking forward, Gordon shouted, 'Your arms *are* your weapons, and I will take them from you!'

Anukke turned back, and with a single command, bolts of lightning flashed from his fingertips. A thunderous boom sounded as the lightning crashed into the shield, pushing Gordon back with tremendous force. Loud arcs of violent blue and purple blinded him as they battered the shield. Unable to look up, he heard a shrill scream, and the lightning ceased. Looking over the shield, he saw that Baldrake had his enormous mouth clenched over the right shoulder of the wizard, but before he could bite down to crush the bones, Anukke shoved his left palm against the chest of the wolf, and an exploding ball of fire erupted between them, flinging them apart. Slowly rising to his feet, the wizard tried to regain his composure, but immediately doubled over as the shield crashed into his stomach.

With the first opportunity to have presented itself, Gordon had thrown the shield to land the blow. Looking down, the wizard saw blood running from his stomach, and although it was not a deep wound, it felt as if his energy was being sapped from his body. His power waning, he stared at the shield on the ground and saw the blade's edge running along the rim. He watched as his blood ran through small groves to congregate in the centre. The carved-in symbol came to life. Frantically flapping its wings to get away from danger, a great spear plunged into the heart of the phoenix. 'No. This cannot be.' He tried to cast a spell; but nothing happened, then paled as he said, 'Where did you get this shield?!'

Gordon moved to the wizard's side as he sagged to the ground, and said, 'A gift from Lady Rose. She sends her regards.'

Baldrake came limping closer, with his right paw hanging in the air. The armour had saved his life. Apart from a hurt leg caused by the fall, he had some singes all over his body, the burnt hair leaving a putrid smell around him. Barely able to put any pressure on the injured leg, the wolf stopped a distance away and said, 'Your reign has ended, you foul creature.'

Anukke stared into the soul of the wolf. 'Have you recently spoken to your friend the abbot?'

Gordon pitched his head up and looked at Baldrake as he said, 'What of them?'

A burst of jarring, mocking laughter sounded from the sorcerer. 'Your precious Beldrin was at the monastery in the mountains, right? Ortega himself destroyed the monastery. He and his rat, Anthelos. Burned it to the ground. You saw what they are capable of in Millanthros. Go ahead and guess what they did with your preci—'

Ignoring the pain in his leg, Baldrake launched himself onto the wizard, knocking him over to stand on his chest, his metal nails piercing flesh and seeping blood through the blue robe. Baldrake snarled and bared his fangs as he said, 'You lie, wizard! Beldrin is safe!'

'Believe what you will, but know this: it was not I who gave the orders. I am not the only one you want to kill; I am a mere pawn. Ortega has risen—he is the one you truly want.'

Baldrake felt his legs giving in under him. The sudden realisation that the wizard was telling the truth came crashing down on him. Limping off the wizard, he staggered a little distance away, vomited, and howled aloud up to the moon, until he fell down on the ground, his legs unable to carry him further, his grief colossal.

Gordon picked up the shield and struck Anukke a heavy blow to the head, sending the wizard back to the ground and into unconsciousness.

How do you console someone after news like that? How do you console the father who just lost his son? Nothing will be enough, nothing can be. He walked to the wolf and stared into his eyes and saw no life in them, no will to go on, nothing left to fight for. His heart broke at the sight of the once-proud wolf, now lying on the ground like a broken toy. 'We will find this Ortega, and we will strip him of his powers; we will hunt him down and break every bone in his body, tear the flesh from his face and burn him alive. We will make him suffer! This I promise you. But I cannot do it alone. I need your help, my friend.'

Baldrake pushed himself to his haunches. 'What are we going to do with him?' He jerked his head in the direction of the unconscious wizard.

Gordon sighed and said, 'We will let him live for now. He probably knows where this Ortega is.'

Rubbing his head as he sat up, Anukke said, 'It will not be that easy, you fool. Why do you think I stayed behind after the soldiers departed? Why do you think I killed the remaining soldiers after your assault? Why do you think I stayed here if I knew you were coming?'

Gordon rose and walked to the wizard. 'What are you talking about?'

'If it were that easy to kill him, I would have done it long before now, and taken his powers for myself! As it is, he is not that easy to kill. That is why I am here...' He climbed to his feet, then mumbled, 'Ineeyohel.'

Pulling his face, Gordon asked, 'What was that?'

'I need your help! Okay! Or rather, you need mine. Look, I wanted to rule this world, not be a servant or suffer in it with the rest of you.'

'How do we kill this Ortega, then?' Baldrake asked, still turned away from them.

CHAPTER FIFTEEN

'Hold that line! Don't let them through!' Gwen shouted to her men. The Ell-Shadack were pushing hard to gain the valley. Fire burst from the sky as the draghnai flew past, igniting trees and fields. Atop a chestnut gelding, Gwen drove through the flames to face the Ell-Shadack. Alone, heavily outnumbered, she fought with a burning vengeance. Seeing their major's plight, the troops crashed through the burning bushes with their shields to aid her. Steel clashed against steel, arrows filled the sky, and blood soaked the ground. At great cost, they were gaining the upper hand as one of the draghnai was shot down by the archers, the other retreating to safety.

Huddled deeper in the valley between the trees were some survivors who had made the forest their refuge after their villages were burned to the ground. Men, women, and children of all ages were trying to hide from the carnage they had survived, now fearing again for their lives as they heard the battle raging on, drawing closer to their location. The sound of the battle faded and was replaced by the thunderous hoofs of horses running in.

Tired and drenched with blood, the resounding victors rode into camp on horseback after the battle. 'Plenty of good men died today and plenty more will die tomorrow, but even more of the enemy will die every day,' Gwen said to the survivors, who stood wide-eyed and fear-gripped as she rode deeper into their little encampment. She looked at Borka as he slid off his horse. A vicious gash from a sword ran from his forehead between his already too wide-apart eyes, spreading them even further. 'Get that looked at Borka. I can't afford you dying on me.'

Borka nodded and went off to a healer—a survivor from Caldonia—to ask for his help.

Gwen stalked off towards one of the small ponds a distance away and stripped off her clothes as fast as possible, then jumped into the shimmering, icy water.

She welcomed the cold on her naked skin after the brutal battle. 'Oh, where are you, Tuds?' she muttered as she swam, then dipped her head under, trying to rid herself of the blood in her hair. The scene of his sudden disappearance ran through her head again, as it has since that day. A voice rang out from the encampment, and she dipped her head again. *There he goes again.*

Borka, being second in command now, was speaking loudly to his men, pacing up and down in front of them as they stood amongst the trees in the forest, 'You fought valiantly today, men. We will all mourn the death of our comrades; know that their deaths did not go in vain. They gave their lives to protect these people here...'

Gwen stood watching as she came back from the pond, unnoticed behind a tree. The Caldonian healer had tied a cloth over the stitched-up gash and around his head, giving him a much bigger head than he already had. Without saying a word to the men, she left and went to her tent.

The sun lowered, and the moon rose to take its place as the light in the sky. Looking up at the big round ball giving its light to rid the darkness, she spoke to the nearing footsteps, 'There will always be a light in this dark world, Borka.'

He lifted his one visible eyebrow and said, 'How d'you know it was I?'

'By trying to be silent and sneaky, you walk loud and unbalanced.'

With a gruff mutter from the man, she turned to look at him, and said, 'There is still hope for this world. I know it. I can feel it. But we need to get more men; we need to recruit. We have not even seen this self-proclaimed king who is busy destroying this world.'

Borka put his hands to his sides. 'So what do you propose, Major?'

'We go to Karta. Maybe they haven't been attacked yet. Or, if they have, maybe there are survivors. Who knows, maybe there's a full squadron left.'

Borka fidgeted with his hands and nervously brought up the question, 'What... happened to the king's Seekers? We could sure use them right now.' Turning her head, she glared into his eyes. He quickly and evasively said, 'Sorry, Major. You don't need to answer that.'

'No, you have a right to ask. We... the Seekers were the best. The elite force of the king, the true king. Until the night that his wife was murdered and rumours spread that it was one of us who killed her. There was an investigation. It went on for a very long time, but they could not find the murderer. Finally, as the last act from the king, he disbanded the Seekers and made them swear an oath to never again wield a sword.'

'But then, what are you doing here?'

With a sardonic grin, Gwen said, 'I was yet to be sworn in when all this took place. But before I had my "graduation," they disbanded us. Officially, I wasn't a Seeker yet, so I didn't need to take the oath. It was also shortly after they banished us that the king mysteriously died, and having no heir, the throne sits empty till today. Everything is falling into ruin.'

'That's terrible. I'm sorry, Major. Of politics I know very little, but isn't someone supposed to hold the throne until such a time that the new king is elected?'

'Indeed. Unfortunately, it was that bed warmer, Keiophillus Rent, that useless swine. He hasn't done a thing to aid anyone or exercise his guard. Karta has probably fallen by now, with him fleeing first and foremost.'

'Aye, then we go to Karta. We must leave the people here with most of our men. If we find any survivors or any soldiers, we can bring them back here. If Karta is still intact, we can ask for aid.'

'I will need my powers back if we are to stop him.'

'Keep your mouth shut. I don't want to hear anything more out of you,' Gordon said as he jerked the rope bound to the wizard's hands.

It was a slow and treacherous journey as they travelled east towards Caldonia. With Baldrake gone for most of the time as he scouted for any sign of enemy movement or trouble ahead, and with a group of people that had probably never even left the comfort of their city; Gordon had endured the worst time of his life so far. In the back of his mind, even he started thinking of a way to get rid of these people. The constant nagging, "Is this poisonous?", "Can we eat that?", "How much further?", "Are there wild animals in the forest?" And his favourite—that nearly sent him off the rails, "Are we stopping for tea soon?"

'Halt!' he ordered the company. One man from Millanthross, a skinny fellow with a glass eye, leaned close and said, 'Why are we stopping? Is it time for lunch?'

Without answering, Gordon stared out over the rolling grasslands at a trail of dust being kicked up by Baldrake as he ran at high speed back to the group. Still far away, Gordon yelled, 'Get to the trees! Something's wrong.'

Out of breath, Baldrake stopped at the tree line and said to evidently no one, 'A scout, up ahead.'

Gordon moved out from behind the tree and replied, 'Well then, let's go say hello. We don't want to be rude, now do we? Melche, keep your men here; we'll circle back and get you. If we don't return, follow the path northeast through the winding forest and over Regnak Pass to Caldonia.'

Baldrake lowered himself to the ground and said, 'Get on my back. It will be much quicker.'

Gordon jumped up on the wolf's back and held on tight as Baldrake launched in the scout's direction. A distance before they reached the scout, still out of sight, Gordon said to the running wolf, 'Let me off here, before he sees me. Get behind him and drive the horse to me.'

Gordon sat next to a tree, waiting patiently for the scout's arrival, and before long he heard the pounding of hoofs coming his way. Frightened, the scout was looking behind him with the horse running at a full gallop to get away from the terror at their backs.

Holding a branch he broke off a half-dead tree, Gordon stepped into the horse's path, unnoticed by the scout still looking behind him, oblivious to what was in front. Gordon whistled to get his attention just before the horse reached him and swung the branch. With a solid blow to the chest armour, he took the scout completely off the horse, sending him to the ground, gasping for air.

The scout coughed and rolled about, holding his armoured chest as Gordon walked closer and demanded, 'Where is your camp!'

'I will tell you nothing, you murderous bastards!'

'Who is your commander?' Helping the scout up from the ground, Gordon sheathed his sword as he saw Baldrake coming closer. He knew there was no way this man could ever outrun the wolf and thought him of little threat to them.

The scout stood and said, 'You're not with any army, then?'

Baldrake sat on his haunches next to Gordon and said, 'Does it look like we belong to an army?'

The scout extended his arm and said, 'I'm Dartan. We have a few survivors we're trying to keep safe deep in the forest.'

'Finally, some good news. How many men do you have, and who do they follow?' Gordon said as he grabbed the man's arm.

'We have a less than a thousand. Major Gweniviere is in command. We've been searching for survivors ever since the fall of Caldonia.'

Gordon, with shock showing on his face, retorted, 'That can't be! It's only been a few days. When did the first attacks start?'

'We've been fighting them for about forty days now, and they're slowly gaining ground. We don't know if Karta still stands.'

Confused and irritated, Gordon changed the topic. 'I have a few survivors from Millanthross. Can you take them to your camp? I believe they will fight, but they lack training. In fact, Major Gweniviere should remember us. Tell her to train everyone who has the slightest possibility of wielding a sword or bow. Tell her that Gordon and Baldrake might just have a way of stopping this war once and for all.'

With daylight fading to crawl under the cover of darkness, Dartan followed them to the remaining survivors and pointedly said, 'What do you say about making camp? I'll ride out with the Millanthrosians in the morning back to our camp. Besides, my horse needs rest.'

All the survivors huddled together, terrified of moving in the dark, and raised their opinions. 'Yes, yes. We think camping for the night is a good idea...'

Outnumbered, Gordon conceded to the burgeoning mob. 'Fine! We camp here for the night.' Concern for his companions had been steadily growing in him over the last few days; Baldrake had left camp every night since he heard about the monastery, sitting alone, talking to himself and evidently the stars. Melche was awfully quiet, always sitting alone with Malachai's hunting knife. He had barely said a word since they left Millanthross, and hadn't made a joke or re-enacted a single event, always moping around and just obeying commands given to him. Gordon walked over to the teary-eyed old mekkel, and said, 'Melche, how long did the attack on Millanthross last?'

Wiping his face, he put down the knife and said, 'Melche thinks it went on for about ten days.'

Raising his head as he furiously tried to work this out, he said, 'That makes little sense; the math doesn't fit. We were only gone for a few days—it's impossible.'

Melche raised his one brow and sagged the other, looking dumbly at Gordon as he said, 'Days? No, no, no, no, no! You left Melche for months!'

'What?!'

From across the two, Anukke started laughing a devilish laugh, cocking his head to the ground.

Gordon, burning with anger, walked over to the wizard and dealt him a vicious blow to the face. 'What's so funny, wizard?'

Anukke immediately ceased his laughing and complacently said, 'You fool. When I imprisoned Rose, I made time *slower* on the island. A bonus for when she escapes one day with the idea of finally besting me, only to find out I had won yet again. It will be devastating. Everyone she ever knew will be long dead by the time she gets out.'

A fire was burning, and food was being prepared by the Millanthrosians—they believed that luxury was a way of life, so for them to sleep in a tent and eat around the fire outside in the forest was a feat in its own. They insisted on cooking the food in fear of having to eat meat that came straight out of a wolf's mouth and half-cooked by some barbarian with no seasoning.

Baldrake rose and left the group to sit alone and stare out to the stars, mumbling to himself. Gordon sat always watching Anukke with a careful eye, ready to draw his sword and spill the blood of the sadistic wizard at the drop of a hat. 'Dartan, keep an eye on the prisoner. If he moves, cut his throat,' he said as he stood and moved into the darkness to where the wolf lingered.

'*Rest in peace, my son. May you find solitude with your forefathers. Please forgive my failure as a father for not protecting you. It should have been me that died, not you. I have lived my life, you only started yours, forgive me... And to those who come to fall, they shall be lifted into the sky and remembered for all time. Honour those who die; respect those who fight to the death. Show mercy upon your enemy; let your kills be quick...*' Baldrake whispered as he looked towards the stars.

'I am sorry for your loss, my friend. He was a fine wolf. I am sure Valanaar will be a little safer with him running around. You taught him well,' Gordon said as he neared.

'Kind words, but that won't bring back my son.' Dropping his head, the wolf continued, 'Forgive me. That was unkind. You only meant well.'

'Finally, I understand what it is to become a man.'

'And how is that?'

'Well, being guarded and stuck inside a city makes one forget about the real world, the one out there,' Gordon clumsily gestured out to nothing and said, 'Once you live in the *real* world, there is no turning back. You lose those close to you, you see the hurt in the world. Yes, there is good, but mostly, you see the bad, and it's how you react towards the bad that defines the person you are.'

Baldrake turned his gaze to Gordon, who reached out and lay his hand upon the wolf's back. 'You once said that you would stay and protect me until I set you free. Now, because of me, your son is dead. Words can't describe how sorry I am about that. From this moment on, I set you free from any bonds you might have put upon yourself. Leave this journey we follow. It will break us all. Find peace, and enjoy the time you have.'

Turning slightly away, Baldrake said, 'I cannot do that, even if I wanted to. I am a warrior! How could I live like that? Knowing that I abandoned you in the time of your greatest need for allies. Besides, I cannot hold you accountable for his death. I chose this. It was not forced upon me. No, I have nowhere else I need to be or want to be, so I will stay and fight by your side.'

'You are always welcome wherever I may be,' Gordon replied with a felicitous smile.

'I did get him! He's probably lying dead just around the corner,' the one hunter said to the other.

'You missed him by a mile!' replied the other hunter as they walked with bows in hand. Searching through the snow-covered forest for the wild boar they'd been hunting for the better part of two days, Makiha and Bak-Bak were both unaware that they had crossed over the border to Northern Milleria.

'I'm telling you, Makiha, I shot it in its lungs. It couldn't have got this far.'

'Ha, my mother is a better shot than you. Keep a watchful eye out.'

The sun was high, and the cool air blew through the forest, chilling even the native hunters as they went about their search.

Hearing a scuffle some distance ahead to the left, Makiha pointed and said, 'There! Move!'

Catching only glimpses of the boar, they ran for miles to keep its relentless pace. The wild boar suddenly stopped in front of a tree and acted as if it was unsure of which way to go, turning its head left and right, snorting as it did. The hunters stopped some distance away and Bak-Bak made to aim, and said, 'This time he is going down and he is not getting back up.' Taking his time with the shot and lining it up perfectly, Makiha suddenly knocked into him and sent the arrow flying crooked over the head of the boar as he yelled, 'Wait!' When he looked back, the boar was gone.

Angrily, Bak-Bak shouted, 'What in the name of Gan-Gad's cave are you doing? I would have had him.'

'Look!' Makiha pointed towards the tree where the boar had stood.

Against the tree lay an unmoving figure—the reason the boar had stopped—and if Bak-Bak had shot straight, the possibility that he would have hit the body was very high.

Running for the tree, they knelt at the side of the body, and immediately Makiha pressed his ear upon the chest, listening intently for a heartbeat. 'He's alive! We have to get him back to the village. She will know what to do.'

Bak-Bak threw down his bow and quiver and ran into the forest when Makiha called to him, 'Bring strong branches, he looks heavy.' Bak-Bak nodded and started gathering up branches big and strong enough to hold the load of the man.

The two tribesmen set to work on a makeshift stretcher, binding the branches together with the thinner roots of the Akiamundu—an ugly old tree that grew everywhere and looked as though someone had stuck holes all over it with a pitchfork. Tree-gum ran out of the stab wounds as blood. The branches were a dark brown-grey and misshapen, with few leaves. The thick roots of the Akiamundu ran deep and straight down into the ground, but the thinner, more flexible roots lay on top of the soil, used all over the island as ropes.

The man's breathing was shallow and in brief spasms, a sign of a damaged or punctured lung, his hair caked from blood coming from a wound at his temple. Bruises and scrape marks covered his body completely, and the thin, torn piece of clothing he wore would not hold off death for long.

Bak-Bak was putting the final touches on the stretcher to ensure its sturdiness as Makiha looked at the surrounding area, trying to figure out what happened to the man. Looking up the sloped surface of the mountain, he saw the pieces of broken branches and roots lying a distance away under a gigantic tree before the cliff that ran straight up and out of sight through the clouds. On the snow below the trees, he saw the crawl marks to where he sat now. Putting the pieces together, he could not believe that anyone could have survived the ordeal of falling from that height, with the only thing to soften your blow being trees and a few feet of snow.

They lay the big man down on their makeshift stretcher and covered him with one of the blankets they carried with them for when they had to spend a night in the forest.

War is always a stressful event, no matter how you cut it, and for some survivors at the camp, it meant the end. But others who still saw hope took the little chances to enjoy the time they had. The sun shone bright, and though the icy wind still blew, it warmed the man-sized rock slabs on the banks of the pond—giving some folks just enough courage to jump in, only to realise that the sun had not warmed the water at all. As quick as they jumped in, they got out even quicker, running for the sun-baked stone.

Gwen had sent out two of her finest warriors as spies to Karta to bring back a report of what they found, and as yet, they had not returned. She was growing anxious, but could only hope that they had survived the mission.

Tightening the reins on her horse, she heard the whistle coming from the watch, sitting in a tree overlooking the camp and beyond. With great speed, she reacted and signalled her men to be ready for an attack, but to her surprise, they had already taken up positions with their weapons in hand. Everyone in the camp was silent and fearful for what would happen next.

'It is I, Dartan. It's all right, Major, I found these folks on the road to Millanthross.'

Coming out from their cover, they closed in on the survivors of Millanthross. Gwen threw back her hair and muttered, 'Great, Millanthrosians. Just what we *didn't* need in this camp. Bunch of stuck-up old farts, with a toothache about everything in life.'

Saluting as Gwen neared him, Dartan explained what had transpired, 'I had a run-in with this blind fighter, Gordon, and his Gar hound. For a blind warrior, he surely—'

'He ain't blind, you know. Can see just as well as you or me. He just has... special eyes,' Gwen cut him off with a giggle.

'What! Do you mean to say he could see everything I did? I waved my hands before his face, like an idiot.'

'Yip, that's exactly what I am saying.'

'But he didn't flinch! He just stared straight ahead, ignoring me.'

'Just the way he likes it, too,' Gwen said as she inspected the bunch of people who came in with Dartan, and said aloud so that everyone could hear her, 'Welcome to Camp Hope. I have a few simple rules, and I expect you to follow them. If you don't want to follow them, you're welcome to leave and take your chances with the Ell-Shadack. We are all survivors here; we all went through hell to make it out alive. I expect all of you to do your part in making life a little easier for everyone here. For those who can fight, I expect you to wield a sword and start training. If you don't, I will hunt you down myself for being a worthless coward. I will not tolerate laziness or fighting against each other, so don't cross me or you'll wish you were facing the Ell-Shadack instead. Do your part, and we'll all get along. Borka, show them around.'

CHAPTER SIXTEEN

The cold air was quickly dissipating with each coming morning as the sun regained its strength. A small rock flew past the wizard's head as Gordon kicked at it, and said, 'Well, at least we had a short winter this year, thanks to you.'

Baldrake shook his head and looked back over his shoulder past Melche and the wizard, and said, 'What do you mean, our winter is shorter? What has he got to do with any of it?'

Their route would take them around the back of the D'hore Mountains to wade through the fermenting puddles of the marshland all the way to Kalaghstine and then to Anukke's castle.

The mekkel skipped over the small pockets of puddles to get to the wolf's side and said with teary eyes, 'Can Melche please ride on your back? Melche is old and doesn't feel like walking anymore. Melche is tired. Melche will tell you what he means, if you let Melche.'

Now, who could say no to that performance? Or was it a performance at all? Melche had not been himself of late, and even the wise Baldrake was at a loss for words for the mekkel. *How am I supposed to comfort him for losing a friend if I myself can't find comfort? I am sorry, my mekkel friend, but this hurt will be your own journey. How can a bereaved comfort the bereaved?* thought Baldrake as he looked at the slouching mekkel. 'Only this once and don't pull on my mane... it is uncomfortable.' Awaiting some comment from the mekkel, he received none.

Melche clambered onto the wolf's back and said, 'Melche won't, promise.' His sullen and sad voice drifted over the vast marshland as they trudged through a shallow pocket of water filled with fermenting plant life. He explained how Anukke had slowed time on the island as another point to further torment Rose and that they had been gone far longer than a month, although it only felt like days to them. A waft of obnoxious gas rose to meet them. He suddenly cupped his little hands around his mouth and nose, and angrily said, 'Did you make a stink, wizard? Gordon, let's get rid of him, he is foul.'

Anukke jerked his head back to the mekkel and said, 'It is not I, you little devil, it's the wasteland, the marsh that is making that putrid stench!'

Baldrake snorted with a grin and said, 'Oh, it might be the marsh, but you still smell funny, wizard. Remember, I have great senses.'

For the first time since their journey started again, the mekkel burst out laughing and jumped off the back of the wolf to run up behind the wizard, waving his hands in front of his face. 'You do smell funny, wizard,' his high-pitched voice rang out. 'Did you eat something rotten?'

With his hands bound at his back, Anukke kicked at the mekkel, but Gordon had jerked hard on the ropes, sending him to the mixture of mud and wet, smelly grass. Falling heavy, the wizard cursed them and got to his feet. Melche ran back to the wolf and clambered back up.

Manoeuvring through the marshlands was taking longer than they expected. The sun was going down on them, and there was no solid ground to set up camp for the night. 'Unless we want to sleep sitting upright in this foul stench, we have to pick up the pace,' Gordon said from the back of the line as he scanned the marshland.

Very calmly, Baldrake halted and waited for the wizard to pass by, and fell in next to Gordon. 'We are being watched.'

'Yeah, I know. They've been trailing us for some time. Any relation to you?'

'They are Gar hounds, that is for sure. As yet I cannot make out any faces though.'

Gordon lifted his head and looked into the distance, where he saw glimpses of the wolves in the bushes through the misty steam drifting up from the marsh puddles. Not once did he get a full view of a wolf.

'There must be at least ten of them. Why are they following us? I thought you said your kind do not just kill for pleasure.'

Looking straight ahead, Baldrake replied, 'We don't, but we do kill for food.'

'Just great.'

Anukke overheard their discussion and intervened, 'Cut me loose and give me back my powers. I can stop them.'

'You mean kill them. Do not test me, wizard,' Baldrake said with an irritated snort. He returned his attention back to the front and said, 'There, their commander waits for us. I will speak with him.'

Moving through the swamps, they had cleared the worst of it when they came to face fifteen Gar hounds. Patrolling on the sides were another fifteen on each side, moving closer. From the centre of the pack came a big red-brown wolf with deep brown eyes, who went down to his haunches before the group. Baldrake moved forward, and with a deep husky tone of remembrance, said, 'Minx,' he cocked his head to the left and right and continued, 'To what do we owe the pleasure of your company today?'

Tranquilly, the wolf regarded the companions and with a slow voice—which irritated Baldrake right to the point of wanting to launch himself onto the wolf to break its neck—said, 'Oh, Baldrake. Our once-fearless leader. I hear you have been spinning lies about having a pup with one of this world. I thought to take it upon myself to confront you about it.'

Biting hard on his teeth, Baldrake tried to calm himself for the sake of his companions and said, 'I did not lie about my son. His name was Beldrin. I am glad Chaulle made it back alive, then. Is he here?'

Minx rose and moved closer as he said, 'No, he is in the den, recovering from the wounds you inflicted upon him.' Howls went up in the air as the surrounding Gar voiced their anger. Minx waited for them to finish before continuing, 'Why do you say "was his name"?'

Gordon saw that Baldrake could not take much more of this before he would break free from his own bonds and attack. He swiftly moved in and interjected, 'What he speaks is the truth—'

But he was cut off by a vicious bark from Minx. 'Stay out of this, human, or I will tear you apart!'

'I'd like to see you try, wolfie.'

Angrily, Minx started moving towards Gordon, fangs bared, the other wolves milling around at the back, waiting for the order to attack.

'Sit down!' came the bouldering voice of Baldrake.

The authority of his voice drove Minx to obey out of habit, and he cursed himself aloud immediately for doing so. He had been under Baldrake's command for a long time, and since the mutiny, he had taken over the leadership.

'Please, do not interfere. They need to hear this from me, and me alone,' Baldrake said as he looked at Gordon, who nodded his understanding and backed away.

The sun was setting rapidly now, and they were not out of the marsh or trouble yet. Baldrake moved past Minx, ignoring him completely, and called out to all the wolves, 'Come closer, brothers! Not all of you stood against me, and I know that not all of you believe that *I* purposefully did this to us. So I ask you. Please listen to me. I never said she was a *normal* wolf. No Gar, but not normal either. They are a breed far larger than the average wolf. During my travels up north, I had met her, and for the first time in a very long time, I could fully communicate with one of them. I couldn't believe it, but they have evolved, brothers. I spent months with her, and we finally sired a pup. It was a hard birth, very nearly costing her life.' Everyone was silent; not even the wizard made a sound out of fear of being devoured by the wolves. Intently, they all listened as he continued, 'We can begin anew, my brothers. There are more of them.'

Minx snarled, 'So what now, great Baldrake? You want to lead the pack again?'

'No, I do not.'

Minx suddenly relaxed his muscles, and more out of shock than anger, replied, 'What do you mean, no? Is that not what you wanted?'

Baldrake went down on his haunches and said, 'No, I have other things to take care of. I do not want your place, Minx. You have earned it. But I would ask for your help, brothers.'

The wolves moved closer, as well as Gordon, who whispered in Baldrake's ear, 'What are you doing?'

'Do not fear. I have this covered, as you would say.' He spoke to his brethren. 'This world is under siege. Soon there will be no place left here for us to roam as well. Like it or not, this is your home now, and we need to protect it as if it was Gar. We once fought side-by-side with the humans of this world. Let us stand united once again and do battle with evil!'

Howls went up from every wolf there, except from Minx. The ground trembled beneath them as the sound filed out.

Minx silenced the platoon, and stalked over to Baldrake and said, 'Seems like you have won this round. They have been eager for war. But tell me, what is our part in all this?'

Baldrake looked at Gordon and said, 'Send your best to all neighbouring cities and villages. Tell them to make the people understand what is happening and what *will* happen if they don't come to our aide. Perhaps send them in pairs; city guards will not take kindly to a lone Gar walking into their town. Bring us reinforcements.'

'And what will you be doing during all this?' came the voice of Minx.

This time Gordon spoke up. 'We have somewhere to be. If we succeed, then perhaps we'll save a lot of lives. If we don't... then you don't have to worry about Baldrake taking your title away from you.'

Through all the speeches and threats, Melche had gone and hid in a bush a distance away, hoping the wolves would miss him. But not being naturally quiet, a wolf heard him and picked him out of the bush by his teeth, clamping on to the criss-crosses of his pant's extensions.

'Let Melche go, you overgrown furball!' yelled the little mekkel.

Dropping Melche in front of the companions, the wolf asked,

'What do we do with this creature?'

Baldrake rolled his eyes and said, 'He is with us.'

Lying flat on their stomachs on the rocky gravel surface of the mountain, Geldrick and Kurrel looked over the city below. In an effort not to be noticed, they had covered themselves with leaves and twigs, blending in with their surroundings. As they lay watch, Geldrick verbally pointed out the army to the east. Patrols were moving around on the city walls, keeping an eye out for the next assault. They watched a man clear the gates from Karta, making a run for the forest, but was cut off halfway by the scouts of the invading army. Shot with an arrow in the back, the man doubled over and hit the ground. Bodies of messengers lay piled up next to the road, close to where the man fell to draw his last breath. Scores of men had braved the mission to send for help, but none made it through. No one could have known that Karta was still in the fight.

'Good gods, man. We need to get word to the major. If we can get our men here, we can still save Karta, and the survivors will be well protected,' Geldrick said as he crawled back from the edge of the mountain and out of view of any scouts. Being the senior assassin, he had the final say, and Kurrel had a lot of respect for the man. He watched as Geldrick rose from the ground. Average height, short, white uncombed hair and a week-old unshaven face, his green eyes shining bright despite the toll war takes on the mind.

Tousling his hair, Geldrick stared back at Kurrel and said, 'Go back to camp and tell the major all we've seen. Tell her I will be in Karta, finding out all I can. She needs to hurry; Karta won't last long.'

Kurrel knew there was no point in arguing, and swore under his breath as he muttered to himself, 'Of all the stupidity, going in there alone.' He quickly gathered his equipment and moved down the mountain to his tethered horse at the bottom of the forest.

☿

Geldrick had been hiding in the bushes, waiting for darkness to fall, watching the routes of the patrols some distance from the wall. There were six he could see from his side, and they all walked short distances before turning back. When the one came, the other went, leaving little room for someone to sneak through unnoticed. 'If I can take out these two patrols covering this side, it might just give me enough time to get past and over the wall, but I will have to do it in complete darkness.' Geldrick whispered to himself as he lay out his plans.

The dreary wait for night to arrive had taken its toll on the man. He was fighting to keep his eyes open, to not fall asleep and alert the scouts with his melodic snores. He took his knife and ran the blade across his thumb, cutting just deep enough to make him more alert as it bit into flesh. Trickles of blood flowed to the ground, staining the earth and his dirty uniform even more.

Darkness came, and he waited for the perfect time to attack. Creeping silently up to the first patrol, he lay only five feet from his target, and when he saw the second target turn his back to him, he jumped up and skilfully sank the knife into the man's chest, severing the aorta while holding his free hand over the patrol's mouth. Quickly he lay the man down on the ground, just in time to see the other turning back. A glint from his steel knife flashed through the air in the moon's light. He heard the dull thud of the blade as it plunged into the throat of his victim. The patrolman tried to wrench the weapon from his throat, which made him unable to scream for help. Just before the man dropped to the ground, Geldrick was at his side to retrieve his knife and pulled it free as the man died and said, 'I do like this knife.'

Quickly he ran to the side of the wall and looked around for any sign of threat. A whining sound came from the grappling hook on the rope that he swung and expertly latched to the top of the wall. Now all he hoped for was—as he pulled himself to the top—that the guard on the wall didn't see him and mistake him for the enemy. Fortunately, he got in without being noticed and made a mental note to tell the general about his apparent luck. If he could get in, then so could any other spy as good as him.

Keeping to the alleys and the dark corners, he moved about the city looking for an open inn. Wondering ponderously, he talked to himself, 'Why has Karta not yet been sacked? They took the other towns and villages quick enough.'

Deep in thought, he walked straight into the barkeep of the Silver Wing Inn and immediately apologised as the fat man incredulously stared at him and said, 'Do you mind, watch where you're going?'

'I'm sorry, sir.' Geldrick cleared his throat and continued, 'I'm looking for a place to sleep for the night.'

'Look, I don't want any trouble, so—'

'I won't be any, I promise.'

The fat man turned to look around and regarded him from head to toe, then coughed slightly before he said, 'There is the question of coin, you know.'

'Oh, of course. I have a few silvers,' he said as he dug into his pocket and produced twenty.

'It will be two silvers a night, one extra if you'd want breakfast in the morning.'

'That would suit my needs perfectly. Thank you.' Geldrick followed the fat barkeep into the tavern and made light conversation with the man. 'I suppose business has been dropping since the war started.'

'Aye, that it has. May I offer you an ale?'

The next morning, Geldrick walked among the frightened people of Karta as soldiers ran about the city from station to station. A young boy of no more than fifteen years came running down the dusty road and tripped over his own spear, falling hard as his spear went flying a distance away from him to skid on the ground. People stopped to point and laugh at the clumsy young soldier.

Geldrick moved to the boy's side and shouted, 'What is wrong with you people?! We are at war, and this young man is putting his life on the line for you worthless pieces of dung! Now...' he unsheathed his sword, 'Anyone who has a problem with this here boy, or laughs once more, *will* answer to me! Move along!'

Ashamed and more frightened of this man with his sword, the people moved along swiftly, as some apologised to the young boy and thanked him for his courage. Geldrick extended his arm and helped the lad up, dusting him off some, then walked to retrieve the spear, and said, 'You never run with a spear, cadet. Except if you plan to use it. And when you do run with it, use both hands, taking care that the spear is next to your body, so that when an enemy attacks, you're already in a fighting stance.' He demonstrated the hold and fighting stance to the boy as he spoke.

The boy wiped his grimy face and took his spear and said, 'Thank you, sir. I will remember this lesson.'

'What's your name, boy?'

'Soneth Morta. Son to Bard Morta, the poet.'

Grinning, the assassin stated, 'Well then, soon your father will sing songs and make poems from his son's bravery.'

Shyly, the boy blushed and turned away.

Geldrick looked around at the people and said, 'Can you take me to your general? I do not know this city very well.'

'It's the least I can do,' the boy said, smiling.

Geldrick entered the garrison grounds with young Soneth, and as he walked, another soldier came towards him bearing an axe over his shoulder and said, 'A noble thing you did back in town, standing up for the lad. It's much appreciated. We need all the support we can get, and it's time that these townsfolk realised that. We've been holding out by the skin of our teeth. Every night they get closer to breaking through our gates and climbing over our walls.' Extending his arm, the soldier continued, 'I'm Captain Braka. Where are you from, soldier?'

Gripping the captain's forearm, he replied, 'If all goes according to plan, we might just win this battle. I'm Geldrick. Major Gweniviere sent me to check on Karta. We weren't sure if the city still stood.'

The young lad joined his squad and resumed his duties while Geldrick and Braka moved through the grounds on their way to the general's quarters. Plenty of soldiers stood around, practising their swordsmanship and honing their blades. Others practised their archery, while others still sparred with various weapons.

They rounded a corner and came to stand before the larger of the tents on the grounds, with two guards standing at the front with their spears crossed at the entrance.

'Is the general available?'

One guard set his spear aside and moved into the tent. A few moments later, he appeared again and ushered them in. The general cleared his throat and said, 'Who is this fellow, Braka?'

Astonished, Geldrick interrupted before Braka could speak, 'General Blackbeard? I am Geldrick, currently under the command of Major Gweniviere. They struck us hard and without warning, sir. Caldonia fell within the day. We led a few survivors out into the forest. The major and the soldiers guard the area with their lives. Kurrel and I were sent to Karta to report back our findings to her. As soon as I saw Karta still standing, I sent Kurrel back so he could relay the information and ask for aid in the fight. If we can get our troops in here, Karta might have a fighting chance.'

'Ahh, I remember you, Geldrick; you are a fine soldier, and a brave one to sneak in here at night as you did,' said the general.

Braka moved forward with his arms folded across his chest and said, 'You didn't think we would just let anybody waltz into Karta that easily, did you? I was informed as soon as they saw you clambering over the far wall. I sent a spy of my own to follow you and report back to me. That is how I knew about your spectacle in town.'

Grinning and nodding, Geldrick admitted that it surprised him to get in as easily as he had. Dark wine flowed from a decanter as the general poured some in glasses and sank into one of his chairs as he said, 'If what you say is true, then we have a fighting chance. But how are we going to get them into the city? We haven't been able to get a messenger out as yet.'

'Leave that to me,' said Geldrick as he gulped down his wine. 'Oh yes, general. Have you thought about why they are not attacking at this stage?'

General Blackbeard moved about his chair anxiously, not knowing what to say. Seeing the uncertainty in his general, Braka intervened, 'It's because we sent them running scared with their last attack.'

'That might be,' Geldrick nodded, then continued, 'But I would wager they are waiting for backup, some support. I think that more likely. Don't you, Captain?'

The footsteps fell loudly on the ears of the people sitting quietly, huddled together in small groups in the corners of the solitary pub deep in the middle of the forest, a few miles due southeast from Millanthross. No one spoke or made a sound as they heard the deafening creaks moving closer and closer to the door, where it stopped.

With a loud crash, the door gave way to the intruder standing outside. Splinters flew through the dark, looming room, the door crashing heavily on the wooden floor. People began screaming and wanted to flee, but the only way out was where the figure stood. Bending down to clear his head from the door frame, he stepped inside the pub and shouted, 'By the teeth of a jackrabbit, would you stop screaming?'

One man in the corner made a run for the door but was stopped as a massive hammer came crashing through a table just in front of him, sending more splinters and wood flying into the crowded onlookers. Suddenly, his feet dangled in the air. Looking up, he stared straight into the eyes of a man driven by anger, the fire from his cigar glinting in his eyes. 'Got somewhere to be, laddie? No one will leave until I get some answers. Got that?'

The man nearly fainted in the arms of this stranger, then slid down the wall and staggered over to the corner again, huddling with the others. Finally, the barkeep came out from under his desk and crept towards the big man. A small man, frail and doubtful, stood in front of the intruder and said, 'Please, sir, we don't want any trouble. I run a peaceful establishment here. If you have questions, please direct them to me, not my customers.'

'Aye, I can admire a man standing up for others, putting his life in danger for them.'

The frail barkeep gestured to one of his tables that was still standing and said, 'Please, have a seat. I will join you soon with two tankards of our finest. On the house, of course, and you can ask me all the questions you want.'

The man seated himself and gazed around the room, seeing the disgusted looks he was getting.

Upon returning, the barkeep spoke to his other customers, 'All is under control, please continue enjoying yourselves.'

'I am sorry about your door... and table. Here are some silvers for their repairs.'

'Don't you worry about that now. Let's get these pesky questions that are bothering you so out of the way,' the barkeep said as he placed the tankards on the table.

Taking a big gulp of his ale, the big man said, 'I have lost some friends of mine—a blind-looking fella and his pooch, a Gar hound named Baldrake. They must have come through here a few days ago. They think me dead, and I am afraid they are in trouble. I need to warn them: the death swarm is coming.'

Sitting back in his chair, the barkeep rubbed his clean-shaven chin. 'There were some strange folks going out and exterminating some of the pests that set Millanthross ablaze. Killed them good, they did. I believe they travelled east, to Caldonia, maybe Karta, I'm not sure. Sorry, but I did not speak to them. I only saw the general direction they were heading.'

Getting to his feet, the big man walked to the door that lay on the floor, picked it up and set it against the wall, and said, 'Sorry again about the door and for frightening your customers.'

As the big man turned, the barkeep called out to him, 'What is your name, if one of your friends comes around—'

'I go by Malachai. You have yourselves a good day, now.'

Geldrick stood atop the wall, overlooking the war-hungry Ell-Shadack as they taunted Karta to come out from behind their gates. When he looked further northeast, something caught his eye. A pack of five Gar hounds came crashing through the fields towards Karta. The three Ell-Shadack that stood in their path posed little threat and discarded of them swiftly. Five more undead warriors went down quickly as the Gar hounds pounced on them before reaching the wall.

Minx turned to his wolves and said, 'Get to the gates. Call for them to open and help them defend this city. I will be back soon, I have matters to attend to.'

Geldrick stood above them on the wall, making sure he wasn't seen as he listened in. Trailing the wolves, he ran on the wall above towards the gate and saw them swing open, then cursed himself for eating too much. The food made him drowsy and short of breath. He looked over at the gate and saw the four Gar hounds entering. *I do not like this at all.* His stomach churned, not just because of all the food, but something else. Gar leaders usually stayed with the pack and sent out one of their wolves to do his bidding; very seldom would the wolf in charge leave his pack with a mere excuse of "I have matters to attend to."

Minx turned and crept in the tall grass to stay out of sight from the Ell-Shadack, heading east. Geldrick jumped over the side of the wall, using his grappling hook to lower himself to the ground, taking great care to stay upwind of the Gar hound. Cautiously he followed the wolf, staying in his line, which he knew would take them out of sight of the Ell-Shadack. The day was coming to a close as he followed the wolf, who seemed reluctant to stop for the night. Both pressed on.

Where are you going, wolf? Geldrick thought as he looked at his surroundings. The green fields had disappeared with the coming of night and were replaced with rocks and holes. It seemed that all things were now an obstacle set in his path. 'Of course, the bloody Gar will not have this problem, will he? Stupid human eyes.'

During the night's running, the hoot of an owl almost gave him away. He ducked behind a tree and waited for the wolf to continue on his way.

Minx stood for quite some time, looking for movement. Complacent that he wasn't being followed, he turned and set off again.

Geldrick's lungs were burning, and by now, he was glad he had eaten so much. There had been no time to eat, being forced to keep up with the wolf. Throughout the night, they pressed on, his legs trembling beneath his body, ready to give in; and still, he kept going.

As the sun rose slowly through the trees, Geldrick finally realised where they were headed. The forbidden lands of Krell lay ahead of them. 'Oh, this is not good,' he said to himself.

The wolf, he saw now, was not hiding its whereabouts anymore, and walked straight into the open fields in front of the castle. Quickly, a dozen Ell-Shadack surrounded the wolf with their weapons drawn. A draghnai flew overhead, scanning the area for any more intruders. Geldrick had stayed behind, watching from the tree line, and therefore could not hear what was being said.

They escorted Minx away to the castle, and he knew he had to find out why the wolf was here, but how? The area was crawling with Ell-Shadack busy in the affairs of making weapons, rams, ballistae; even a few ships were being built.

'I suppose I will have to climb the cliff from the sea up to the castle,' Geldrick pondered aloud and set off through the forest under the cover of the trees. He ran to the side of the cliff and climbed down about fifteen feet; placing his hands and feet in the crevices of the cliff, he moved towards the castle's back about three hundred feet to his left.

With nothing to tie himself down whilst hanging a staggering five hundred feet above the raging sea, he held his breath for most of it, or so it felt. Winds buffeted him from the back, wanting to tear his grip from the cliff-side, but he would not relent.

Finally reaching the castle's back wall, he climbed over with his grappling hook and rope. Once inside the inner bailey, he was free to gain access to the castle's air vents. Crawling through the tight spaces, he had made his way to the great hall, and upon seeing the throne from the back through the vent slits, he saw the Gar hound ushered into the hall, flanked by four Ell-Shadack.

The wolf came to stand before Ortega, and said, 'Great King, I bear information regarding a plot against you.'

'Is that so? Well, please don't keep me waiting.'

'Of course. I have some requirements, though.'

'Of course you do. You always do. Now tell me this plot.'

'Word has been sent to all neighbouring cities to assemble at Karta; all soldiers will attend. They will march against you and take back what was once theirs by force. I just ask one thing—that you send me and my brothers back to our world. You may do to this place what you want. I will ensure my Gar hounds do not interfere with your plans.'

'I will reward your efforts. Thank you for informing me about these... events they plan. Now leave me.'

Nervously shifting around on the floor, Minx averted his eyes from Ortega and said, 'Is there a possibility that Your Grace could—'

Sighing, Ortega held out his hand and snapped his fingers. With the crack of lighting and blinding blue light, Minx was gone. Not a trace of him ever being there.

Creeping back out of the vents and out of the castle, Geldrick got himself some distance away, before cursing that wolf, then said to himself, 'Where did I hear that voice before? I know it from somewhere, I just cannot place it. A shame I could not make out the face of this king. But no time to waste; I have to warn the others of this betrayal.'

CHAPTER SEVENTEEN

W alking next to Gordon, Anukke bowed his head, letting out a whisper from his mouth, 'Asfilianto,' but nothing happened.

'What was that you said?' Gordon asked, as they moved through the countryside towards Kalaghstine.

'Nothing, merely talking to myself.'

Though they were walking on the footpaths of animals, Baldrake realised he had not smelled or seen any animal for some time now. His first impression had been that they were nearing the city, and therefore the animals were scarcer; but in the back of his mind, he knew it to be false.

The gates were barred. Guards patrolled on the wall, scanning the group as they neared. A guard leaned over and shouted, 'What is your business here? It is not a good day for strangers to wander about.'

'We are here for supplies, food and water, a quick rest maybe. Then we will be on our way again. I am Gordon, and these are my companions, Baldrake, Melche, and Anukke. We will leave the city before the day's end.' Gordon turned to the group and whispered, 'Do not let them see that we've tied him up.'

'See that you do. I will have men following you, so try nothing stupid,' came the voice from the wall.

The gates swung open with a low groan, and they entered the city. Soldiers were gearing up to move to Karta. Wagons filled with food and water, weapons, and belongings lined the main avenue of the city while oxen were being hitched, as the loads would be too much for the horses.

A guard jumped down from the ladder leaning against the wall and approached the group and said, 'I am Captain Chip. Where do you come from?'

'We journeyed from Millanthross, Captain.'

'Is it really as bad as the claims? We had two Gar hounds come in two days ago, explaining the situation, but I still held out some hope that it was a lie.'

'It's true, Captain. They sacked Millanthross, burned it to the ground. The golden city is no more.'

The captain paled, the words striking like a blow to the chest. 'Please, get your supplies; I need to get back to my duties.' Chip turned and staggered away, but a hand fell on his shoulder.

'Do not lose hope yet.'

He nodded and left the group.

They continued on through the street. Women and children were being forced to take shelter in the barracks until the column would march out. People watched in fear as the soldiers bustled about. Rounding a familiar corner and heading past the liberatum, Gordon heard the screams of a madman. 'He is watching us! Watching us, I tell you. He wants our souls!'

He grinned and said to Anukke, 'You know, he's talking about you.'

'One could only hope,' responded the wizard.

They headed towards the market to restock their supplies. Melche stalked around the open stalls, not saying much to anyone, merely looking at the dismal availability of goods, and was saddened even more.

'Melche, we have what we need, let's get moving.' Gordon walked hastily and without looking at Anukke said, 'Tell me how we are going to kill this Ortega.'

The mekkel ran back and clambered on the back of the wolf as the wizard spoke. 'When we get to my castle,' Anukke suddenly rubbed at his nose, revealing the ropes tied around his hands. Gordon quickly forced them back down.

'My nose is itching! Anyway, there is a secret passage in the dungeon that leads to a deep cave in the mountain where there is a very rare occurrence. You have heard of hot waterholes?'

Gordon didn't answer, and after a few heartbeats, the wizard continued, 'Well, in this cave are mercury pools. Hot mercury pools.'

'And what is the significance of this?' Baldrake asked as he drew closer.

'Above these pools lies the Ornieël dagger, an ornate curved wooden knife. In its current form, it is utterly useless, looking more like a children's toy than a weapon of the gods, but when bonded with the mercury in the pools, it becomes a thing of terrible power. We will strike him down with this dagger, piercing it through his heart. The liquid metal will course through his veins until he oozes liquid metal from every orifice in his body. He will suffocate, his organs will burst, and he will die a horrible but fitting death for the atrocities he has committed. Even with his power, he cannot prevent his fate when stabbed with that weapon. Is that not what you want for him, Baldrake?' Anukke cocked his head towards the wolf, eyeing him profusely out of the corner of his yellow catlike eyes.

'Do not speak to me about this subject again. And no, that is not what I want for him. I want something bloody.'

'Oh, there will be blood. Don't you worry about that.'

The day dragged on, and as they got to the castle, Baldrake saw that it was not invisible anymore—it was an ugly thing. It did not look old at all, just tasteless. There was no outer bailey, just the courtyard. The main top chamber overlooked everything, and a long spiralling staircase wound to the bottom where the dungeons were. There was no main hall, just a mess hall for soldiers to eat in. Not that there were any soldiers in the compound. Everything stood empty—no sign of life at all. The company walked around the compound directing all their comments at Anukke, annoying the wizard and setting him off in a fit of rage a few times. Melche was beside himself as he started making comments about the castle. 'If Melche was a rat, Melche would rather swim in poop-infested water than live in this pigsty.' Baldrake chuckled as the wizard squirmed and berated the mekkel, which did not stop the old scoundrel.

Melche ran to the corner of the courtyard, pulled down his pants, and relieved himself on a dying tree. Urine splattered all over as he whirled around, saying, 'Melche needs to water these plants, they are all dying!'

'Stop that, you wretched little mongrel!' roared Anukke.

The companions laughed at the crazy old mekkel, holding tight on the ropes of the wizard as he tried with all his might to break free and strangle him.

'Enough of this, let's get to the dungeon. We still have a long way back,' came Gordon's voice from just within the dark castle. Daylight was fading; and soon, where they were heading, there would be no light at all. When he lit a torch on the wall, the staircase suddenly came alive with spiders and all kinds of insects crawling all over the cracked walls and floors.

Gordon thought back to when they rescued Baldrake, and said, 'I don't remember it looking this bad the last time we were here.'

Anukke sighed. 'You humans know absolutely nothing of magic. Once you took my power away, the magic I constantly generated for this castle to keep it in shape died.'

Slowly making their way to the dungeon, they carefully stepped over a loose step that could go tumbling down. Gordon heaved heavily on the door before it gave way with a loud squealing sound echoing up the staircase.

269

Once in the dungeon, Baldrake felt his heart go heavy when he saw the metal cages they had been imprisoned in not so long ago—Beldrin lying unmoving, slowly dying of the poison administered by Anukke. Fighting to calm his rage, he dropped the rope from his mouth and stalked off, as far away from the wizard as possible. The feeling of losing control was taking over, and he knew what that meant. He remembered the last time it happened, eight of his wolves were lying dead after he regained control of himself. Sure, they had attacked him—or so he believed—but the fact that he was not in control made him tremble at the thought. Sometimes, thinking back, trying to recall that dreadful day, he thought, *Maybe they were just trying to calm me. Maybe I am the one who lost control and murdered them.* It had tormented him for years.

They walked past the cages to the back of the dungeon, where an old, rusted metal door lay shut at an acute angle. Anukke pointed to it and said, 'There, open it.'

Gordon started pulling on the door, heaving his muscles into a spasm. Baldrake suddenly cocked his head and pitched his ears as he said, 'Quiet!'

This time everyone heard it. A faint, horribly tormented scream from afar, drawing closer.

'What is that?' Gordon asked Anukke, who just shrugged his shoulders and said, 'If you don't want to find out, I suggest opening that door.'

Once more the scream came, this time much closer. Gordon was pounding on the door with a large rock, hoping to loosen its grip as Baldrake took up a defensive stand in front of the group. Terrified, Melche hid behind Gordon, his little heart racing as the screams echoed through the dungeon. Anukke picked up a piece of timber that lay on the floor, holding it with his bound hands.

Gordon dug his fingers into the grooves of the frame and heaved. It shifted slightly before falling back into place. The scream sounded again. 'Sounds like a giant bat,' Melche said, as he trembled with fear. A loud clang sounded from the dungeon door at the stairs, and the group stopped to see if it would break through. All went silent; no one moved as everyone looked around them and at the door, but saw nothing.

A mighty crash sent the door flying open on its hinges. The creature darted inside with great speed. They could not see what it was, but one thing was for certain: it was fast. Out of nowhere, it came crashing into Gordon and knocked him to the ground. He fought with the beast, trying to avoid its fangs and claws as it ripped at his face. The attacks came from everywhere: its head, feet and taloned wings. Blow after blow, it struck against the armour as it lashed out.

Baldrake charged and took the creature off Gordon and then some, rolling on the ground, his metal armour clinking loudly. Jaws snapped and claws slashed through the air. Snarling and hissing noises came from the dark as the two fought on.

Adrenalin pumping through his body, Gordon ran back to the door and pulled with all his might. A few wailing sounds came from the dark, and the wizard and Melche did not dare to investigate. Hammering sounds echoed as he hit the door again with a rock, then pulled more on it. The creature darted back into sight, streaming blood from several wounds on its body, hissing at the group. Just as Gordon jumped up to unsheathe his sword, the wolf came flying in from the side, this time expertly locking his jaws around the creature's neck. Closing his jaws with their terrible power, the bones of the creature finally gave way, cracking and splintering, Baldrake's fangs slipping with ease further through the flesh to tear its head from its body. The wizard flinched as the creature's head sailed from the darkness to land at his feet.

'What creature is this?' came the pelting voice of the wolf.

'Alone, it's called Vanta a' koreen—Bringer of death. Together, they are called the Death Swarm,' Anukke said, worry showing on his face for the first time.

Gordon walked up to him and slapped him hard, and said, 'What exactly do you mean "together" and "swarm"?'

Back to reality, Anukke looked at the others, and said, 'Just that, my pet. These creatures usually come in swarms, and if they are sent by Ortega, you can be sure there will be plenty more. Time is running out.'

Gordon cut the wizard's bonds. 'If you run or do anything that gives me the slightest inkling that you will betray us, you're dead. Remember that.'

Nodding, the wizard rubbed his raw, chafed wrists and moved to the door to help. Together, they heaved at the door. Melche grabbed the cut rope and tied it around the chest of the wolf and then to the door. 'Very smart,' said the wolf and dug into the ground with his steel-tipped claws, scratching grooves out on the floor. With great effort did the door open, and once the weight shifted over, it crashed down to the floor with tremendous force.

'After you, wizard. Hopefully, if something eats you first, they will be too full and sick to eat us,' Melche said, eyeing the scrawny wizard as he tapped his index finger to his mouth, then continued, 'Then again, you are probably just skin and dust, no meat anymore.'

Knowing he would only waste his breath, Anukke turned and walked through the door, followed by the companions.

Gwen lay watching the patrolling guards, her men and the survivors awaiting her orders deeper in the forest. Suddenly and without warning or concealment, a big, muscular man walked out into the open field, holding his cigar to the dry grass. Small flames flared up quickly to rage out of control.

'What's he doing? Who is that?' Gwen asked Borka.

Pulling his hammer free, he walked a distance away from the raging fire as a patrolling Ell-Shadack charged at him with a raised club. Malachai dodged the club. Holding his hammer close to the head, using it as an extension of his hand, he clobbered the undead soldier on the chin, breaking the man's jaw. He turned to Gwen and yelled, 'What are you waiting for? An invitation? Get moving!'

Gwen raised her sword and yelled as she charged forward, 'Come on, men, protect the people! Bring the women and children first.'

Flames were burning high, blocking the main Ell-Shadack force from reaching them. The few remaining Ell-Shadack scouts stood no chance against the many soldiers streaming out of the forest, and they knew it. The entire field to the city wall was burning now, scattering the Ell-Shadack from the blaze. Malachai reached the gates first and started hammering on them with his fists, shouting, 'Open these damned gates, you imbeciles! Do you want these people to die?'

The drawbar fell off on the other side and the gates swung open. The survivors streamed into the city, holding only what was dearest to them. Barnicus Bree had rambled from the start of the charge until he entered the city, and then he still continued, 'Why does everyone need to be so inhospitable? And so dirty!'

Busy with crowd control, Malachai herded the people through the gates, looking out for any stragglers or if someone fell. Most who died in such situations were trampled to death and not killed by an enemy's sword.

'What the hell was that!' Came the angry voice from Gwen. 'You could have gotten all of us killed out there!'

Malachai turned and regarded the woman without saying a word, then looked away again.

'Did you ever think that the winds could swing against us, burning us alive as the fire raced at us? No, you didn't,' angrily Gwen jerked on his arm to turn him around. 'Look at me when I'm talking to you, soldier!'

'I ain't no soldier. Sometimes the simplest plan is the best plan,' Malachai said as he crossed his arms again. 'You're welcome.'

Contorting her face, Gwen stared at him and said, 'Wait, I remember you! You reached camp Waterhole with some companions. As I recall, there was a Gar hound with you named Baldrake, and that blind looking fellow. Think his name was Gordo. Oh yeah, and who could forget the pesky little mekkel. Where's the rest of your party?'

'It's Gordon, although Gordo sounds like a better name,' he chuckled then, and continued, 'We got... separated. I had hoped they would be here in Karta; I will look around for them.'

A crack of thunder sounded around the corner of the gates, drawing their attention. 'Hold that thought,' he said as he went to investigate;

his hammer held ready for any foolish sod who would dare to get this close. Huffing and puffing, Minx trembled with his eyes to the ground, shaken.

'If you value your life, little doggie. I would suggest being very careful about telling me why you are here and how you got here.'

Minx looked up at Malachai. Unwilling to fight at all after his magical trip from the forbidden lands of Krell, he said, 'Vasgath, is that really you? It's me, Minx. I served under Baldrake. Four of my comrades are already inside; more could have arrived. See for yourself.'

'Minx, yes. I remember you,' he said as he lowered his hammer and then continued, 'But forgive me if I am a bit untrusting at this moment. Until I find out the truth, you wouldn't mind walking ahead of me so I may keep my eye on you?'

'I expect nothing less from you, Vasgath,' Minx said as he turned to regard the Ell-Shadack force on the other side of the fire. As soon as everyone was clear, they closed the gate, barricading it with the massive bars. The big man walked up to the nearest guard and said, 'You! There come any Gar hounds in, by chance?'

'Yes, a few, actually. Strange to see so many of them. That one over there,' the guard said, gesturing to Minx. 'He is their general. You may want to ask him what's going on.'

'Thanks. Where's *your* general?'

The soldier looked about the city, and said, 'Easiest way is to just follow this road. You will get to the training grounds; he should be there.'

Nodding, Malachai turned back to Gwen and rubbed his stomach. 'I would kill for a steak and an ale. Care to join?'

Grinning, Gwen took a knife from her boot and let it fly from her hand. The knife flashed through the air and slammed into the sign of "The Ox an' Crow," a tavern fifty feet from them.

With his brows raised, Malachai placed his hammer in its holster on his back, and said, 'I take that as a yes, then.' Turning around, he saw the wolf a distance away, looking for his troops, and shouted, 'General Minx! Would you care to join us? I would like to hear your story.'

Minx cursed the man but knew he would not let him out of his sight if he skipped out on this invitation. 'I would love nothing more,' he said as he followed them into the tavern.

Gwen got to the sign and pulled free her knife, leaving a big gash in the wood. As they entered, the barkeep greeted them and awkwardly stared at the Gar hound before seating them. After all, this was an immaculate establishment. Fine red leather couches adorned the walls, the tables all crafted using wood of the Black Walnut tree. The tavern was spacious with the bar area in the centre at the back. He gave them a table in the corner where there was a long couch against the wall. The wolf jumped up as Malachai and Gwen took the seats on the opposite side. 'Two mugs of your worst ale, one in a bowl for the dog, the other's for me. Get the lady something better.'

Half charmed, Gwen corrected, 'That's fine, bring me the same.' Twirling her hair around her finger, she slid the chair softly a bit closer to Malachai, who if he noticed did not react to it, but said, 'I'm kinda glad you said that. Places like these are very expensive. And their worst ale is usually better than most places' best.'

Shortly after, the barkeep brought their beverages and placed them on the table.

Minx started explaining how he had run into Baldrake and what they had planned, and how his wolves were sent all over to find allies to join the fight against this madman and then said, 'Baldrake and this Gordon will be here in a few days, I guess, if all goes well.'

Malachai frowned and rubbed at his beard. 'I have some news of my own. When I was on the island, I heard rumours from the sailors that arrived from time to time. They were talking about a death swarm, creatures that screamed your ears off your head with huge fangs and claws. Black as the night, strong enough to pick up a grown man, with hard hides. They soar through the sky like eagles and are basically invisible at night time. They're heading to the mainland and destroying everything in their paths. I fear they will be here soon, if they are not already. We must speak to the general and rid ourselves of these pesky Ell-Shadack before this death swarm comes.'

275

'If what you say is true, then I agree with you. Let's get to the general and explain the situation. Minx, better get your troops geared up for war. Looks like we're taking the fight to them,' Gwen said as she took a sip of her ale.

Hot and damp air with a distinct metallic taste to it filled their noses and mouths as they made their way deeper into the cave. Constantly spitting, the mekkel wiped his mouth, and said, 'Taste like Melche is eating iron shavings from the shop.'

Anukke walked at the front clutching the sides as he said, 'This mountain's rocks are rich in iron; mix that with water and air, and you get this taste. Perfectly safe, though.'

Gordon pulled his hand from the green-yellow moss covering most of the wall and smelled at it, immediately regretting his decision. His face pinched as he tried to rid himself of the smell. 'It's rather hot in here,' he noted. Baldrake flared his nostrils and took a deep breath. 'I don't think there's been fresh air in here for centuries. The air is stale.'

The ominous darkness was kept at bay just by the torch held up by the little mekkel, swinging back and forth in his hands as he moved, making the shadows jump to life.

'Melche hungry, want to rest.'

'We will rest in a bit, little one, let's move on for now,' Baldrake calmly stated as he walked past the little mekkel. Travelling in the cave felt like there was no end; no sun, no stars, no wind, just endless nothing. Gordon took the torch from Melche and halted the party as the cave branched off in various directions, 'Where to, wizard?'

'I need my powers back! I am a wizard; I don't keep track like humans—I am magically tuned for direction. Do you know what you call a wizard without his power? Mmmm?' Silence greeted him. 'Nothing! He has no title.'

'Well then, I guess we just go back and forget about this then, cause you're never getting your powers back. What do you take us for? Fools?'

Gordon lay against the wall, awaiting another retort from the wizard.

'I should have just burned you alive! Why do I have to put up with this nonsense? I am your superior!' Anukke was red with fury, but it could just have been the light from the torch.

'Hey, Baldrake, *he* is our superior. Do you want to bow down to *His* Majesty?' Gordon laughed as he spoke.

'I would not dream of it.' Baldrake growled the words.

Anukke swung around, preparing to walk into the dark, then halted and said, 'Okay, it's this way. Now come on.'

'Aha, YOUR MAJESTY remembers,' Gordon announced, falling in behind the wizard.

Melche came running past and called out, 'Thank you, Your Majesty!'

'Here, eat something,' Gordon said as he broke off pieces of the bread he had bought back in Kalaghstine and divided it between them.

'Great directions, wizard, it's a dead-end.' A wall of rocks extending to the ceiling lay in their way.

'It's because I closed the way, you imbecile. Did you think I would leave it open for anyone to stumble upon? I need my magic to open it,' Anukke tried his luck again.

Gordon took his sword and pushed it under one rock; turning the blade slightly, he squeezed his fingers into the gap and lifted it up to throw it to the side, then the next one, and the next one. Melche joined in and moved the smaller rocks off to the side. Digging for a long time, they saw no end to the wall before them, and yet, they pressed on. With their fingers raw and bleeding from the rocks, doubt started setting in and just when he was about to give up, hot air rushed over Gordon and made him cough uncontrollably for a few moments.

Laughing, Anukke clapped his hands and said, 'My, but you are an interesting breed!'

The hole they had dug was just big enough for them to squeeze through on their stomachs. Baldrake went first, forcing the hole a bit wider, followed by the complaining wizard, then the mekkel, and Gordon came last. Once inside, he held up the torch to get a better view of his surroundings and saw lights flickering back at him from a distance. Liquid metal pools were abundant in the cavern beyond. Walking past the hundreds of smaller pools, all at least the size of an oxcart, they came to a pool at the end of the cavern, at least a hundred to two hundred feet in diameter, and one could only guess how deep. At the centre of the pool, the mercury pushed up like a fountain, bowling over itself and falling back into the pool. Above this fountain lay the dull Ornieël dagger, suspended in the air, twisting and turning.

'What do we do now?' Baldrake snorted.

Anukke stared at the dagger, and this time spoke with no amusement in his voice, 'Now I really need my magic.'

'Enough of this! You will not get your powers back,' Gordon said as he moved forward, and just as he was about to stick his foot into the pool, the wizard grabbed him and yanked him back.

Wanting to reprimand the wizard for his actions, Gordon drew his sword and saw Anukke bending down at the edge of the pool, not paying him any attention.

'Look,' came the softer voice of the wizard as he stuck the tip of a root into the pool. Mercury started consuming it, covering the root completely, devouring the last life it had. Anukke threw it to the ground just before it touched his hand, and said, 'That could have been you.'

Gordon sheathed his sword. 'So, what then?'

Anukke paced the edge of the pool, his reflection dancing in the mercury as he said, 'I told you I need my powers back! There is no other way. Look, I want Ortega dead just as much as you. Now please, give me back my powers.'

Gordon walked over to Baldrake, eyeing the wizard, and whispered, 'What do you think, my friend?'

'I do not see another way. We cannot enter the pool.'

Gordon wiped his face, and said, 'The first sign he shows of turning against us, he's dead, got that?'

'You do not have to tell me. I am willing to kill him now.'

Gordon took the shield and walked over to Anukke, who stood wide-eyed with anticipation. To his surprise, he received a menacing blow to the gut. The wizard fell to the ground and curled around the pain. Gordon turned the shield and exposed the blade on the rim to cut the wizard's arm. Blood streamed into the shield as Gordon lay it down on the ground and stepped back.

Clutching his stomach, Anukke rose from the ground. He watched as the blood flowed from his arm to the shield and demanded, 'Well, say it! Say the words that will release me.'

Gordon took another step back. 'I do not know the words.'

Anukke staggered forward. 'What! How can you not know the words?'

'Lady Rose said that once you needed to be released, you would know the words yourself.'

Perplexed, the wizard thought about this recent development, then laughed out loud and said, 'She has finally bested me! By the gods, I love that woman, she's as cunning as I am evil in your eyes.'

The companions all looked at each other, puzzled. 'What do you mean?'

Turning to the misty-eyed warrior, he said with a broad smile upon his face, 'In order to release myself, I must utter the words that would release her, giving her free rein.' Anukke turned back to the shield on the ground and bellowed out, 'Kebo aste Kru nomi Tende, Varley!'

After a few moments of silence, the cave shook; boulders fell from the roof into the mercury pools, splashing the liquid everywhere. Ducking and diving for cover, Gordon, Melche, and Baldrake jumped from spot to spot while Anukke stood motionless, nothing coming close to touching him.

Far away on the island known as Milleria, the earth shook and tore asunder the house of Lady Rose, scattering the villagers as they fled for their lives. A voice drifted on the currents of the winds, 'Free at last!'

At the top of the hill where they had planted the hammer for Malachai, she stood staring at the vacant grave. The way he had looked when they brought him in sent shivers down her spine. She thought for an instant that they would use the grave after all. But then, a few days later, he had climbed up the hill to reclaim his hammer. She turned to look across the sea towards the mainland and said, 'Time for me to go home.'

Rose looked over at her people as they ran about the village, scared that another earthquake might hit. She lifted her staff and said a few words, soft and calm. Like mist before the rising sun, she disappeared.

The rumblings had ceased, and everyone walked closer to the large liquid metal pool. Anukke stretched out his arms in front of him and spoke in a voice not his own, and as he bellowed out the strange language, the dagger responded, as if being called by its master. The wooden dagger rose from the pool high above the ground, slowly ascending until they couldn't see it anymore. All went silent except for the wizard's constant chanting, and with sudden, blinding speed it came down, blade tip first. The dagger plunged into the centre of the mercury fountain, driving deep into the depths of the pool.

Waiting anxiously for what would happen next, they stood motionless. A loud drumming noise, as if someone were beating against a door in the distance, was coming from the bottom of the pool, a faint light emanating, pulsing from within. All went calm in the pool and slowly, five feet from their position emerged the dagger. It rose, guided by Anukke to float in the air in front of them. The wizard held out his hand and took hold of the weapon, but this time the mercury did not spread further, being held in place by magic. The companions stared at the dagger, its constantly moving metal form miraculous to their eyes.

Gordon, still amazed by the dagger, dreamily said, 'We have to get to Karta; everyone should arrive soon. We don't want the fight to start without us.'

CHAPTER EIGHTEEN

From the distance, smoke rose over the trees, billowing upward to the open sky. The cheerful sounds of singing birds and animals running through the forest made Gordon think of what lay ahead, where the smoke rose. He knew the only sound there was the sound of good men dying; the only smell the stench of the dead, the reek of fields burning. No happy thoughts dwelled there.

The day was nearing its end, and they still had a few miles left to get to Karta. Gordon and Anukke were running at the front, while Baldrake was keeping a keen eye on the wizard from the rear with Melche sitting hunched over on his back. Coming to a narrow stone bridge that crossed a small ravine, Gordon unsheathed his sword and slowed in his run, saying, 'Something is not right; ready yourselves.' All animal sounds had fallen away, replaced by an eerie silence.

Cautiously crossing the bridge, Baldrake cocked his head up, and said, 'There's something foul in the air.'

A shrill cry came from the treetops high above them, piercing their ears as four of the death swarm jumped from the tops, gliding to the ground below. Gordon stared at them with disgust. Their heads looked like those of inbred dogs, their bodies those of bats. Massive teeth lined their mouths, and as they screamed, black saliva dripped from their fangs. Claws reached out on the tips of their wings and feet. Their hides, black with little fur, glistened in the fading sunlight.

Wasting no time at all, the wizard stepped forward and cast a ball of fire, setting to light one beast as it neared; it screamed and hurled itself on the ground, where it died slowly. Another charged, while two took flight. Gordon stood ready with shield raised, then decided it was slowing him down and threw it to the ground to await the beast. Just as the creature reached him, he crouched and sliced his blade through the air, narrowly missing the creature and throwing it off balance. He quickly struck again, this time cutting the wing from its tip to its body. Shrill cries rang out as the beast thrashed in pain, flapping its severed wing, the sounds deafening, hurting their ears.

One beast swooped down and Baldrake charged at full speed, Melche still on his back. Anukke toiled with the other creature in the sky, sending lightning and fire up to it.

'Hold on, this is going to be rough!' Baldrake yelled to the mekkel clutching at his mane, who drew the big knife and raised it to the air as he screamed a fierce battle cry, 'To death with all of you!' Baldrake and the creature crashed heavily in the air. The little mekkel went flying forward but had expected this. Holding onto his knife with both hands, he swept over the beast and plunged the knife into the back of the creature, holding on for dear life as it thrashed about, trying to reach him.

Gordon spun and ducked a vicious blow from the beast, brought up his sword, and stuck it through the jugular and out the back of the skull. Yanking it free, he swung the blade, cutting off the head of the foul creature. Trails of smoke followed the one surviving creature as it flew away, its tail caught alight.

Baldrake walked up to the little mekkel on the ground and said, 'That was a very brave thing you did back there, old one. I thank you for your aide.'

Happy with himself, Melche smiled and retrieved his knife from the dead beast.

'Let's make haste, Karta isn't far now.' Gordon turned and ran to crest the hill, with the wizard and the wolf not far behind. He slowed as he looked down at the battle being waged on the outskirts of the city. Karta was attacking the Ell-Shadack, driving them from the grounds with great fervour. They headed for the Kraydenian rear echelons, where the general would be. From a hundred feet away, reserved archers at the rear spun away from the battle and took aim at them. They all raised their arms in the air and Gordon shouted, 'Hold on, we've come to help!'

Grackis recognised the young man and bellowed, 'Lower your weapons, boys. I know this lad. Back to your posts.' He sauntered over to the young warrior, eyeing the company he kept, and said with a smile on his face, 'Glad to see you alive, lad. They with you?'

'Aye, they are. It's good to be back, although one could ask for better circumstances. Grackis, where is the general?'

The big blacksmith grabbed him in a bear hug and lifted him in the air, and said, 'Damned good to see you survived, my boy. Come, I'll take you to him.'

Following the big bulky blacksmith, the companions were led to a table standing on the open hill, two figures leaning over it in deep conversation, studying a map and discussing tactics.

Gordon stood at their backs. 'General.' Both men turned to regard him. Suddenly weak in the knees, his heart skipped a beat as he stared at the two men.

'Son? Is that really you?' Laying out tactical advances for the troops and assisting the general with decisions about the battle, his father had become the general's second. Shaking and unable to control himself, he dropped the map and embraced his son, tears streaming down his face as he said, 'I thought you dead. Oh, thank the gods. Where have you been? I've been worried sick.'

Gordon stepped back, trying to take control of the situation, and said, 'Father, it's good to see you well.' He gestured to his companions and said, 'This is Baldrake and Melche. They've been by my side from the beginning and have saved my life more times than I can count.'

Brindell moved to the wolf and threw his arm around its chest, holding the little mekkel with his other hand all teary-eyed as he whispered, 'Thank you, my friends, for protecting him.' He rose and looked at the wizard and said, 'And why were you not mentioned by my son?'

'I only recently joined their party. I am Anukke,' the wizard said with a courteous nod.

'What matters is that he will aid us in ridding the world of this enemy. We've been fighting this evil since the day I started my rite, and it seems it is not near an end yet. But we'll discuss all that later. What's happening here?'

General Blackbeard had graciously stepped aside for the reunion of father and son. Brindell looked over the fields of the battle and said, 'We were under siege for quite some time, and we would not have held out much longer. Luckily, a man named Geldrick sent word for allies hiding in the forests near Caldonia. Major Gweniviere came to our aide with a full battalion. With her help, we're winning this battle. Another man also came with her, with information regarding some nasty creatures on their way. He suggested we get rid of these Ell-Shadack before they arrived. Had the strangest armour—said he got it as a gift.'

With his arms folded, listening to his father, Gordon asked, 'Who is this man?'

Brindell shook his head. 'To the balls of the abyss, I can't remember his name, but... Oh, wait, here he comes now. Hell of a fighter.'

Gordon stared over the rolling hills, the dying light of the sun shining in their eyes. From the distance, he saw a figure coming up the hill at a jog. Cupping his hand over his eyes to block the sun's rays, he said, 'It can't be!'

At the sound of his breaking voice, Baldrake and Melche turned to regard the man as he closed in.

'Well, if it isn't the boy and his pup. You finally come to join in the fun?'

Melche jumped down from the wolf and ran up to Malachai, jumping high, forcing the big man to catch him. 'Okay now, old fellow, enough of that,' Malachai said as he tried to remove the mekkel from him, with no luck.

Gordon prodded the big man in the chest with his finger and said, 'Is it really you?'

Baldrake bowed his head in respect. 'Vasgath, I can honestly say that I am more than happy to see you well, my brother.'

Malachai bent slightly and laid his hands on the wolf's head and Gordon's shoulder, and said, 'Me too, my brothers. Now can someone get Melche off of me?'

Jumping down, the mekkel laughed and ran to clamber onto the back of the wolf.

The big man pushed past them and suddenly, out of nowhere, his enormous fist slammed into the side of the wizard's face, buckling his knees and dropping the man to the ground.

'No! Malachai. He is going to help us. Shit! Is he dead?'

The big man spat on the unconscious wizard and said, 'One can only hope.' A low groan sounded from the ground and he continued, 'Guess I'm not that lucky.' He stared down at the man as blood seeped from his ear. 'Betray us, wizard, and I will break every bone in your body.'

Brindell was puzzled as he looked at them and said, 'Do you know each other?'

'Yes, Father, Malachai was the very first to join me on the quest. I thought him dead after we got separated in Milleria. I'm glad to be proven wrong.'

The big man slapped Gordon on his back as he said, 'Looks like you came just in time to see us take victory.'

The Ell-Shadack were pulling back, retreating into the forest and heading back to the forbidden lands of Krell. Karta's army pursued them to the edge of the field and turned to celebrate their victory. The night would be a peaceful one.

Malachai took the companions to the inn and got them settled in for the night as Gordon and his father made their way to their home, speaking at length as they travelled. Halfway he stopped and said to his father, 'I would like nothing more than to come home and sit and talk with you, Father, but I've started this journey and I need to finish this; my friends will need me. I must go to them. There's much to discuss.'

Brindell sighed, and Gordon saw his father's shoulders sag as he said, 'I understand, my son. I respect your decision. Just please, be careful. If you need anything, you know where to find me.'

'Thank you, sir.'

Gordon turned and left for the inn where his friends were waiting for him.

Throughout the night, they took turns watching the wizard. Gordon had explained the situation to Malachai, who was unwilling to let the wizard live any longer. Calming him was a great endeavour, and it still worried him that the big guy would kill the wizard in his sleep during his watch, so he stayed awake for both their turns just in case.

The morning that followed, Gordon sat in the grass woven chair in the corner, staring at the sleeping companions. Malachai rose, stretching his muscles, staring out of the window overlooking the city.

'We all took your death hard, you know, but he,' Gordon pointed to the little old mekkel as he spoke, then continued, 'took your death hardest. Barely said a word since I told him of your accident. I am ashamed that I left you, a failure I will not live down. I should have searched for you. How did you manage to not die in that fall?'

'Poor little fellow.' Malachai sighed and said, 'It was not your choice to let go. It was mine. There was no way of knowing that I had survived, and I never blamed you for leaving me. I can't really remember what happened exactly. It was so dark. As I fell, I could swear I heard a voice telling me to hold out my arms and ready myself. I did so, and struck a big branch from a tree, but could not hold on. Grabbing at anything from there, I hit plenty more branches going down, snapping them and some of my bones. Hurt like hell! The last thing I remember was hitting my head against a tree, then instant darkness. A while later, I woke up to two hunters picking me up and taking me back to Lady Rose. She healed me as best she could, putting all kinds of herbs over my body. And here I am. All new and shiny.'

In the calm of early morning, they heard the shouts of men rising up in alarm. Then came a wailing cry that shook to the bone. Gordon jumped from his chair and shouted, 'The death swarm.'

Malachai ran to the window and saw a huge, winged creature flying over the city, blowing fire down to the earth from its mouth, and said, 'I'm afraid not.' The huge red serpent turned its attention to the watchtowers and the walls, scorching all the archers that shot at him. Stone and mortar exploded from the heat, debris flying everywhere.

The earth shook the rest of the companions awake with a start. Quickly, they gathered their gear. Melche jumped for his knife and shoved it down his pants, almost cutting off his mekkelhood. Screaming to himself, he yanked out the knife, grabbed the scabbard, clipped it to his belt, and sheathed the weapon. He looked down his pants and sighed with relief that everything was still intact.

With a third of the city burnt to the ground, people were running for their lives, trying to find cover from the death above. Anukke ran outside and stood in the clearing, working his magic, calling up an old spell he could barely remember, and hoped that it would not turn on him. The wizard spoke his alien language, gliding his hands over each other in the shape of a ball. A green-blue spark appeared at first in the centre of his hands, growing to the size of a pig. He spun on his heels, hurling the ball towards the dragon, which had its back turned to them.

Suddenly aware of the awakening magic, the dragon turned in time to catch the green-blue ball of magic in the face. It floundered, struggling for breath as it fell to the ground. Before the impact, it regained its composure and beat its enormous wings to rise back to the sky. The serpent's voice hissed back at them, 'You will die for that, wizard.' Drawing back his breath to burn the wizard to ashes, the dragon exhaled nothing but puffs of blue smoke. Again he inhaled, and again the blue smoke filled the sky. Outraged, the dragon called down, 'My master awaits your arrival at his castle. You will meet your doom in four days!' He flew away, blue puffs trailing in his wake.

Anukke walked back to the door of the inn and said to the cowering innkeeper, 'He will spit blue smoke for months.'

The innkeeper came running to the door with a mug of ale and shoved it in the wizard's hands as he said, 'Thank you, grand wizard! You have truly saved our lives. Three cheers for the wizard!' Cheers went up from the cowering patrons, now laughing and slapping the wizard on his back.

Gordon and Malachai stood at the door, annoyed at the situation. Sure, he had chased away the dragon. If only they knew that it was the wizard's fault in the first place that brought this death to their doors, then they might not be so welcoming to him.

Further down the street, people were running around after the dragon had turned their homes to ash, trying to save what they could. Smoke drifted into the air, and the stench of a few burnt people lingered. Being so close to the main gate, they heard a commotion start up. A voice shouted out as someone hammered on the gate, drawing the attention of the guards, now trailing their arrows over the wall and shouting back. Malachai leaned against the doorframe of the inn with arms folded and said, 'Boy, this day just gets better and better. Let's go see what the ruckus is about.'

The frantic pleas of someone on the other side of the gate got louder as they neared. 'Let me in, it's me, Geldrick! Major Gweniviere will vouch for me. I have urgent news for the general. Let me in!' Geldrick hammered on the gates with his fists until they bled. He turned to leave just as he heard the drawbar being lifted to fall away. As the gates opened, he stumbled forward and fell into the arms of Malachai, who caught the exhausted man and shouted, 'Bring a bucket of water! Damn it. Gordon, grab his arm. We need to move him out of the sun—he's burning up.'

They moved the man to the closest shade under a tree as one guard brought a canteen filled with water and handed it over. 'When last did you drink water, man?' Malachai asked as he drizzled just a little into the man's cracked and bleeding mouth. Geldrick, slow in his movements, took the bottle and drank deep, then said, 'I can't remember. I have been running for over four days.'

'Slow down then, take small amounts first.'

Gordon looked at the man and the state of his torn clothes, there was no doubt that he had been on the run for some time. 'Tell us your message; we will see it delivered to the general.'

Slow rolling eyes found him, and Geldrick said, 'I'm sorry, I don't want to doubt you, but I don't trust anyone after what I saw.'

They stared at each other and Gordon said, 'Okay, then, let's go to the general.' Lifting Geldrick by his arms, they began walking when Baldrake emerged from the inn.

'What has happened to him?'

Geldrick snapped at Baldrake, 'Get away from me, you filthy coward dog!'

Confused and belittled, Baldrake did not understand what was happening. Malachai and Gordon had stopped at the reprimanding, and the big man looked into the eyes of the wolf, gesturing with his hand for him to follow them. Geldrick hopped along, carried on either side by the two men.

'General Blackbeard!' They stood before the general's tent, being shoved away by the sentries on duty. 'Get off me, you fool!' Malachai shouted aloud.

'What in the name of...' General Blackbeard drew open the tent flap and stopped as soon as he saw Geldrick, 'Leave them!' He rushed forward and helped Geldrick from the ground, then said, 'What happened to him?'

'He has something important to tell you, sir, and we all would like to hear what that is, especially Baldrake.' They moved the man into the tent and closed the flap after the wolf had entered.

The general moved forward and sat down at the table. 'Please sit.'

As they all sat, Geldrick stared at the wolf sitting across from him on his haunches, and said, 'I am sorry, General, but I do not wish to speak in the presence of these... cowards.' The disgust was heavy in his voice. Malachai immediately intervened as he saw the wolf rise. 'These Gars may be a lot of things, but one is for sure, Reaper is no coward, my friend. I have known him for a very long time and fought many battles at his side. I would choose him above most men to watch my back, so I beg you, watch your tongue. Whatever you have to say, you say in front of him.'

The general combed his beard with his fingers, and said, 'Talk. We don't have time to waste.'

'Fine then. A few days ago, I saw the first Gar hounds get to the city. I then saw their general lead them in and heard him telling them he had a few errands to run and that they should wait for him here. I thought it strange, and so started trailing the wolf. Day and night, we travelled without stopping. He was in a hurry. I was as cautious as possible not to be seen, and still a few times he almost caught wind of me. We travelled deep into the forbidden lands of Krell, where I saw him give himself over to the Ell-Shadack near the castle. I climbed the cliffs at the back and sought my way in from there. Finally getting to the main hall, I saw this king, sitting on his throne when the wolf was brought in before him. He sold us out, general. He told this Ortega everything, about how he was forced to send his wolves to bring allies back to us, about how we intended on attacking him by surprise. Revealed our entire plan. All in return for their lives to be spared!'

Baldrake couldn't take it anymore. All the name-calling and the constant humiliation was driving him mad. Launching himself on the table, he swiftly moved to stand before Geldrick, lowering his face to stare him in the eyes. Malachai and Gordon were flung from the table and struggled to get up; watching from the ground, they heard the wolf speak. 'I hope for your sake that what you say is true. If it isn't, it will be your last lie!' Baldrake jumped clear over Geldrick's head, landing just before the tent flap, and stormed out without stopping, knocking the sentries from their feet.

'Come quick, we need to follow him!' Gordon shouted as he got up and gave chase with the big man close on his heels. Geldrick staggered out and slowly made his way in their direction.

The Gar camp was always kept separate from the main camp; everyone feared the wolves. Gordon and Malachai stormed into the Gar camp after Baldrake, following the cloud of dust as he ran through the streets. Reaching the centre of the camp, they saw the two wolves already circling each other.

'Is it true, Minx?! Tell your brothers what you have done!' Baldrake roared aloud for all to hear.

'Tell them what, Baldrake? You always had a flair for the dramatic. What is it this time?'

'Tell them how you betrayed us! How you consorted with the enemy in his own castle, giving him all the details of our plan.'

All the Gar hounds started speaking to each other, some snarling at Baldrake, the others growling at Minx. For the Gar hounds, their pride was most valued, and betrayal was dealt with with the utmost severity. Snarling, fangs bared, Minx said, 'Fine, you want to hear me say it! I went to Ortega, I told him about your plot. And you want to know why?'

The Gar hounds who were snarling at Baldrake ceased and turned their attention to Minx, who said, 'Brothers, we were cast to this unholy place because of him—your old general... We do not belong here. This is not our fight! I told Ortega everything because he is the only one who can send us back to Gar, all of us!'

By now, the wolves were howling and barking and growling and snarling. Baldrake roared out, 'You fool! Ortega does not do favours. He will send you back just to go with you and destroy Gar, just as he will destroy this world if we do not stop him now. He will kill everyone you left behind, and you will be to blame!'

Suddenly all the wolves went silent, all listening to Baldrake speak.

'Twelve years ago, I made the mistake of sending my squadron into that void. Our information suggested that was where the enemy camp was. Only we were lied to, the same way you are being lied to now. Not a day goes by that I do not think about that day.'

Minx growled and stormed. 'Enough talking!'

He caught Baldrake off guard, lunged for his neck, but got hold of a shoulder blade instead. The two wolves rolled around on the ground, swiping claws and snapping jaws. Minx spat out tufts of black fur as he was thrown to the side, his teeth ripping out of Baldrake's shoulder. Charging in, he bit the back leg of the black wolf. Baldrake turned and latched on to his hind end as they tumbled over the erect tents, snapping the supporting lines. Gordon started forward to intervene in this madness but was stopped as Malachai thrust out his arm in front of him, and said, 'This is his fight. It needs to be done.'

On the ground, where the two wolves had rolled, lay trails of blood mixing in with the sand. A faint yelp came from the fight as Baldrake came to his feet and bit down hard on Minx's back. Jerking his head to the left, he threw the wolf. Minx crashed through clay cooking pots lying on the ground, breaking most of them, scattering the rest. He surged up and went for Baldrake's jugular, but only found skin and fur as he lifted the bigger wolf to the air and slammed him on the ground. Fighting for his life, Baldrake fended off the vicious bites trying to get to his throat.

Seeing a small opening—Minx had left his front left leg unprotected—Baldrake stretched out his jaws, exposing his neck. A bone-shattering crunch sounded as the black wolf bit down hard. A scream of pain erupted from Minx as he staggered back, unable to put weight on his foot.

'Give it up Minx, you are done.'

'Never!' he shouted back as he charged, and they collided heavily. Being the bigger of the two, Baldrake drove him back down on the broken cooking pots. A piercing cry sounded through the camp. Minx rose, swaying on his back legs, blood running down his side. Many of the pots' sharp edges had driven deep into the side of the wolf; some still dangled from his side, his fur caked with blood. 'I did this for us...

Baldrake. All we wanted was to go back home. I am finished. Forgive me, my brethren, I have failed you. May your kill be merciful, my brother.'

Baldrake stared upon the swaying Minx, his legs giving in under him, then rushed in, dipped his head to lock on to the wolf's jugular, and ripped it out with a vicious jerk, taking half of the neck with it. Minx had not even tried to defend himself in this last act; he knew it was over. Baldrake spat out the bloody throat and said, 'Farewell, Minx.' But he could not call him brother and instead turned to his fellow Gar hounds. 'Hear me now. I never wanted this for us, but here we are nonetheless. Now, this world needs us again. You have taken the vow to fight with the humans, so let's show these men how real warriors fight.'

Howls went into the air, some in mourning of their fallen comrade, others excited for the coming battle.

Geldrick walked into the Gar camp and said, 'I'm sorry for the things I said about you; I see now that I was wrong.'

Baldrake nodded and returned to his Gars, cheering them on.

'Who's watching the wizard?' Gordon suddenly asked as they walked back from the Gar camp.

Malachai squeezed his eyes as he looked into the sun, and said, 'Well, we're here, and Baldrake is over at the Gar camp. That means that only... oh... that's not good.'

They ran through the streets back to the inn, thoughts running through their heads of how the wizard had killed the little mekkel, fried him alive with his lightning bolts. Rounding a corner, Malachai knocked a pedestrian to the ground as he ran, shouting over his back, 'Sorry!'

The door slammed open and the dining crowd gave a frightful gasp at the sudden disturbance. Gordon unsheathed his sword and continued up the stairs with Malachai a little behind him. Upon entering the room, he stopped and gazed at the two sitting at the window, looking down at the passers-by, making snobbish comments about everyone. Melche turned to him and said, 'You run funny. Why is Malachai chasing you?'

Anukke also turned at the question, eager to hear his answer, or waiting more likely to hear what little lies he would use.

'We, uh... were exercising.'

Malachai burst into the room at that point, huffing and puffing from the run. Melche rubbed his ears and said, 'There is no time for that. We need to go fight the bad man to the east.'

During the last three days, soldiers had heeded the call for war, be it travellers on the road, soldiers for hire, or farmers and their sons. All came to pledge their steel against the terrible tyrant Ortega. Now they stood in front of General Blackbeard, listening to him giving his speeches while roll calls and name-tagging were taking place, eager for the coming battle. The assembled soldiers, Gar hounds, men, women, and some children—who had lost everything and were willing to die for justice—were not much to look at, but they had spirit. As the general finished his speeches, people cheered and shouted; wolves howled and growled, urging each other on.

Baldrake had once more taken command of his squadron and howled with them from next to General Blackbeard. Melche decided that his best position would be on the wolf's back, and proceeded—without question—to jump on, arguing that if he hadn't killed the big flying bat on their last encounter, he would have been dead and therefore owed him. Baldrake saw in the little old mekkel's eyes how much it meant to him to stand and fight this war with his friends. Although he knew he was going to have to protect this little creature, which meant putting his own life on the line, he dropped his head to the ground and conceded to Melche, 'It would be an honour to have you fight with me.'

Malachai had taken no position or title, although he was offered many. He readily stood at Gwen's side; albeit she was not all too pleased with being looked after, but found it charming that he was so protective. Silent messages had been passing between these two for some time; a brush of a hand, a whisper in the ear. They would run into each other every so often by accident; one would swear it was deliberate.

Gordon and Anukke would have one task: while everyone was distracted by the battle, they had to get to Ortega and plunge the mercury dagger into his heart. What could possibly go wrong?

As nighttime approached, everyone returned to their lodgings for one final good night's rest. Malachai slipped out of their room, moving through the deathly quiet streets of Karta until he came to a stop before another inn. Reaching out, he wanted to push on the doorknob but stopped just as he touched the cold iron. Retracting his hand, he paced back and forth in front of the building, muttering to himself, 'Stupid... You're a man... she's a woman... what am I—'

'Hey! Down there, you mind? Some people are trying to sleep,' came a woman's voice from the window. Malachai looked up and said, 'Sorry, miss. I will take my leave.'

'Malachai, is that you?' Gwen called.

Ruffling his hair and looking around for an escape, he said, 'Uh, oh, uh. Yah, it's me. Our inn's coffee is finished. Do you have any to spare for a guy like me? I mean... Oh, never mind.'

Gwen giggled and called down, 'Come up. I'm sure we can arrange something hot.'

Blushing, the big man wasted no time entering the inn this time.

Tonight would be the last night spent in Karta, the last night in comfortable beds, the last night loved ones would have to hold one another. For when the sun rose in the morning, thirty thousand soldiers would march to the forbidden lands of Krell, where they would take back their world from this savage monster.

CHAPTER NINETEEN

For three days and two nights, they had travelled the lands undisturbed. Ortega wanted a war and wasn't willing to kill his enemy from miles away. He wanted to see their destruction, smell their death.

Camping for the last night, everyone was silent and focused on what lay ahead, for over the hill lay the battlefield, and with that, the coming of death. Quiet in their business, everyone knew what was expected of them. Together, the companions sat around a fire with very little in the way of conversation. Gordon stuck a twig in the fire and stared at it as it blazed, then looked up to his friends, and Anukke, then said, 'We have been through hell to get as far as we have. We have fought side-by-side and also each other,' he looked at Anukke and then Baldrake. 'But come tomorrow, we will all face the same enemy. My brothers, I only ask one thing of you tomorrow. Come back alive and give them hell.'

Malachai lifted his cup and said, 'Hear, hear. Same goes for you, lad.'

'That was two things,' Melche said as he walked around the fire, eyeing the cask of ale next to the big man.

'So it was.'

'You said one.' He waited for them to be distracted.

'Oh, yeah. Guess I made a mistake.' Gordon chuckled and blushed as he asked for another ale from Malachai.

Baldrake nodded and Melche stole the ale, drinking it as fast as possible before the big man could get it back. A loud belch went up from the little mekkel as the big man fell over a rock on the grassy field.

'Whoa, that was loud enough to scare off most of the Ell-Shadack,' Malachai said as he lay laughing on the ground, trying to catch the mekkel.

Anukke, silent and ever watchful, sat eyeing his "companions." *What fools they are. Most of them will die tomorrow.*

The sun rose as normal, but no birds chirped today. Infact, no animal life was visible. All was quiet, except for the general riding on horseback up and down the front lines, bellowing out his best war speeches. At the end of his speeches, he raised his sword and pointed it at the castle over the hill, only the top of the towers visible at this distance. A lush green meadow and thousands of Ell-Shadack separated them. 'They don't seem to outnumber us that much! By nightfall, we go home victorious! Come on, men, let's get this over with.'

As if in response to his speech, thousands of black creatures streamed from the top of the castle in the distance, blotting out the sky as they swarmed. *We stirred the hornet's nest.* The murmuration of the swarm floated up and down as they flew in their direction, almost beautiful if you didn't know what they were. Their horrifying, shrill screams echoed over the plains.

The general lowered his sword and whispered, 'May the gods be with us all.' Then he shouted, 'Ready the archers!'

The belligerent swarm of death came at them with menacing speed and vigour. Arrows filled the sky, cutting through the black mass, and then they clashed; steel against raw hide, fangs and claws, they fought. Tearing into the ranks, limbs went flying as the creatures sliced with their sharp talons. Soldiers cut left and right to even the score.

Holding on to one of the creatures' necks with his bare hands, Malachai twisted his arms and heard the snap. As the body fell to the ground amidst the turmoil, he saw out of the corner of his eye a group of draghnai, around twenty, advancing on them with the Ell-Shadack not far behind. He unslung his hammer and shouted, 'I will take the lot of you with me to wherever it is I'm going!'

A large bringer of death headed towards him in a raging fury, and just as the creature reached him, six big falcons lifted the Vanta a' koreen into the air, tearing at and killing it. The body dropped to the ground in the battle's midst, causing everyone to look to the sky. Silver-winged gryphons attacked the draghnai, and thousands of their smaller companions, the falcons, attacked the death swarm, the smaller birds pairing up, attacking them four and more at a time. Cheers went up to their new allies as they rained death from above to their enemies.

Finally free of the death swarm to fight the Ell-Shadack, the Kraydenian soldiers came at them with renewed vigour.

A deadly dust cloud headed for the Ell-Shadack flank at great speed. Baldrake ran at the front of the wedge-shaped formation as they hit with great force, dividing the enemy as they pushed deeper, his armour glinting in the sunlight with the mekkel screaming his war cries from his back, stabbing and slicing with his big knife. The Gar hounds fought like demons possessed with extraordinary power. Every Ell-Shadack, every one of the death swarm that strayed, was at the hands of instant death.

Ortega and Anthelos stood on his balcony, overlooking the layered battle in the distance. High above, fire adorned the blue sky as the draghnai fought with the silver-winged gryphons. Below them, the falcons and the death swarm raged in their battles. On the ground, soldiers, wolves, and Ell-Shadack fought for victory. Anthelos, as calm as ever, regarded his lord and said, 'We have to gather in the main hall for your upcoming victory, my liege.'

Ortega didn't take his eyes off the battle, hunger burning holes in his soul, the need for blood rushing over him. 'No, I will join the battle down below. I will break them myself.'

They cut through the forest, moving stealthily, not to be noticed by any stragglers. Anukke led the way to the secret tunnel entrance that would lead them into the castle. As they entered the tunnel, Gordon unsheathed his sword and set off at a jog, Anukke following close behind. Twice the height of a man and nearly triple in width, the walls, carved from the rock, were scorched black, a putrid smell of decay clinging to the air.

Gordon, focused on the tunnel ahead, spoke without turning his head to the wizard. 'You know your part in this. Do not slip up.'

'Oh, I know my part in this, little warrior. Don't you worry about a thing.' Anukke grinned and fell back with his hands folded neatly in his robe's sleeves. *I know my part all too well...*

As they reached the entrance to the castle, a small wooden trapdoor at the top of the tunnel with a rusty old steel ladder running down to the surface greeted them.

Anukke climbed up first, slowly lifted the door, and peered inside. Silently they climbed up and realised they were standing in what must be a kitchen. Frying pans, cooking pots, and burnt meat lay all over the long tables in the cold room.

'That passage leads to the main hall and through to the stairs, to his chambers.' Anukke pointed to one of the three passages leading out of the kitchen area.

'Let's move, then.'

Along the passageways, they saw no movement; everything was eerily quiet, too quiet. Reaching the massive open hall, they stopped and leaned against the side of the wall to peer inside. All kinds of artwork ordained the hall. A long red carpet ran the length to stop before the elaborate throne. Six gigantic square pillars ran along both edges of the carpet, holding up the roof high above. The sun pierced through the large windows in the ceiling, bringing light to the room. Past the throne was the door leading to the stairs. 'Looks empty. Let's go.'

Gordon suddenly grabbed the wizard and pulled him in behind one pillar as he jumped to the next. Even as the wizard wanted to protest this action, he realised someone was coming down the corridor from the stairs towards the hall. *How did he hear them? I hadn't even sensed their presence yet.*

They waited from behind the pillars as their enemy moved to sit on the throne, the other walking up and down in front of him.

Ortega and Anthelos were deep in conversation regarding the future. 'What are we going to do with the remaining people of this world?' asked Anthelos, as he walked with his hands behind his back.

Ortega drank deep from a golden goblet and said, 'We put to work those who do not oppose us and kill those who do. Conquer the remaining cities across the seas and spread our empire further.'

Gordon stepped out from behind the pillar, his sword unsheathed and held at his side. 'I am afraid that will not happen for you.' Anukke sighed, rolled his eyes, and also came out from behind his cover. Anthelos turned, drawing his sword in the same breath, ready to face the intruders, but was brushed aside as Ortega moved past to look upon them.

His stomach churned as he saw his enemy for the first time. Gordon could not believe his eyes, and said, 'Tuds, is that you?' Before him stood the man he had fought with, side-by-side, in the cave against those rapists so long ago now, yet the memory ran through his head as if it was only yesterday.

Ortega moved closer, and said with a wave of the hand, 'Tudeske is dead; I am all that remains. You have failed him, as you will fail the thousands outside giving their lives for this war. I was just about to step outside and join the battle, now you have brought me this delightful warmup.' With a courteous but mocking bow, he continued, 'I thank you for this timely gift.'

Gordon saw the physical changes in the man. He was no skinny noble brat; this man was a well-built, hardened warrior. A scar had manifested from the side of his face down to his neck and disappeared under his armour, an old wound that had walked with Ortega for a very long time. Ortega pulled free his sword and motioned for Anthelos to move to the wizard, and said, 'And you, wizard, you would betray me? I should have killed you the first time I saw you.'

Anukke smiled but said nothing, his hands still in the sleeves.

Adorned in his golden armour, the usurper king moved closer to the young warrior, sword ready, and said, 'I will not waste my power on you; this will be a fair fight. I hope you are worthy. By the way, I love your eyes. Maybe when you're dead, I'll wear them around my neck.'

'You're going to die once and for all, Ortega. No prison for you this time.'

Anthelos circled the wizard and threw him a crude old sword from the wall, saying, 'At least try to defend yourself.'

Anukke avoided the thrown sword and let it clatter on the floor. 'Thanks, but I brought my own.' He pulled out his hands from the robe and spoke his magic into being, forming a sword of lightning, the colour of the sun.

Anthelos stared at the sword in the wizard's hands, and said, 'Hmph, impressive.'

With not a word further, Gordon attacked with great ferocity, lunging blows left and right, stabbing forth, slicing left and spinning around, and struck the king on the golden armour, glancing off with no physical damage. But there was a mental one.

Malachai slammed his knee against the face of an Ell-Shadack warrior, crushing his skull and leaving the man on the ground. He stepped over to meet another with a flailing axe and knocked it away with his hammer, then reversed his hand, breaking the brow ridge of the man, collapsing his eye socket. The Ell-Shadack screamed as he tried to shove his dangling eye back into place, with no success. Malachai brought down the hammer again, then shouted, 'Come on, you bastards! Is this all you have?'

A large death-bringer answered with a shrieking cry and dove from the sky at him. Ready with his hammer, Malachai awaited the beast with its scything talons. He swung with all his might as the creature neared, but it covered its flank as the blow struck, skidding it over rocks and ruts in the ground. It got back to its feet and lunged at Malachai's throat. As he ducked under the talons, his stomach suddenly burned from a deep gash. Blood poured from the wound. He fell back, clutching the slash with his one hand, fending off the beast with the other.

Men were falling all around him, dying in scores on both sides. Malachai tripped over the foot of a dying soldier, and the beast dove on top of him at great speed. Cuts rained down on him. His shoulder burst into pain as the creature sank its vile teeth into it, shaking its head to break his arm. A repulsive black tarry liquid flowed from the beast's mouth, dripping over Malachai's face, the stench horrible. Suddenly he gripped the creature's neck and head-butted it with incredible force. He was back on his feet as it staggered back. Then, using his mighty hammer, he swung it up, lifting the creature high as the snap of bones sounded, then brought down the hammer on the creature's head, splitting the skull, and it sagged to the ground.

Malachai looked up, air wheezing from his lungs as fatigue set in, and saw Gwen in the distance, surrounded by the Ell-Shadack, fighting for her life. *We are only a few that remain.* Over the rise, he saw thousands more of the once-dead marching from the right. *Gordon, we need you to finish this soon.* He let out a loud whistle as he looked to his left, gesturing to the new threat. Raising his hammer, he screamed as he charged the Ell-Shadack surrounding Gwen.

The Ell-Shadack forces had scattered Baldrake's squadron. At the sound of the whistle, he looked up and saw the big man's gesture, then followed his gaze to the right. 'Form up! Form up now!' he roared. His wolves fell into their wedge formation as they charged the advancing once-dead. They swung around the main force and drove into the flank, tearing at limbs and necks, killing with extreme prejudice. The slaughter was surreal as they gave a much-needed respite. A sword bounced off his armour, making his legs buckle. Then he remembered about the little mekkel on his back. 'Melche! Are you still with me?' He roared over his shoulder.

Bounced around and thrown up to land hard on the back of the canine, the mekkel was holding on with everything he had and shouted, 'Melche still here! But Melche wishes Melche wasn't!'

Baldrake laughed and roared, 'Today, my mekkel friend, we become the stuff of legends!'

Melche raised his long hunting knife and shouted as he sliced through the throat of an enemy as Baldrake jumped for another. As Melche looked back, he saw a wolf fall under a blade in a splash of blood. *They have no armour; Melche wishes Melche had time to make their armour.* A deep sadness swept over him.

They successfully divided the advancing enemy, giving much needed time for their force to regain their line. Arrows rained down, killing hundreds closer to the frontline before the clash of steel was heard as the two forces hit. Fire scorched the earth and more of his wolves died as a draghnai escaped the clutches of a gryphon momentarily before having its throat ripped open. They drove the wedge deeper, a trail of blood and corpses left in their wake, then turned to re-join the main force.

Ortega staggered back and smiled as he looked at the young warrior, then charged. Swinging that greatsword through the air with ease, he pushed his opponent back, who parried the blows but struggled to keep his footing.

A pommel breached Gordon's defences and struck him in the face. He staggered back, clutching his nose as blood spilled from it, and still the broadsword came at him unabated. He stepped back, trying his best not to fall, ducking and diving between the blows. A wild cut sliced into his thigh, and his foot slipped on the blood. With his vision fading as his left eye shut from the swelling, he saw sparks fly as the lightning sword bit into the steel of Anthelos' blade. *Who knew the wizard could fight?*

The king's guardian cursed as the lightning blade cut across his chest, deep enough for blood to stream, but not to hit organs. More and more shallow cuts burned into his flesh, weakening him with every one of them.

Suddenly from above, they heard a great roar; the castle shook violently, throwing them all to the floor as the roof of the hall caved and, with loud cracks, the red dragon tore open part of the roof, snaking its way into the hall. In a far corner, it seemed as if the walls, floor and pillars were melting together, swirling and forming something new. A bright light blinded them from the corner, and as it vanished, Lady Rose stood before them, spinning her staff and bellowing words of unknown origin. She reprimanded the dragon as it turned to face her. It bore down on her with its maw open, the great fangs biting down into a magical protective shield around her. Furious, it came down again and again, trying to tear through the barrier. She still spun the staff in her hands as she stood beneath the barrage of strikes from the beast. A great wind was born from the staff, forcing back the dragon. Its taloned claws dug into the stone floor and walls as it slid ever back from the driving wind. It clutched the broken roof with all its might. Mouth open, the winds drove the blue smoke from its lungs, and small embers drifted from its mouth once more. A great blow to its chest lifted it through the air, and it crashed into the walls a distance away. The castle walls were giving in; the roof had collapsed in most parts, nevertheless; they fought on. The serpent crawled over the roof, and fire rained down on them. Lady Rose contained the blaze as best she could, but the heat was getting intense.

Gordon and Ortega fought on, ignoring the dragon raging above them. A vicious cut from Gordon sliced through the golden armour, cutting deep across the chest and shoulder of Ortega. The armour was in tatters as the binding straps gave way. Ortega jerked at the breastplate, tearing it off and throwing it to the ground. The swords sang through the air as they clashed. Gordon went to the ground on his knees and stabbed Ortega through the thigh. Enraged, the usurper king picked Gordon up by the throat and hurled him across the room and into a wall.

Air exploded from his lungs as Gordon sagged to the ground. He heard a clangour next to him and saw the shield had come undone from his back after the blow to the wall. Groggy, his head pounded in his skull as he made to pick up the shield. Ortega was fast approaching with that sword. He launched himself onto the shield and skidded away as the sword came down crashing through the floorboards. Barely back on his feet, a mighty blow to the shield sent reverberations through his arms. Then another. And another. Gordon could feel his energy slipping from his being. He could barely hang on to the shield anymore. He blocked a savage thrust by Ortega and sliced his sword up, nicking the king's sword arm. A trickle of blood flowed down his bicep. This momentary loss of focus gave Gordon an opening, and he swung the shield of Nethas at the king. But this was not to be.

Ortega had seen it coming and jumped back, then rammed his shoulder into the shield, the force driving Gordon to his knees. Blood stained the floor as it dripped from his mouth. Gordon could no longer focus. Loud percussions deafened him as the dragon climbed over the ceiling and spewed its flames. The heat was so intense it felt like his insides were boiling. His arms burned like they never had before, and still, Ortega stood before him with barely a scratch now as he advanced. A blinding light exploded from Ortega. Gordon screamed as the skin was torn from his body, peeling away to reveal raw flesh. He could see the usurper's mouth moving, casting the spell. He heard a voice from the corner, 'Trust the shield!'

Through the pain, he pushed himself to his feet, bringing up the shield before his body and cut his arm over the rim, letting his blood seep into it. Instantly, the phoenix came alive, and Gordon could feel the effects of the magic diminish.

Ortega's eyes widened as he roared, 'Impossible!' He sheathed his sword and shouted his chant, squeezing his hands together as one would form a clay ball. Loud creaks sounded from the shield as an unseen force drove it and Gordon back, the edges of the metal buckling and bending under the pressure; but it held. Then, from the corner of the room, a piece of the wall hurtled into the shield, flinging Gordon back.

Anukke and Anthelos were in a death-lock, sparks flying as their swords bit into each other. Although Anthelos was much stronger physically than the wizard, Anukke had considerable skill with a blade. Seeing Gordon in trouble, he lost his focus on the fight, and a sudden left hook clobbered into the wizard's ribs. Coughing and searching for air, he struggled to regain his posture, then shouted, 'To hell with this!'

He shook his hands, and the sword vanished. Magical words left his mouth and immediately Anthelos charged in, raising his sword to deal the death blow; but the wizard ducked and thrust out his hand, the lightning blade jumping back to life. Anthelos stopped and dropped his sword to the floor. Looking down, he saw the red lightning coursing through his chest. Anukke stood and dragged the blade up to the man's face and out through his skull, and waited for him to collapse to the ground. He shook his head and pulled free the mercury dagger from his back—and vanished.

Lady Rose had seen him pull free the dagger and shouted to Gordon, 'No, stop him, don't let—' She had taken the chance to thrust a lightning bolt in the wizard's direction, but just before she could cast her spell, she was thrown from her feet and flung to the ground as Gordon tackled her.

Seeing Anthelos fall, Ortega turned to flee as they outnumbered him—and felt a jabbing pain shoot through his body. Slowly, as if he were a mirage, Anukke materialised before him, the mercury dagger protruding from Ortega's chest. The wizard bent over, catching the collapsing Ortega while holding on to the knife's hilt.

Gordon and Lady Rose still rolled around on the ground as she tried to squirm out of his grasp. 'You fool!' she shouted. 'Do you know what you have done?'

'That was the only way to kill him!'

'Fool, the Ornieël Dagger does not *stop* power, it takes, and gives it to the wielder!'

Gordon paled. The dragon fled as the magical claim on him ended. Shrieks of terror were heard as the death swarm flew away. Ell-Shadack collapsed to the ground, dead for good, as Ortega drew his last breath and died. The pair looked upon the wizard Anukke as he stood laughing, lifting the dagger to the sky triumphantly.

Violently shaking, the castle was breaking apart as everything around them crumbled.

Anukke laughed unfazed as the castle broke apart around him. His eyes gleamed as he shouted, 'So long have I waited!' Waves of power poured into him from the dagger.

Bathed in sweat, he suddenly stopped laughing and bent over, gripping his stomach. 'No, what is happening. No! Why? What is happening to me? No!' Convulsive fits tortured the wizard, sending him to his knees. Blood streamed down his face as his skin cracked, seeping from wounds all over. Screaming from all the pain, he soon couldn't bear it anymore.

They stared in disbelief and horror as the wizard tore himself apart, piece by piece. Anukke lay on the ground, convulsing. As if a small bomb had exploded in his skull, his eyes suddenly bulged outward, and blood streamed from the sockets.

'He did say there would be blood. I just didn't know it would be his.' Gordon said as he grabbed Lady Rose by the wrist and pulled her from the floor. They ran to the kitchen and out through the tunnel as the castle collapsed.

Gordon and Lady Rose ran through the forest, heading towards the battlefield. Cheers went up as he saw the few remaining soldiers. The Gar hounds and gryphons stood by, looking down at the field of dead.

Lady Rose approached the magnificent silver winged gryphons and said, 'I thank you for heeding my call, great ones.' From behind her, Gordon said, 'Thank you, Lady Rose.' He looked to the noble beasts and continued, 'I do not know if you understand me, but thank you for coming to our aide, without you we all would have perished.' A stream of cries went up from the gryphons as they took to the sky.

Malachai came from the side as soon as he saw Gordon and embraced him, lifting him to the air in a great bear hug, then winced from the gash on his stomach. 'We beat those bastards! Now you may smoke that cigar.'

Bruised and battered, Baldrake and the little mekkel came from the distance. Melche, walking with a certain triumphant air about him, said, 'You can thank Melche now for saving your life and killing all the Ell-Shadack.'

Smiling, Gordon bowed down. 'I thank you, noble warrior.' He turned to the wolf. 'Ah, Baldrake, you fought valiantly. No one will ever forget what you Gar did for us here, especially not me. Thank you for all you've sacrificed.'

'This is our world as well. The quicker we learn that, the better for us.'

The wolf turned his gaze to Malachai and said, 'Glad to see you came out of this alive.'

Gwen ran up to the big man and flung herself in his arms, kissing him violently. In between the momentary breaths, he said, 'I think I came out better than just alive, old friend. Wait, Gwen, my arm... Ouch!'

Surprised, the companions stood and watched the big man being overwhelmed by the major, then burst out laughing.

EPILOGUE

S pring was on its way as the sun's heat intensified. The rebuilding of Karta and the other fallen cities had started, but they would never forget the destruction wrought on the lands.

He walked through the streets and stopped at the blacksmith's shop, hearing the high-pitched voice of Melche in the background when Grackis walked out of the shop and said, 'Ah, Gordon, so good to see you, lad. You ready for the ceremony?'

'Aye, I am,' he said as he looked over the shoulder of the smith. 'Melche giving you a hard time?'

'Don't you worry about him; I'll get used to him. I rather like the little rascal. See you at the ceremony.'

Grackis turned and left as Gordon said, 'See you later.'

As night approached, he made his way to the centre of town, where he found Malachai and Gwen running about, shouting orders for the last touches before the ceremony started. Without making himself known to them, he moved away to sit on his own, waiting for the feast to begin.

☿

'Ladies and gentlemen!' Regan called out from the heavily decorated stage. 'We are gathered here tonight not just to conclude the longest Rite of Passage ever to occur to one of our youths, but also to celebrate life. To mourn those who passed, and to thank them for their courage. Please give a warm welcome for the man who did so much more than complete his Rite of Passage!'

Everyone clapped and shouted as Gordon climbed the stairs to the centre. Regan gripped his hand and shook it before walking away.

Gordon looked over the crowd before him and saw his friends at the front, cheering him on. 'Thank all of you. This must have been the toughest rite in history. And if it weren't for the friends I encountered on my way, I would never have made it out alive. I want you all to realise that, no matter what race or species, there's good to be found in all of us. We all go through trials and tribulations in life, but it's how you handle them that makes you who you are. This might be my night, but it belongs to all of us. It belongs to the fallen heroes on the battlefield.' He raised his glass and said, 'To the fallen!'

A roar went up as everyone shouted, 'To the fallen!'

He left the stage and walked out back to sit alone on a bench overlooking a grassy park. Lost in thought, he didn't hear the big wolf approach, and jumped as he heard, 'Why so sad?'

'Oh, hey, Baldrake. Didn't hear you coming.'

'You seem distraught. What is wrong?'

Gordon sighed and asked, 'What's our purpose now that evil has been conquered? What do we do?'

The wolf snorted. 'There will always be evil out there in the world; it will never be fully conquered. There is always someone out there who thrives on chaos, who believes they are meant to rule. There is always another adventure.'

A stone flew from Gordon's hands as he said, 'I'm sorry you didn't get the revenge you sought for Beldrin and Cuorco.'

A low rumble escaped Baldrake's mouth. 'We all were where we were supposed to be. He is dead. That is all that matters.'

'I did say I wanted to free those people in the mines of Milleria. I think that might be my next adventure. You want to tag along?'

Grinning his wolfish grin, Baldrake roared, 'Only if I choose the boat this time! But first, I have to travel to the monastery, to pay my respects.'

'If you don't mind, I'll come with and help you bury him.'

'Thank you, Gordon. I would like that.'

'I hope youse two aren't thinking of leaving without me,' came a voice from behind. Malachai approached as he sucked on the cigar, the fire lighting up his ice-blue eyes.

'I would be honoured to have you there, Vasgath.'

A tangible dark that would terrify the demons of the night encompassed the oppressive, soundless, and seemingly endless room. No sound was heard, and no breath of air was felt.

Groggy and confused, Anukke pushed himself up off the black floor. 'What... where am I?' Looking around, he saw nothing but darkness, a void that swallowed everything. Standing in the ever-reaching black, he walked forward, his footsteps silent, but everything looked the same, or nothing did. Afraid for the first time in his life, he started running, and shouted, 'What is this place? Am I dead?'

'Yes, in a manner of speaking,' came a voice from all around him.

Lightning arced from Anukke's fingertips, racing into the nothingness as he summoned forth his power.

'That will not help you here, my son,' came the calm old voice once again.

'Show yourself, coward!'

Sighing the sad sigh of the old, ashamed father of a disobedient child, the voice said, 'Why must they always be so difficult? I will tell you where you are if you will stop throwing around those lights. They hurt my eyes.'

Anukke twisted and turned, trying to find the person speaking to him, but could see nothing. 'Fine, I will stop. Now tell me.'

'You are here and you are there; you are everywhere, yet you are nowhere. Does that answer your question, son?'

'What?! That answers nothing, you old fool!' Anukke cursed and sent forth another lightning bolt with some fireballs for good measure.

'Oh dear, oh dear. They never learn. I shall speak with you again when I am ready to. Goodbye, my son.'

Lifting his hands in the air, Anukke shouted, 'What is with this *my son* nonsense?' But no answer came. He walked again, cursing as he did.

For what seemed like days, Anukke travelled the void, the all-consuming nothingness, when at last he saw something standing out from a distance in the darkness. Running to the object, he saw that it was a single flower in bloom. One rose to punctuate the vast nothingness. He shouted, 'Rose, is this your doing? Is this payback? Fine, you got me this time! Now let me out, damn you!'

The voice came again, this time much closer. 'Who is this Rose you speak of? If she could do this to you as I have, I would like to meet her.'

Holding the rose, Anukke thought of that last statement, then said, 'If you let me out, I can take you to her, arrange a meeting.'

'Oh, you are clever, but so am I. Goodbye for now.'

'Why am I not getting hungry or thirsty or anything?' Anukke asked himself.

'Because the dead do not need sustenance,' came the voice.

'How did I get here?'

The voice calmly stated, 'I brought you here.'

Anukke, growing angry, said, 'I killed Ortega with the Ornieël dagger! I was not supposed to die!'

'Yes, of course.'

'Why am I here?' He wanted to cry with frustration.

'To learn, my child.'

'To learn what?' There was no use in fighting anymore.

'To learn how to control and use your power, and your temper... these tantrums are just not working for me. You will be reborn into something else, or maybe not. We shall see and judge. Until then, goodbye, my son.'

The End

AFTERWORD

Thank you for reading Mercury Dagger - A Tale From Kraydenia. I really hope you enjoyed this novel. If you have a moment, please leave a review on Amazon or your preferred store as this will allow me the opportunity to write more books such as this. I would really appreciate it. Reviews are especially critical in today's world. Help other fantasy readers and tell them why you enjoyed this book. Thank you!

Want to stay updated with news about my books?

* Join my mailing list at:

https://www.mariushvisser.com/contact

* Like me on Facebook:

https://www.facebook.com/mariushvisserbooks

* Follow me on Twitter:

https://twitter.com/MariusHVisser

Thank you again, reader. I hope we meet again soon amidst the battles to come in a new adventure.

* Hint, there's a sneak preview of the upcoming novel *Daughter Of The Ageian* on the next page…

Enjoy Chapter One from DAUGHTER OF THE AGEIAN, Book One of the Dragon Wars Saga.

The blood of King Madock was still hot on his hands; the taste of victory lay naked before him. Galvos reached down and gripped the hand of the dead king as he repeated a phrase, over and over, 'Entou ta kamien a saldjien.' The body of the king spasmed, his muscles pulled taut making him seem animate once more.

As the chant continued, a mist of blood flowed from every orifice of the former king. Larger and larger it grew until a sphere the size of a man's head circled above the warlock. Beautiful to behold, the colours swirling and misty, as if a war was being waged inside the sphere. Finally, he dropped the dried-up corpse, drained of all bodily fluid. With a heave and a sigh of agony, he got to his feet, his legs trembling from exhaustion, making him stumble as he took hold of the hovering sphere with his gloved hand. But this day was not yet at an end.

Galvos walked from the dais through the corridors of the large, ornate palace towards the gardens. The smell of hot iron and piss from the dead and the dying stung his nose, but there was another smell that he recognised above all else, the stench of sorcery. Standing in the hall of the king, he focused his gaze and hearing on the supernatural in the air. The hairs on his muscled arms were suddenly erect, like the hackles of an alarmed dog. He swung his axe down at seemingly nothing, yet it stopped in mid-air, as if hitting a solid wall of iron. Slowly a bladed chain appeared, wrapped around the axe, cutting deep grooves in the wooden haft and holding it firm. Sweat ran down the side of his face as a dark, hooded apparition materialised in front of him. Using all his strength, he stepped in to slam the axe into the face of this new

315

adversary. The axe shook in his hands as it hit a wall of magic, sending the apparition skidding backwards on its feet. Already weakened by the ritual of removing the orb, the warlock's energy was fading fast. 'You are not of the king's company. What do you want?'

A slow and steady laugh greeted the warlock as the apparition removed the hood to reveal a woman with long black hair, braided to the back and left flowing down further, her eyes the colour of night. She glided closer and replied, 'Now why would I tell you all my dirty little secrets? All you need to know is that I need that orb. I do not care for your squabbling.'

A low snort escaped his mouth as he said, 'It's a little presumptuous to think I have this orb you're referring to.'

Cocking her head to the side, she said, 'Do you mean to say that you do not have it? That it is not in that sack at your side?'

Galvos shrugged and continued, 'No, I just said it is presumptuous of you.'

'Arrogant, even in the face of danger. I like you, you have balls. But I do not like to be toyed with. I will destroy you.'

With blinding speed, the chain lashed out to wrap around the warrior's left arm, cutting deep. In agony, he screamed as he gripped the chain with his right hand and pulled with all his might, sending her flying into his grasp. Suddenly, she was dangling in the air as he held her by the throat.

Shocked at the turn of events, she quickly drew some symbols in the air.

The warlock's arm started turning red, his veins burning from the inside. Fighting to calm his mind through the pain, he chanted steadily. Archaic symbols appeared on his arms as if seared in by fire, the burn slowly subdued by his defences. The sorceress twisted the chain further around his arm and snapped it down. Blood sprayed as the blades from the chain cut deeper still. Any lesser man would have lost his arm. In agony the warlock let her go and reeled back as she stumbled to the ground and said, 'Well now, warlock, that was an interesting turn of events. Tell me, what are you planning to do with the orb? Or as my people called it, the Balamuth.'

Galvos staggered back to catch his breath, then pulled a cloth from the sack and quickly bandaged his arm as he said, 'You mean witches, right?'

She chuckled. 'You are interesting, I will give you that. No, I mean people. I am no witch.'

The chain snapped out in a succession of strikes, left and right, and the warlock stumbled back, defending for his life as the attacks came unabated. From his left, he heard shouts as his Kamatayon warriors ran into the hall. Seeing their captain in trouble, they rushed in to come to his aid. The sorceress cursed and ran from the hall in the other direction, disappearing through the doors at the rear that lead higher into the palace. Galvos shouted to his men, 'Go after her and bring me her head!'

Five warriors gave chase as the rest remained in the hall, should she circle back.

The blood was running freely down his arm, and he could feel his strength fading. Galvos stumbled forth through the hall and out to the garden, watching as soldiers fought in the courtyard, then used his axe to cut some branches from a tree and stuck them into the ground in the shape of a large square, about the size of a horse cart around him. He cut three more and placed them in the square in the shape of a triangle. Pushing the blade of the axe into the ground, he dragged it from branch to branch, connecting them to each other.

'What are you doing, Galvos?' Came a shout from his lieutenant.

'Destroy it, we have to destroy it.' Tired beyond comprehension, he continued with the lines in the ground as his muscles burned from fatigue.

'Stop that! You cannot destroy it, we need to take it back to the city!' Underestimating the warlock's ability to fight under such circumstances, he grabbed hold of the axe in Galvos' left hand, but an unanticipated thunderous right came from below, striking Ganda'har full in the face, stunning the big warrior as blood sprayed from his nose. He staggered back and gripped his nose, swearing as he said, 'Agh! You broke it, you bastard!'

'I told you we need to destroy it. I am still the commanding officer in this squadron, so you will obey my orders.'

The air was growing tense. King Madock's Deraset warriors were still putting up a fight in the losing battle, fighting to avenge their king and save what they could of their city. As Galvos pulled the orb from the sack, he heard a shout to his right, 'Get him, we need that orb!' A grisly warrior, tall and muscled, advanced on the warlock with his fellow soldiers joining in the charge.

Mumbling more than speaking, Galvos looked at his lieutenant as he said, 'Please, you need to stop them from getting to me.'

Shocked at the pale visage of his captain, Ganda'har merely nodded, then turned to shout aloud, 'Kamatayon form up, we defend our own!'

Warriors from all sides converged on Galvos, a dust cloud kicked up as the warriors raced towards their prize. The first to reach the defending line was the grisly Deraset warrior, who suddenly flew through the air as Ganda'har used his momentum against him and lifted him into the air, impaling the warrior on the spear of another Kamatayon. The warrior slid off the spear as it was swung to the left, crashing into another attacker and falling to the ground. His end was inevitable and soon he lay still, his eyes turned dull. The fighting grew more intense as the others converged around the square.

Galvos placed the sphere in the centre of the triangle and stood at the foot end. Carnage surrounded him as he saw the young men and women dying to defend him in this hour of need. With his palms together, the warlock spoke with authority, sending a prayer to Kelcai: the warrior turned legend, ascended to become a god amongst mortal men. 'Be with these brave soldiers today, guide their sword arms. Make their blades swing true. Protect them.' Then he closed his eyes and chanted.

Soldiers on both sides were tiring, but the bodies still piled up, for the fighting would not cease until the orb was recovered or destroyed. A fierce battle cry sounded as one of the Deraset broke through the line of defence and dashed forth into the square, to plunge his dagger into the warlock's stomach, then rib cage.

In the state of trance Galvos was in, he did not stop the incantation but continued through the bubbling blood he spewed up. A distant sound echoed in his ears.

'My name is Sukayi Kavali. Remember me as you die, demon,' the man said as he plunged the blade into the warlock again.

Blood flowed down Galvos' chest at an alarming rate. Sukayi Kavali pulled the dagger out for another thrust, when a sword slid through from his back to emerge at his stomach. Looking down, he reached out and felt the cold of the iron and laughed hysterically. Ganda'har ripped out the sword, and the warrior fell to the ground clutching his stomach, then scrambled for safety as the earth beneath him quaked. Cracks spread from the sides of the square in the ground, large enough to fit a man's foot and growing quickly.

Ganda'har shouted to his men to push the fight further away and leapt across the growing crack as a light, ever so bright, shot up in the air, blinding everyone for a few seconds, followed by another, then another, and another until all the branches in the ground were lit up. With a thunderous crack in the air, an immense force rushed down from the heavens through the pillars of light until it reached the ground, spreading outward, throwing all the warriors from their feet. Soldiers everywhere clung to trees and walls, anything firmly rooted. As all winds died down and the warriors slowly rose, the orb was gone and the warlock lay unmoving on the ground ten feet from where he stood, blood spilling from his wounds. Everyone was silent and astonished, there was nothing left to fight for.

The Kamatayon warriors that Galvos had sent in after the sorceress walked out of the palace with a scared servant girl clutching her raggedy clothes in fear. They stared down at the lieutenant as he held Galvos' head from the ground and said, 'We found no witch, sir, just one of the servant girls.'

Ganda'har looked up at her and said, 'What's your name, girl?'

Stuttering from fear, she said, 'B-B-B-Beuneth. P-p-please don't kill me.'

The big man looked at her with deep sadness in his eyes, then back down to his dying friend. 'The killing is done for the day, girl, you need not fret. You will be safe with us back in Artorea.'

Ganda'har whispered in the warlock's ear for a while as the blood bubbled on the man's lips, then rose and shouted, 'Get a wagon here. Now! We ride for home and we ride hard.' He rose from the ground and stared at all the surrounding soldiers, the Kamatayon and the Deraset. He could see the eagerness to do battle still burning in their eyes. 'There is nothing left to fight over! Go home, those of you still alive. Go to your families and hug your children. We did not come for your lives, merely the king's.' A man wielding a broadsword stood a few feet from Ganda'har. He could see how the man struggled internally to accept this offer, then sheathed his blade and shouted, 'Kamatayon! Sheath your weapons.' One and all, their blades slipped into their scabbards, axes and hammers placed back on their belts, spears lowered to the ground.

The man was fuming, jittering as he looked about, gripping his broadsword tighter in his hand. A shout suddenly burst forth from the man as he charged at the lieutenant. Before any other soldier could react, they saw a flash of metal from the sun's rays and the charging man sagged to his knees a few feet past Ganda'har, who was standing with sword in hand. A sigh escaped the lieutenant before he sheathed the weapon again.

Gurgling noises came from the soldier as he collapsed to the ground, his throat cut through.

'If there is anyone else who wants to join this man in death, step forth! Or let us pass.' The clangour of steel echoed as the Deraset warriors dropped their weapons to the ground. Ganda'har was relieved for a moment before he shouted, 'Get the healer here quickly!'

The march back home was a sombre one, with nothing to show for their victory but the dead at their backs, burning on their pyres as they left Tergaron. The smell of burning flesh finally left their nostrils as they put more distance between themselves and the city. After a week of travelling, they had passed the glades of the Nakurothi and were now in the thick of the Northern forests of the Baga — indigenous tribes that had claimed the area as their sacred hunting grounds. From here they would still have to make their way across the mountains of the Chimna dwarves before finally venturing through the vast desert of Artokla to their city Artorea; the heart of the desert. Their king — Naka the Second, ruler of Artokla — wanted the source of Madock's sudden boom in power and zeal. Instead, they come home empty-handed, with wagons filled with injured soldiers. An outcome he would not be happy with. King Naka had known King Madock for years and found the man to be ostentatious, but not one to sack kingdoms for his own gains. He knew something else must be at play, something supernatural, forcing the sudden explosion of tyranny from King Madock, as well as his drive to expand his empire. Two other kingdoms to the far northwest had already fallen to his madness. The next could have been Artorea, but King Naka would not sit idly by. He acted swiftly and without mercy. As Madock's occupying forces moved further out west to capture more lands, they left their king vulnerable in his palace with a diminished force to safeguard against intruders. The Kamatayon legion slipped into the city of Tergaron with the help of spies on the inside. With reinforcements far away, Galvos and his force of Kamatayon warriors sneaked around in the dead of night, taking their positions to ambush the remaining guards. The Kamatayon struck like lightning to a tree. An alarm bell sounded, and the fighting ensued. Now they bear new scars as they return home.

Further down the train of soldiers walked the servant girl, Beuneth, keeping a keen eye on the wagon transporting their injured captain. With every chance she got, she inched ever closer to the wagon. Eyes continually tracked her movement, but every so often they would get distracted with conversation or become lost in their own thoughts, and soon she was only a few feet from the wagon. Once in the cool shade of

321

the wagon, she closed her eyes and breathed deeply from the relief of being away from the harsh sun's rays. A horse's hooves beat on the ground moments before a man rode past towards the lieutenant catching the attention of the men around her. She quickly slipped into the back of the wagon while no one was watching. Beuneth stared down at the bleeding man barely clinging to life as ragged breaths came from his mouth, then moved to sit next to him. Ragged sutures closed the wounds, but one had already torn free, leaking blood over his chest. *The healer was not talented.* She spied a small box in the corner and collected it.

Ganda'har was quiet as he rode his chestnut gelding, contemplating the reactions of the king once he found out they had failed to procure the item of Madock's power, when one of his men pulled up alongside him and said, 'Lieutenant!' With a startle Ganda'har jerked his head up and looked at the man.

'Sorry, sir, but you have not responded to any of my calls. We need to rest the horses, everyone is tired, morale is low.'

Shaking his head, trying to clear it, Ganda'har spat in his hands and worked his fingers through his oily black hair and sighed as he said, 'Gailan, find a clearing in the forest and let them rest.'

Gailan stared at the man, then said, 'We lost too much today, sir. I know you were close to Galvos, I am sorry for your loss.'

'He ain't dead yet, soldier. So I don't want to hear that from any of you again. We fought side by side for many a year and we always came out on top.' Grinning with the remembrance of a fond memory, Ganda'har chuckled as he continued, 'We had just come back from the battle of Ormondeo and the king wanted to see us immediately. Galvos really needed to "go" and was not happy about this at all, but kept his composure. The sounds of his bowels rumbling could have drowned out the royal bard's most boisterous songs. The king walked with us through the palace as we recounted the battle, as if telling a story to a child before bed, his eyes full of wonder and excitement. Galvos had saved my life that day as he had done many times before...' Bursting out with laughter, Ganda'har said, 'As soon as the king turned his back to leave us, Galvos dashed into the closest chamber's outhouse to drop one, turns out it was the king's. Ha-ha-ha.'

The sound of laughter from the two men rang out over the silent troops. Here and there, heads lifted from their march, joining in with a chuckle. As Gailan called for the train to halt, Ganda'har motioned him to join as he walked over to the wagon's rear and flung the flap open at the back. 'Gods girl, what are you doing in here! Get out!' Ganda'har shouted as he climbed in and grabbed her by the wrist. He hurled her from the wagon, causing her to fall on the ground at the back. Gailan was on her quickly to restrain her hands as the lieutenant climbed back out.

'I was just cleaning his wounds! I wanted to help him. He needed water!' Beuneth shouted with her head pressed to the ground.

'If you did anything to that man other than what you said, I will cut your throat,' Ganda'har said as he climbed back into the wagon. By now, some of his men surrounded them, waiting for the order to string her up.

He ducked his head to clear the low timbers as he made his way to Galvos' side and examined his friend. A strange odour hung in the air, musky and sour. The thick leather armour and shirt had been undone to reveal the wounds on his chest. Blood was smeared, as if she had tried to mop it up. He saw the bloodied rag on the floor of the wagon as he looked around. The big wound higher on his chest had been closed for a second time. He saw the previous thread and tear marks. A poor job, but he bled less. He took hold of Galvos' hand and said, 'Hold on, my friend, we are going home.' As he climbed out, he gestured to Gailan to release her and said, 'She tells the truth. She has stitched a wound and cleaned him some. I apologise, girl. Can't be too careful you know.'

She shoved Gailan aside and wiped her face with the back of her hand, then said, 'Yes, I know.' Beuneth walked away to sit under the shade of a tree, breathing deep to calm herself.

☿

Shouts and cheers of elation were heard as the warrior train moved through the gates of Artorea. Flowers of all colours serenaded the sky and covered the roads with their beauty. In the front rows of the crowd, a big man pushed his way through and rushed to the warriors, calling out, 'Father! Where are you? Ganda'har, where is the old man?'

The lieutenant walked up to the man and embraced him fully as he whispered, 'I am sorry, Khan, your father was gravely wounded in battle. The carts with the injured came in ahead of us through the Western gate, heading straight to the healers' hall. Khan, prepare yourself. I do not know if he will pull through this time.'

Khanaseri paled, his hands and legs trembled as he sought to wipe the sweat from his brow. Unable to say another word, he turned to run as fast as his legs could carry him through the crowds, shoving people out of the way to get to the hall. The knot in his stomach pulled tighter and tighter the closer he got, then he saw the queue of carts with injured soldiers on them, waiting to get into the hall of the sick.

Dust plagued the air as oxen stamped their hooves, anxiously waiting to move forward. He slipped past the waiting men as the healers in their white robes shouted at him to slow down.

Pulled from his work, a healer spun around as the big man grabbed him by the arm, and said, 'Where is my father? Where is the captain?' But before the healer in his grasp could answer, an old man with no hair and a crooked stance shuffled towards him and said, 'Oh dear man, he is in the back room. We thought to give him some privacy. Go to him. Do not dally.'

Everywhere he looked, he could see blood-soaked rags strewn on the floor of the hall. Khanaseri pushed through the indefatigable workers as they carried the dead out to the back and piled them on carts as the healers frantically ran around trying to save others. Finally reaching the room at the back, he leaned on the door to move in, then stopped to steel himself. With a heavy creak, the old oak door swung open, and he saw a well-dressed man in a red silk tunic and green trousers with an elegant sword hanging from his belt, leaning over the bed.

A weak hand waved him closer as Galvos lay in the bed, the stink of infection rancid in the air. He spoke with a garbled voice, 'Khan, meet King Naka. Show some manners, my boy.'

He dragged his gaze away from the form that was his father and looked at the king, bowing slightly as he said, 'Father, you are unwell and need to rest.'

A sudden cough racked the warlock. Blood spewed from his mouth as he struggled to wave his hand, then pointed a finger at Khanaseri to silence him. King Naka grabbed Galvos' hand and whispered, 'He means no disrespect, my friend. He is merely concerned for his father. I can't fault that. Now spend some time with your son before the day is done.'

Galvos locked eyes with the king and slowly let go of his hand. Turning to leave, the king lay his hand upon Khanaseri's shoulder. 'Your father will be in our thoughts this night.'

'Thank you, my king.'

As King Naka left the room, Khanaseri pulled an armchair closer and bit on his teeth as he muttered, 'What does he demand from you now? More Blood?'

Blood seeped from the warlock's mouth as he tried to speak, the words coming slow and spaced, 'You... are... too... fast... to anger.'

Khanaseri grabbed a cloth from the bowl by his side and wiped his father's mouth, the dark blood staining his beard and chest. The old warlock's eyes suddenly turned inward, showing only the whites as his body pulled tight and vehemently convulsed.

'Someone! Please help!'

Two healers came through the door and pushed him out of the way as they turned Galvos on his side. Another came running holding a small vial, the contents a deep orange tinge. Holding his father down, they pried open his mouth and poured the liquid down his throat, then held his jaw closed. A few pounding heartbeats later, the seizure passed.

Khanaseri looked at his father in this state of dying and thought back to a better time, a time when he had been full of life, trying to teach young Khanaseri how to wield an axe. His father would always

325

have the stance of a general as he looked at him. He would walk up and down before him, speaking as to his troops before a battle, a cold and stern face with little humour hiding behind his deep blue eyes, saying, 'Both hands! Now swing left! Swing right! Move forward! Straight down!' The small wooden axe usually slipped out of his tired little fingers by this stage and went flying to hit his father in the face. The sudden short-lived curse that was followed by his father chasing after him as he clutched his bruised nose always improved his day. But the fond memories of youth were quickly being replaced by the truth of adulthood. The world was growing fast to be a bitter one.

A creak from the door behind them made them turn to see Ganda'har stroll into the room, followed by a tall, gaunt man wearing trinkets around his arms, legs and neck — his sleeveless black kaftan revealing letters and symbols inked into his arms. The lieutenant walked over to the injured warlock as the nurses moved out of his way and motioned to the man to come closer, then said, 'Stilts, see what you can do for him.'

Khanaseri stepped aside and let the man pass without a word. Stilts lay his gangly hand upon Galvos' head, then took a dagger from his belt and cut his finger just enough to bleed. He chanted as he drew a symbol that looked like the sun, with its brilliant rays shining outward on the old warlock's forehead. The blood caked instantly and the man nervously looked at Khanaseri and took a step back before he said, 'Come here, please.'

'What's wrong?' asked Ganda'har before Khanaseri could mouth the same.

'He... or something, is resisting me, my blood.' Stilts picked up the rag from the chair next to him and wiped the dried blood off, then continued, 'Hold out your hand.' A swift, slight cut and Khanaseri's finger bled and Stilts grabbed his hand to draw the same symbol as before on Galvos' forehead, while chanting.

Khanaseri felt a tingling sensation course through his legs and up his spine. He breathed deep as the hairs on the back of his neck stood erect. Stilts lowered his hand, gestured him to move away as he continued chanting. The blood did not dry up this time, but a thin trail of smoke — almost invisible — rose from the old warlock's head before the man stepped back.

'What's wrong?' Khanaseri asked as he took a step closer again.

'I cannot be certain why...' Stilts looked up at Khanaseri, then at Ganda'har and continued, 'I am afraid he is beyond any warlock's help, unless they are blood of his blood. Some might do more, but I cannot help him. I am sorry.' Stilts turned to leave the room and placed his hand briefly on Khanaseri's shoulder as he passed the man, then disappeared through the door.

A groan sounded from the chair and Ganda'har tensed his muscles as he leaned on the back, squeezing the frame until they heard a loud snap. Everyone jumped around to see Ganda'har holding a piece of the backrest in hand. He gazed at them, then threw the piece of timber on the floor before storming from the room.

Khanaseri dipped his head, keeping his eyes closed as he thought about what Stilts had said, then turned and left the room without a word.

The days slowly progressed as Khanaseri sat by his father's bedside for most of the day, be it to bring water or food, or simply stare at him as he slept. People from all over, people he did not even know, started confronting him on the streets wherever he went, proclaiming their sympathy for his loss, or saying how sorry they were to hear about the news of his father. *He is not dead yet!* He wanted to yell at them, but kept his mouth shut. Truth was, he was not sure how long his father had left. Every night he would go to the temple to pray, then to the archives to search through the Acronodium; the scroll that held all information about the warlocks and their gifts, hoping that he might find something to bring his power into the light and help his father. But he was yet to find something.

The nights passed in a blink of an eye as he stood practising everything he learnt in the book. But nothing came of it. He was his father's son, but he had not inherited his abilities. Days blurred together as sleep eluded him. Exhausted and plagued by hallucinations caused by sleep deprivation, his mind bent the truth of the world. Up was down and down was up, constantly forgetting what he was just about to do.

Rounding the corner to the bakery across the street from the infirmary, he stopped to buy half a loaf of wheat bread for his father. The sudden feeling of being watched swept over him, the feeling of being spied upon. He snapped his head around and watched as people made their way in various directions, walking up and down the gravel road hurriedly to get to their destinations, but he saw no one paying him any special heed. Smells from the freshly baked bread filled the air and pulled his attention back to the bakery, and he entered the shop. Wandering around, he reached for a loaf, but upon touching it he stopped and stood, frozen in time. In a daze of sleeplessness and worry, his mind had shut down any non-essential thinking. He did not wonder about what people were doing around him, or what they thought when they saw him in his current state of unwash, wearing clothes that had not been changed for days. Muffled sounds, as if he was underwater, echoed in his ears, getting closer and louder, but yet remained unrecognisable.

'I said, are you going to buy something or just foul all of my bread with your touch today?' The old baker snapped his fingers next to Khanaseri's ear, again and again. Annoyed, he finally cuffed Khanaseri over the head with the flat of his palm and said, 'I am speaking to you. Are you okay?'

Snapping out of the trance, Khanaseri looked around as he came back to reality, and said, 'Uhm, yes. Sorry, I will take this one.'

'You okay? Been coming in here a lot of late and every time you look worse than before.'

He took the bread and held out the coins to the baker as he said, 'Yes, I'm fine thanks.'

'You are the great Galvos' boy. Well, can't really say boy, now can I, you're as big as a horse! How is he doing?' he said, ignoring the coins before him.

At first Khanaseri wanted to turn and run from the shop, not wanting to speak with another fake sympathiser, but turned back as the old baker said, 'Your father came in to this shop almost every day ya know. He is one of my best customers. You know he swore to me he would never buy bread anywhere else. He had a standing discount here, and today I think he earned his free loaf. Tell your da, Oloff sends his blessings.' The old baker tossed the loaf over to Khanaseri who snapped it from the air and said, 'Thank you Oloff, he has spoken plenty about "the old baker". Now I can at least put a face to the title. I will tell my father you send your regards.' Khanaseri sighed as he pushed open the door and walked through.

Once outside, he looked around again. The crowds had thinned, and the noise had died down. *How long was I in that shop for?* Staring at the door of the infirmary across the street, it felt as though the weight on his shoulders had doubled. Suddenly it was hard to breathe or swallow with the lump that sat in his throat. Uncontrollable breathing forced air rapidly in and out of his lungs as black spots engulfed his vision. His heart thundered in his chest. His hands shook and his mind started bending time and the world around him. He wanted to cry out for help, but no sound came from his lips other than his panting breaths. People walking around him were speaking to him. He could see their mouths moving, but he could not hear them. A nauseating feeling surged through his body, as if something were clawing its way from the inside, trying to get out. Suddenly he collapsed on the road as a fit warred through his body. His eyes turned back in his head. All his muscles pulled taut as his body went into shock. People on the street ran to his side, screaming for help from the infirmary.

An old man came running out as fast as he could and knelt at the young man's side, then shouted, 'Help me turn him on his side!' After they turned him, the old man soothingly spoke to him, 'Hold on, Khan. Calm down. You will be okay, just calm down.'

A scream of absolute horror escaped Khanaseri's mouth, terrifying those around him. The sky grew darker as clouds quickly formed in the heavens. Gusts of wind blew through the city at great strength and unexpected lightning came crashing down all over, sparks flying as it hit ground and metal. A tree burst into flames as it exploded from a strike to their right. Sudden rain poured down in big drops, quickly creating puddles on the road and making it slippery. People were falling all over as they ran to find shelter from the sudden storm. The old healer lay his frail old body over the man to protect him. 'Wake up! We need to get cover! Wake up!'

The spasms lasted a while longer before Khanaseri's eyes turned back, blinking rapidly as his body stopped spasming. The old healer shouted loudly to be heard over the storm, 'You will be okay, do not fear! We need to get to shelter. Has this happened before?'

Khanaseri looked around at the people moving away to seek shelter and then to the old man who helped him up, and said, 'N-N-n-o-o.' Minor tremors, as the aftershock following an earthquake, made him tremble all over in short succession. He scanned the crowd hiding under awnings, huddled together to wait out the sudden storm, feeling ashamed and humiliated for being so weak. The taste of iron in his mouth made him even more nauseous as his stomach churned, the contents begging to be released into the world. And so it was. Hunched over, the bile spilled from his mouth to the curb.

The old man, however, still stood close by, lending a hand to the poor man. He quickly shuffled into the bakery to reappear with a glass of sweetened water and said, 'Here, drink this! It will soothe your stomach.'

Khanaseri found the sweet taste of the sugared water almost euphoric as he downed the glass and walked with the supporting arms of the healer to under the roof of the bakery. Feeling better, he said, 'Thank you, old man. I do not know what happened. It was the worst feeling. As if I was being attacked from the inside.'

With a sigh, the old healer placed his hand on Khanaseri's shoulder and said, 'I have seen this before. You put too much burden on yourself. You must learn to calm yourself. Repeat after me. Close your eyes.'

'Close your eyes.'

'No, actually close your eyes. Good. Now, breathe in. Hold it.'

'Breathe in and hold.'

'Don't repeat what I am saying, man. Do what I say. So, breathe in. Hold. Hold. Hold. Now breathe out. Do this a couple times until you feel your heart relaxing.'

'I have been coming to the infirmary for over a month and I do not even know your name. I am ashamed of my behaviour.'

'Oh, come now. You have more important things to worry about than finding out this old fool's name.'

'That does not excuse me for being rude.'

The old man eyed him and released a long breath before he said, 'Well enough. I am Gantris.'

Gripping the old healer's arm, he said, 'Thank you for everything.' The gusts of wind softened their angry howls and died down. The storm ceased its raging torrent, abated and calmed as the clouds overhead dispersed and the two men headed across the street.

Together they walked through the infirmary in silence to reach the door to his father's chamber. The momentary seed of doubt made the young man pause as his fingers touched the doorknob and said, 'I don't know if I can do this, I am not as strong as he is. I am no warlock. I am a disappointment.'

An old bony hand settled on his shoulders as the old healer sighed and said, 'Close your eyes. Breathe in. Hold. Now breathe out.'

The creak of the door was deafening to Khanaseri as he slowly pushed it open. Afraid that he might wake his father, he stopped opening the door, then opened it quickly, hoping it would not creak as much. But it did. Scowling at the healer, he said, 'Can't you get this fixed?' But the old healer simply shrugged and said, 'Cutbacks...'

Moving through the room, he leaned on the bed and sighed as he looked down at the figure before him. Frail, thin and grey. His body was deteriorating fast. Sweat covered him from head to toe and the smell of rancid flesh hung in the air. 'Why is he not getting better?'

Gantris had his hands in the sleeves of his robe as he said, 'We have done all we can medically. He needs to fight this now.'

'Father,' he said as he shook the man lightly. 'You need to eat. I brought you some bread from your friend, Oloff. He sends his regards. Father! Why are you not waking up?'

The old healer moved closer and placed his fingers on Galvos' neck in search of a pulse and said, 'His heartbeat is weak, but he is still hanging on. Although he seems to be non-responsive. Nurse, bring me my bag!'

After some time, a helper came running in with an old leather bag and handed it to Gantris, who said, 'Thank you.'

'What is happening?' Khanaseri shouted, but the old man did not answer. Instead, he was rummaging through the bag and pulled out a vial with a yellow liquid and a large syringe. He drew the liquid out of the vial and injected it into Galvos' neck.

Instantly going into shock, Galvos' back arched as his arms thrashed about.

'Hold him down!'

Khanaseri leaned on his father to push him back down and held him steady as the thrashing continued, and said, 'What did you give him, Gantris?'

'A cocktail to ease him. It is not supposed to do this!' Looking back at the young Khanaseri with dread in his eyes, he continued, 'This seems spell-bound.'

With a puzzled look on his face, Khanaseri squinted his eyes and said, 'Do you mean he did this to himself?'

Sighing, the old man said, 'I rather hope so, son. For if he did not, then someone else did...'

The cold, damp cavern taunted Galvos as he slowly made his way from chamber to chamber in search of something. Exactly what, eluded him. The echo in the cave made it near impossible to place where a sound was coming from. Bats squeaking, slow-flowing water dropping from a height in the distance to splatter down on rocks below and the distinct sound of a mocking laugh in the dark taunted his ears and mind, although he was not sure if the laugh was real or just in his head. Alone and unarmed, he felt the presence of someone, something, following him, stalking him. The darkness was all-consuming, sending the warlock stumbling into ruts and rocks. Cursing, he slapped his hands together and shouted, 'Asvaniante!'

A light burst into being in the cup of his hands, trying to escape as he slowly opened them, and said, 'You will obey me today. Follow me!'

Like a dog on a leash, the light followed him around, but it was not bright enough to see everything in these vast chambers, merely enough for him not to stumble down a cliff. Shadows danced on the walls and floors, playing tricks on his mind. The mocking laughter sounded out loud to his left, moving past him at great speed. Jumping around to face this nuisance, he said, 'Who are you? Why am I here?'

'Warlock, I implore you to bring me the Balamuth. There is no need for violence here today.'

Galvos studied the cave, watching the movement of the shadows on the walls. 'You will never get this Balamuth. No one should have its power. That is why I sent it away.'

'You misunderstand, warlock. That Balamuth belongs to the one I love. Without it, he is nothing but a soulless husk. I need it back. It chose him.'

'I have seen what that thing does to people! It is too much power to wield. You will never have it!'

He caught the chain that flashed from the darkness and yanked on it. The woman stumbled into the light from the other end. A harsh back-handed blow threw her off her feet. Quick as a lion attacking its prey, he was on top of the sorceress. Her throat felt so soft, so thin under his calloused hand as he squeezed the life out of her.

Searing pain ripped through his right side as the sizzle of burning flesh filled the damp air. Enraged, he screamed as he dropped her and spun around, searching for the threat, but there was nothing. He spun to his right, then looked back down, and she was gone.

'Just know that I did not want this.' Her voice echoed from the walls.

Galvos recoiled as more pain ripped through his left side, the stench of his burning skin making him sick. Lifting his shirt, blood leaked from what looked like a deep, burnt claw mark on his sides. 'You will pay for this! Where are you?'

The omnipotent voice sounded from everywhere as it said, 'You, warlock, are in my world now. Help me and I will help you.'

Thousands of small eyes reflected the light next to him, following his movement as he made his way deeper into the cave.

Beaded with sweat and muttering sounds escaping his mouth, Galvos was restrained to the bed to ensure he did not hurt himself or others as he thrashed about. Khanaseri was frantic but utterly helpless and resorted to wiping his father's face with a wet cloth as he spoke to calm him, telling stories of his youth to bring him back. Screams of pain erupted from Galvos as the smell of burning flesh filled the air. The blanket covering him turned red with blood as it seeped from his side. Panicked and afraid for his father, Khanaseri stood frozen. Shock filled his being as he saw the claw marks appearing on the old warlock's side.

Gantris shouted aloud, 'He is being attacked and there is nothing I can do to aid him! He needs a warlock that is of his blood, and you... I am sorry.'

Khanaseri pulled out an old book from his pack with a green emerald on the cover.

Astonished, Gantris looked upon the old book and said, 'You are not supposed to have that. They will hang you.'

'Borrowed, Gantris. I am going to return it. Now hold him down.'

He flipped through the book and found the page he was looking for, then started reciting the words, 'Ilk anon Senovat!' Over and over he recited it, but nothing happened. Launching the old book across the room in a fit of rage, he shouted, 'See, Gantris! I am useless!'

The old healer hurried to pick up the book and scanned through the pages, then said, 'No, there is something in you that is blocking your ability. You have the magic in you. Normal people, like myself, cannot see anything written on these pages. You can! Don't you see? Try again. Hold on to your father's arm, maybe, and really focus. Force yourself through the blockage.'

'Can you really not see anything in the book?' Khanaseri asked, perturbed by the idea.

'I promise you, young man, I cannot. Now go!'

He grabbed his father's arm and focused as he shouted out, 'Ilk anon Senovat! Ilk anon Senovat! Ilk anon Senovat!' A burgeoning light appeared in his mind's eye. He could feel it growing, thrashing at the blockage that was stopping his abilities. He imagined the blockage as a dam wall holding back a vast quantity of water and increased his chanting, visualising it explode to release a flood.

A bursting pain shot through his head, lighting his brain on fire. Blood gushed out of his nose and he gagged through the liquid, gurgling as he barely kept his focus on the incantation.

'Senoc's balls!' the old healer shouted as he grabbed a rag and wiped the gushing blood from the man's face.

Khanaseri drifted away from the pain he felt in his head and thought, *am I dying?* He opened his eyes and saw a fire in the strangling darkness a distance away. Another world surrounded him. Sounds of footsteps and shouts of rage came from the direction of the fire as it moved about. Khanaseri steadily moved closer to investigate.

'Father!' he shouted as he ran to the man. A burning branch swung at him and he dived to the left to avoid the blows, then pleaded, 'It's me da! Khan!'

Galvos took another swing as he growled, 'You idiot apparition! I stopped my son from using magic! I blocked his ability! You cannot fool me!'

Khan stumbled back and his foot caught on a jutting rock. Sharp stones cut through his hands as he stopped his fall. He looked on at his father, eyes wide with shock, and mumbled, 'I broke through.'

The warlock advanced on his son and saw the terror in his eyes as he said, 'You broke through what exactly?!'

Scrambling back as his father took a swing at his head, he said, 'Through your barrier! To save you! I went through the Acronodium, I could read it Father. I have been practising since you came back from the battle. Today I finally broke through when I saw you in need.'

Galvos relaxed his fists, and said, 'What do you mean, you saw me in need? I stand here in front of you now.'

'No, da, you are in a dream state. Blood is leaking from your side and the healers are trying to save you, but I am afraid they will fail.'

Pointing to a small scar on his forehead, Galvos asked, 'Where did I get this?'

'When I was five, the small wooden axe slipped out of my hand as you were training me and hit your head. Almost took out your eye, but luckily it didn't.'

'Slipped, huh? Still sticking to that story?' Extending his arm, he reached out to pull Khanaseri up from the ground, then sighed deeply as he continued, 'You probably have lots of questions, but you should not be here. Just know that I took your magic for your own safety. Not that it lasted, apparently. You must be stronger than I anticipated.'

A voice from the shadows said, 'What is this I see? An uninvited guest! You should not be here.'

The smell of sorcery stung Galvos' nose. His eyes flared wide, and he reacted as quickly as possible, jumping forward to crash into Khanaseri as a bladed chain whip whizzed past the younger man's face with terrible force to slice into Galvos' side. A scream of agony filled the air as she ripped the whip out, blood spurting from the warlock's side and onto the ground. Coughing up the red liquid, Galvos slowly got to his feet as he watched their assailant draw closer. The look of triumph radiated from her.

The dark hooded figure stood facing the bleeding old warlock; the whip a blur as she spun it with tremendous precision and grace. In a fight to keep his intestines on the inside, Galvos clutched his side as blood oozed from his wounds, spilling over his hands.

The assailant angrily stated, 'If you had just given me the Balamuth, none of this would have been necessary. Look, I am not unreasonable, I desperately need the Balamuth. If you get it back to me, I will spare you and your son.'

The old warlock looked at his son as he said, 'Why should I trust you?'

She moved back and caught the whip, then said, 'I do not want to murder you or anyone else. I am not doing this for fun or out of spite, nor am I a crazy old wench that just wants to sow chaos. I am here to find the Balamuth because I need to set things straight. Lives hang in the balance. But know this, all who stand in the way of my quest, will fall.'

'And you expect me to believe this?'

'Do you have any reason not to?'

The question sent doubts through his mind, and the warlock preferred not to answer.

'In fact,' she continued, 'If you help me, I will save your life right here, right now.'

Hearing this, Khanaseri shouted out, 'Save him, please! Come on, old man, give her what she wants and be done with it. Don't be so stubborn!'

Galvos, without taking his eyes off of her, shouted back, 'Stay out of this, Khan!'

For a heartbeat, Khanaseri thought his father was about to charge the woman when the warlock suddenly wheeled around, running straight at him, the deadly whip following close behind. Galvos slammed his hand to Khanaseri's forehead and shouted, 'Exvele!'

It all happened so quickly. The last thing Khanaseri saw was the whip slicing into his father's back repeatedly, just before it went dark.

'No!' The scream erupted from Khanaseri as he jumped up from the ground, startled. Bewildered faces stared down at him from the corners of the room as he looked about, then hurried to the bed and grabbed his father's hand. Foam and blood flowed from the old warlock's mouth, his body stiff and shaking as a fit overtook him. He watched his father being torn apart from the inside. The utter uselessness he felt crawled deep within his heart and soul, branding him forever. Vowing that he would never feel like this again, he unsheathed the knife at his side and brought it up to his father's throat.

'What are you doing! You mean to murder your own father now?' Gantris shouted as he looked into the frightened eyes of the man.

Khanaseri looked down at his hands and said, 'He is being tortured to death, Gantris! What would you have me do? Let him suffer? Let my father endure more of this horrific violence? He is going to die, whether or not I ease his suffering. At least this way, it will be quick.'

An unnatural shout erupted from Galvos, shrieking through the room as he suddenly sat upright in the bed, eyes wide open and bloodshot. Foaming at the mouth, he grabbed the knife from Khanaseri and stuck it into his own throat, twisting the blade before pulling it out.

Everyone jumped back from the grisly scene, unable to comprehend what they had just witnessed as blood flowed from the warlock, leading him to die moments later.

'No! You were not supposed to die! Can't you do anything right?' Pulling her hair, the hooded figure fumed as the grasp of the sphere stretched further and further from her fingers. In a fit of rage, she flung everything from the desk and cabinets, shattering glass ornaments and scattering documents all over the floor. She grabbed the nearest piece of paper to wipe her hands on, then realised the blood had already dried and forwent the effort to rub them down.

'Now look at this, you imbecile. How am I supposed to walk out into the streets now?'

The lifeless, twisted, obese man sitting in the chair opposite her stared with unseeing eyes as she screamed at him, blood still slowly pumping from his cut throat. She rolled up the chained whip and placed it back on her hip as she said, 'At least I know now that he has a son with some magical abilities. Hopefully, all is not yet lost. Can't you see I do not want to do these horrible acts? But no one wants to help me in my quest!' Raging on as she yelled at the dead man, she raised her hands up in the air, surrendering as she said, 'You should not have tried to have sex with that little girl. You might have been alive now. So don't blame me.' Beuneth looked up to the little girl sitting on the staircase, shaking with terror, then said, 'Get! And stop whoring around!'

She stared at the dead man with a smirk, then looked down at her bloodied hands and left the little house.

Trembling from anger and anguish, Khanaseri walked through the deathly silent infirmary, oblivious to all the eyes following him. In a complete trance, he closed on the door and reached for the handle. Time passed by as he stood in front of the big unmoving door, pushing and pushing, but nothing budged. The hall suddenly felt so very small, as if the walls were closing in on him. Sweat ran down his face. He felt like a deer being hunted, the hunter close by, chills running down his spine. A cornered animal. He grabbed the handle with both hands as he shook the door, pushing on it with all his might, when Gantris appeared out of nowhere and grabbed his arm as he said, 'Calm down, Khan. Brea—'

'Valoush!' Khanaseri shouted. The earth quaked from the explosive force that followed. The door was torn from its hinges and thrown into the street between the passersby, striking down a woman in the crowd. Coughing as he got to his feet, rubble and dust fell from his jacket and pants. His face was stained red from a shallow cut to his temple, his head was pounding. He looked around and saw everything that surrounded him was now lying scattered.

'No, no, no no no. What have I done? I didn't mean to do this!'

Running outside, he saw the carnage caused by his actions. A little boy's screams tore through his very being, sending him into a frenzy, running to help people up from the ground. Some bled a bit from their ears, others held their heads, but luckily no lost limbs — yet. In the distance, he saw the broken door of the infirmary, an arm hanging from the side underneath. The sight of the unmoving body under the door sent shivers through his very soul. As he ran to the door, he saw more people running from all directions to see what was going on. He grabbed the door on one end and heaved as he flipped it over and off the woman. The cut marks on her face and arms didn't look lethal, mostly superficial. As he gently tore the dress away over her stomach to check for more serious injuries, she gasped for air and sat up, frantically grabbing at nothing as air rushed back into her lungs.

Bewildered and shocked, she was unsure of where she was and what had occurred. Realising that a man had torn her dress, she feared for the worst and immediately scratched and kicked at her assailant.

'Wait! Stop that! I am only trying to help! Wait!' Khanaseri grabbed her arms and held her tightly as she tried to bite him in the face and neck.

A vicious kick from a knee found its target, crashing into Khanaseri's testicles. Losing all ability to hold on to her, or his breath, he dropped to the ground, gripping his privates. More vicious kicks rained down on him as the woman screamed at the top of her voice, 'You filthy fucking bastard! Taking advantage of a woman when she could have been dying, you worthless swine of a human being! How do you like me now, you piece of shit! Not so fun if I can hit back, huh!'

A crowd started gathering, seeing the brutal assault on Khanaseri, but none intervened. A few more kicks followed before he reached out and grabbed her foot, twisting it to make her lose her balance. Hitting the ground, she spun to see him staring down at her with his hand extended to help her up and heard him say, 'Please, I was not doing what you think. I was trying to see if you had any serious injuries on your stomach. With all the blood on your dress, I thought you badly hurt. I am Khanaseri.'

One man from the crowd shouted out, 'Heya girl, ya need us to call the guards on him?'

Looking around, she saw all the attention they had attracted and reluctantly accepted his hand as she said, 'Well, don't expect an apology from me. I am sure you deserved it one way or another. I am named Beuneth.' She turned to the crowd and said, 'No, it's okay. Just a misunderstanding.' Opening the torn section of the dress, she looked at her stomach and said, 'Seems like a lot of minor cuts, nothing deep, luckily. What happened here?'

'Well, uh,' Khanaseri stuttered, then remembered the old healer being very close to him when all this occurred. Eyes going wide, he shouted, 'Oh no, I need to check on the old healer. I think he might be hurt.'

'Wait!' Beuneth shouted, and followed him as he ran back into the infirmary.

He saw a charred half-moon burned into the floor as he entered. Beds were flipped, and the patients lay on the ground, being aided and helped back to their beds by the nurses. Arms flailed about as Gantris groaned from under a bed, then gasped as Khanaseri lifted the heavy frame from the old man's chest. The healer shouted, 'What have you done, dear boy!'

At that very moment, guards ran through the doorway. One shouted to the others, 'Arrest him!'

Guards charged in at Khanaseri as he said, 'Wait, I did not mean for any of this.' A guard swung down a baton, hitting him over the head. A sudden explosion of pain, then darkness followed.

Creaks sounded, echoing in the cavernous prison as the heavy wooden door swung slowly open. King Naka entered the small gaol cell, pulling his face into a sneer as the rank odour stung his nose, then said, 'You know the only reason you are alive today is because of the years of

341

service your father gave to this kingdom,' shrugging, he continued, 'Well, that and because I will it so.'

A snort and brief laughter followed from Khanaseri as he said, 'Oh, I see. So I should be thankful because I am basically drinking my piss and shitting in a bucket in the corner of my "lodging".'

'Yes, in a manner of speaking. Rather this than being strung by the neck or lopped off with a blunt sword. Wouldn't you say? The crowds wanted blood for the devastation you caused, not to even mention the Keeper of Archives. What were you thinking when you stole the Acronodium? That alone is punishable by death.'

Shifting around on the dirty bed, Khanaseri lowered his head as he said, 'My father was being attacked by sorcery. I was his only hope. He did not die naturally.'

'And so you were able to cast a spell from the book and enter his mind? That's what you would have me believe? You, a man who has shown no warlockian abilities. You know warlocks show abilities from a very young age, right?' Moving around the small cell, King Naka dragged a chair from the corner with his foot. Sneering as he looked at the chair — grime all over it — he kicked it back to the corner and continued, 'For all the years of service your father gave me, I would really like not to kill his son. Please give me something to work with and get you out of this.'

'I am telling you the truth, Your Majesty!' Khanaseri shouted as he lunged up from the bed.

King Naka stood unflinching with his hands behind his back and said, 'Well, then do something. Create magic for me or control it or whatever it is warlocks do.'

Khanaseri walked past the king, and said, 'Fine, I will blast this door off its hinges, the same as I did the one in the infirmary.'

'Oh, come now, I spoke to Gantris myself and he assured me that the door was really old and the hinges were worn. You merely kicked the door hard enough to break it off the hinges.'

'He only said that not to get me into more trouble, I am sure.' Mumbling under is his breath, Khanaseri turned around to face the door, poised for the blast.

'Anytime you are ready,' King Naka said as he looked through the barred little window to find the sun, then continued, 'It is getting a bit late and I would like to get back to my duties, you know... as king.'

With eyes closed, expecting a big bang, Khanaseri shouted aloud, 'Valous!'

Laughter rang out from behind him and in between breaths the king said, 'Was that it?'

Ignoring him, Khanaseri shouted again, 'Valous!' But nothing happened. From over his shoulder, he heard the king say, 'Performance issues? Hey, you know I have a remedy for that, but don't tell anyone. Bambil horns... changed my life, I tell you.' King Naka strode forward and Khanaseri moved aside to let the king pass as he said, 'Guards! Open up.'

The door swung open and King Naka strode gracefully through, then turned to say, 'Honestly, if you want to get out of here, you will need to give me a reason. And well, the best reason would be magic. We could use more warlocks. They are a dying breed.'

Embers burst into fires in his head. Rage filled him, the sort that could devour the world. The heavy door creaked as it closed; the latch falling into place as the guards turned the key. The monolithic rage, fuelled by agony and hate for himself and everyone around him, burned brighter and brighter. Grabbing his head, Khanaseri felt ripples of energy flowing through him. Power tried to claw its way out, the yearning to be released, tremendous. *Why does this hurt so much? What is happening to me?* Vision blurring, unable to see clearly, he looked around the room as it started morphing into a cave; the walls changing shape, almost disappearing altogether. Turning round and round, the beast still trying to fight its way out, head pounding, skin on fire, round and round. The hooded figure that killed his da was suddenly right in front of him, reaching out to grasp hold of him.

He stammered back, tripped over the edge of the bed and fell to the floor, hitting his head. The cave disappeared. His vision swam. Sweet darkness...

☿

Unnerved, shaken, she stared down at her blood-soaked hands; remembering the feeling as she twisted the bladed chain around the fat man's neck, pulling it tighter and tighter. The blood running down and over her hands and chains, spilling to the floor, but she only noticed the heat of the blood at that stage, blocking out the rest. Thrusting her hands into the bowl of warmed water before her, she scrubbed and scrubbed to get rid of the red stains.

Finally satisfied that her hands were clean, Beuneth slumped down to the ground, her breathing ragged, the rasp of the inhale and exhale making her clamp her hand over her mouth to stifle the sounds.

The room was suddenly cold, the hairs on her arms raising like the hackles of a beast. Alarmed, she jumped up from the floor as a tear in the fabric of space opened up in front of her. Seeing Khanaseri in the goal cell, she reached out to grab him. He stammered back, and the rift closed instantly. With her adrenalin surging, she did not realise that the stab wound in her side had opened up again, turning the dressing red. Feeling the stickiness of blood on her arm, she took off her shirt and stood bare-breasted as she examined the wound. Her long black hair was caked with blood. In disgust, she pulled the strands away from the wound. Bruises covered her left flank with a big stab wound just below her kidneys. Feeling her back, she was assured the stitches still held. Thinking back to that fight, she said, 'You were truly a great warlock. I am sorry I had to do what I did.'

Daughter Of The Ageian is scheduled for release mid 2022. Chapter subject to change upon release. Join my mailing list for updated information:

https://www.mariushvisser.com/contact.

A professionally trained Information Technology Specialist Marius H. Visser spent the better part of a decade honing his writing skills and pushing the bounds of imagination after his debut fantasy novel Mercury Dagger - A Tale From Kraydenia back in 2010. When Marius H. Visser is not off exploring the wilds of Australia, he is dreaming up new adventures and monsters to cause chaos in a fantastical world filled with twists, loyalty, honour and great and terrible battles.

Made in the USA
Coppell, TX
04 October 2021